SCIENCE FICTION NOVELLAS

EDITED BY

Harry Harrison

EDITOR *Year's Best Science Fiction*

Willis E. McNelly

PROFESSOR OF ENGLISH

CALIFORNIA STATE UNIVERSITY, FULLERTON

EDITOR *Above the Human Landscape*

Charles Scribner's Sons

NEW YORK

ACKNOWLEDGMENTS

"Black Destroyer," by A. E. van Vogt, copyright 1939 by Street & Smith Publications, Inc.; reprinted by permission of the author and the author's agent, Forrest J. Ackerman.

"Call Me Joe," by Poul Anderson, copyright © 1957 by Street & Smith Publications, Inc.; reprinted by permission of the author and the author's agents, Scott Meredith Literary Agency, Inc.

"The Far Look," by Theodore L. Thomas, copyright © 1956 by Street & Smith Publications, Inc.; reprinted by permission of the author.

"East Wind, West Wind," by Frank M. Robinson, copyright © 1972 by Harry Harrison; reprinted by permission of the author.

"The Streets of Ashkelon," by Harry Harrison, copyright © 1962 by Nova Publications Ltd.; reprinted by permission of the author and his agent, Robert P. Mills, Ltd.

"Omnilingual," by H. Beam Piper, copyright © 1957 by Street & Smith Publications, Inc.; reprinted by permission of Charter Communications, Inc.

"The Asian Shore," by Thomas M. Disch, copyright © 1970 by Thomas M. Disch; reprinted by permission of the author and Brandt & Brandt.

Library of Congress Cataloging in Publication Data

Cover painting by Jack Gaughan

Harrison, Harry, comp.
    Science fiction novellas.

    CONTENTS: Things to come.—Van Vogt, A. E. Black destroyer.—Anderson, P. Call me Joe. [etc.]
    1. Science fiction, American. I. McNelly, Willis Everett, 1920- joint comp. II. Title.
PZ1.H247Sb [PS648.S3] 813'.0876 74-13151
ISBN 0-684-13847-6

1 3 5 7 9 11 13 15 17 19 M/P 20 18 16 14 12 10 8 6 4 2

Printed in the United States of America

As usual . . .

to the ladies

Contents

Things to Come

THAT wonderful Englishman H. G. Wells was the father of science fiction, and he started writing it at the end of the last century. He was well ahead of the rest of the world when he did this, so that the SF engine only idled for a number of years. It was in the 1930's, in the United States, when the science fiction pulp magazines burst upon an unsuspecting world. This was well before comic books, before television too, a time when *all* of the bang-zowie entertainment was in the pulps. These were cheap magazines, usually costing only a dime, with bright, eye-hurting covers and shredding pages. The brightest—and shreddi-est—of all were the SF mags. They promised great wonders on the outside and then delivered these wonders inside.

Science fiction is still delivering its wonders. And it still has a lot of bang-zowie left. It might be called a literature of ideas in an adventurous package. But "literature of ideas" sounds boring, and good SF is never boring. Look at some of the ideas in this book and you will see why. You can join a voyage in a great ship to a distant star, where you will meet the most intelligent and most evil animal in creation—who wants to wipe out all mankind. Or you can experience just what it feels like to be living on the surface of the deadly planet Jupiter. A literature of ideas like these *cannot* be boring.

SF is also about the real world of the present, and about the tomorrow that is already coming into existence. Other kinds of fiction have not yet even caught up with rocket ships—while science fiction authors stopped writing about rockets years ago. As the pace of science and technology—and pollution—increases daily, we are moving faster and faster into this science fictional future. SF, by examining possibilities and futures, gives us something to grab on to in our flight through time.

Science fiction is many things: fantasy and adventure, monsters and rockets, distant stars and close-up robots. A literature of ideas, yes—but always a literature of entertainment as well.

Harry Harrison
Willis E. McNelly

Science Fiction Novellas

Black Destroyer

A. E. van Vogt

A. E. van Vogt is a tall solid Canadian of Dutch descent who has lived
in the United States for many years. His novels and short stories
are science fiction classics, his imagination galaxy spanning always.
He looks at our night sky and sees it filled with stars—and every
star a sun that may have planets moving in orbit about it. What
kind of strange and different life forms can we expect to find on
these planets, he asks. Will we meet creatures like Coeurl, a
savage, intelligent, incredibly strong monster, who must kill to live?

O N and on Coeurl prowled! The black, moonless, almost
starless night yielded reluctantly before a grim reddish dawn that
crept up from his left. A vague, dull light, it was, that gave no
sense of approaching warmth, no comfort, nothing but a cold,
diffuse lightness, slowly revealing a nightmare landscape.

Black, jagged rock and black, unliving plain took form around
him, as a pale-red sun peered at last above the grotesque horizon. It was then Coeurl recognized suddenly that he was on
familiar ground.

He stopped short. Tenseness flamed along his nerves. His
muscles pressed with sudden, unrelenting strength against his
bones. His great forelegs—twice as long as his hindlegs—
twitched with a shuddering movement that arched every razor-
sharp claw. The thick tentacles that sprouted from his shoulders
ceased their weaving undulation, and grew taut with anxious
alertness.

Utterly appalled, he twisted his great cat head from side to side, while the little hairlike tendrils that formed each ear vibrated frantically, testing every vagrant breeze, every throb in the ether.

But there was no response, no swift tingling along his intricate nervous system, not the faintest suggestion anywhere of the presence of the all-necessary id. Hopelessly, Coeurl crouched, an enormous catlike figure silhouetted against the dim reddish skyline, like a distorted etching of a black tiger resting on a black rock in a shadow world.

He had known this day would come. Through all the centuries of restless search, this day had loomed ever nearer, blacker, more frightening—this inevitable hour when he must return to the point where he began his systematic hunt in a world almost depleted of id-creatures.

The truth struck in waves like an endless, rhythmic ache at the seat of his ego. When he had started, there had been a few id-creatures in every hundred square miles, to be mercilessly rooted out. Only too well Coeurl knew in this ultimate hour that he had missed none. There were no id-creatures left to eat. In all the hundreds of thousands of square miles that he had made his own by right of ruthless conquest—until no neighboring coeurl dared to question his sovereignty—there was no id to feed the otherwise immortal engine that was his body.

Square foot by square foot he had gone over it. And now—he recognized the knoll of rock just ahead, and the black rock bridge that formed a queer, curling tunnel to his right. It was in that tunnel he had lain for days, waiting for the simple-minded, snakelike id-creature to come forth from its hole in the rock to bask in the sun—his first kill after he had realized the absolute necessity of organized extermination.

He licked his lips in brief gloating memory of the moment his slavering jaws tore the victim into precious toothsome bits. But the dark fear of an idless universe swept the sweet remembrance from his consciousness, leaving only certainty of death.

He snarled audibly, a defiant, devilish sound that quavered on the air, echoed and re-echoed among the rocks, and shuddered back along his nerves—instinctive and hellish expression of his will to live.

And then—abruptly—it came.

He saw it emerge out of the distance on a long downward slant, a tiny glowing spot that grew enormously into a metal ball. The great shining globe hissed by above Coeurl slowing visibly in quick deceleration. It sped over a black line of hills to the right, hovered almost motionless for a second, then sank down out of sight.

Coeurl exploded from his startled immobility. With tiger speed, he flowed down among the rocks. His round, black eyes burned with the horrible desire that was an agony within him. His ear tendrils vibrated a message of id in such tremendous quantities that his body felt sick with the pangs of his abnormal hunger.

The little red sun was a crimson ball in the purple-black heavens when he crept up from behind a mass of rock and gazed from its shadows at the crumbling, gigantic ruins of the city that sprawled below him. The silvery globe, in spite of its great size, looked strangely inconspicuous against that vast, fairylike reach of ruins. Yet about it was a leashed aliveness, a dynamic quiescence that, after a moment, made it stand out, dominating the foreground. A massive, rock-crushing thing of metal, it rested on a cradle made by its own weight in the harsh, resisting plain which began abruptly at the outskirts of the dead metropolis.

Coeurl gazed at the strange, two-legged creatures who stood in little groups near the brilliantly lighted opening that yawned at the base of the ship. His throat thickened with the immediacy of his need; and his brain grew dark with the first wild impulse to burst forth in furious charge and smash these flimsy, helpless-looking creatures whose bodies emitted the id-vibrations.

Mists of memory stopped that mad rush when it was still only electricity surging through his muscles. Memory that brought fear in an acid stream of weakness, pouring along his nerves, poisoning the reservoirs of his strength. He had time to see that the creatures wore things over their real bodies, shimmering transparent material that glittered in strange, burning flashes in the rays of the sun.

Other memories came suddenly. Of dim days when the city that spread below was the living, breathing heart of an age of glory that dissolved in a single century before flaming guns whose wielders knew only that for the survivors there would be an ever-narrowing supply of id.

It was the remembrance of those guns that held him there, cringing in a wave of terror that blurred his reason. He saw himself smashed by balls of metal and burned by searing flame.

Came cunning—understanding of the presence of these creatures. This, Coeurl reasoned for the first time, was a scientific expedition from another star. In the olden days, the coeurls had thought of space travel, but disaster came too swiftly for it ever to be more than a thought.

Scientists meant investigation, not destruction. Scientists in their way were fools. Bold with his knowledge, he emerged into the open. He saw the creatures become aware of him. They turned and stared. One, the smallest of the group, detached a shining metal rod from a sheath, and held it casually in one hand. Coeurl loped on, shaken to his core by the action; but it was too late to turn back.

Commander Hal Morton heard little Gregory Kent, the chemist, laugh with the embarrassed half gurgle with which he invariably announced inner uncertainty. He saw Kent fingering the spindly metalite weapon.

Kent said: "I'll take no chances with anything as big as that."

Commander Morton allowed his own deep chuckle to echo along the communicators. "That," he grunted finally, "is one of the reasons why you're on this expedition, Kent—because you never leave anything to chance."

His chuckle trailed off into silence. Instinctively, as he watched the monster approach them across that black rock plain, he moved forward until he stood a little in advance of the others, his huge form bulking the transparent metalite suit. The comments of the men pattered through the radio communicator into his ears:

"I'd hate to meet that baby on a dark night in an ally."

"Don't be silly. This is obviously an intelligent creature. Probably a member of the ruling race."

"It looks like nothing else than a big cat, if you forget those tentacles sticking out from its shoulders, and make allowances for those monster forelegs."

"Its physical development," said a voice, which Morton recognized as that of Siedel, the psychologist, "presupposes an animallike adaptation to surroundings, not an intellectual one. On the other hand, its coming to us like this is not the act of an animal but of a creature possessing a mental awareness of our possible identity. You will notice that its movements are stiff, denoting caution, which suggests fear and consciousness of our weapons. I'd like to get a good look at the end of its tentacles. If they taper into handlike appendages that can really grip objects, then the conclusion would be inescapable that it is a descendant of the inhabitants of this city. It would be a great help if we could establish communication with it, even though appearances indicate that it has degenerated into a historyless primitive."

Coeurl stopped when he was still ten feet from the foremost creature. The sense of id was so overwhelming that his brain drifted to the ultimate verge of chaos. He felt as if his limbs were bathed in molten liquid; his very vision was not quite clear, as the sheer sensuality of his desire thundered through his being.

The men—all except the little one with the shining metal rod in his fingers—came closer. Coeurl saw that they were frankly and curiously examining him. Their lips were moving, and their voices beat in a monotonous, meaningless rhythm on his ear tendrils. At the same time he had the sense of waves of a much higher frequency—his own communication level—only it was a machinelike clicking that jarred his brain. With a distinct effort to appear friendly, he broadcast his name from his ear tendrils, at the same time pointing at himself with one curving tentacle.

Gourlay, chief of communications, drawled: "I got a sort of static in my radio when he wiggled those hairs, Morton. Do you think—"

"Looks very much like it," the leader answered the unfinished question. "That means a job for you, Gourlay. If it speaks by means of radio waves, it might not be altogether impossible that you can create some sort of television picture of its vibrations, or teach him the Morse code."

"Ah," said Siedel. "I was right. The tentacles each develop into seven strong fingers. Provided the nervous system is complicated enough, those fingers could, with training, operate any machine." Morton said: "I think we'd better go in and have some lunch. Afterward, we've got to get busy. The material men can set up their machines and start gathering data on the planet's metal possibilities, and so on. The others can do a little careful exploring. I'd like some notes on architecture and on the scientific development of this race, and particularly what happened to wreck the civilization. On earth civilization after civilization crumbled, but always a new one sprang up in its dust. Why didn't that happen here? Any questions?"

"Yes. What about kitty? Look, he wants to come in with us."

Commander Morton frowned, an action that emphasized the deep-space pallor of his face. "I wish there was some way we could take it in with us, without forcibly capturing it. Kent, what do you think?"

"I think we should first decide whether it's an it or a him, and call it one or the other. I'm in favor of him. As for taking him in with us—" The little chemist shook his head decisively. "Impossible. This atmosphere is twenty-eight percent chlorine. Our oxygen would be pure dynamite to his lungs."

The commander chuckled. "He doesn't believe that, apparently." He watched the catlike monster follow the first two men through the great door. The men kept an anxious distance from him, then glanced at Morton questioningly. Morton waved his hand. "O.K. Open the second lock and let him get a whiff of the oxygen. That'll cure him."

A moment later, he cursed his amazement. "By Heaven, he doesn't even notice the difference! That means he hasn't any lungs, or else the chlorine is not what his lungs use. Let him in! You bet he can go in! Smith, here's a treasure house for a biologist—harmless enough if we're careful. We can always handle him. But what a metabolism!"

Smith, a tall, thin, bony chap with a long, mournful face, said in an oddly forceful voice: "In all our travels, we've found only two higher forms of life. Those dependent on chlorine, and those who need oxygen—the two elements that support combustion.

I'm prepared to stake my reputation that no complicated organism could ever adapt itself to both gases in a natural way. At first thought I should say here is an extremely advanced form of life. This race long ago discovered truths of biology that we are just beginning to suspect. Morton, we mustn't let this creature get away if we can help it."

"If his anxiety to get inside is any criterion," Commander Morton laughed, "then our difficulty will be to get rid of him."

He moved into the lock with Coeurl and the two men. The automatic machinery hummed; and in a few minutes they were standing at the bottom of a series of elevators that led up to the living quarters.

"Does that go up?" One of the men flicked a thumb in the direction of the monster.

"Better send him up alone, if he'll go in."

Coeurl offered no objection, until he heard the door slam behind him; and the closed cage shot upward. He whirled with a savage snarl, his reason swirling into chaos. With one leap, he pounced at the door. The metal bent under his plunge, and the desperate pain maddened him. Now, he was all trapped animal. He smashed at the metal with his paws, bending it like so much tin. He tore great bars loose with his thick tentacles. The machinery screeched; there were horrible jerks as the limitless power pulled the cage along in spite of projecting pieces of metal that scraped the outside walls. And then the cage stopped, and he snatched off the rest of the door and hurtled into the corridor.

He waited there until Morton and the men came up with drawn weapons. "We're fools," Morton said. "We should have shown him how it works. He thought we'd double-crossed him."

He motioned to the monster, and saw the savage glow fade from the coal-black eyes as he opened and closed the door with elaborate gestures to show the operation.

Coeurl ended the lesson by trotting into the large room to his right. He lay down on the rugged floor, and fought down the electric tautness of his nerves and muscles. A very fury of rage against himself for his fright consumed him. It seemed to his burning brain that he had lost the advantage of appearing a mild and harmless creature. His strength must have startled and dismayed them.

It meant greater danger in the task which he now knew he must accomplish: To kill everything in the ship, and take the machine back to their world in search of unlimited id.

With unwinking eyes, Coeurl lay and watched the two men clearing away the loose rubble from the metal doorway of the huge old building. His whole body ached with the hunger of his cells for id. The craving tore through his palpitant muscles, and throbbed like a living thing in his brain. His every nerve quivered to be off after the men who had wandered into the city. One of them, he knew, had gone—alone.

The dragging minutes fled; and still he restrained himself, still he lay there watching, aware that the men knew he watched. They floated a metal machine from the ship to the rock mass that blocked the great half-open door, under the direction of a third man. No flicker of their fingers escaped his fierce stare, and slowly, as the simplicity of the machinery became apparent to him, contempt grew upon him.

He knew what to expect finally, when the flame flared in incandescent violence and ate ravenously at the hard rock beneath. But in spite of his preknowledge, he deliberately jumped and snarled as if in fear, as that white heat burst forth. His ear tendrils caught the laughter of the men, their curious pleasure at his simulated dismay.

The door was released, and Morton came over and went inside with the third man. The latter shook his head.

"It's a shambles. You can catch the drift of the stuff. Obviously, they used atomic energy, but . . . but it's in wheel form. That's a peculiar development. In our science, atomic energy brought in the nonwheel machine. It's possible that here they've progressed *further* to a new type of wheel mechanics. I hope their libraries are better preserved than this, or we'll never know. What could have happened to a civilization to make it vanish like this?"

A third voice broke through the communicators: "This is

Siedel. I heard your question, Pennons. Psychologically and sociologically speaking, the only reason why a territory becomes uninhabited is lack of food."

"But they're so advanced scientifically, why didn't they develop space flying and go elsewhere for their food?"

"Ask Gunlie Lester," interjected Morton. "I heard him expounding some theory even before we landed."

The astronomer answered the first call. "I've still got to verify all my facts, but this desolate world is the only planet revolving around that miserable red sun. There's nothing else. No moon, not even a planetoid. And the nearest star system is *nine hundred light-years* away.

"So tremendous would have been the problem of the ruling race of this world, that in one jump they would not only have had to solve interplanetary but interstellar space traveling. When you consider how slow our own development was—first the moon, then Venus—each success leading to the next, and after centuries to the nearest stars; and last of all to the anti-accelerators that permitted galactic travel. Considering all this, I maintain it would be impossible for any race to create such machines without practical experience. And, with the nearest star so far away, they had no incentive for the space adventuring that makes for experience."

Coeurl was trotting briskly over to another group. But now, in the driving appetite that consumed him, and in the frenzy of his high scorn, he paid no attention to what they were doing. Memories of past knowledge, jarred into activity by what he had seen, flowed into his consciousness in an ever developing and more vivid stream.

From group to group he sped, a nervous dynamo—jumpy, sick with his awful hunger. A little car rolled up, stopping in front of him, and a formidable camera whirred as it took a picture of him. Over on a mound of rock, a gigantic telescope was rearing up toward the sky. Nearby, a disintegrating machine drilled its searing fire into an ever-deepening hole, down and down, straight down.

Coeurl's mind became a blur of things he watched with half attention. And ever more imminent grew the moment when he knew he could no longer carry on the torture of acting. His brain strained with an irresistible impatience; his body burned with the fury of his eagerness to be off after the man who had gone alone into the city.

He could stand it no longer. A green foam misted his mouth, maddening him. He saw that, for the bare moment, nobody was looking.

Like a shot from a gun, he was off. He floated along in great, gliding leaps, a shadow among the shadows of the rocks. In a minute, the harsh terrain hid the spaceship and the two-legged beings.

Coeurl forgot the ship, forgot everything but his purpose, as if his brain had been wiped clear by a magic, memory-erasing brush. He circled widely, then raced into the city, along deserted streets, taking short cuts with the ease of familiarity, through gaping holes in time-weakened walls, through long corridors of moldering buildings. He slowed to a crouching lope as his ear tendrils caught the id vibrations.

Suddenly, he stopped and peered from a scatter of fallen rock. The man was standing at what must once have been a window, sending the glaring rays of his flashlight into the gloomy interior. The flashight clicked off. The man, a heavy-set, powerful fellow, walked off with quick, alert steps. Coeurl didn't like that alertness. It presaged trouble; it meant lightning reaction to danger.

Coeurl waited till the human being had vanished around a corner, then he padded into the open. He was running now, tremendously faster than a man could walk, because his plan was clear in his brain. Like a wraith, he slipped down the next street, past a long block of buildings. He turned the first corner at top speed; and then, with dragging belly, crept into the half-darkness between the building and a huge chunk of débris. The street ahead was barred by a solid line of loose rubble that made it like a valley, ending in a narrow, bottlelike neck. The neck had its outlet just below Coeurl.

His ear tendrils caught the low-frequency waves of whistling. The sound throbbed through his being; and suddenly terror caught with icy fingers at his brain. The man would have a gun. Suppose he leveled one burst of atomic energy—*one burst*— before his own muscles could whip out in murder fury.

A little shower of rocks streamed past. And then the man was beneath him. Coeurl reached out and struck a single crushing blow at the shimmering transparent headpiece of the spacesuit. There was a tearing sound of metal and a gushing of blood. The man doubled up as if part of him had been telescoped. For a moment, his bones and legs and muscles combined miraculously to keep him standing. Then he crumpled with a metallic clank of his space armor.

Fear completely evaporated, Coeurl leaped out of hiding. With ravenous speed, he smashed the metal and the body within it to bits. Great chunks of metal, torn piecemeal from the suit, sprayed the ground. Bones cracked. Flesh crunched.

It was simple to tune in on the vibrations of the id, and to create the violent chemical disorganization that freed it from the crushed bone. The id was, Coeurl discovered, mostly in the bone.

He felt revived, almost reborn. Here was more food than he had had in the whole past year.

Three minutes, and it was over, and Coeurl was off like a thing fleeing dire danger. Cautiously, he approached the glistening globe from the opposite side to that by which he had left. The men were all busy at their tasks. Gliding noiselessly, Coeurl slipped unnoticed up to a group of men.

Morton stared down at the horror of tattered flesh, metal and blood on the rock at his feet, and felt a tightening in his throat that prevented speech. He heard Kent say:

"He *would* go alone, damn him!" The little chemist's voice held a sob imprisoned; and Morton remembered that Kent and Jarvey had chummed together for years in the way only two men can.

"The worst part of it is," shuddered one of the men, "it looks like a senseless murder. His body is spread out like little lumps of flattened jelly, but it seems to be all there. I'd almost wager there'd still be one hundred and seventy-five pounds by earth gravity. That'd be about one hundred and seventy pounds here."

Smith broke in, his mournful face lined with gloom: "The killer attacked Jarvey, and then discovered his flesh was alien—

uneatable. Just like our big cat. Wouldn't eat anything we set before him—" His words died out in sudden, queer silence. Then he said slowly: "Say, what about that creature? He's big enough and strong enough to have done this with his own little paws."

Morton frowned. "It's a thought. After all, he's the only living thing we've seen. We can't just execute him on suspicion, of course—"

"Besides," said one of the men, "he was never out of my sight."

Before Morton could speak, Siedel, the psychologist, snapped, "Positive about that?"

The man hesitated. "Maybe he was for a few minutes. He was wandering around so much, looking at everything."

"Exactly," said Siedel with satisfaction. He turned to Morton. "You see, commander, I, too, had the impression that he was always around; and yet thinking back over it, I find gaps. There were moments—probably long minutes—when he was completely out of sight."

Morton's face was dark with thought, as Kent broke in fiercely: "I say, take no chances. Kill the brute on suspicion before he does any more damage."

Morton said slowly: "Korita, you've been wandering around with Cranessy and Van Horne. Do you think kitty is a descendant of the ruling class of this planet?"

The tall Japanese archeologist stared at the sky as if collecting his mind. "Commander Morton," he said finally, respectfully, "there is a mystery here. Take a look, all of you, at the majestic skyline. Notice the almost Gothic outline of the architecture. In spite of the megalopolis which they created, these people were close to the soil. The buildings are not simply ornamented. They are ornamental in themselves. Here is the equivalent of the Doric column, the Egyptian pyramid, the Gothic cathedral, growing out of the ground, earnest, big with destiny. If this lonely, desolate world can be regarded as a mother earth, then the land had a warm, a spiritual place in the hearts of the race.

"The effect is emphasized by the winding streets. Their machines prove they were mathematicians, but they were artists first; and so they did not create the geometrically designed cities of the ultra-sophisticated world metropolis. There is a genuine artistic abandon, a deep joyous emotion written in the curving and unmathematical arrangements of houses, buildings and avenues; a sense of intensity, of divine belief in an inner certainty. This is not a decadent, hoary-with-age civilization, but a young and vigorous culture, confident, strong with purpose.

"There it ended. Abruptly, as if at this point culture had its Battle of Tours, and began to collapse like the ancient Mohammedan civilization. Or as if in one leap it spanned the centuries and entered the period of contending states. In the Chinese civilization that period occupied 480–230 B.C., at the end of which the State of Tsin saw the beginning of the Chinese Empire. This phase Egypt experienced between 1780–1580 B.C., of which the last century was the 'Hyksos'—unmentionable—time. The classical experienced it from Chaeronea—338—and, at the pitch of horror, from the Grachi—133—to Actium—31 B.C. The West European Americans were devastated by it in the nineteenth and twentieth centuries, and modern historians agree that, nominally, we entered the same phase fifty years ago; though, of course, we have solved the problem.

"You may ask, commander, what has all this to do with your question? My answer is: there is no record of a culture entering abruptly into the period of contending states. It is always a slow development; and the first step is a merciless questioning of all that was once held sacred. Inner certainties cease to exist, are dissolved before the ruthless probings of scientific and analytic minds. The skeptic becomes the highest type of being.

"I say that this culture ended abruptly in its most flourishing age. The sociological effects of such a catastrophe would be a sudden vanishing of morals, a reversion to almost bestial criminality, unleavened by any sense of ideal, a callous indifference to death. If this . . . this kitty is a descendant of such a race, then he will be a cunning creature, a thief in the night, a cold-blooded murderer, who would cut his own brother's throat for gain." "That's enough!" It was Kent's clipped voice. "Commander, I'm willing to act the role of executioner."

Smith interrupted sharply: "Listen, Morton, you're not going to kill that cat yet, even if he is guilty. He's a biological treasure house."

Kent and Smith were glaring angrily at each other. Morton frowned at them thoughtfully, then said: "Korita. I'm inclined to accept your theory as a working basis. But one question: Kitty comes from a period earlier than our own? That is, we are entering the highly civilized era of our culture, while he became suddenly historyless in the most vigorous period of his. *But* it is possible that his culture is a later one on this planet than ours is in the galactic-wide system we have civilized?"

"Exactly. His may be the middle of the tenth civilization of his world; while ours is the end of the eighth sprung from earth, each of the ten, of course, having been builded on the ruins of the one before it."

"In that case, kitty would not know anything about the skepticism that made it possible for us to find him out so positively as a criminal and murderer?"

"No; it would be literally magic to him."

Morton was smiling grimly. "Then I think you'll get your wish, Smith. We'll let kitty live; and if there are any fatalities, now that we know him, it will be due to rank carelessness. There's just the chance, of course, that we're wrong. Like Siedel, I also have the impression that he was always around. But now—we can't leave poor Jarvey here like this. We'll put him in a coffin and bury him."

"No, we won't!" Kent barked. He flushed. "I beg your pardon, commander. I didn't mean it that way. I maintain kitty wanted something from that body. It looks to be all there, but something must be missing. I'm going to find out what, and pin this murder on him so that you'll have to believe it beyond the shadow of a doubt."

It was late night when Morton looked up from a book and saw Kent emerge through the door that led from the laboratories below.

Kent carried a large, flat bowl in his hands; his tired eyes flashed across at Morton, and he said in a weary, yet harsh, voice: "Now watch!"

He started toward Coeurl, who lay sprawled on the great rug, pretending to be asleep.

Morton stopped him. "Wait a minute, Kent. Any other time, I wouldn't question your actions, but you look ill; you're overwrought. What have you got there?"

Kent turned, and Morton saw that his first impression had been but a flashing glimpse of the truth. There were dark pouches under the little chemist's gray eyes—eyes that gazed feverishly from sunken cheeks in an ascetic face.

"I've found the missing element," Kent said. "It's phosphorus. There wasn't so much as a square millimeter of phosphorus left in Jarvey's bones. Every bit of it had been drained out—by what superchemistry I don't know. There are ways of getting phosphorus out of the human body. For instance, a quick way was what happened to the workman who helped build this ship. Remember, he fell into fifteen tons of molten metalite—at least, so his relatives claimed—but the company wouldn't pay compensation until the metalite, on analysis, was found to contain a high percentage of phosphorus—"

"What about the bowl of food?" somebody interrupted. Men were putting away magazines and books, looking up with interest.

"It's got organic phosphorus in it. He'll get the scent, or whatever it is that he uses instead of scent—"

"I think he gets the vibrations of things," Gourlay interjected lazily. "Sometimes, when he wiggles those tendrils, I get a distinct static on the radio. And then, again, there's no reaction, just as if he's moved higher or lower on the wave scale. He seems to control the vibrations at will."

Kent waited with obvious impatience until Gourlay's last word, then abruptly went on: "All right, then, when he gets the vibration of the phosphorus and reacts to it like an animal, then —well, we can decide what we've proved by his reaction. Can I go ahead, Morton?"

"There are three things wrong with your plan," Morton said. "In the first place, you seem to assume that he is only animal; you seem to have forgotten he may not be hungry after Jarvey; you seem to think that he will not be suspicious. But set the bowl down. His reaction may tell us something."

Coeurl stared with unblinking black eyes as the man set the bowl before him. His ear tendrils instantly caught the id-vibrations from the contents of the bowl—and he gave it not even a second glance.

He recognized this two-legged being as the one who had held the weapon that morning. Danger! With a snarl, he floated to his feet. He caught the bowl with the fingerlike appendages at the end of one looping tentacle, and emptied its contents into the face of Kent, who shrank back with a yell.

Explosively, Coeurl flung the bowl aside and snapped a hawser-thick tentacle around the cursing man's waist. He didn't bother with the gun that hung from Kent's belt. It was only a vibration gun, he sensed—atomic powered, but not an atomic disintegrator. He tossed the kicking Kent onto the nearest couch —and realized with a hiss of dismay that he should have disarmed the man.

Not that the gun was dangerous—but, as the man furiously wiped the gruel from his face with one hand, he reached with the other for his weapon. Coeurl crouched back as the gun was raised slowly and a white beam of flame was discharged at his massive head.

His ear tendrils hummed as they canceled the efforts of the vibration gun. His round, black eyes narrowed as he caught the movement of men reaching for their metalite guns. Morton's voice lashed across the silence.

"Stop!"

Kent clicked off his weapon; and Coeurl crouched down, quivering with fury at this man who had forced him to reveal something of his power.

"Kent," said Morton coldly, "you're not the type to lose your head. You deliberately tried to kill kitty, knowing that the majority of us are in favor of keeping him alive. You know what our rule is: If anyone objects to my decisions, he must say so *at the time*. If the majority object, my decisions are overruled. In this case, no one but you objected, and, therefore, your action in taking the law into your own hands is most reprehensible, and automatically debars you from voting for a year."

Kent stared grimly at the circle of faces. "Korita was right

when he said ours was a highly civilized age. It's decadent."
Passion flamed harshly in his voice. "My God, isn't there a man
here who can see the horror of the situation? Jarvey dead only
a few hours, and this creature, whom we all know to be guilty,
lying there unchained, planning his next murder; and the victim
is right here in this room. What kind of men are we—fools,
cynics, ghouls—or is it that our civilization is so steeped in
reason that we can contemplate a murderer sympathetically?"

He fixed brooding eyes on Coeurl. "You were right, Morton,
that's no animal. That's a devil from the deepest hell of this
planet, whirling its solitary way around a dying sun."

"Don't go melodramatic on us," Morton said. "Your analysis is
all wrong, so far as I am concerned. We're not ghouls or cynics;
we're simply scientists, and kitty here is going to be studied. Now
that we suspect him, we doubt his ability to trap any of us.
One against a hundred hasn't a chance." He glanced around. "Do
I speak for all of us?"

"Not for me, commander!" It was Smith who spoke, and, as
Morton stared in amazement, he continued: "In the excitement
and momentary confusion, no one seems to have noticed that
when Kent fired his vibration gun, the beam hit this creature
squarely on his cat head—and didn't hurt him."

Morton's amazed glance went from Smith to Coeurl, and back
to Smith again. "Are you certain it hit him? As you say, it all
happened so swiftly—when kitty wasn't hurt I simply assumed
that Kent had missed him."

"He hit him in the face," Smith said positively. "A vibration
gun, of course, can't even kill a man right away—but it can
injure him. There's no sign of injury on kitty, though, not even
a singed hair."

"Perhaps his skin is a good insulation against heat of any
kind."

"Perhaps. But in view of our uncertainty, I think we should
lock him up in the cage."

While Morton frowned darkly in thought, Kent spoke up. "Now
you're talking sense, Smith."

Morton asked: "Then you would be satisfied, Kent, if we put
him in the cage?"

Kent considered, finally: "Yes. If four inches of micro-steel can't hold him, we'd better give him the ship."

Coeurl followed the men as they went out into the corridor. He trotted docilely along as Morton unmistakably motioned him through a door he had not hitherto seen. He found himself in a square solid metal room. The door clanged metallically behind him; he felt the flow of power as the electric lock clicked home.

His lips parted in a grimace of hate, as he realized the trap, but he gave no other outward reaction. It occurred to him that he had progressed a long way from the sunk-into-primitiveness creature who, a few hours before, had gone incoherent with fear in an elevator cage. Now, a thousand memories of his powers were reawakened in his brain; ten thousand cunnings were, after ages of disuse, once again part of his very being.

He sat quite still for a moment on the short, heavy haunches into which his body tapered, his ear tendrils examining his surroundings. Finally, he lay down, his eyes glowing with contemptuous fire. The fools! The poor fools!

It was about an hour later when he heard the man—Smith—fumbling overhead. Vibrations poured upon him, and for just an instant he was startled. He leaped to his feet in pure terror —and then realized that the vibrations *were* vibrations, not atomic explosions. Somebody was taking pictures of the inside of his body.

He crouched down again, but his ear tendrils vibrated, and he thought contemptuously: the silly fool would be surprised when he tried to develop those pictures.

After a while the man went away, and for a long time there were noises of men doing things far away. That, too, died away slowly.

Coeurl lay waiting, as he felt the silence creep over the ship. In the long ago, before the dawn of immortality, the coeurls, too, had slept at night; and the memory of it had been revived the day before when he saw some of the men dozing. At last, the vibration of two pairs of feet, pacing, pacing endlessly, was the only human-made frequency that throbbed on his ear tendrils.

Tensely, he listened to the two watchmen. The first one walked slowly past the cage door. Then about thirty feet behind him came the second. Coeurl sensed the alertness of these men; knew that he could never surprise either while they walked separately. It meant—he must be doubly careful!

Fifteen minutes, and they came again. The moment they were past, he switched his senses from their vibrations to a vastly higher range. The pulsating violence of the atomic engines stammered its soft story to his brain. The electric dynamos hummed their muffled song of pure power. He felt the whisper of that flow through the wires in the walls of his cage, and through the electric lock of his door. He forced his quivering body into straining immobility, his senses seeking, searching, to tune in on that sibilant tempest of energy. Suddenly, his ear tendrils vibrated in harmony—he caught the surging change into shrillness of that rippling force wave.

There was a sharp click of metal on metal. With a gentle touch of one tentacle, Coeurl pushed open the door, and glided out into the dully gleaming corridor. For just a moment, he felt contempt, a glow of superiority, as he thought of the stupid creatures who dared to match their wit against a coeurl. And in that moment, he suddenly thought of other coeurls. A queer, exultant sense of race pounded through his being; the driving hate of centuries of ruthless competition yielded reluctantly before pride of kinship with the future rulers of all space.

Suddenly, he felt weighed down by his limitations, his need for other coeurls, his aloneness—one against a hundred, with the stake all eternity; the starry universe itself beckoned his rapacious, vaulting ambition. If he failed, there would never be a second chance—no time to revive long-rotted machinery, and attempt to solve the secret of space travel.

He padded along on tensed paws—through the salon—into the next corridor—and came to the first bedroom door. It stood half open. One swift flow of synchronized muscles, one swiftly lashing tentacle that caught the unresisting throat of the sleeping man, crushing it; and the lifeless head rolled crazily, the body twitched once.

Seven bedrooms; seven dead men. It was the seventh taste of

murder that brought a sudden return of lust, a pure, unbounded desire to kill, return of a millennium-old habit of destroying everything containing the precious id.

As the twelfth man slipped convulsively into death, Coeurl emerged abruptly from the sensuous joy of the kill to the sound of footsteps.

They were not near—that was what brought wave after wave of fright swirling into the chaos that suddenly became his brain.

The watchmen were coming slowly along the corridor toward the door of the cage where he had been imprisoned. In a moment, the first man would see the open door—and sound the alarm.

Coeurl caught at the vanishing remnants of his reason. With frantic speed, careless now of accidental sounds, he raced—along the corridor with its bedroom doors—through the salon. He emerged into the next corridor, cringing in awful anticipation of the atomic flame he expected would stab into his face.

The two men were together, standing side by side. For one single instant, Coeurl could scarcely believe his tremendous good luck. Like a fool the second had come running when he saw the other stop before the open door. They looked up, paralyzed, before the nightmare of claws and tentacles, the ferocious cat head and hate-filled eyes.

The first man went for his gun, but the second, physically frozen before the doom he saw, uttered a shriek, a shrill cry of horror that floated along the corridors—and ended in a curious gurgle, as Coeurl flung the two corpses with one irresistible motion the full length of the corridor. He didn't want the dead bodies found near the cage. That was his one hope.

Shaking in every nerve and muscle, conscious of the terrible error he had made, unable to think coherently, he plunged into the cage. The door clicked softly shut behind him. Power flowed once more through the electric lock.

He crouched tensely, simulating sleep, as he heard the rush of many feet, caught the vibration of excited voices. He knew when somebody actuated the cage audioscope and looked in. A few moments now, and the other bodies would be discovered.

"Siedel gone!" Morton said numbly. "What are we going to

do without Siedel? And Breckenridge! And Coulter and—
Horrible!"

He covered his face with his hands, but only for an instant. He
looked up grimly, his heavy chin outthrust as he stared into the
stern faces that surrounded him. "If anybody's got so much as a
germ of an idea, bring it out."

"Space madness!"

"I've thought of that. But there hasn't been a case of a man
going mad for fifty years. Dr. Eggert will test everybody, of
course, and right now he's looking at the bodies with that possibility in mind."

As he finished, he saw the doctor coming through the door.
Men crowded aside to make way for him.

"I heard you, commander," Dr. Eggert said, "and I think I
can say right now that the space-madness theory is out. The
throats of these men have been squeezed to a jelly. No human
being could have exerted such enormous strength without using
a machine."

Morton saw that the doctor's eyes kept looking down the corridor, and he shook his head and groaned:

"It's no use suspecting kitty, doctor. He's in his cage, pacing
up and down. Obviously heard the racket and— Man alive!
You can't suspect him. That cage was built to hold literally *anything*—four inches of micro-steel—and there's not a scratch on
the door. Kent, even you won't say, 'Kill him on suspicion,'
because there can't be any suspicion, unless there's a new science
here, beyond anything we can imagine—"

"On the contrary," said Smith flatly, "we have all the evidence
we need. I used the telefluor on him—you know the arrangement we have on top of the cage—and tried to take some pictures. They just blurred. Kitty jumped when the telefluor was
turned on, as if he felt the vibrations.

"You all know what Gourlay said before? This beast can apparently receive and send vibrations of any lengths. The way he
dominated the power of Kent's gun is final proof of his special
ability to interfere with energy."

"What in the name of all the hells have we got here?" One
of the men groaned. "Why, if he can control that power, and

send it out in any vibrations, there's nothing to stop him killing all of us."

"Which proves," snapped Morton, "that he isn't invincible, or he would have done it long ago."

Very deliberately, he walked over to the mechanism that controlled the prison cage.

"You're not going to open the door!" Kent gasped, reaching for his gun.

"No, but if I pull this switch, electricity will flow through the floor, and electrocute whatever's inside. We've never had to use this before, so you had probably forgotten about it."

He jerked the switch hard over. Blue fire flashed from the metal, and a bank of fuses above his head exploded with a single bang.

Morton frowned. "That's funny. Those fuses shouldn't have blown! Well, we can't even look in, now. That wrecked the audios, too."

Smith said: "If he could interfere with the electric lock, enough to open the door, then he probably probed every possible danger and was ready to interfere when you threw that switch."

"At least, it proves he's vulnerable to our energies!" Morton smiled grimly. "Because he rendered them harmless. The important thing is, we've got him behind four inches of the toughest of metal. At the worst we can open the door and ray him to death. But first, I think we'll try to use the telefluor power cable—"

A commotion from inside the cage interrupted his words. A heavy body crashed against a wall, followed by a dull thump.

"He knows what we were trying to do!" Smith grunted to Morton. "And I'll bet it's a very sick kitty in there. What a fool he was to go back into that cage and does he realize it!"

The tension was relaxing; men were smiling nervously, and there was even a ripple of humorless laughter at the picture Smith drew of the monster's discomfiture.

"What I'd like to know," said Pennons, the engineer, "is, why did the telefluor meter dial jump and waver at full power when kitty made that noise? It's right under my nose here, and the dial jumped like a house afire!"

There was silence both without and within the cage, then Morton said: "It may mean he's coming out. Back, everybody, and keep your guns ready. Kitty was a fool to think he could conquer a hundred men, but he's by far the most formidable creature in the galactic system. He may come out of that door, rather than die like a rat in a trap. And he's just tough enough to take some of us with him—if we're not careful."

The men backed slowly in a solid body; and somebody said: "That's funny. I thought I heard the elevator."

"Elevator!" Morton echoed. "Are you sure, man?"

"Just for a moment I was!" The man, a member of the crew, hesitated. "We were all shuffling our feet—"

"Take somebody with you, and go look. Bring whoever dared to run off back here—"

There was a jar, a horrible jerk, as the whole gigantic body of the ship careened under them. Morton was flung to the floor with a violence that stunned him. He fought back to consciousness, aware of the other men lying all around him. He shouted: "Who the devil started those engines!"

The agonizing acceleration continued; his feet dragged with awful exertion, as he fumbled with the nearest audioscope, and punched the engine-room number. The picture that flooded onto the screen brought a deep bellow to his lips:

"It's kitty! He's in the engine room—and we're heading straight out into space."

The screen went black even as he spoke, and he could see no more.

It was Morton who first staggered across the salon floor to the supply room where the spacesuits were kept. After fumbling almost blindly into his own suit, he cut the effects of the body-torturing acceleration, and brought suits to the semiconscious men on the floor. In a few moments, other men were assisting him; and then it was only a matter of minutes before everybody was clad in metalite, with anti-acceleration motors running at half power.

It was Morton then who, after first looking into the cage, opened the door and stood, silent as the others crowded about him, to stare at the gaping hole in the real wall. The hole was a frightful thing of jagged edges and horribly bent metal, and it opened upon another corridor.

"I'll swear," whispered Pennons, "that it's impossible. The ten-ton hammer in the machine shops couldn't more than dent four inches of micro with one blow—and we only heard one. It would take at least a minute for an atomic disintegrator to do the job. Morton, this is a super-being."

Morton saw that Smith was examining the break in the wall. The biologist looked up. "If only Breckenridge weren't dead! We need a metallurgist to explain this. Look!"

He touched the broken edge of the metal. A piece crumbled in his finger and slithered away in a fine shower of dust to the floor. Morton noticed for the first time that there was a little pile of metallic débris and dust.

"You've hit it." Morton nodded. "No miracle of strength here. The monster merely used his special powers to interfere with the electronic tensions holding the metal together. That would account, too, for the drain on the telefluor power cable that Pennons noticed. The thing used the power with his body as a transforming medium, smashed through the wall, ran down the corridor to the elevator shaft, and so down to the engine room."

"In the meantime, commander," Kent said quietly, "we are faced with a super-being in control of the ship, completely dominating the engine room, and its almost unlimited power, and in possession of the best part of the machine shops."

Morton felt the silence, while the men pondered the chemist's words. Their anxiety was a tangible thing that lay heavily upon their faces; in every expression was the growing realization that here was the ultimate situation in their lives; their very existence was at stake, and perhaps much more. Morton voiced the thought in everybody's mind:

"Suppose he wins. He's utterly ruthless, and he probably sees galactic power within his grasp."

"Kent is wrong," barked the chief navigator. "The thing doesn't dominate the engine room. We've still got the control room, and that gives us *first* control of all the machines. You fellows may not know the mechanical set-up we have; but, though he can eventually disconnect us, we can cut off all the switches in the engine room *now*. Commander, why didn't you just shut off the power instead of putting us into spacesuits? At the very least you could have adjusted the ship to the acceleration."

"For two reasons," Morton answered. "Individually, we're safer within the force fields of our spacesuits. And we can't afford to give up our advantages in panicky moves."

"Advantages. What other advantages have we got?"

"We know things about him," Morton replied. "And right now, we're going to make a test. Pennons, detail five men to each of the four approaches to the engine room. Take atomic disintegrators to blast through the big doors. They're all shut, I noticed. He's locked himself in.

"Selenski, you go up to the control room and shut off everything except the drive engines. Gear them to the master switch, and shut them off all at once. One thing, though—leave the acceleration on full blast. No anti-acceleration must be applied to the ship. Understand?"

"Aye, sir!" The pilot saluted.

"And report to me through the communicators if any of the machines start to run again." He faced the men. "I'm going to lead the main approach. Kent, you take No. 2; Smith, No. 3; and Pennons, No. 4. We're going to find out right now if we're dealing with unlimited science, or a creature limited like the rest of us. I'll bet on the last possibility."

Morton had an empty sense of walking endlessly, as he moved, a giant of a man in his transparent space armor, along the glistening metal tube that was the main corridor of the engine-room floor. Reason told him the creature had already shown feet of clay, yet the feeling that here was an invincible being persisted.

He spoke into the communicator: "It's no use trying to sneak up on him. He can probably hear a pin drop. So just wheel up your units. He hasn't been in that engine room long enough to do anything.

"As I've said, this is largely a test attack. In the first place, we could never forgive ourselves if we didn't try to conquer him now, before he's had time to prepare against us. But, aside from the possibility that we can destroy him immediately, I have a theory.

"The idea goes something like this: Those doors are built to withstand accidental atomic explosions, and it will take fifteen minutes for the atomic disintegrators to smash them. During that period the monster will have no power. True, the drive will be on, but that's straight atomic explosion. My theory is, he can't touch stuff like that; and in a few minutes you'll see what I mean —I hope."

His voice was suddenly crisp: "Ready, Selenski?"

"Aye, ready."

"Then cut the master switch."

The corridor—the whole ship, Morton knew—was abruptly plunged into darkness. Morton clicked on the dazzling light of his spacesuit; the other men did the same, their faces pale and drawn.

"Blast!" Morton barked into his communicator.

The mobile units throbbed; and then pure atomic flame ravened out and poured upon the hard metal of the door. The first molten droplet rolled reluctantly, not down, but up the door. The second was more normal. It followed a shaky downward course. The third rolled sideways—for this was pure force, not subject to gravitation. Other drops followed until a dozen streams trickled sedately yet unevenly in every direction—streams of hellish, sparkling fire, bright as fairy gems, alive with the coruscating fury of atoms suddenly tortured, and running blindly, crazy with pain.

The minutes ate at time like a slow acid. At last Morton asked huskily:

"Selenski?"

"Nothing yet, commander."

Morton half whispered: "But he must be doing something. He can't be just waiting in there like a cornered rat. Selenski?"

"Nothing, commander."

Seven minutes, eight minutes, then twelve.

"Commander!" It was Selenski's voice, taut. "He's got the electric dynamo running."

Morton drew a deep breath, and heard one of his men say:

"That's funny. We can't get any deeper. Boss, take a look at this."

Morton looked. The little scintillating streams had frozen rigid. The ferocity of the disintegrators vented in vain against metal grown suddenly invulnerable.

Morton sighed. "Our test is over. Leave two men guarding every corridor. The others come up to the control room."

He seated himself a few minutes later before the massive control keyboard. "So far as I'm concerned the test was a success. We know that of all the machines in the engine room, the most important to the monster was the electric dynamo. He must have worked in a frenzy of terror while we were at the doors."

"Of course, it's easy to see what he did," Pennons said. "Once he had the power he increased the electronic tensions of the door to their ultimate."

"The main thing is this," Smith chimed in. "He works with vibrations only so far as his special powers are concerned, and the energy must come from outside himself. Atomic energy in its pure form, not being vibration, he can't handle any differently than we can."

Kent said glumly: "The main point in my opinion is that he stopped us cold. What's the good of knowing that his control over vibrations did it? If we can't break through those doors with our atomic disintegrators, we're finished."

Morton shook his head. "Not finished—but we'll have to do some planning. First, though, I'll start these engines. It'll be harder for him to get control of them when they're running."

He pulled the master switch back into place with a jerk. There was a hum, as scores of machines leaped into violent life in the engine room a hundred feet below. The noises sank to a steady vibration of throbbing power.

Three hours later, Morton paced up and down before the men gathered in the salon. His dark hair was uncombed; the space pallor of his strong face emphasized rather than detracted from the outthrust aggressiveness of his jaw. When he spoke, his deep voice was crisp to the point of sharpness:

"To make sure that our plans are fully co-ordinated, I'm going to ask each expert in turn to outline his part in the overpowering of this creature. Pennons first!"

Pennons stood up briskly. He was not a big man, Morton thought, yet he looked big, perhaps because of his air of authority. This man knew engines, and the history of engines. Morton had heard him trace a machine through its evolution from a simple toy to the highly complicated modern instrument. He had studied machine development on a hundred planets; and there was literally nothing fundamental that he didn't know about mechanics. It was almost weird to hear Pennons, who could have spoken for a thousand hours and still only have touched upon his subject, say with absurd brevity:

"We've set up a relay in the control room to start and stop every engine rhythmically. The trip lever will work a hundred times a second, and the effect will be to create vibrations of every description. There is just a possibility that one or more of the machines will burst, on the principle of soldiers crossing a bridge in step—you've heard that old story, no doubt—but in my opinion there is no real danger of a break of that tough metal. The main purpose is simply to interfere with the interference of the creature, and smash through the doors."

"Gourlay next!" barked Morton.

Gourlay climbed lazily to his feet. He looked sleepy, as if he was somewhat bored by the whole proceedings, yet Morton knew he loved people to think him lazy, a good-for-nothing slouch, who spent his days in slumber and his nights catching forty winks. His title was chief communication engineer, but his knowledge extended to every vibration field; and he was probably, with the possible exception of Kent, the fastest thinker on the ship. His voice drawled out, and—Morton noted—the very deliberate assurance of it had a soothing effect on the men —anxious faces relaxed, bodies leaned back more restfully:

"Once inside," Gourlay said, "we've rigged up vibration screens of pure force that should stop nearly everything he's got on the ball. They work on the principle of reflection, so that everything he sends will be reflected back to him. In addition, we've got plenty of spare electric energy that we'll just feed him from mobile copper cups. There must be a limit to his capacity for handling power with those insulated nerves of his."

"Selenski!" called Morton.

The chief pilot was already standing, as if he had anticipated Morton's call. And that, Morton reflected, was the man. His nerves had that rocklike steadiness which is the first requirement of the master controller of a great ship's movements; yet that very steadiness seemed to rest on dynamite ready to explode at its owner's volition. He was not a man of great learning, but he "reacted" to stimuli so fast that he always seemed to be anticipating.

"The impression I've received of the plan is that it must be cumulative. Just when the creature thinks that he can't stand any more, another thing happens to add to his trouble and confusion. When the uproar's at its height, I'm supposed to cut in the anti-accelerators. The commander thinks with Gunlie Lester that these creatures will know nothing about anti-acceleration. It's a development, pure and simple, of the science of interstellar flight, and couldn't have been developed in any other way. We think when the creature feels the first effects of the anti-acceleration—you all remember the caved-in feeling you had the first month—it won't know what to think or do."

"Korita next."

"I can only offer you encouragement," said the archeologist, "on the basis of my theory that the monster has all the characteristics of a criminal of the early ages of any civilization, complicated by an apparent reversion to primitiveness. The suggestion has been made by Smith that his knowledge of science is puzzling, and could only mean that we are dealing with an actual inhabitant, not a descendant of the inhabitants of the dead city we visited. This would ascribe a virtual immortality to our enemy, a possibility which is borne out by his ability to breathe both oxygen and chlorine—or neither—but even that makes no difference. He comes from a certain age in his civilization; and he has sunk so low that his ideas are mostly memories of that age.

"In spite of all the powers of his body, he lost his head in the elevator the first morning, until he remembered. He placed himself in such a position that he was forced to reveal his special powers against vibrations. He bungled the mass murders a few hours ago. In fact, his whole record is one of the low cunning of the primitive, egotistical mind which has little or no conception of the vast organization with which it is confronted.

"He is like the ancient German soldier who felt superior to the elderly Roman scholar, yet the latter was part of a mighty civilization of which the Germans of that day stood in awe.

"You may suggest that the sack of Rome by the Germans in later years defeats my argument; however, modern historians agree that the 'sack' was an historical accident, and not history in the true sense of the word. The movement of the 'Sea-peoples' which set in against the Egyptian civilization from 1400 B.C. succeeded only as regards the Cretan island-realm—their mighty expeditions against the Libyan and Phœnician coasts, with the accompaniment of viking fleets, failed as those of the Huns failed against the Chinese Empire. Rome would have been abandoned in any event. Ancient, glorious Samarra was desolate by the tenth century; Pataliputra, Asoka's great capital, was an immense and completely uninhabited waste of houses when the Chinese traveler Hsinan-tang visited it about A.D. 635.

"We have, then, a primitive, and that primitive is now far out in space, completely outside of his natural habitat. I say, let's go in and win."

One of the men grumbled, as Korita finished: "You can talk about the sack of Rome being an accident, and about this fellow being a primitive, but the facts are facts. It looks to me as if Rome is about to fall again; and it won't be no primitive that did it, either. This guy's got plenty of what it takes."

Morton smiled grimly at the man, a member of the crew. "We'll see about that—right now!"

In the blazing brilliance of the gigantic machine shop, Coeurl slaved. The forty-foot, cigar-shaped spaceship was nearly finished. With a grunt of effort, he completed the laborious installation of the drive engines, and paused to survey his craft.

Its interior, visible through the one aperture in the outer wall, was pitifully small. There was literally room for nothing but the engines—and a narrow space for himself.

He plunged frantically back to work as he heard the approach of the men, and the sudden change in the tempest-like thunder of the engines—a rhythmical off-and-on hum, shriller in tone, sharper, more nerve-racking than the deep-throated, steady throb that had preceded it. Suddenly, there were the atomic disintegrators again at the massive outer doors.

He fought them off, but never wavered from his task. Every mighty muscle of his powerful body strained as he carried great loads of tools, machines and instruments, and dumped them into the bottom of his makeshift ship. There was no time to fit anything into place, no time for anything—no time—no time.

The thought pounded at his reason. He felt strangely weary for the first time in his long and vigorous existence. With a last, tortured heave, he jerked the gigantic sheet of metal into the gaping aperture of the ship—and stood there for a terrible minute, balancing it precariously.

He knew the doors were going down. Half a dozen disintegrators concentrating on one point were irresistibly, though slowly, eating away the remaining inches. With a gasp, he released his mind from the doors and concentrated every ounce of his mind on the yard-thick outer wall, toward which the blunt nose of his ship was pointing.

His body cringed from the surging power that flowed from the electric dynamo through his ear tendrils into that resisting wall. The whole inside of him felt on fire, and he knew that he was dangerously close to carrying his ultimate load.

And still he stood there, shuddering with the awful pain, holding the unfastened metal plate with hard-clenched tentacles. His massive head pointed as in dread fascination at that bitterly hard wall.

He heard one of the engine-room doors crash inward. Men shouted; disintegrators rolled forward, their raging power unchecked. Coeurl heard the floor of the engine room hiss in protest, as those beams of atomic energy tore everything in their path to bits. The machines rolled closer; cautious footsteps sounded behind them. In a minute they would be at the flimsy doors separating the engine room from the machine shop.

Suddenly, Coeurl was satisfied. With a snarl of hate, a vindictive glow of feral eyes, he ducked into his little craft, and pulled the metal plate down into place as if it was a hatchway.

His ear tendrils hummed, as he softened the edges of the surrounding metal. In an instant, the plate was more than welded —it was part of his ship, a seamless, rivetless part of a whole that was solid opaque metal except for two transparent areas, one in the front, one in the rear.

His tentacle embraced the power drive with almost sensuous tenderness. There was a forward surge of his fragile machine, straight at the great outer wall of the machine shops. The nose of the forty-foot craft touched—and the wall dissolved in a glittering shower of dust.

Coeurl felt the barest retarding movement; and then he kicked the nose of the machine out into the cold of space, twisted it about, and headed back in the direction from which the big ship had been coming all these hours.

Men in space armor stood in the jagged hole that yawned in the lower reaches of the gigantic globe. The men and the great ship grew smaller. Then the men were gone; and there was only the ship with its blaze of a thousand blurring portholes. The ball shrank incredibly, too small now for individual portholes to be visible.

Almost straight ahead, Coeurl saw a tiny, dim, reddish ball— his own sun, he realized. He headed toward it at full speed. There were caves where he could hide and with other coeurls build secretly a spaceship in which they could reach other planets safely—now that he knew how.

His body ached from the agony of acceleration, yet he dared not let up for a single instant. He glanced back, half in terror. The globe was still there, a tiny dot of light in the immense blackness of space. Suddenly it twinkled and was gone.

For a brief moment, he had the empty, frightened impression that just before it disappeared, it moved. But he could see nothing. He could not escape the belief that they had shut off all their lights, and were sneaking up on him in the darkness. Worried and uncertain, he looked through the forward transparent plate.

A tremor of dismay shot through him. The dim red sun toward which he was heading was not growing larger. *It was becoming smaller* by the instant. And it grew visibly tinier during the next five minutes, became a pale-red dot in the sky—and vanished like the ship.

Fear came then, a blinding surge of it, that swept through his being and left him chilled with the sense of the unknown. For minutes, he stared frantically into the space ahead, searching for some landmark. But only the remote stars glimmered there, unwinking points against a velvet background of unfathomable distance.

Wait! One of the points was growing larger. With every muscle and nerve tensed, Coeurl watched the point becoming a dot, a round ball of light—red light. Bigger, bigger, it grew. Suddenly, the red light shimmered and turned white—and there, before him, was the great globe of the spaceship, lights glaring from every porthole, the very ship which a few minutes before he had watched vanish behind him.

Something happened to Coeurl in that moment. His brain was spinning like a flywheel, faster, faster, more incoherently. Suddenly, the wheel flew apart into a million aching fragments. His eyes almost started from their sockets as, like a maddened animal, he raged in his small quarters.

His tentacles clutched at precious instruments and flung them insensately; his paws smashed in fury at the very walls of his ship. Finally, in a brief flash of sanity, he knew that he couldn't face the inevitable fire of atomic disintegrators.

It was a simple thing to create the violent disorganization that freed every drop of id from his vital organs.

They found him lying dead in a little pool of phosphorus.

"Poor kitty," said Morton. "I wonder what he thought when he saw us appear ahead of him, after his own sun disappeared. Knowing nothing of anti-accelerators, he couldn't know that we could stop short in space, whereas it would take him more than three hours to decelerate; and in the meantime he'd be drawing farther and farther away from where he wanted to go. He couldn't know that by stopping, we flashed past him at millions of miles a second. Of course, he didn't have a chance once he left our ship. The whole world must have seemed topsy-turvy."

"Never mind the sympathy," he heard Kent say behind him. "We've got a job—to kill every cat in that miserable world."

Korita murmured softly: "That should be simple. They are but primitives; and we have merely to sit down, and they will come to us, cunningly expecting to delude us."

Smith snapped: "You fellows make me sick! Kitty was the toughest nut we ever had to crack. He had everything he needed to defeat us—"

Morton smiled as Korita interrupted blandly: "Exactly, my dear Smith, except that he reacted according to the biological impulses of his type. His defeat was already foreshadowed when we unerringly analyzed him as a criminal from a certain era of his civilization.

"It was history, honorable Mr. Smith, our knowledge of history that defeated him," said the Japanese archeologist, reverting to the ancient politeness of his race.

For a Journal Entry . . .

"Black Destroyer," among many other things, is about how man defeats an unknown, powerful, often vicious beast. What other examples of this theme can you suggest? What are the differences or similarities between the battle with Coeurl and, for example, Ulysses' battle with Polyphemus or Dr. Frankenstein's battle with the monster he created?

Suppose you were the captain of the return ship to this planet with orders to exterminate all of the coeurls on it. How would you go about your job?

For Your Consideration . . .

1. "Scientists in their way were fools," Coeurl thinks early in the story. From Coeurl's point of view, would you agree?
2. Consider the scientists in the story. Do you think they acted foolishly?
3. What examples of scientific arrogance or ignorance can you find?
4. Korita's long lectures on history on pages 13 and 14 and later on 29 and 30 seem like interruptions in the story. Do they in fact serve any purpose or add any dimension to the story? If so, what?
5. Do you agree with Korita's statement that it was "our knowledge of history that defeated him"?

6. On the other hand, is it true that, rather than a knowledge of history, it was a science fiction device—the anti-accelerator, which drives space ships at faster-than-light speeds—that actually defeated Coeurl? If so, is the ending a cop-out? How else could the story have ended?

Notes

PAGE

1   *undulation*—a waving motion

1   *taut*—tightly drawn

2   *id*—food source necessary for Coeurl's life, later identified as phosphorus

2   *silhouetted*—an outline drawing or a shadow seen against a light

2   *intricate*—complex

2   *sovereignty*—authority

3   *deceleration*—slowing down

3   *quiescence*—quietness

5   *sensuality*—relating to his senses

5   *drawled*—spoke in a lazy way

6   *pallor*—lack of color, paleness

7   *criterion*—test, standard of judgment

8   *palpitant*—pulsing, throbbing

9   *expounding*—to make clear

9   *galactic*—a galaxy is a cluster of millions of stars, sometimes known as a nebula. Our Milky Way is a galaxy.

10 *presaged*—foretold

13 *decadent*—older, deteriorating

17 *melodramatic*—sentimental, exaggerated drama

18 *micro-steel*—a super-hard steel alloy

20 *millennium*—a period of a thousand years

20 *audioscope*—an instrument for making sound waves visible

21 *telefluor*—a fluoroscope or X-ray machine that works at a distance

22 *discomfiture*—confusion or frustration

26 *coruscating*—vividly flashing

31 *feral*—animal, beast-like

33 *insensately*—without thought or reason

Call Me Joe

Poul Anderson

With a degree in physics, Poul Anderson knows what he is writing
about in science fiction. The many awards he has received for his
writing show how well he has applied that knowledge. He is at his
literary and scientific best in this story of Joe, a creature without
intelligence, whose brain is controlled from a distance of thousands
of miles. Joe can live on the terribly cold, impossibly rugged surface of the planet Jupiter, where men can never go. Men still
control Joe's mind—but the control is breaking down.

THE wind came whooping out of eastern darkness, driving
a lash of ammonia dust before it. In minutes, Edward Anglesey
was blinded.

He clawed all four feet into the broken shards which were
soil, hunched down and groped for his little smelter. The wind
was an idiot bassoon in his skull. Something whipped across his
back, drawing blood, a tree yanked up by the roots and spat a
hundred miles. Lightning cracked, immensely far overhead where
clouds boiled with night.

As if to reply, thunder toned in the ice mountains and a red
gout of flame jumped and a hillside came booming down, spilling
itself across the valley. The earth shivered.

Sodium explosion, thought Anglesey in the drumbeat noise.
The fire and the lightning gave him enough illumination to
find his apparatus. He picked up tools in muscular hands, his
tail gripped the trough, and he battered his way to the tunnel
and thus to his dugout.

It had walls and roof of water, frozen by sun-remoteness and compressed by tons of atmosphere jammed onto every square inch. Ventilated by a tiny smokehole, a lamp of tree oil burning in hydrogen made a dull light for the single room.

Anglesey sprawled his slate-blue form on the floor, panting. It was no use to swear at the storm. These ammonia gales often came at sunset, and there was nothing to do but wait them out. He was tired anyway.

It would be morning in five hours or so. He had hoped to cast an axhead, his first, this evening, but maybe it was better to do the job by daylight.

He pulled a dekapod body off a shelf and ate the meat raw, pausing for long gulps of liquid methane from a jug. Things would improve once he had proper tools; so far, everything had been painfully grubbed and hacked to shape with teeth, claws, chance icicles, and what detestably weak and crumbling fragments remained of the spaceship. Give him a few years and he'd be living as a man should.

He sighed, stretched, and lay down to sleep.

Somewhat more than one hundred and twelve thousand miles away, Edward Anglesey took off his helmet.

He looked around, blinking. After the Jovian surface, it was always a little unreal to find himself here again, in the clean quiet orderliness of the control room.

His muscles ached. They shouldn't. He had not really been fighting a gale of several hundred miles an hour, under three gravities and a temperature of 140 Absolute. He had been here, in the almost nonexistent pull of Jupiter V, breathing oxynitrogen. It was Joe who lived down there and filled his lungs with hydrogen and helium at a pressure which could still only be estimated because it broke aneroids and deranged piezoelectrics.

Nevertheless, his body felt worn and beaten. Tension, no doubt—psychosomatics—after all, for a good many hours now he had, in a sense, been Joe, and Joe had been working hard.

With the helmet off, Anglesey held only a thread of identification. The esprojector was still tuned to Joe's brain but no longer focused on his own. Somewhere in the back of his mind, he knew an indescribable feeling of sleep. Now and then, vague forms or colors drifted in the soft black—dreams? Not impossible, that Joe's brain should dream a little when Anglesey's mind wasn't using it.

A light flickered red on the esprojector panel, and a bell whined electronic fear. Anglesey cursed. Thin fingers danced over the controls of his chair, he slewed around and shot across to the bank of dials. Yes—there—K-tube oscillating again! The circuit blew out. He wrenched the faceplate off with one hand and fumbled in a drawer with the other.

Inside his mind, he could feel the contact with Joe fading. If he once lost it entirely, he wasn't sure he could regain it. And Joe was an investment of several million dollars and quite a few highly skilled man-years.

Anglesey pulled the offending K-tube from its socket and threw it on the floor. Glass exploded. It eased his temper a bit, just enough so he could find a replacement, plug it in, switch on the current again—as the machine warmed up, once again amplifying, the Joe-ness in the back alleys of his brain strengthened.

Slowly, then, the man in the electric wheel chair rolled out of the room, into the hall. Let somebody else sweep up the broken tube. To hell with it. To hell with everybody.

Jan Cornelius had never been farther from Earth than some comfortable Lunar resort. He felt much put upon, that the Psionics Corporation should tap him for a thirteen-months exile. The fact that he knew as much about esprojectors and their cranky innards as any other man alive, was no excuse. Why send anyone at all? Who cared?

Obviously the Federation Science Authority did. It had seemingly given those bearded hermits a blank check on the taxpayer's account.

Thus did Cornelius grumble to himself, all the long hyperbolic path to Jupiter. Then the shifting accelerations of approach to its tiny inner satellite left him too wretched for further complaint.

And when he finally, just prior to disembarkation, went up to the greenhouse for a look at Jupiter, he said not a word. Nobody does, the first time.

Arne Viken waited patiently while Cornelius stared. *It still gets me, too,* he remembered. *By the throat. Sometimes I'm afraid to look.*

At length Cornelius turned around. He had a faintly Jovian appearance himself, being a large man with an imposing girth. "I had no idea," he whispered. "I never thought . . . I had seen pictures, but—"

Viken nodded. "Sure, Dr. Cornelius. Pictures don't convey it."

Where they stood, they could see the dark broken rock of the satellite, jumbled for a short ways beyond the landing slip and then chopped off sheer. This moon was scarcely even a platform, it seemed, and cold constellations went streaming past it, around it. Jupiter lay across a fifth of that sky, softly ambrous, banded with colors, spotted with the shadows of planet-sized moons and with whirlwinds as broad as Earth. If there had been any gravity to speak of, Cornelius would have thought, instinctively, that the great planet was falling on him. As it was, he felt as if sucked upward, his hands were still sore where he had grabbed a rail to hold on.

"You live here . . . all alone . . . with this?" He spoke feebly.

"Oh, well, there are some fifty of us all told, pretty congenial," said Viken. "It's not so bad. You sign up for four-cycle hitches—four ship arrivals—and believe it or not, Dr. Cornelius, this is my third enlistment."

The newcomer forbore to inquire more deeply. There was something not quite understandable about the men on Jupiter V. They were mostly bearded, though otherwise careful to remain neat; their low-gravity movements were somehow dreamlike to watch; they hoarded their conversation, as if to stretch it through the year and month between ships. Their monkish existence had changed them—or did they take what amounted to vows of poverty, chastity, and obedience, because they had never felt quite at home on green Earth?

Thirteen months! Cornelius shuddered. It was going to be a long cold wait, and the pay and bonuses accumulating for him were scant comfort now, four hundred and eighty million miles from the sun.

"Wonderful place to do research," continued Viken. "All the facilities, hand-picked colleagues, no distractions . . . and of course—" He jerked his thumb at the planet and turned to leave.

Cornelius followed, wallowing awkwardly. "It is very interesting, no doubt," he puffed. "Fascinating. But really, Dr. Viken, to drag me way out here and make me spend a year-plus waiting for the next ship . . . to do a job which may take me a few weeks—"

"Are you sure it's that simple?" asked Viken gently. His face swiveled around, and there was something in his eyes that silenced Cornelius. "After all my time here, I've yet to see any problem, however complicated, which when you looked at it the right way didn't become still more complicated."

They went through the ship's air lock and the tube joining it to the station entrance. Nearly everything was underground. Rooms, laboratories, even halls had a degree of luxuriousness— why, there was a fireplace with a real fire in the common room! God alone knew what *that* cost!

Thinking of the huge chill emptiness where the king planet laired, and of his own year's sentence, Cornelius decided that such luxuries were, in truth, biological necessities.

Viken showed him to a pleasantly furnished chamber which would be his own. "We'll fetch your luggage soon, and unload your psionic stuff. Right now, everybody's either talking to the ship's crew or reading his mail."

Cornelius nodded absently and sat down. The chair, like all low-gee furniture, was a mere spidery skeleton, but it held his bulk comfortably enough. He felt in his tunic, hoping to bribe the other man into keeping him company for a while. "Cigar? I brought some from Amsterdam."

"Thanks." Viken accepted with disappointing casualness, crossed long thin legs and blew grayish clouds.

"Ah . . . are you in charge here?"

"Not exactly. No one is. We do have one administrator, the cook, to handle what little work of that type may come up. Don't forget, this is a research station, first, last, and always."

"What is your field, then?"

Viken frowned. "Don't question anyone else so bluntly, Dr. Cornelius," he warned. "They'd rather spin the gossip out as long as possible with each newcomer. It's a rare treat to have someone whose every last conceivable reaction hasn't been— No, no apologies to me. 'S all right. I'm a physicist, specializing in the solid state at ultra-high pressure." He nodded at the wall. "Plenty of it to be observed—there!"

"I see." Cornelius smoked quietly for a while. Then: "I'm supposed to be the psionics expert, but frankly, at present I've no idea why your machine should misbehave as reported."

"You mean those, uh, K-tubes have a stable output on Earth?"

"And on Lunar, Mars, Venus . . . everywhere, apparently, but here." Cornelius shrugged. "Of course, psibeams are always persnickety, and sometimes you get an unwanted feedback when— No. I'll get the facts before I theorize. Who are your psimen?"

"Just Anglesey, who's not a formally trained esman at all. But he took it up after he was crippled, and showed such a natural aptitude that he was shipped out here when he volunteered. It's so hard to get anyone for Jupiter V that we aren't fussy about degrees. At that, Ed seems to be operating Joe as well as a Ps.D. could."

"Ah, yes. Your pseudojovian. I'll have to examine that angle pretty carefully too," said Cornelius. In spite of himself, he was getting interested. "Maybe the trouble comes from something in Joe's biochemistry. Who knows? I'll let you into a carefully guarded little secret, Dr. Viken: psionics is not an exact science."

"Neither is physics," grinned the other man. After a moment, he added more soberly: "Not my brand of physics, anyway. I hope to make it exact. That's why I'm here, you know. It's the reason we're all here."

Edward Anglesey was a bit of a shock, the first time. He was a head, a pair of arms, and a disconcertingly intense blue stare. The rest of him was mere detail, enclosed in a wheeled machine.

"Biophysicist originally," Viken had told Cornelius. "Studying atmospheric spores at Earth Station when he was still a young man—accident, crushed him up, nothing below his chest will ever work again. Snappish type, you have to go slow with him."

Seated on a wisp of stool in the esprojector control room, Cornelius realized that Viken had been soft-pedaling the truth.

Anglesey ate as he talked, gracelessly, letting the chair's tentacles wipe up after him. "Got to," he explained. "This stupid place is officially on Earth time, GMT. Jupiter isn't. I've got to be here whenever Joe wakes, ready to take him over."

"Couldn't you have someone spell you?" asked Cornelius.

"Bah!" Anglesey stabbed a piece of prot and waggled it at the other man. Since it was native to him, he could spit out English, the common language of the station, with unmeasured ferocity. "Look here. You ever done therapeutic esping? Not just listening in, or even communication, but actual pedagogic control?"

"No, not I. It requires a certain natural talent, like yours." Cornelius smiled. His ingratiating little phrase was swallowed without being noticed by the scored face opposite him. "I take it you mean cases like, oh, re-educating the nervous system of a palsied child?"

"Yes, yes. Good enough example. Has anyone ever tried to suppress the child's personality, take him over in the most literal sense?"

"Good God, no!"

"Even as a scientific experiment?" Anglesey grinned. "Has any esprojector operative ever poured on the juice and swamped the child's brain with his own thoughts? Come on, Cornelius, I won't snitch on you."

"Well . . . it's out of my line, you understand." The psionicist looked carefully away, found a bland meter face and screwed his eyes to that. "I have, uh, heard something about . . . well, yes, there were attempts made in some pathological cases to, uh, bull through . . . break down the patient's delusions by sheer force—"

"And it didn't work," said Anglesey. He laughed. "It *can't* work, not even on a child, let alone an adult with a fully developed personality. Why, it took a decade of refinement, didn't it, before the machine was debugged to the point where a psychiatrist could even 'listen in' without the normal variation between his pattern of thought and the patient's . . . without that variation setting up an interference scrambling the very thing he wanted to study. The machine has to make automatic compensations for the differences between individuals. We still can't bridge the differences between species.

"If someone else is willing to co-operate, you can very gently guide his thinking. And that's all. If you try to seize control of another brain, a brain with its own background of experience, its own ego—you risk your very sanity. The other brain will fight back, instinctively. A fully developed, matured, hardened human personality is just too complex for outside control. It has too many resources, too much hell the subconscious can call to its defense if its integrity is threatened. Blazes, man, we can't even master our own minds, let alone anyone else's!"

Anglesey's cracked-voice tirade broke off. He sat brooding at the instrument panel, tapping the console of his mechanical mother.

"Well?" said Cornelius after a while.

He should not, perhaps, have spoken. But he found it hard to remain mute. There was too much silence—half a billion miles of it, from here to the sun. If you closed your mouth five minutes at a time, the silence began creeping in like fog.

"Well," gibed Anglesey. "So our pseudojovian, Joe, has a physically adult brain. The only reason I can control him is that his brain has never been given a chance to develop its own ego. I *am* Joe. From the moment he was 'born' into consciousness, I have been there. The psibeam sends me all his sense data and sends him back my motor-nerve impulses. But nevertheless, he has that excellent brain, and its cells are recording every trace of experience, even as yours and mine; his synapses have assumed the topography which is my 'personality pattern.'

"Anyone else, taking him over from me, would find it was like an attempt to oust me myself from my own brain. It couldn't be done. To be sure, he doubtless has only a rudimentary set of Anglesey-memories—I do not, for instance, repeat trigonometric theorems while controlling him—but he has enough to be, potentially, a distinct personality.

"As a matter of fact, whenever he wakes up from sleep—there's usually a lag of a few minutes, while I sense the change through my normal psi faculties and get the amplifying helmet adjusted—I have a bit of a struggle. I feel almost a . . . a resistance . . . until I've brought his mental currents completely into phase with mine. Merely dreaming has been enough of a different experience to—"

Anglesey didn't bother to finish the sentence.

"I see," murmured Cornelius. "Yes, it's clear enough. In fact, it's astonishing that you can have such total contact with a being of such alien metabolism."

"I won't for much longer," said the esman sarcastically, "unless you can correct whatever is burning out those K-tubes. I don't have an unlimited supply of spares."

"I have some working hypotheses," said Cornelius, "but there's so little known about psibeam transmission—is the velocity infinite or merely very great, is the beam strength actually independent of distance? How about the possible effects of transmission . . .oh, through the degenerate matter in the Jovian core? Good Lord, a planet where water is a heavy mineral and hydrogen is a metal! What do we know?"

"We're supposed to find out," snapped Anglesey. "That's what this whole project is for. Knowledge. Bull!" Almost, he spat on the floor. "Apparently what little we have learned doesn't even get through to people. Hydrogen is still a gas where Joe lives. He'd have to dig down a few miles to reach the solid phase. And I'm expected to make a scientific analysis of Jovian conditions!"

Cornelius waited it out, letting Anglesey storm on while he himself turned over the problem of K-tube oscillation:

"They don't understand back on Earth. Even here they don't. Sometimes I think they refuse to understand. Joe's down there without much more than this bare hands. He, I, we started with no more knowledge than that he could probably eat the local life. He has to spend nearly all his time hunting for food. It's a miracle he's come as far as he has in these few weeks—made a shelter, grown familiar with the immediate region, begun on metallurgy, hydrurgy, whatever you want to call it. What more do they want me to do, for crying in the beer?"

"Yes, yes—" mumbled Cornelius. "Yes, I—"

Anglesey raised his white bony face. Something filmed over in his eyes.

"What—" began Cornelius.

"Shut up!" Anglesey whipped the chair around, groped for the helmet, slapped it down over his skull. "Joe's waking. Get out of here."

"But if you'll only let me work while he sleeps, how can I—"

Anglesey snarled and threw a wrench at him. It was a feeble toss, even in low-gee. Cornelius backed toward the door. Anglesey was tuning in the esprojector. Suddenly he jerked.

"Cornelius!"

"Whatisit?" The psionicist tried to run back, overdid it, and skidded in a heap to end up against the panel.

"K-tube again." Anglesey yanked off the helmet. It must have hurt like blazes, having a mental squeal build up uncontrolled and amplified in your own brain, but he said merely: "Change it for me. Fast. And then get out and leave me alone. Joe didn't wake up of himself. Something crawled into the dugout with me—I'm in trouble down there!"

It had been a hard day's work, and Joe slept heavily. He did not wake until the hands closed on his throat.

For a moment, then, he knew only a crazy smothering wave of panic. He thought he was back on Earth Station, floating in null-gee at the end of a cable while a thousand frosty stars haloed the planet before him. He thought the great I-beam had broken from its moorings and started toward him, slowly, but with all the inertia of its cold tons, spinning and shimmering in the Earthlight, and the only sound himself screaming and screaming in his helmet trying to break from the cable the beam nudged him ever so gently but it kept on moving he moved with it he was crushed against the station wall nuzzled into it his mangled suit frothed as it tried to seal its wounded self there was blood mingled with the foam his blood *Joe roared.*

His convulsive reaction tore the hands off his neck and sent a black shape spinning across the dugout. It struck the wall, thunderously, and the lamp fell to the floor and went out.

Joe stood in darkness, breathing hard, aware in a vague fashion that the wind had died from a shriek to a low snarling while he slept.

The thing he had tossed away mumbled in pain and crawled along the wall. Joe felt through lightlessness after his club.

Something else scrabbled. The tunnel! They were coming

through the tunnel! Joe groped blind to meet them. His heart drummed thickly and his nose drank an alien stench.

The thing that emerged, as Joe's hands closed on it, was only about half his size, but it had six monstrously taloned feet and a pair of three-fingered hands that reached after his eyes. Joe cursed, lifted it while it writhed, and dashed it to the floor. It screamed, and he heard bones splinter.

"Come on, then!" Joe arched his back and spat at them, like a tiger menaced by giant caterpillars.

They flowed through his tunnel and into the room, a dozen of them entered while he wrestled one that had curled itself around his shoulders and anchored its sinuous body with claws. They pulled at his legs, trying to crawl up on his back. He struck out with claws of his own, with his tail, rolled over and went down beneath a heap of them and stood up with the heap still clinging to him.

They swayed in darkness. The legged seething of them struck the dugout wall. It shivered, a rafter cracked, the roof came down. Anglesey stood in a pit, among broken ice plates, under the wan light of a sinking Ganymede.

He could see, now, that the monsters were black in color and that they had heads big enough to accommodate some brain, less than human but probably more than apes. There were a score of them or so, they struggled from beneath the wreckage and flowed at him with the same shrieking malice.

Why?

Baboon reaction, thought Anglesey somewhere in the back of himself. See the stranger, fear the stranger, hate the stranger, kill the stranger. His chest heaved, pumping air through a raw throat. He yanked a whole rafter to him, snapped it in half, and twirled the iron-hard wood.

The nearest creature got its head bashed in. The next had its back broken. The third was hurled with shattered ribs into a fourth, they went down together. Joe began to laugh. It was getting to be fun.

"Yeee-ow! Ti-i-i-iger!" He ran across the icy ground, toward the pack. They scattered, howling. He hunted them until the last one had vanished in the forest.

Panting, Joe looked at the dead. He himself was bleeding, he ached, he was cold and hungry and his shelter had been wrecked . . . but, he'd whipped them! He had a sudden impulse to beat his chest and howl. For a moment, he hesitated—why not? Anglesey threw back his head and bayed victory at the dim shield of Ganymede.

Thereafter he went to work. First build a fire, in the lee of the spaceship—which was little more by now than a hill of corrosion. The monster pack cried in darkness and the broken ground, they had not given up on him, they would return.

He tore a haunch off one of the slain and took a bite. Pretty good. Better yet if properly cooked. Heh! They'd made a big mistake in calling his attention to their existence! He finished breakfast while Ganymede slipped under the western ice mountains. It would be morning soon. The air was almost still, and a flock of pancake-shaped skyskimmers, as Anglesey called them, went overhead, burnished copper color in the first pale dawnstreaks.

Joe rummaged in the ruins of his hut until he had recovered the water-smelting equipment. It wasn't harmed. That was the first order of business, melt some ice and cast it in the molds of ax, knife, saw, hammer he had painfully prepared. Under Jovian conditions, methane was a liquid that you drank and water was a dense hard mineral. It would make good tools. Later on he would try alloying it with other materials.

Next—yes. To hell with the dugout, he could sleep in the open again for a while. Make a bow, set traps, be ready to massacre the black caterpillars when they attacked him again. There was a chasm not far from here, going down a long ways toward the cold of the metallic-hydrogen strata: a natural icebox, a place to store the several weeks' worth of meat his enemies would supply. This would give him leisure to— Oh, a hell of a lot!

Joe laughed, exultantly, and lay down to watch the sunrise.

It struck him afresh how lovely a place this was. See how the small brilliant spark of the sun swam up out of eastern fogbanks colored dusky purple and veined with rose and gold; see how the light strengthened until the great hollow arch of the sky became one shout of radiance; see how the light spilled warm and living over a broad fair land, the million square miles of rustling low forests and wave-blinking lakes and feather-plumed hydrogen geysers; and see, see, see how the ice mountains of the west flashed like blued steel!

Anglesey drew the wild morning wind deep into his lungs and shouted with a boy's joy.

"I'm not a biologist myself," said Viken carefully. "But maybe for that reason I can better give you the general picture. Then Lopez or Matsumoto can answer any questions of detail."

"Excellent," nodded Cornelius. "Why don't you assume I am totally ignorant of this project? I very nearly am, you know."

"If you wish," laughed Viken.

They stood in an outer office of the xenobiology section. No one else was around, for the station's clocks said 1730 GMT and there was only one shift. No point in having more, until Anglesey's half of the enterprise had actually begun gathering quantitative data.

The physicist bent over and took a paperweight off a desk. "One of the boys made this for fun," he said, "but it's a pretty good model of Joe. He stands about five feet tall at the head."

Cornelius turned the plastic image over in his hands. If you could imagine such a thing as a feline centaur with a thick prehensile tail— The torso was squat, long-armed, immensely muscular; the hairless head was round, wide-nosed, with big deep-set eyes and heavy jaws, but it was really quite a human face. The overall color was bluish gray.

"Male, I see," he remarked.

"Of course. Perhaps you don't understand. Joe is the complete pseudojovian: as far as we can tell, the final model, with all the bugs worked out. He's the answer to a research question that took fifty years to ask." Viken looked sidewise at Cornelius. "So you realize the importance of your job, don't you?"

"I'll do my best," said the psionicist. "But if . . . well, let's say that tube failure or something causes you to lose Joe before I've solved the oscillation problem. You do have other pseudos in reserve, don't you?"

"Oh, yes," said Viken moodily. "But the cost— We're not on an unlimited budget. We do go through a lot of money, because it's expensive to stand up and sneeze this far from Earth. But for that same reason our margin is slim."

He jammed hands in pockets and slouched toward the inner door, the laboratories, head down and talking in a low, hurried voice:

"Perhaps you don't realize what a nightmare planet Jupiter is. Not just the surface gravity—a shade under three gees, what's that? But the gravitational potential, ten times Earth's. The temperature. The pressure . . . above all, the atmosphere, and the storms, and the darkness!

"When a spaceship goes down to the Jovian surface, it's a radio-controlled job; it leaks like a sieve, to equalize pressure, but otherwise it's the sturdiest, most utterly powerful model ever designed; it's loaded with every instrument, every servo-mechanism, every safety device the human mind has yet thought up to protect a million-dollar hunk of precision equipment.

"And what happens? Half the ships never reach the surface at all. A storm snatches them and throws them away, or they collide with a floating chunk of Ice VII—small version of the Red Spot—or, so help me, what passes for a flock of *birds* rams one and stoves it in!

"As for the fifty per cent which does land, it's a one-way trip. We don't even try to bring them back. If the stresses coming down haven't sprung something, the corrosion has doomed them anyway. Hydrogen at Jovian pressure does funny things to metals.

"It cost a total of—about five million dollars—to set Joe, one pseudo, down there. Each pseudo to follow will cost, if we're lucky, a couple of million more."

Viken kicked open the door and led the way through. Beyond was a big room, low-ceilinged, coldly lit and murmurous with ventilators. It reminded Cornelius of a nucleonics lab; for a moment he wasn't sure why, then recognized the intricacies of remote control, remote observation, walls enclosing forces which could destroy the entire moon.

"These are required by the pressure, of course," said Viken, pointing to a row of shields. "And the cold. And the hydrogen itself, as a minor hazard. We have units here duplicating conditions in the Jovian, uh, stratosphere. This is where the whole project really began."

"I've heard something about that," nodded Cornelius. "Didn't you scoop up airborne spores?"

"Not I." Viken chuckled. "Totti's crew did, about fifty years ago. Proved there was life on Jupiter. A life using liquid methane as its basic solvent, solid ammonia as a starting point for nitrate synthesis—the plants use solar energy to build unsaturated carbon compounds, releasing hydrogen; the animals eat the plants and reduce those compounds again to the saturated form. There is even an equivalent of combustion. The reactions involve complex enzymes and . . . well, it's out of my line."

"Jovian biochemistry is pretty well understood, then."

"Oh, yes. Even in Totti's day, they had a highly developed biotic technology: Earth bacteria had already been synthesized, and most gene structures pretty well mapped. The only reason it took so long to diagram Jovian life processes was the technical difficulty, high pressure and so on."

"When did you actually get a look at Jupiter's surface?"

"Gray managed that, about thirty years ago. Set a televisor ship down, a ship that lasted long enough to flash him quite a series of pictures. Since then, the technique has improved. We know that Jupiter is crawling with its own weird kind of life, probably more fertile than Earth. Extrapolating from the airborne microorganisms, our team made trial syntheses of metazoans and—"

Viken sighed. "Damn it, if only there were intelligent native life! Think what they could tell us, Cornelius, the data, the—Just think back how far we've gone since Lavoisier, with the low-pressure chemistry of Earth. Here's a chance to learn a high-pressure chemistry and physics at least as rich with possibilities!"

After a moment, Cornelius murmured slyly: "Are you certain there *aren't* any Jovians?"

"Oh, sure, there could be several billion of them," shrugged

Viken. "Cities, empires, anything you like. Jupiter has the surface area of a hundred Earths, and we've only seen maybe a
dozen small regions. But we do know there aren't any Jovians
using radio. Considering their atmosphere, it's unlikely they ever
would invent it for themselves—imagine how thick a vacuum
tube has to be, how strong a pump you need! So it was finally
decided we'd better make our own Jovians."

Cornelius followed him through the lab, into another room.
This was less cluttered, it had a more finished appearance: the
experimenter's haywire rig had yielded to the assured precision
of an engineer.

Viken went over to one of the panels which lined the walls
and looked at its gauges. "Beyond this lies another pseudo," he
said. "Female, in this instance. She's at a pressure of two hundred atmospheres and a temperature of 194 Absolute. There's a
. . . an umbilical arrangement, I guess you'd call it, to keep her
alive. She was grown to adulthood in this, uh, fetal stage—we
patterned our Jovians after the terrestrial mammal. She's never
been conscious, she won't ever be till she's 'born.' We have a
total of twenty males and sixty females waiting here. We can
count on about half reaching the surface. More can be created
as required.

"It isn't the pseudos that are so expensive, it's their transporta-
tion. So Joe is down there alone till we're sure that his kind *can*
survive."

"I take it you experimented with lower forms first," said Cornelius.

"Of course. It took twenty years, even with forced-catalysis
techniques, to work from an artificial air-borne spore to Joe.
We've used the psibeam to control everything from pseudo-
insects on up. Interspecies control is possible, you know, if your
puppet's nervous system is deliberately designed for it, and isn't
given a chance to grow into a pattern different from the
esman's."

"And Joe is the first specimen who's given trouble?"

"Yes."

"Scratch one hypothesis." Cornelius sat down on a workbench, dangling thick legs and running a hand through thin sandy hair. "I thought maybe some physical effect of Jupiter was responsible. Now it looks as if the difficulty is with Joe himself."

"We've all suspected that much," said Viken. He struck a cigarette and sucked in his cheeks around the smoke. His eyes were gloomy. "Hard to see how. The biotics engineers tell me *Pseudocentaurus Sapiens* has been more carefully designed than any product of natural evolution."

"Even the brain?"

"Yes. It's patterned directly on the human, to make psibeam control possible, but there are improvements—greater stability."

"There are still the psychological aspects though," said Cornelius. "In spite of all our amplifiers and other fancy gadgets, psi is essentially a branch of psychology, even today . . . or maybe it's the other way around. Let's consider traumatic experiences. I take it the . . . the adult Jovian fetus has a rough trip going down?"

"The ship does," said Viken. "Not the pseudo itself, which is wrapped up in fluid just like you were before birth."

"Nevertheless," said Cornelius, "the two hundred atmospheres pressure here is not the same as whatever unthinkable pressure exists down on Jupiter. Could the change be injurious?"

Viken gave him a look of respect. "Not likely," he answered. "I told you the J-ships are designed leaky. External pressure is transmitted to the, uh, uterine mechanism through a series of diaphragms, in a gradual fashion. It takes hours to make the descent, you realize."

"Well, what happens next?" went on Cornelius. "The ship lands, the uterine mechanism opens, the umbilical connection disengages, and Joe is, shall we say, born. But he has an adult brain. He is not protected by the only half-developed infant brain from the shock of sudden awareness."

"We thought of that," said Viken. "Anglesey was on the psibeam, in phase with Joe, when the ship left this moon. So it wasn't really Joe who emerged, who perceived. Joe has never been much more than a biological waldo. He can only suffer mental shock to the extent that Ed does, because it *is* Ed down there!"

"As you will," said Cornelius. "Still, you didn't plan for a race of puppets, did you?"

"Oh, heavens, no," said Viken. "Out of the question. Once we know Joe is well established, we'll import a few more esmen and get him some assistance in the form of other pseudos. Eventually females will be sent down, and uncontrolled males, to be educated by the puppets. A new generation will be born normally— Well, anyhow, the ultimate aim is a small civilization of Jovians. There will be hunters, miners, artisans, farmers, housewives, the works. They will support a few key members, a kind of priesthood. And that priesthood will be esp-controlled, as Joe is. It will exist solely to make instruments, take readings, perform experiments, and tell us what we want to know!"

Cornelius nodded. In a general way, this was the Jovian project as he had understood it. He could appreciate the importance of his own assignment.

Only, he still had no clue to the cause of that positive feedback in the K-tubes.

And what could he do about it?

His hands were still bruised. *Oh, God,* he thought with a groan, for the hundredth time, *does it affect me that much? While Joe was fighting down there, did I really hammer my fists on metal up here?*

His eyes smoldered across the room, to the bench where Cornelius worked. He didn't like Cornelius, fat cigar-sucking slob, interminably talking and talking. He had about given up trying to be civil to the Earthworm.

The psionicist laid down a screwdriver and flexed cramped fingers. "*Whuff!*" he smiled. "I'm going to take a break."

The half-assembled esprojector made a gaunt backdrop for his wide soft body, where it squatted toad-fashion on the bench. Anglesey detested the whole idea of anyone sharing this room, even for a few hours a day. Of late he had been demanding his meals brought here, left outside the door of his adjoining bedroom-bath. He had not gone beyond for quite some time now.

And why should I?

"Couldn't you hurry it up a little?" snapped Anglesey.

Cornelius flushed. "If you'd had an assembled spare machine, instead of loose parts—" he began. Shrugging, he took out a cigar stub and relit it carefully; his supply had to last a long time. Anglesey wondered if those stinking clouds were blown from his mouth of malicious purpose. *I don't like you, Mr. Earthman Cornelius, and it is doubtless quite mutual.*

"There was no obvious need for one, until the other esmen arrive," said Anglesey in a sullen voice. "And the testing instruments report this one in perfectly good order."

"Nevertheless," said Cornelius, "at irregular intervals it goes into wild oscillations which burn out the K-tube. The problem is why. I'll have you try out this new machine as soon as it is ready, but frankly, I don't believe the trouble lies in electronic failure at all—or even in unsuspected physical effects."

"Where, then?" Anglesey felt more at ease as the discussion grew purely technical.

"Well, look. What exactly is the K-tube? It's the heart of the esprojector. It amplifies your natural psionic pulses, uses them to modulate the carrier wave, and shoots the whole beam down at Joe. It also picks up Joe's resonating impulses and amplifies them for your benefit. Everything else is auxiliary to the K-tube."

"Spare me the lecture," snarled Anglesey.

"I was only rehearsing the obvious," said Cornelius, "because every now and then it is the obvious answer which is hardest to see. Maybe it isn't the K-tube which is misbehaving. Maybe it is you."

"What?" The white face gaped at him. A dawning rage crept red across its thin bones.

"Nothing personal intended," said Cornelius hastily. "But you know what a tricky beast the subconscious is. Suppose, just as a working hypothesis, that way down underneath, you don't *want* to be on Jupiter. I imagine it is a rather terrifying environment. Or there may be some obscure Freudian element involved. Or, quite simply and naturally, your subconscious may fail to understand that Joe's death does not entail your own."

"Um-m-m—" *Mirable dictu*, Anglesey remained calm. He rubbed his chin with one skeletal hand. "Can you be more explicit?"

"Only in a rough way," replied Cornelius. "Your conscious mind sends a motor impulse along the psibeam to Joe. Simultaneously, your subconscious mind, being scared of the whole business, emits the glandular-vascular-cardiac-visceral impulses associated with fear. These react on Joe, whose tension is transmitted back along the beam. Feeling Joe's somatic fear-symptoms, your subconscious gets still more worried, thereby increasing the symptoms— Get it? It's exactly similar to ordinary neurasthenia, with this exception: that since there is a powerful amplifier, the K-tube, involved, the oscillations can build up uncontrollably within a second or two. You should be thankful the tube does burn out—otherwise your brain might do so!"

For a moment Anglesey was quiet. Then he laughed. It was a hard, barbaric laughter. Cornelius started as it struck his eardrums.

"Nice idea," said the esman. "But I'm afraid it won't fit all the data. You see, I like it down there. I like being Joe."

He paused for a while, then continued in a dry impersonal tone: "Don't judge the environment from my notes. They're just idiotic things like estimates of wind velocity, temperature variations, mineral properties—insignificant. What I can't put in is how Jupiter looks through a Jovian's infrared-seeing eyes."

"Different, I should think," ventured Cornelius after a minute's clumsy silence.

"Yes and no. It's hard to put into language. Some of it I can't because man hasn't got the concepts. But . . . oh, I can't decribe it. Shakespeare himself couldn't. Just remember that everything about Jupiter which is cold and poisonous and gloomy to us is *right* for Joe."

Anglesey's tone grew remote, as if he spoke to himself:

"Imagine walking under a glowing violet sky, where great flashing clouds sweep the earth with shadow, and rain strides beneath them. Imagine walking on the slopes of a mountain like polished metal, with a clean red flame exploding above you and thunder laughing in the ground. Imagine a cool wild stream, and low trees with dark coppery flowers, and a waterfall, methane-fall . . . whatever you like . . . leaping off a cliff, and the strong live wind shakes its mane full of rainbows! Imagine a

whole forest, dark and breathing, and here and there you
glimpse a pale-red wavering will-o'-the-wisp, which is the life
radiation of some fleet shy animal, and . . . and—"

Anglesey croaked into silence. He stared down at his clenched
fists, then he closed his eyes tight and tears ran out between
the lids.

"Imagine being *strong!*"

Suddenly he snatched up the helmet, crammed it on his head
and twirled the control knobs. Joe had been sleeping, down in
the night, but Joe was about to wake up and—roar under the
four great moons till all the forest feared him.

Cornelius slipped quietly out of the room.

In the long brazen sunset light, beneath dusky cloud banks
brooding storm, he strode up the hillslope with a sense of day's
work done. Across his back, two woven baskets balanced each
other, one laden with the pungent black fruit of the thorntree
and one with cablethick creepers to be used as rope. The ax on
his shoulder caught the waning sunlight and tossed it blindingly
back.

It had not been hard labor, but weariness dragged at his mind
and he did not relish the household chores yet to be performed,
cooking and cleaning and all the rest. Why couldn't they hurry
up and get him some helpers?

His eyes sought the sky, resentfully. The moon Five was hidden—down here, at the bottom of the air ocean, you saw nothing
but the sun and the four Galilean satellites. He wasn't even sure
where Five was just now, in relation to himself . . . *wait a minute, it's sunset here, but if I went out to the viewdome I'd see
Jupiter in the last quarter, or would I, oh, hell, it only takes us
half an Earth-day to swing around the planet anyhow—*

Joe shook his head. After all this time, it was still damnably
hard, now and then, to keep his thoughts straight. *I, the essential
I, am up in heaven, riding Jupiter V between cold stars. Remember that. Open your eyes, if you will, and see the dead control room superimposed on a living hillside.*

He didn't, though. Instead, he regarded the boulders strewn

wind-blasted gray over the tough mossy vegetation of the slope. They were not much like Earth rocks, nor was the soil beneath his feet like terrestrial humus.

For a moment Anglesey speculated on the origin of the silicates, aluminates, and other stony compounds. Theoretically, all such materials should be inaccessibly locked in the Jovian core, down where the pressure got vast enough for atoms to buckle and collapse. Above the core should lie thousands of miles of allotropic ice, and then the metallic hydrogen layer. There should not be complex minerals this far up, but there were.

Well, possibly Jupiter had formed according to theory, but had thereafter sucked enough cosmic dust, meteors, gases and vapors, down its great throat of gravitation, to form a crust several miles thick. Or more likely the theory was altogether wrong. What did they know, what *could* they know, the soft pale worms of Earth?

Anglesey stuck his—Joe's—fingers in his mouth and whistled. A baying sounded in the brush, and two midnight forms leaped toward him. He grinned and stroked their heads; training was progressing faster than he'd hoped, with these pups of the black caterpillar beasts he had taken. They would make guardians for him, herders, servants.

On the crest of the hill, Joe was building himself a home. He had logged off an acre of ground and erected a stockade. Within the grounds there now stood a lean-to for himself and his stores, a methane well, and the beginnings of a large comfortable cabin.

But there was too much work for one being. Even with the half-intelligent caterpillars to help, and with cold storage for meat, most of his time would still go to hunting. The game wouldn't last forever, either; he had to start agriculture within the next year or so—Jupiter year, twelve Earth years, thought Anglesey. There was the cabin to finish and furnish; he wanted to put a waterwheel, no, methane wheel in the river to turn any of a dozen machines he had in mind, he wanted to experiment with alloyed ice and—

And, quite apart from his need of help, why should he remain alone, the single thinking creature on an entire planet? He was a male in this body, with male instincts—in the long run, his health was bound to suffer if he remained a hermit, and right now the whole project depended on Joe's health.

It wasn't right!

But I am not alone. There are fifty men on the satellite with me. I can talk to any of them, any time I wish. It's only that I seldom wish it, these days. I would rather be Joe.

Nevertheless . . . I, the cripple, feel all the tiredness, anger, hurt, frustration, of that wonderful biological machine called Joe. The others don't understand. When the ammonia gale flays open his skin, it is I who bleed.

Joe lay down on the ground, sighing. Fangs flashed in the mouth of the black beast which humped over to lick his face. His belly growled with hunger, but he was too tired to fix a meal. Once he had the dogs trained—

Another pseudo would be so much more rewarding to educate.

He could almost see it, in the weary darkening of his brain. Down there, in the valley below the hill, fire and thunder as the ship came to rest. And the steel egg would crack open, the steel arms—already crumbling, puny work of worms!—lift out the shape within and lay it on the earth.

She would stir, shrieking in her first lungful of air, looking about with blank mindless eyes. And Joe would come carry her home. And he would feed her, care for her, show her how to walk—it wouldn't take long, an adult body would learn those things very fast. In a few weeks she would even be talking, be an individual, a soul.

Did you ever think, Edward Anglesey, in the days when you also walked, that your wife would be a gray four-legged monster?

Never mind that. The important thing was to get others of his kind down here, female *and* male. The station's niggling little plan would have him wait two more Earth years, and then send him only another dummy like himself, a contemptible human mind looking through eyes which belonged rightfully to a Jovian. It was not to be tolerated!

If he weren't so tired—

Joe sat up. Sleep drained from him as the realization entered. *He* wasn't tired, not to speak of. Anglesey was. Anglesey, the human side of him, who for months had only slept in catnaps, whose rest had lately been interrupted by Cornelius—it was the human body which drooped, gave up, and sent wave after soft wave of sleep down the psibeam to Joe.

Somatic tension traveled skyward; Anglesey jerked awake.

He swore. As he sat there beneath the helmet, the vividness of Jupiter faded with his scattering concentration, as if it grew transparent; the steel prison which was his laboratory strengthened behind it. He was losing contact—Rapidly, with the skill of experience, he brought himself back into phase with the neural currents of the other brain. He willed sleepiness on Joe, exactly as a man wills it on himself.

And, like any other insomniac, he failed. The Joe-body was too hungry. It got up and walked across the compound toward its shack.

The K-tube went wild and blew itself out.

The night before the ships left, Viken and Cornelius sat up late.

It was not truly a night, of course. In twelve hours the tiny moon was hurled clear around Jupiter, from darkness back to darkness, and there might well be a pallid little sun over its crags when the clocks said witches were abroad in Greenwich. But most of the personnel were asleep at this hour.

Viken scowled. "I don't like it," he said. "Too sudden a change of plans. Too big a gamble."

"You are only risking—how many?—three male and a dozen female pseudos," Cornelius replied.

"And fifteen J-ships. All we have. If Anglesey's notion doesn't work, it will be months, a year or more, till we can have others built and resume aerial survey."

"But if it does work," said Cornelius, "you won't need any J-ships, except to carry down more pseudos. You will be too busy evaluating data from the surface to piddle around in the upper atmosphere."

"Of course. But we never expected it so soon. We were going to bring more esmen out here, to operate some more pseudos—"

"But they aren't *needed*," said Cornelius. He struck a cigar to

life and took a long pull on it, while his mind sought carefully
for words. "Not for a while, anyhow. Joe has reached a point
where, given help, he can leap several thousand years of history
—he may even have a radio of sorts operating in the fairly near
future, which would eliminate the necessity of much of your
esping. But without help, he'll just have to mark time. And it's
stupid to make a highly trained human esman perform manual
labor, which is all that the other pseudos are needed for at this
moment. Once the Jovian settlement is well established, certainly, then you can send down more puppets."

"The question is, though," persisted Viken, "can Anglesey himself educate all those pseudos at once? They'll be helpless as
infants for days. It will be weeks before they really start thinking and acting for themselves. Can Joe take care of them mean-
while?"

"He has food and fuel stored for months ahead," said Cornelius. "As for what Joe's capabilities are, well, hm-m-m . . . we
just have to take Anglesey's judgment. He has the only inside
information."

"And once those Jovians do become personalities," worried
Viken, "are they necessarily going to string along with Joe?
Don't forget, the pseudos are not carbon copies of each other.
The uncertainty principle assures each one a unique set of genes.
If there is only one human mind on Jupiter, among all those
aliens—"

"One *human* mind?" It was barely audible. Viken opened his
mouth inquiringly. The other man hurried on.

"Oh, I'm sure Anglesey can continue to dominate them," said
Cornelius. "His own personality is rather—tremendous."

Viken looked startled. "You really think so?"

The psionicist nodded. "Yes, I've seen more of him in the
past weeks than anyone else. And my profession naturally ori-
ents me more toward a man's psychology than his body or his
habits. You see a waspish cripple. I see a mind which has reacted to its physical handicaps by developing such a hellish
energy, such an inhuman power of concentration, that it almost
frightens me. Give that mind a sound body for its use and
nothing is impossible to it."

"You may be right, at that," murmured Viken after a pause. "Not that it matters. The decision is taken, the rockets go down tomorrow. I hope it all works out."

He waited for another while. The whirring of ventilators in his little room seemed unnaturally loud, the colors of a girlie picture on the wall shockingly garish. Then he said, slowly:

"You've been rather close-mouthed yourself, Jan. When do you expect to finish your own esprojector and start making the tests?"

Cornelius looked around. The door stood open to an empty hallway, but he reached out and closed it before he answered with a slight grin: "It's been ready for the past few days. But don't tell anyone."

"How's that?" Viken started. The movement, in low-gee, took him out of his chair and halfway across the table between the men. He shoved himself back and waited.

"I have been making meaningless tinkering motions," said Cornelius, "but what I waited for was a highly emotional moment, a time when I can be sure Anglesey's entire attention will be focused on Joe. This business tomorrow is exactly what I need."

"Why?"

"You see, I have pretty well convinced myself that the trouble in the machine is psychological, not physical. I think that for some reason, buried in his subconscious, Anglesey doesn't want to experience Jupiter. A conflict of that type might well set a psionic amplifier circuit oscillating."

"Hm-m-m." Viken rubbed his chin. "Could be. Lately Ed has been changing more and more. When he first came here, he was peppery enough, and he would at least play an occasional game of poker. Now he's pulled so far into his shell you can't even see him. I never thought of it before, but . . . yes, by God, Jupiter must be having some effect on him.

"Hm-m-m," noded Cornelius. He did not elaborate: did not, for instance, mention that one altogether uncharacteristic episode when Anglesey had tried to describe what it was like to be a Jovian.

"Of course," said Viken thoughtfully, "the previous men were not affected especially. Nor was Ed at first, while he was still controlling lower-type pseudos. It's only since Joe went down to the surface that he's become so different."

"Yes, yes," said Cornelius hastily. "I've learned that much. But enough shop talk—"

"No. Wait a minute." Viken spoke in a low, hurried tone, looking past him. "For the first time, I'm starting to think clearly about this . . . never really stopped to analyze it before, just accepted a bad situation. There *is* something peculiar about Joe. It can't very well involve his physical structure, or the environment, because lower forms didn't give this trouble. Could it be the fact that—Joe is the first puppet in all history with a potentially human intelligence?"

"We speculated in a vacuum," said Cornelius. "Tomorrow, maybe, I can tell you. Now I know nothing."

Viken sat up straight. His pale eyes focused on the other man and stayed there, unblinking. "One minute," he said.

"Yes?" Cornelius shifted, half rising. "Quickly, please. It is past my bedtime."

"You know a good deal more than you've admitted," said Viken. "Don't you?"

"What makes you think that?"

"You aren't the most gifted liar in the universe. And then— you argued very strongly for Anglesey's scheme, this sending down the other pseudos. More strongly than a newcomer should."

"I told you, I want his attention focused elsewhere when—"

"Do you want it that badly?" snapped Viken. Cornelius was still for a minute. Then he sighed and leaned back.

"All right," he said. "I shall have to trust your discretion. I wasn't sure, you see, how any of you old-time station personnel would react. So I didn't want to blabber out my speculations, which may be wrong. The confirmed facts, yes, I will tell them; but I don't wish to attack a man's religion with a mere theory."

Viken scowled. "What the devil do you mean?"

Cornelius puffed hard on his cigar, its tip waxed and waned like a miniature red demon star. "This Jupiter V is more than a research station," he said gently. "It is a way of life, is it not?

No one would come here for even one hitch unless the work was important to him. Those who re-enlist, they must find something in the work, something which Earth with all her riches cannot offer them. No?"

"Yes," answered Viken. It was almost a whisper. "I didn't think you would understand so well. But what of it?"

"Well, I don't want to tell you, unless I can prove it, that maybe this has all gone for nothing. Maybe you have wasted your lives and a lot of money, and will have to pack up and go home."

Viken's long face did not flicker a muscle. It seemed to have congealed. But he said calmly enough: "Why?"

"Consider Joe," said Cornelius. "His brain has as much capacity as any adult human's. It has been recording every sense datum that came to it, from the moment of 'birth'—making a record in itself, in its own cells, not merely in Anglesey's physical memory bank up here. Also, you know, a thought is a sense datum too. And thoughts are not separated into neat little railway tracks; they form a continuous field. Every time Anglesey is in rapport with Joe, and thinks, the thought goes through Joe's synapses as well as his own—and every thought carries its own associations, and every associated memory is recorded. Like if Joe is building a hut, the shape of the logs might remind Anglesey of some geometric figure, which in turn would remind him of the Pythagorean theorem—"

"I get the idea," said Viken in a cautious way. "Given time, Joe's brain will have stored everything that ever was in Ed's."

"Correct. Now a functioning nervous system with an engrammatic pattern of experience—in this case, a *nonhuman* nervous system—isn't that a pretty good definition of a personality?"

"I suppose so—Good Lord!" Viken jumped. "You mean Joe is —taking over?"

"In a way. A subtle, automatic, unconscious way." Cornelius drew a deep breath and plunged into it. "The pseudojovian is so nearly perfect a life form: your biologists engineered into it all the experience gained from nature's mistakes in designing *us*. At first, Joe was only a remote-controlled biological machine. Then Anglesey and Joe became two facets of a single

personality. Then, oh, very slowly, the stronger, healthier body
. . . more amplitude to its thoughts . . . do you see? Joe is becoming the dominant side. Like this business of sending down
the other pseudos—Anglesey only thinks he has logical reasons
for wanting it done. Actually, his 'reasons' are mere rationaliza-
tions for the instinctive desires of the Joe-facet.

"Anglesey's subconscious must comprehend the situation, in a
dim reactive way; it must feel his human ego gradually being
submerged by the steamroller force of *Joe's* instincts and *Joe's*
wishes. It tries to defend its own identity, and is swatted down
by the superior force of Joe's own nascent subconscious.

"I put it crudely," he finished in an apologetic tone, "but it
will account for that oscillation in the K-tubes."

Viken nodded slowly, like an old man. "Yes, I see it," he
answered. "The alien environment down there . . . the different
brain structure . . . good God! Ed's being swallowed up in Joe!
The puppet master is becoming the puppet!" He looked ill.

"Only speculation on my part," said Cornelius. All at once,
he felt very tired. It was not pleasant to do this to Viken, whom
he liked. "But you see the dilemma, no? If I am right, then any
esman will gradually become a Jovian—a monster with two
bodies, of which the human body is the unimportant auxiliary
one. This means no esman will ever agree to control a pseudo
—therefore, the end of your project."

He stood up. "I'm sorry, Arne. You made me tell you what I
think, and now you will lie awake worrying, and I am maybe
quite wrong and you worry for nothing."

"It's all right," mumbled Viken. "Maybe you're not wrong."

"I don't know." Cornelius drifted toward the door. "I am
going to try to find some answers tomorrow. Good night." The
moon-shaking thunder of the rockets, crash, crash, crash, leaping
from their cradles, was long past. Now the fleet glided on metal
wings, with straining secondary ramjets, through the rage of the
Jovian sky.

As Cornelius opened the control-room door, he looked at his
telltale board. Elsewhere a voice tolled the word to all the
stations, *one ship wrecked, two ships wrecked,* but Anglesey
would let no sound enter his presence when he wore the helmet.

An obliging technician had haywired a panel of fifteen red and fifteen blue lights above Cornelius' esprojector, to keep him informed, too. Ostensibly, of course, they were only there for Anglesey's benefit, though the esman had insisted he wouldn't be looking at them.

Four of the red bulbs were dark and thus four blue ones would not shine for a safe landing. A whirlwind, a thunderbolt, a floating ice meteor, a flock of mantalike birds with flesh as dense and hard as iron—there could be a hundred things which had crumpled four ships and tossed them tattered across the poison forests.

Four ships, hell! Think of four living creatures, with an excellence of brain to rival your own, damned first to years in unconscious night and then, never awakening save for one uncomprehending instant, dashed in bloody splinters against an ice mountain. The wasteful callousness of it was a cold knot in Cornelius' belly. It had to be done, no doubt, if there was to be any thinking life on Jupiter at all; but then let it be done quickly and minimally, he thought, so the next generation could be begotten by love and not by machines!

He closed the door behind him and waited for a breathless moment. Anglesey was a wheelchair and a coppery curve of helmet, facing the opposite wall. No movement, no awareness whatsoever. Good!

It would be awkward, perhaps ruinous, if Anglesey learned of this most intimate peering. But he needn't ever. He was blindfolded and ear-plugged by his own concentration.

Nevertheless, the psionicist moved his bulky form with care, across the room to the new esprojector. He did not much like his snooper's role, he would not have assumed it at all if he had seen any other hope. But neither did it make him feel especially guilty. If what he suspected was true, then Anglesey was all unawares being twisted into something not human; to spy on him might be to save him.

Gently, Cornelius activated the meters and started his tubes warming up. The oscilloscope built into Anglesey's machine gave him the other man's exact alpha rhythm, his basic biological clock. First you adjusted to that, then you discovered the subtler elements by feel, and when your set was fully in phase you could probe undetected and—

Find out what was wrong. Read Anglesey's tortured subconscious and see what there was on Jupiter that both drew and terrified him.

Five ships wrecked.

But it must be very nearly time for them to land. Maybe only five would be lost in all. Maybe ten would get through. Ten comrades for—Joe?

Cornelius sighed. He looked at the cripple, seated blind and deaf to the human world which had crippled him, and felt a pity and an anger. It wasn't fair, none of it was.

Not even to Joe. Joe wasn't any kind of soul-eating devil. He did not even realize, as yet, that he *was* Joe, that Anglesey was becoming a mere appendage. He hadn't asked to be created, and to withdraw his human counterpart from him would very likely be to destroy him.

Somehow, there were always penalties for everybody, when men exceeded the decent limits.

Cornelius swore at himself, voicelessly. Work to do. He sat down and fitted the helmet on his own head. The carrier wave made a faint pulse, inaudible, the trembling of neurones low in his awareness. You couldn't describe it.

Reaching up, he tuned to Anglesey's alpha. His own had a somewhat lower frequency, it was necessary to carry the signals through a heterodyning process. Still no reception . . . well, of course he had to find the exact wave form, timbre was as basic to thought as to music. He adjusted the dials, slowly, with enormous care.

Something flashed through his consciousness, a vision of clouds roiled in a violet-red sky, a wind that galloped across horizonless immensity—he lost it. His fingers shook as he tuned back.

The psibeam between Joe and Anglesey broadened. It took Cornelius into the circuit. He looked through Joe's eyes, he stood on a hill and stared into the sky above the ice mountains, straining for sign of the first rocket; and simultaneously, he was still Jan Cornelius, blurrily seeing the meters, probing about for emotions, symbols, any key to the locked terror in Anglesey's soul.

The terror rose up and struck him in the face.

Psionic detection is not a matter of passive listening in. Much as a radio receiver is necessarily also a weak transmitter, the nervous system in resonance with a source of psionic-spectrum energy is itself emitting. Normally, of course, this effect is unimportant; but when you pass the impulses, either way, through a set of heterodyning and amplifying units, with a high negative feedback—

In the early days, psionic psychotherapy vitiated itself because the amplified thoughts of one man, entering the brain of another, would combine with the latter's own neural cycles according to the ordinary vector laws. The result was that both men felt the new beat frequencies as a nightmarish fluttering of their very thoughts. An analyst, trained into self-control, could ignore it; his patient could not, and reacted violently.

But eventually the basic human wave-timbres were measured, and psionic therapy resumed. The modern esprojector analyzed an incoming signal and shifted its characteristics over to the "listener's" pattern. The *really* different pulses of the transmitting brain, those which could not possibly be mapped onto the pattern of the receiving neurones—as an exponential signal cannot very practicably be mapped onto a sinusoid—those were filtered out.

Thus compensated, the other thought could be apprehended as comfortably as one's own. If the patient were on a psibeam circuit, a skilled operator could tune in without the patient being necessarily aware of it. The operator could either probe the other man's thoughts or implant thoughts of his own.

Cornelius' plan, an obvious one to any psionicist, had depended on this. He would receive from an unwitting Anglesey-Joe. If his theory were right, and the esman's personality was being distorted into that of a monster—his thinking would be too alien to come through the filters. Cornelius would receive spottily or not at all. If his theory was wrong, and Anglesey was still Anglesey, he would receive only a normal human stream-of-consciousness, and could probe for other trouble-making factors.

His brain roared!

What's happening to me?

For a moment, the interference which turned his thoughts to sawtoothed gibberish struck him down with panic. He gulped for breath, there in the Jovian wind, and his dreadful dogs sensed the alienness in him and whined.

Then, recognition, remembrance and a blaze of anger so great that it left no room for fear. Joe filled his lungs and shouted it aloud, the hillside boomed with echoes:

"Get out of my mind!"

He felt Cornelius spiral down toward unconsciousness. The overwhelming force of his own mental blow had been too much. He laughed, it was more like a snarl, and eased the pressure.

Above him, between thunderous clouds, winked the first thin descending rocket flare.

Cornelius' mind groped back toward the light. It broke a watery surface, the man's mouth snapped after air and his hands reached for the dials, to turn his machine off and escape.

"Not so fast, you." Grimly, Joe drove home a command that locked Cornelius' muscles rigid. "I want to know the meaning of this. Hold still and let me look!" He smashed home an impulse which could be rendered, perhaps, as an incandescent question mark. Remembrance exploded in shards through the psionicist's forebrain.

"So. That's all there is? You thought I was afraid to come down here and be Joe, and wanted to know why? But I *told* you I wasn't!"

I should have believed—whispered Cornelius.

"Well, get out of the circuit, then." Joe continued growling it vocally. "And don't ever come back in the control room, understand? K-tubes or no, I don't want to see you again. And I may be a cripple, but I can still take you apart cell by cell. Now—

sign off—leave me alone. The first ship will be landing in minutes."

You a cripple . . . you, Joe Anglesey?

"What?" The great gray being on the hill lifted his barbaric head as if to sudden trumpets. "What do you mean?"

Don't you understand? said the weak, dragging thought. *You know how the esprojector works. You know I could have probed Anglesey's mind in Anglesey's brain without making enough interference to be noticed. And I could not have probed a wholly nonhuman mind at all, nor could it have been aware of me. The filters would not have passed such a signal. Yet you felt me in the first fractional second. It can only mean a human mind in a nonhuman brain.*

You are not the half-corpse on Jupiter V any longer. You're Joe—Joe Anglesey.

"Well, I'll be damned," said Joe. "You're right."

He turned Anglesey off, kicked Cornelius out of his mind with a single brutal impulse, and ran down the hill to meet the spaceship.

Cornelius woke up minutes afterward. His skull felt ready to split apart. He groped for the main switch before him, clashed it down, ripped the helmet off his head and threw it clanging on the floor. But it took a little while to gather the strength to do the same for Anglesey. The other man was not able to do anything for himself.

They sat outside sickbay and waited. It was a harshly lit barrenness of metal and plastic, smelling of antiseptics: down near the heart of the satellite, with miles of rock to hide the terrible face of Jupiter.

Only Viken and Cornelius were in that cramped little room. The rest of the station went about its business mechanically, filling in the time till it could learn what had happened. Beyond the door, three biotechnicians, who were also the station's medical staff, fought with death's angel for the thing which had been Edward Anglesey.

"Nine ships got down," said Viken dully. "Two males, seven females. It's enough to start a colony."

"It would be genetically desirable to have more," pointed out Cornelius. He kept his own voice low, in spite of its underlying cheerfulness. There was a certain awesome quality to all this.

"I still don't understand," said Viken.

"Oh, it's clear enough—now. I should have guessed it before, maybe. We had all the facts, it was only that we couldn't make the simple, obvious interpretation of them. No, we had to conjure up Frankenstein's monster."

"Well," Viken's words grated, "we have played Frankenstein, haven't we? Ed is dying in there."

"It depends on how you define death." Cornelius drew hard on his cigar, needing anything that might steady him. His tone grew purposely dry of emotion:

"Look here. Consider the data. Joe, now: a creature with a brain of human capacity, but without a mind—a perfect Lockean *tabula rasa*, for Anglesey's psibeam to write on. We deduced, correctly enough—if very belatedly—that when enough had been written, there would be a personality. But the question was: whose? Because, I suppose, of normal human fear of the unknown, we assumed that any personality in so alien a body had to be monstrous. Therefore it must be hostile to Anglesey, must be swamping him—"

The door opened. Both men jerked to their feet.

The chief surgeon shook his head. "No use. Typical deep-shock traumata, close to terminus now. If we had better facilities, maybe—"

"No," said Cornelius. "You cannot save a man who has decided not to live any more."

"I know." The doctor removed his mask. "I need a cigarette. Who's got one?" His hands shook a little as he accepted it from Viken.

"But how could he—decide—anything?" choked the physicist. "He's been unconscious ever since Jan pulled him away from that . . . that thing."

"It was decided before then," said Cornelius. "As a matter of fact, that hulk in there on the operating table no longer has a mind. I know. I was there." He shuddered a little. A stiff shot of tranquilizer was all that held nightmare away from him. Later he would have to have that memory exorcised.

The doctor took a long drag of smoke, held it in his lungs a moment, and exhaled gustily. "I guess this winds up the project," he said. "We'll never get another esman."

"I'll say we won't." Viken's tone sounded rusty. "I'm going to smash that devil's engine myself."

"Hold on a minute!" exclaimed Cornelius. "Don't you understand? This isn't the end. It's the beginning!"

"I'd better get back," said the doctor. He stubbed out his cigarette and went through the door. It closed behind him with a deathlike quietness. "What do you mean?" Viken said it as if erecting a barrier.

"*Won't* you understand?" roared Cornelius. "Joe has all Anglesey's habits, thoughts, memories, prejudices, interests . . . oh, yes, the different body and the different environment, they do cause some changes—but no more than any man might undergo on Earth. If you were suddenly cured of a wasting disease, wouldn't you maybe get a little boisterous and rough? There is nothing abnormal in it. Nor is it abnormal to want to stay healthy—no? Do you see?"

Viken sat down. He spent a while without speaking.

Then, enormously slow and careful: "Do you mean Joe is Ed?"

"Or Ed is Joe. Whatever you like. He calls himself Joe now, I think—as a symbol of freedom—but he is still himself. What *is* the ego but continuity of existence?

"He himself did not fully understand this. He only knew—he told me, and I should have believed him—that on Jupiter he was strong and happy. Why did the K-tube oscillate? A hysterical symptom! Anglesey's subconscious was not afraid to stay on Jupiter—it was afraid to come back!

"And then, today, I listened in. By now, his whole self was focused on Joe. That is, the primary source of libido was Joe's virile body, not Anglesey's sick one. This meant a different pattern of impulses—not too alien to pass the filters, but alien enough to set up interference. So he felt my presence. And he saw the truth, just as I did—

"Do you know the last emotion I felt, as Joe threw me out of his mind? Not anger any more. He plays rough, him, but all he had room to feel was joy.

"I *knew* how strong a personality Anglesey has! Whatever made me think an overgrown child-brain like Joe's could override it? In there, the doctors—bah! They're trying to salvage a hulk which has been shed because it is useless!"

Cornelius stopped. His throat was quite raw from talking. He paced the floor, rolled cigar smoke around his mouth but did not draw it any farther in.

When a few minutes had passed, Viken said cautiously: "All right. You should know—as you said, you were there. But what do we do now? How do we get in touch with Ed? Will he even be interested in contacting us?"

"Oh, yes, of course," said Cornelius. "He is still himself, remember. Now that he has none of the cripple's frustrations, he should be more amiable. When the novelty of his new friends wears off, he will want someone who can talk to him as an equal."

"And precisely who will operate another pseudo?" asked Viken sarcastically. "I'm quite happy with this skinny frame of mine, thank you!"

"Was Anglesey the only hopeless cripple on Earth?" asked Cornelius quietly.

Viken gaped at him.

"And there are aging men, too," went on the psionicist, half to himself. "Someday, my friend, when you and I feel the years close in, and so much we would like to learn—maybe we, too, would enjoy an extra lifetime in a Jovian body." He nodded at his cigar. "A hard, lusty, stormy kind of life, granted—dangerous, brawling, violent—but life as no human, perhaps, has lived it since the days of Elizabeth the First. Oh, yes, there will be small trouble finding Jovians."

He turned his head as the surgeon came out again.

"Well?" croaked Viken.

The doctor sat down. "It's finished," he said.

They waited for a moment, awkwardly.

"Odd," said the doctor. He groped after a cigarette he didn't have. Silently, Viken offered him one. "Odd. I've seen these cases before. People who simply resign from life. This is the first one I ever saw that went out smiling—smiling all the time."

For a Journal Entry . . .

In "Call Me Joe," the meeting of two cultures takes place between our scientifically oriented Earth culture and the artificially created life forms of the pseudojovians. What differences or similarities are there between this type of cultural contact and the one written about in "Black Destroyer"? How do the differences affect the way each author chooses to tell his story?

For Your Consideration . . .

1. Why does Anglesey refuse to let anyone else control Joe?
2. How does what happens to Joe affect Anglesey? Why do you think Anglesey reacts the way he does?
3. Anderson's use of the names Joe and Anglesey interchangeably could confuse the reader. Why do you think he does this?
4. Why is controlling Joe so much more difficult than controlling lower-type pseudojovians?
5. What makes Anglesey so uniquely suited to operate a pseudojovian? How do you think the story would have ended if one of the other characters had been controlling Joe?
6. If you were given the opportunity to spend an extra lifetime in a Jovian body, would you take it? Why or why not?
7. Anderson is famous for writing "hard science" science fiction. How does his use of specific detail affect your attitude toward the story and the characters in it?

Notes

PAGE

36 *shards*—broken fragment, usually of pottery or stone
37 *dekapod*—a creature with five pairs of legs
37 *140 Absolute*—a very low temperature based on the centigrade scale

37   *aneroids*—meters used for measuring pressure
37   *piezoelectrics*—meters used for measuring pressure
37   *esprojector*—an instrument for projecting Extra-Sensory Perception
38   *K-tube*—see definition in the story on p. 54
38   *hyperbolic*—a type of geometric curve
40   *psionic*—adjective, indicating a form of ESP
41   *pseudojovian*—artificial native of Jupiter
42   *pedagogic*—teaching or learning
43   *synapses*—acquired muscle patterns
43   *topography*—surface features
44   *oscillation*—rapid movement
44   *metallurgy*—science of metals
44   *hydrurgy*—a word coined by the author to mean the science of hydrogen in metallic form
45   *null-gee*—no gravity
48   *xenobiology*—the study of life on other planets
49   *Ice VII*—an isotope, or alternate form, of ice
50   *metazoan*—many-celled organisms
52   *Pseudocentaurus sapiens*—artificial half-man, half-cat being
52   *waldo*—derived from Robert A. Heinlein's story by that name; thus, a creature controlled from a long distance
54   *mirable dictu*—marvelous to tell (Latin)
55   *somatic*—physical or bodily
55   *neurasthenia*—nervous exhaustion
57   *allotropic*—a different form of a familiar substance; thus, water, ice, and steam are allotropes of H_2O
71   *libido*—life force

The Far Look

Theodore L. Thomas

If you grow up in a tropical rain forest, you see life one way. If you are an eskimo living on the polar ice cap, you see it in a totally different manner. Some day men will live and work on the surface of the Moon. Will this change them—and if it does, how will they change? The author of this story, Theodore L. Thomas, is an engineer who specializes in patents. In "The Far Look" he proves that he knows a good deal about the human condition as well.

> *So, like things of stone in a valley lone,*
> *Quiet we sat and dumb:*
> *But each man's heart beat thick and quick,*
> *Like a madman on a drum.*
> OSCAR WILDE
> *Ballad of Reading Gaol*

THE ship appeared first as a dot low on the horizon. The television cameras immediately picked it up. At first the ship did not give the impression of motion; it seemed to hover motionless and swell in size. Then in a few seconds it passed the first television station, the screaming roar of its passage rocking the camera slightly.

Thirty miles beyond, its belly skids touched the packed New Mexican sand. An immense dust cloud stirred into life at the rear of the ship and spread slowly across the desert.

As soon as the ship touched, the three helicopters took off to meet it. The helicopters were ten miles away when the ship halted and lay motionless. The dust began to dissipate rear-

ward. The late afternoon sun distorted the flowing lines of the
ship and made it look like some outlandish beast of prey
crouched on the desert.

As the lead helicopter drew within a mile of the ship, its television camera caught the ship clearly for the first time. Tele-
photo lenses brought it in close, and viewers once again
watched closely. They could see the pilot's head as he checked
over his equipment. They looked admiringly at the stubby
swept-back wings and at the gaping opening at the rear from
which poured the fires of hell itself. But most of all they looked
to the area amidship where the door was.

And as they watched, the door swung open. The sun slanted
in and showed two figures standing there. The figures moved
to a point just inside the door and stopped. They stood there
looking out, motionless, for what seemed an interminable
period. Then the two figures looked at each other, nodded, and
jumped out the door.

Though the sand was only four feet below the sill of the door,
both fell to their knees. They quickly arose, knocked the dust
from their clothes, and started walking to where the helicopters
were waiting. And all over the country people watched that
now-familiar moon walk—the rocking of the body from side to
side to get too-heavy feet off the ground, the relaxed muscles
on the down step where the foot just seemed to plop against the
ground.

But the cameras did not focus on the general appearance or
action of the men. The zoom lenses went to work and a close-
up of the faces of the two men side by side flashed across the
country.

The faces even at first glance seemed different. And as the
cameras lingered, it became apparent that there was something
quite extraordinary there. These were men, but the eyes were
different. There was an expression not found in human eyes. It
was a level-eyed expression, undeviating. It was a penetrating,
probing expression, yet one laden with compassion. There was a
look in those eyes of things seen from deep inside, of things
seen beyond the range of normal vision. It was a far look, a compelling look, a powerful look set in the eyes of normal men.

And even when those eyes were closed, there was something different. A network of tiny creases laced out from both corners of each eye. The crinkled appearance of the eyes made each man appear older than he was, older and strangely wizened.

The cameras stayed on the men's faces as they awkwardly walked toward the helicopters. Even though several dignitaries hurried forward to greet the men, the camera remained on the faces, transmitting that strange look for all to see. A nation crammed forward to watch.

In Macon, Georgia, Mary Sinderman touched a wetted finger to the bottom of the iron. She heard it pop as she stared across her ironing board at the television screen with the faces of two men on it.

"Charlie. Oh, Charlie," she called. "Here they are."

A dark squat man in an undershirt came into the room and looked at the picture. "Yeah," he grunted. "They got it all right. Both of 'em."

"Aren't they handsome?" she said.

He threw a black look at her and said, "No, they ain't." And he went out the door he had come in.

In Stamford, Connecticut, Walter Dwyer lowered his newspaper and peered over the top of it at the faces of two men on the television screen. "Look at that, honey," he said.

His wife looked up from her section of the paper and nodded silently. He said, "Two more, dear. If this keeps up, we'll all be able to retire and let them run things." She chuckled, and nodded and continued to watch the screen.

In Boise, Idaho, the Tankard Saloon was doing a moderate business. The television set was on up over one end of the bar. The faces of two men flashed on the screen. Slowly a silence fell over the saloon as one person after another stopped what he was doing to watch. One man sitting in close under the screen raised his drink high in tribute to the two faces on the screen. And every man in the place followed suit.

In a long low building on the New Mexican flats, the wall TV set was on. A thin, earnest-faced young man wearing heavy glasses sat stiffly erect on a folding chair in front of the screen watching the two faces. He glanced briefly aside with a faint air of disapproval at the pipe being contentedly puffed on by an older man who stood near. He turned back to the screen and his disapproval vanished. "Dr. Scott," he said, "they both have the look."

The older man nodded wordlessly. They watched the awkwardness of the two men, apparent even from a view confined to their faces.

The young man said, "How long will it be before they arrive here, doctor?"

"About half to three-quarters of an hour. They've got to get the red plush carpet laid out for them first."

"Dr. Scott, do you think you'll be able to find out anything this time?"

A slight urge to tell this young man to keep his big fat mouth shut rose up in Dr. Scott. He noted the urge and catalogued it neatly in the niche filled with the urges of older, experienced men toward young naïve men who believe everything they learned at college, and no more.

But Dr. Scott answered gently, "I don't know, Dr. Webb, I don't know. We've examined sixteen of these fellows without finding out anything. I don't know why we should now."

"Have you no theories to explain it?"

"No. I have no theories. Once I had theories, but I haven't any anymore." And Scott brought out a match, struck it, and began ejecting great sheets of flame and smoke from his pipe.

Webb quietly watched the scene on the screen. He saw the two men shake hands with an impressive assortment of generals, defense officials, air officials, space officials, and the assorted lot that clusters around such dignitaries.

Webb said, "Have you isolated all the factors resulting from your choice of men?"

Scott pulled reflectively on his pipe a time or two, and said, "As far as we've been able, yes."

"And you found nothing, even though you've been highly selective in picking the men?"

Again the reflective puffs of smoke; then, "Well, I'm not sure

I know what you mean when you say 'highly selective.' We look for a combination of qualities, not any one or two or three qualities." More smoke. "Suppose you had to choose a man who was a good electrical engineer and who was also a good mule skinner. You'd find that the best man you could get would not be the best electrical engineer, nor would he be the best mule skinner. Well, that's our problem, only ten times worse. We look for men with the combination of technological and psychological qualities that we know best equips the men for survival on the moon. But as soon as you try to isolate any one of the various qualities, you'll find there are thousands of other men that outshine ours in that particular quality. It's the combination that counts."

Webb hadn't taken his eyes off the handshaking and speechmaking on the screen, but he had been listening to Scott.

Webb said, "Well, isn't it the combination that does it then? The good all-around men?"

"It might be," said Scott, "except for one thing. When we started this project we didn't know as much as we know now. The first ten men were not selected the way we select them now, yet the same ratio of them developed the far look. Two of them died on the Moon, and that helped teach us how to better select the ones that can survive. The point is that our selection system affects survival but doesn't seem to affect the far look."

Webb nodded. He watched the two men board a helicopter and saw it take off. The screen faded to a blare of martial music and then came to life on a toothy announcer praising the virtues of a hair shampoo. Webb snapped the set off, turned to Scott, and said, "Don't all these men go through some experience in common?"

Scott pulled hard at his pipe, but it was out. He reached in a side pocket and pulled out a match the size of a small pine tree. He struck it under the table, held it poised over the bowl, and said, "They go through a great many experiences in common. They go through two years of intensive training. They make a flight through space and land on the Moon. They spend twenty-eight days of hell reading instruments, making surveys, and collecting samples. They suffer loneliness such as no human being has even known before. Their lives are in constant peril. Each pair has had at least one disaster during their stay. Then they get their replacements and come back to Earth. Yes, they have something in common all right. But a few come back without the far look. They've improved; they're better than most men here on Earth. But they are not on a par with the rest of these returning prodigies with crinkles around their eyes. Talk about *Homo superior*. We're making about two of them a month, and we haven't the foggiest idea of how we're doing it. *Ouch.*" And he flung the burnt-out pine tree into an ash tray.

Webb looked at him quizzically and then glanced at his watch. "Ten minutes," he said, "they'll be here in ten minutes." He walked to the window and looked out, listening to the hissing and bubbling of Scott's pipe going through the throes of being relighted. Webb said, "I suppose these two will become just as successful as the others. They've got 'the far look,' as you and the newspapers call it."

"Yes, they've got it. And they'll be as good as the others, too. I don't know whether they'll go into business or politics or science or art; but whatever it is, you can bet they'll be better at it than anybody else has ever been."

Webb continued to look out the window for a while, trying to fit this latest information into his general background of knowledge. It would not fit. He shook his head and turned from the window and said, "We are missing something. Somewhere there is an element we are unaware of. These men must know what it is. They are keeping it from us, knowingly or unknowingly. All we have to do is dig out that missing element and I venture to say we will have the answer. It's as simple as that."

Scott looked at him. He puffed gently a time or two to slow the welling up of anger. He took the pipe from his mouth and said softly, "These men are concealing nothing, as far as our best efforts can show. We've pumped them full of half a dozen truth drugs. We've doped them and subjected them to hypnosis. On top of that they have all been completely frank and open with us. Maybe they're concealing something but I doubt it very much." And he put the pipe back in his mouth and clamped down on it hard.

Webb shook his head again. "I don't know. There's something missing here. I certainly mean to put these subjects through exhaustive tests. I'll dig something out of them."

The anger in Scott brought a flush to his face. He cupped the pipe bowl and studied the gray ashes while he considered whether a wrathful response would merely be a venting of his own anger or a real help to Webb. He decided that Webb might profit with a little cushioning against the shock he was due to receive in a very few minutes now. Scott pointed the stem of the pipe at Webb as he crossed the room toward him. He stopped in front of Webb and touched him on the lapel of the coat with the bit as he said, "Look here, young fella, these 'subjects' as you call them are like no subjects you ever had or conceived of. These men can twist you and me up into knots if they want to. They understand more about people than the entire profession of psychiatrics will learn in the next hundred years. These men are intellectual giants with a personality that can curl you up on the floor."

He put the pipe in his mouth and said, more gently, "You are in for a shock, Dr. Webb. I'm telling you this so you won't be quite as crushed when you meet these men. You've read about them, studied their histories, I know, but no mere description does justice to the force of their personalities. These two particular men are fresh from the Moon and do not yet fully realize the immense impact they have on people. Now you'd best get yourself ready for quite an experience. You'll need all your strength to preserve an ounce of objectivity."

The murmur of approaching motors broke into the ensuing silence. Webb did not hear them at first; he stared at Scott, mouth slightly open. The murmur grew to a roar as the helicopters landed outside the building. Webb turned to look out the window again, but the men dismounted on the far side of the plane and disappeared through a door in the building. In a moment footsteps sounded outside in the hall and the door crashed open.

Webb turned to see the two men with crinkles surrounding
their eyes walk into the room. The taller of the two looked at
Webb and Webb felt as if struck by a hot blast of wind. The
level eyes were brilliant blue and seemed to reach into Webb
and gently strum on the fibers of his nervous system. A sense of
elation swept through him. He felt as he had once felt standing
alone at dusk in a wind-tossed forest. He could not speak. His
breath stopped. His muscles held rigid. And then the blue-eyed
glance passed him and left him confused and restless and dis-
appointed.

He dimly saw Scott cross the room and shake hands with the
shorter man. Scott said, "How do you do. We are very glad for
your safe return. Was everything in order when you left the
Moon?"

The shorter man smiled as he shook Scott's hand. "Thank you,
doctor. Yes, everything was in order. Our two replacements are
off to a good start." He glanced at the taller man. They looked
at each other, and smiled.

"Yes," said the taller man, "they are off to a good start. Fowler
and McIntosh will do all right."

Don Fowler and Al McIntosh still had the shakes. After six
days they still had the shakes whenever they remembered the
first few moments of their landing on the Moon.

The ship had let down roughly. Fowler awkwardly climbed
out through the lock first. He turned to make sure McIntosh
was following him and then started to move around the ship to
look for the two men they were to replace.

The ship lay near a crevice. A series of ripples in the rock
marred the black shiny basalt surface that surrounded the crevice. The surface was washed clean of dust by the jets of the
descending ship. As Fowler walked around the base of the ship
his foot stepped into the trough of one of the ripples in the
rock. It threw him off balance, tilted him toward the crevice.
He struggled to right himself. Under Earth gravity he would
simply have fallen, but under Lunar gravity he managed to
retain his feet. But he staggered toward the crevice, stumbling

in the ripples, unable to recover himself in the unaccustomed gravity. McIntosh grabbed for him. But with arms flailing, body twisting, feet groping he disappeared down the crevice as if drawn into the maw of some hungry beast. McIntosh staggered behind him. His own feet skidded on the ripples in the hard, slick basalt. He, too, bobbled his way to the lip of the crevice and toppled in.

Thirty feet down the crevice narrowed to a point where the men could fall no farther. Both found themselves pinned firmly in place. Fowler was head down and four feet to McIntosh's left. They were unhurt but they began to worry when a few struggles showed them how firmly the slick rock gripped their spacesuits. The pilot of the spaceship, sealed in his tiny compartment, could not help them. The two men they were to replace might be miles away. The radios were useless for anything but line-of-sight work. So they hung there, waiting for something to happen.

Although they were completely helpless and hadn't the slightest idea of how to get out of their predicament, their training on Earth asserted itself. Fowler spoke first.

"Say, Mac. Did you get a chance to see what the Moon looks like before you joined me down here?"

"No. I had sort of hoped you'd noticed. Now we don't have a thing to talk about."

Silence, then,

"This is one for the books," said Fowler. "We spend ten seconds on the surface of the Moon and an undetermined period of time some odd feet beneath it. Can you see anything? All I can see is the bottom of this thing and all I can tell you about it is that it's black down there."

"No. I can't tilt my head back far enough to see out. I have a nice view of the wall, though. Dense, igneous, probably of basic plagioclose. Make a note of that, will you?"

"Can you reach me?"

"No. I can't even see you. Can you—"

"What are you fellows doing down there?" A new voice broke into the conversation. Neither Fowler nor McIntosh could think of an answer. "Stay right there," the voice continued, with something that sounded suspiciously like a chuckle in it. "We'll be down to get you out."

Both of the pinned men could hear a rock-scraping sound through their suits. Two pairs of hands rocked each man free of the walls and lifted him up to where he could bridge the crevice with knees and back. McIntosh was the first to be freed and he watched with close interest the easy freedom of movement of the two spacesuited figures as they released Fowler, turned him right side up, and lifted him up to where he could support himself in the crevice. All four then worked their way up the slick walls by sliding their backs up one wall while bracing their feet against the opposite wall.

It took Fowler and McIntosh appreciably longer to climb to the surface than the other two. There had been no words spoken in the crevice and there was little to say now. Fowler and McIntosh each solemnly shook hands with the other two. The clunk of the metallic-faced palms of the spacesuit and the gritty sound of the finger, wrist, and elbow joints made handshaking a noisy business in a spacesuit.

The two men led Fowler and McIntosh around to the other side of the spaceship and pointed westward across Mare Imbrium. One of them said, "About half a mile over there behind that rise you'll find the dome. About eight miles south of here you'll find the latest cargo rocket—came in two days ago. The terrain is pretty rough so you'd better wait a few days to get used to the gravity before you go after it. We left some hot tea for you at the dome. Watch yourselves now." And again there was their noisy business of shaking hands. Both Fowler and McIntosh tried to see the faces of the two men they were replacing, but they could not. It was daytime on the Moon and the faceplate filters were all in place. Their radio voices sounded the same as they had on Earth.

The two disappeared into the ship with a final wave of hand. Fowler and McIntosh turned and carefully and awkwardly moved westward away from the ship. A quarter of a mile away they turned to watch it and for the first time the men had the chance to see the actual moonscape.

Pictures are wonderful things and they are of great aid in

conveying information. The two men were prepared for what they saw, yet they were deeply shocked. Words and pictures are often adequate to impart a complete understanding of a place or event. Yet where human emotions are intertwined with an experience mere words and pictures are inadequate.

And so Fowler and McIntosh reeled slightly as the garish barrenness of the moonscape impressed itself on their minds. It might well be that on Earth there existed similar wild wastelands, but they were limited, and human beings lived on the fringes, and human beings had crossed them, and human beings could stand out on them unprotected and feel the familiar heat of day and the cold of night. Here there was only death for the unarmored man, swift death like nothing on Earth. And nowhere were there human beings, nor any possibility of human beings. Only the darker and lighter places, no color, black sky, white spots for stars, and the moonscape itself nothing but brilliant gray shades of tones between the white stars and the black sky.

So Fowler and McIntosh, knowing in advance what it would be like, still had to struggle to fight down an urge to scream at finding themselves in a place where men did not exist. They stared out through the smoked filters, wide-eyed, panting, fine drops of perspiration beading their foreheads. Each could hear the harsh breath of the other in the earphones, and it helped a little to know they both felt the same.

A spot of fire caught their attention and they turned slightly to see. The spaceship stood ungainly and awkward with a network of pipework surrounding the base. The spot of fire turned into a column of fire and the ship trembled. The column produced a flat bed of fire on the surface of the Moon and the ship rose slowly. There was no dust. A small stream of fire reached out sideways as a balancing rocket sprang to life. The ship rose farther, faster now, and Fowler and McIntosh leaned back to watch it. Once it cleared the Moon's horizon it lost apparent motion; it seemed to hover merely, and to grow smaller. They watched it until the fire was indistinguishable with the stars, then they looked around again.

It was a little better this time, since they were prepared for an emotional response. But in another sense it was worse for they were truly alone now. The horror of utter aloneness again welled up inside them. And without knowing what they were doing they drew closer together until the spacesuits touched. The gentle thud registered in each consciousness and brought their attention in to themselves. They pressed together for a moment while they fought to organize their thoughts.

And then McIntosh drew a long deep breath and shook his head violently. Fowler could feel the relief it brought. They moved apart and looked around.

McIntosh said, "Let's go get that tea they mentioned."

"Right," said Fowler. "I could use some. That's the dome there." And he pointed west.

They headed for it. They could see the dome in every detail; and as they approached, the details grew larger. It was almost impossible to judge distances on the Moon. Everything stood out with brilliant clarity no matter how far away. The only effect of distance was to cause a shrinking in size.

The dome was startling in its familiarity. It was the precise duplicate to the last bolt of the dome they had lived in and operated for months in the hi-vac chambers on Earth.

The air lock was built to accommodate two men in a pinch. They folded back the antennas that projected up from their packs and they crawled into the lock together; neither suggested going in one at a time. They waited while the pump filled the lock with air from the inside; then they pushed into the dome itself and stood up and looked around.

Automatically their eyes flickered from one gauge to another, checking to make sure everything was right with the dome. They removed their helmets and checked more closely. Air pressure was a little high, eight pounds. Fowler reached out to throw the switch to bring it down when he remembered that a decision had been made just before they left Earth to carry the pressure a little higher than had been the practice in the past. A matter of sleeping comfort.

"How's the pottet?" asked McIntosh. His voice sounded different from the way it had on Earth.

Fowler noted the difference—a matter of the difference in

air density—as he crossed the twenty-foot dome and squatted to look into a bin with a transparent side. The bin bore the label in raised letters, Potassium Tetraoxide.

On Earth, water is the first worry of those who travel to out-of-the-way places. Food is next, with comfort close behind depending on the climate. On the Moon, oxygen was first. The main source of oxygen was potassium textraoxide, a wonderful compound that gave up oxygen when exposed to moisture and then combined with carbon dioxide and removed it from the atmosphere. And each man needed some one thousand pounds of the chemical to survive on the Moon for twenty-eight days. A cylinder, bulky and heavy, of liquid air mounted under the sled supplied the air make-up in the dome. And a tank of water, well insulated by means of a hollow shiny shell open to the Moon's atmosphere, gave them water and served in part as the agent to release oxygen from the pottet when needed.

The dome checked out and by common consent both men swung to the radio, hungry for the reassuring sound of another human voice. McIntosh tuned it and said into the mike, "Moon Station to Earth. Fowler and McIntosh checking in. Everything in order. Over."

About four seconds later the transmitter emitted what the two men waited to hear. "Pole Number One to Moon. Welcome to the network. How are you, boys? Everything shipshape? Over."

McIntosh glanced at Fowler and a vision of the crevice swam between them. McIntosh said, "Everything fine, Pole Number One. Dome in order. Men in good shape. All's well on the Moon. Over."

About three seconds' wait, then, "Good. We will now take up Schedule Charlie. Time, 0641. Next check-in, 0900. Out." McIntosh hung up the mike quickly, and hit the switches to save power.

The two men removed their spacesuits and sat down on a low bench and poured tea from the thermos.

McIntosh was a stocky man with blue eyes and sandy hair cut short. He was built like a rectangular block of granite, thick chest, thick waist, thick legs; even his fingers seemed square in cross section. His movements were deliberate and conveyed an air of relentlessness.

Fowler was slightly taller than McIntosh. His hair and eyes were black, his skin dark. He was lean and walked with a slight stoop. His waist seemed too small and his shoulders too wide. He moved in a flowing sinuous manner like a cat perpetually stalking its prey.

They sipped the hot liquid gratefully, inhaling the wet fragrance of it. They carried their cups to the edge of the dome and looked out the double layer of transparent resin that served as one of the windows. The filter was in place and they pushed against it and looked out.

"Dreary looking place, isn't it?" said Fowler.

McIntosh nodded and said, "Funny, you don't get the feel of the complete barrenness by looking at pictures."

"I noticed that, too."

They sipped their tea, holding it close under their noses when they weren't drinking, looking out at the moonscape, trying to grasp it, adjusting their minds to it, thinking of the days ahead, and sipping their tea.

They finished, and Fowler said, "Well, time to get to work. You all set?"

McIntosh nodded. They climbed into their spacesuits and passed through the lock, one at a time. They checked over the exterior of the dome and every piece of mechanism mounted on the sled. Fowler mounted an outside seat, cleared with McIntosh, and started the drive motor. The great sled, complete with dome, parabolic mirror, spherical boilers, batteries, antennas, and a complex of other equipment rolled slowly forward on great, sponge-filled tires. McIntosh walked beside it. Fowler watched his odometer and when the sled had moved five hundred yards he brought it to a halt. He dismounted and the two of them continued the survey started months back by their predecessors.

They took samples, they read radiation levels, they ran the survey, they ate and slept, they took more samples. They kept to a rigid routine, for that was the way to make time pass, that was the way to preserve sanity.

The days passed. The two men grew accustomed to the low gravitation, so they recovered the cargo rocket. Yet they moved about with more than the usual caution for Moon men; their experience of the first few seconds on the Moon loomed forbiddingly on their minds. They had learned earlier than the others that an insignificant and trivial bit of negligence can cost a man his life.

So the days passed. And as time went by they became aware of another phenomenon of life on the Moon. On Earth, in an uncomfortable and dangerous situation, you become accustomed to the surroundings and can achieve a measure of relaxation. Not on the Moon. The dismal bright and less-bright grays, the oppressive barrenness of the gray moonscape, the utter aloneness of two men in a gray wilderness, slowly took on the tone of a gray malevolence seeking an unguarded moment. And the longer they stayed the worse it became. So the men kept themselves busier than ever. They accomplished more and more work, driving themselves to exhaustion, sinking into restless sleep, and up to work some more. They made more frequent five-hundred-yard jumps; they expanded the survey; they sought frozen water or frozen air deep in crevices, but they found only frozen carbon dioxide. They kept a careful eye on the pottet, for hard-working men consume more oxygen, and the supply was limited. And every time they checked the remaining supply they remembered what had happened to Booker and Whitman.

A pipeline had frozen. Booker took a bucket of water and began to skirt the pottet bin. The bail of the bucket caught on the corner of the lid of the bin. Booker carelessly hoisted the bucket to free it. The lid pulled open and the canvas bucket struck a corner and emptied into the bin. Instantly the dome filled with oxygen and steam. The safety valves opened and bled off the steam and oxygen to the outside, where it froze and fell like snow and slowly evaporated. The bin ruptured from the

heat and broke a line carrying hydraulic fluid. Twenty gallons
of hydraulic fluid flooded the pottet, reacting with it, forming
potassium salts with the silicone liquid, releasing some oxygen,
irretrievably locking up the rest.

Booker's backward leap caromed him off the ceiling and out
of harm's way. After a horrified moment, the two men assessed
the damage and calmly radioed Earth that they had a seven-
Earth-day supply of oxygen left. Whereupon they stocked one
spacesuit with a full supply of salvaged pottet and lay down on
their bunks. For six Earth days they lay motionless; activity
consumes oxygen. They lay calm; panic makes the heart beat
faster and a racing blood stream consumes oxygen.

Two men lay motionless on the Moon. For four days slightly
more than two thousand men on Earth struggled to get an off-
schedule rocket to the Moon. The already fantastic requirements
of fuel and equipment needed to put two men and supplies on
the Moon every month had to be increased. The tempo of round-
the-clock schedules stepped up to inhuman heights; there were
two men lying motionless on the Moon.

It lacked but a few hours of the seven days when Booker and
Whitman felt the shudder that told them a rocket had crashlanded nearby. They sat up and looked at each other, and it
was apparent that Whitman had the most strength left. So
Booker climbed into the spacesuit while Whitman lay down
again. And Booker went out to the crashed rocket feeling strong
from the fresh oxygen in the spacesuit. He scraped up pottet
along with the silica dust and carried it in a broken container
back into the dome. Whitman was almost unconscious by the
time Booker got back and put water into the pottet. The two
men lived. And by the time their replacements arrived the dome
was again in as perfect condition as it had been. Except there
was a different type of cover on the pottet bin.

So Fowler and McIntosh worked endlessly, ranging far out from
the dome on their survey. The tension built up in them, for the
worst was yet to come. The long Lunar day was fast drawing
to a close, and night was about to fall. The night was fourteen

Earth-days long. A black night broken only by the faint harsh starlight, a night where the imagination does things that the eyes would not allow in daylight.

"Well, here it comes," said McIntosh on the twelfth Earth-day. He pointed west. Fowler climbed up on the hummock beside him and looked. He saw the bottom half of the sun mashed by a distant mountain range and a broad band of shadow reaching out toward them. The shadow stretched as far north and south as he could see.

"Yes," said Fowler. "It won't be long now. We'd better get back."

They jumped down from the hummock and started for the dome, samples forgotten. At first they walked, throwing glances back over their shoulder. The pace grew faster until they were traveling in the peculiar ground-consuming lope of men in a hurry under light gravity.

They reached the dome and went in together. Inside they removed their helmets and McIntosh headed for the radio. Fowler dropped a hand on his shoulder and said, "Wait, Mac. We have half an hour before we're due to check in."

McIntosh picked up a cloth and wiped his wet forehead, running the cloth through his sandy hair. "Yes," he said. "You're right. If we check in too soon they'll worry. Let's make some tea."

They removed their suits and brewed two steaming cupsfull. They sat down and sipped the scalding fluid and slowly relaxed a little.

"You know," said Fowler, "it's right about now that I'm glad we have an independent water supply. Repurified stuff would begin to taste bad about now."

McIntosh nodded. "I noticed it a day or two ago. I think I'd have trouble if the water weren't fresh." And the two men fell silent thinking of Tilton and Beck.

Tilton and Beck had been the second pair of men on the Moon. Very little water was sent up in those days, only enough for makeup. Tiny stills and ion-exchange resins purified all body waste products and produced a pure clear water pre-eminently suitable for drinking. Tilton and Beck had lived on that water for weeks on Earth and they, along with dozens of others, had pronounced it as fit to drink as clean cool spring water.

Then they went to the Moon. Two Earth-days after night fell Beck thought the water tasted bad. Tilton did, too. They knew the water was sweet and clean, they knew it was their imagination that gave the water its taste, but they could not help it. They reached a point where the water wrenched at their insides; it tasted so foul they could not drink it. Then they radioed Earth for help, and began living off the make-up water. But Earth was not as experienced in emergency rocket send-offs in those days. The pleas for decent water for the men on the Moon grew weaker. The first rocket might have saved them, except its controls were erratic and it crashlanded five hundred miles from the dome. The second rocket carried the replacements, and when they entered the dome they found Tilton and Beck dead, cheeks sunken, skin parched, lips cracked and broken, dehydrated, dead of thirst. And within easy reach of the two dried-out bodies was twenty-five gallons of clear, pure —almost chemically pure—tasteless, odorless water, sparkling bright with dissolved oxygen.

Fowler and McIntosh finished their tea and radioed in at check time. They announced that night had overtaken them. A new schedule was set up, one with far more frequent radio contacts with Earth. And immediately they set about their new tasks. No more trips far from the dome, no surveying. They broke the telescope from its cover and set up the spectrometer. Inside the dome they converted part of the drafting table to a small but astonishingly complete analytical chemical laboratory.

The sun was gone completely now, but off to the east several mountaintops still glistened like the last flame that shoots up from an expiring fire. In an hour the gleam disappeared and night was completely come.

The planners of the Moon survey from the very beginning recognized that night on the Moon presented a difficult problem. So they scheduled replacements to arrive when the Moon day was about forty-eight hours old. Thus the replacements had twelve Earth-days of sunlight on the Moon to get themselves ready for the emotional ordeal of fourteen Earth-days of darkness. Then once the long night was ended, they had two Earth-days of sunlight before the next replacements arrived. Such a system insured that the spaceship landed on the Moon in daylight and also allowed optimum psychological adjustment for the Moon men. Shorter periods of residence on the Moon were not feasible, since the full twenty-eight days were needed to prepare for the shuttle flight from Earth to the space station, from the space station to the Moon, and return. Then, too, at least one supply rocket a month had to be crashlanded within easy walking distance of the dome. The effort and money expended by the United States to do these things were prodigious. But with the backing of the people, the project went ahead. Future property rights on the Moon might well go to the nation that continuously occupied it.

Fowler looked up from adjusting the telescope and said, "Look at that, Al." His arm pointed to the Earth brightly swimming in a sea of star-pointed blackness.

They saw the Western Hemisphere, white-dotted with clouds, and a brilliant blinding spot of white in the South Pacific off the coast of Peru where the ocean reflected the sun's light to them.

McIntosh said, "Beautiful, isn't it? I can just about see Florida. Good old Orlando. I'll bet the lemon blossoms smell good these days. You know it looks even better at night than it does in day."

Fowler nodded inside his helmet as the two continued to watch the Earth. Fowler said, "You know, we've certainly gone and loused up a good old Earth tradition."

"What do you mean?"

"Well, picture it. A guy and his girl go out walking in the moonlight down there. They'd sigh and feel all choked up and gaze at the Moon and feel like the Moon was made for them alone. Now when they look up they know there's a couple of slobs sprinting around up here. It must take something away."

"I'll bet," chuckled McIntosh. "They must either get mad at us or feel very sorry for us."

Fowler dropped his gaze to the moonscape and looked around and said, "It sure looks different here at night."

They studied the eerie scene. As always, it showed nothing but varying shades of gray, but now the tones were dark and foreboding. The sharp, dim starlight and soft Earthshine threw no shadows but spread a ghostly luminescence over ridge and draw alike. It was impossible to tell just where the actual seeing left off and the imagination began.

Fowler muttered, almost under his breath. "The night is full of forms of fear."

"What?"

"The night is full of forms of fear. It's a line I read some place."

They looked around in silence, turning the ungainly space-suits. McIntosh said, "It sure describes this place. Never saw such a weird sight."

They finally shrugged off the fascination of the moonscape and got to work.

Several Earth-days passed. The two men kept busy making astronomical observation and checking out some of the minerals collected during the long day. They made short trips out into the region around the dome but they took no samples; they let the scintillation counters built into their suits do the probing for hot spots as they simply walked around. They never got too far from the dome or from each other. And often while they were outside striding through the moon-dust on their separate paths, one of them would say, "How're things?" And the other would say, "O.K., how're things there?" The urge to hear a human voice rose powerful and often in the Moon night.

It was on one of these outside trips that their first real panic occurred. The two men were each about a hundred yards away from the dome and on opposite sides. McIntosh did not notice a telltale slight dip in the dust where a shallow crack lay almost filled with light flourlike particles. His foot went in. He twisted and fell on his back so that his caught leg would bend at the knee and not wrench the knee-joint of the suit. He hit with a jolt; his forward speed added to the normal speed of fall. The impact was not great but it clanged loudly inside the suit.

McIntosh grunted, and said "damn," and sat up to free his foot. Fowler's voice sounded in his headphones. "You O.K., Mac?"

"Yeah," said McIntosh. "I fell down but I'm not hurt a bit. Things are fine."

"Mac," Fowler's voice was shrill. "You O.K.?"

"Yes. Not a thing wrong. Just took a—"

"For God's sake, Mac, answer me." Fowler's voice was a near scream, panic bubbling through it.

The fear was contagious. McIntosh yanked his foot out of the crevice, leaped to his feet, and ran for the dome shouting. "What is it, Don? What's the matter? I'm coming. What is it?" And as he ran he could hear Fowler screaming now for Mac to answer.

McIntosh rounded the dome and almost collided with Fowler coming in the opposite direction. The two slipped and skidded to a halt, clouds of dust kicking up around their feet and settling as fast as they rose. Once stopped, the two men jumped toward each other and touched helmets.

"What is it, Don?" shouted McIntosh.

"What happened to you?" came Fowler's voice, choked, gasping. McIntosh could hear it both through the helmet and through his headphones. It sounded hollow.

McIntosh shouted again. "I took a little spill, that's all. I told you I was all right over the set. Didn't you hear me?"

"No," Fowler was getting himself under control. "I kept calling you and getting no answer. Something must be wrong with the sets."

"Yeah. It's either your receiver or my transmitter. Let's go in and check them out."

They entered the dome together and removed their suits. They wiped the sweat from their faces and automatically started to make tea, but they stopped. Power was in short supply during the night and hot water had to be held to a minimum. So they checked the radios instead.

They went over McIntosh's transmitter first, since he had had the fall. They soon found the trouble. A tiny grain of silica shorted a condenser in the printed circuit. It was easily fixed and then the transmitter worked again. They put on the suits and went outside. But the shock they suffered was not so easily remedied. And thereafter when they were outside they were never out of sight of each other.

Time went by. The looming loneliness of the brooding moonscape closed ever more tightly around them. Their surroundings took on the stature of a living thing, menacing, waiting, lurking. Even the radio contacts with Earth lost much of their meaning; the voices were just voices, not really belonging to people, but emanating from some ominous creature poised just over the ridge. The loneliness grew.

On Earth a man can be deep in a trackless and impenetrable jungle, yet there is a chance a fellow human being will happen by. A man can be isolated on the remotest of desert islands and still maintain a reasonable hope that a ship, or canoe, or plane will carry another human being to him. A man sentenced to a life of solitary confinement knows for certain that there are people on the other side of the wall.

But on the Moon there is complete aloneness. There are no human beings and—what is worse—no possibility of any human beings. And never before had men, two men, found themselves in such a position. The human mind, adaptable entity that it is, nevertheless had to reach beyond its boundaries to absorb the reality of perfect isolation.

The lunar night wore on. Fowler and McIntosh were out spreading their dirty laundry for the usual three-hour exposure to Moon conditions before shaking the clothes out and packing them away 'til they were needed again.

Fowler straightened up and looked at the Earth for a moment, then said, "Mac, did you ever eat in a diner on a train?"

"Sure, many times."

"You remember how the headwaiter seated people?"

McIntosh thought for a moment, then said, "I know what you mean. He keeps them apart. He seats individuals at empty tables until there are no more empty tables; then he begins to double them up."

"That's it. He preserves the illusion of isolation. I guess people don't know how much they need one another."

"I guess they don't. People are funny that way."

They grinned at each other through the faceplates, although it was too dark to see inside the spacesuits. They finished spreading the laundry and went into the dome together. Both of them had recently come to realize a striking thing. If one of them died, the other could not survive. It was difficult enough to preserve sanity with two. One alone could not last an Earth-day. The men on the Moon lived in pairs or they died in pairs. And if Fowler and McIntosh had thought to look at each other closely, they would have noticed a few incipient lines radiating from the eyes. Nothing striking, nothing abnormal, and certainly nothing as intense as the far look. Just the suggestion of a few lines around the eyes.

The night had only two Earth-days to run. Fowler and McIntosh for the first time began to turn their thoughts to the journey home, not with longing, not with anticipation, but as a possibility of something that might happen. The actuality of leaving the Moon seemed too unreal to be true. And the cold harsh fact was that the rocket might not come; it had happened before. So though they dimly realized that in a mere four Earth-days they might leave the grim grayness behind, they were not much concerned.

A series of observations ended. Fowler and McIntosh sipped hot tea, drawing the warmth into their chilled bodies. Fowler sat perched on one end of a bench. McIntosh cupped the teacup in his hands and stood looking out at the lowering moonscape, wishing he could pull his eyes from it, too fascinated by its awfulness to do so. There was complete silence in the dome.

"Don." The word came as a gasp, as though McIntosh had called the name before he had completely swallowed a mouthful of tea.

Fowler looked up, mildly curious. He saw McIntosh drop the teacup, saw it bounce off the floor. He saw McIntosh straining forward, taut, neck muscles standing out, mouth open, one hand against the clear plastic.

"Don. *I saw something move out there.*" The words were shrill, harsh, hysteria in every syllable.

Fowler landed beside him in a single leap and looked, not out the window, but at his face. At the staring, terror-filled eyes, the drawn mouth. Fowler threw his arms around McIntosh's chest and squeezed hard and said, "Easy, Mac, easy. Don't let the shadows get you. Things are all right."

"I tell you I saw something. A sudden movement. Near that hillock but at a greater range and to the right. Something moved, Don." And he inhaled a great shuddering gasp.

Fowler kept his arms around McIntosh and looked out. He saw only the jagged dim surface of the Moon. For a long moment he looked out, listening to McIntosh's gasping breath, a chill fear slowly rising inside him. He turned his head to look at McIntosh's face again, and as he did he caught a flicker of motion out of the corner of his eye. He dropped his arms and jerked his head back to look out as McIntosh screamed, "There, there it is again, but it's moved."

The two men, both panting, strained at the window. For a full minute they stood with every muscle pulled tight, gulping down air, perspiration prickling out of their scalps and running down over face and neck. Their eyes saw fantastic shapes in the sharp dim light but their minds told them it was imagination.

Then they saw it clearly. About one hundred yards straight out in front of the window a tiny fountain of moondust sprayed upward and outward from a glowing base that winked out as swiftly as it appeared. Like the blossoming of a death-colored gray rose, the dust from a handspread of surface suddenly rose and spread outward in a circle and just as suddenly fell back to the surface.

"What is it?" hissed Fowler.

"I don't know."

They watched, the tension so great that they shuddered. They saw another one, bigger, out farther and to the left. They watched. Another, small, in much closer, the brief white base instantly flashing through shades of deeper reds and disappearing.

"Spacesuits," gasped Fowler. "Get into the spacesuits."

And he turned and jumped to the rack, McIntosh alongside him. They slipped into the cumbersome suits with the swift smoothness of long practice. They twisted the helmets on.

"Radio O.K.?" said McIntosh.

"Check. Let's look."

And the two jumped back to the window. The activity outside seemed to have stopped. They watched for six full minutes before they saw another of the dust fountains. After they saw it, they twisted their suits to look at each other. They were bringing themselves under control. They were rationally trying to reason out a cause for what they saw.

"Any ideas?" said McIntosh.

"No," said Fowler. "Let's look out the other windows and see if we see anything."

They took up separate places at the two remaining windows.

"Nothing. Just that hideous-looking terrain. I guess it's all on the other—Wait. There's one. Way out, I could just—"

"I've got one, too," said Fowler. "It's all around us. Let's call Earth."

They moved over to the radio. Fowler turned the volume high and McIntosh hit the On switch. Almost immediately they heard a voice, mounting swiftly in loudness. "Station Number One to Moon Station. Station Number One to Moon Station." Over and over it repeated the words.

McIntosh touched a microphone to his helmet, flipped the Transmit switch and said, "Moon Station to Station Number One. We hear you. Over."

"Thank God," came the voice. "Listen. The Leonid meteor swarm may hit you. Find cover. Find a cave or bridge and get out of the open. Repeat. Meteor swarm may hit you. Find cover. Over."

At the word "meteor" McIntosh swung to face Fowler. The two moved closer together to see into the faceplates. Each face broke into a smile of relief at the knowledge of what was happening.

McIntosh touched the microphone to his helmet and said, "We're already in it. There is no cave or other shelter within forty miles. How long do you expect the shower—"

There was a thunderous explosion and a brilliant flash of light that seared the eyeballs of both men. Something heavy dropped on them and gently clung to the spacesuits. They struggled futilely against the softness that enfolded them. McIntosh dropped the microphone and flailed his arms. Fowler sought to lift off the cloying substance; he dropped to one knee and fought it, but it would not give. Both men fought blind; the caressing enfolding material brought complete blackness.

McIntosh felt something grip his ankle and he lashed out with his foot. He felt it crash against something hard, but something that rolled with his kick and then bore back against his legs and knocked him over. His arms were still entangled in the material but he tried to flail the thing that crawled on top of him. With a superhuman effort he encircled the upper portion of the thing with layers of the soft material and began to squeeze. Through the thickness of the material he left the familiar outline of a helmet with a short flexible antenna reaching up from the back. And he realized he was fighting Fowler.

He felt Fowler pull away the material that separated them. Then he heard Fowler's voice.

"Mac, it's me. The dome's punctured and fallen in on us. You hear me?"

"Yes," said McIntosh, gasping for air. "I didn't know what happened. You all right?"

"Yes. Let's get out of here. Shoulder to shoulder 'til we find the lock. Let's go."

They crawled side by side, lifting the heavy leaded plastic in front of them. They bumped into the drafting table and oriented themselves. They passed out through the useless lock and stood up outside and looked at the dome.

It is a terrible thing when a man's home is destroyed. The agony of standing and looking at the ruins of all a man holds near and dear is a heavy burden on the human heart. But on Earth a man can go elsewhere; he has relatives, friends, to turn to. His heart may be heavy, but his life is not in peril.

But Fowler and McIntosh were on the Moon. They looked at their collapsed dome and doom itself froze around their hearts. There was no one to turn to, no place to go. They stood alone on a frozen, shadow-ridden, human-eating world. They stood hand in hand with death.

They looked at the collapsed dome and the way it lay over the equipment they knew so well, softening the sharp angles,

filling in the hollow spaces in the interior. The equipment outside looked stark and awkward, standing high, silhouetted
against the luminous grayness, looking forlorn. The antenna
caught McIntosh's eye.

He swallowed heavily and said, "Let's radio Earth and give
them the news. We were talking to them when we got hit."

Fowler dumbly followed him to a small box on the far side
of the sled and watched him remove the mike and receiver from
a small box. McIntosh faced out from the sled and held the
receiver against one side of the helmet and the mike against the
other. Fowler slipped behind him. They stood back to back,
helmets touching. McIntosh doing the talking. Fowler operating
the switches and listening to all that was said. The receiver was
silent when Fowler turned it on. Earth was listening, waiting.
He switched to Transmit and nudged McIntosh.

"Moon Station to Space Station Number One. Over."

In five seconds a voice came back. "Pole Station to Moon
Station. Space Station Number One is out of line-of sight. What
happened? You all right?"

"Yes. Meteor punctured dome. We're outside. Over."

It was considerably more than five seconds before the voice
came back, quieter but more intense. "Can you fix it?"

"We don't know. We'll go over the damage and talk to you
soon. Out."

McIntosh dropped his hands and Fowler turned the switch
off. "Well," said McIntosh, "we'd better see how bad it is. They
may want to call the whole thing off."

Fowler nodded. Getting the sled and dome and equipment to
the Moon had called for prodigious effort and staggering cost.
It could not be duplicated in a hurry. Their replacements were
already on the way. The dome had to be operating if they were
to stay. And the spaceship could only carry two men back.

"Let's look it over," said Fowler. As they turned to climb up
on the sled a fountain of dust sprang up ten feet to their right.
They looked out over the sullen moonscape; the meteors were
still falling. But they didn't care. They climbed up on the sled
and carefully picked their way on top of the collapsed material
to where they had been standing when the meteor struck. They

pulled out several folds and found the hole. They inspected it with growing excitement.

The hole was a foot in diameter, neatly round. Around the perimeter was a thick ridge charred slightly on the inner edge where the thermoplastic material had fused and rolled back. The ridge had strengthened the material and prevented it from splitting and tearing when the air in the dome rushed out. The hole in the inner layer measured about eighteen inches in diameter and the encircling ridge was even thicker.

Fowler held the hand-powered flashlight on the material surrounding the holes while he examined it carefully. "Mac," he said, "we can fix it. We've got enough scrap dome plastic to seal these holes. Let's see if the meteor went out the bottom."

They moved the holes around on the floor of the dome and found a four-inch hole through the plastic floor. Looking down it, they could see a small crater in the Moon's surface half-filled with a white solid.

McIntosh said, "It went through one of the batteries, but we won't miss it. We've got some scrap flooring plastic and some insulation around. We can fix this, too. Our make-up air is in good supply. Don," he stood up, "we're gonna make it."

"Yes," said Fowler, letting the light go out. "Let's radio Earth."

They went back to the set and Fowler reported their findings. They could hear the joy come back in the man's voice as he wished them luck and told them an extra rocket with make-up air would be on the way soon. Then the voice asked, "What about the meteor shower?"

Fowler and McIntosh looked around; they had forgotten the meteors again. The spurts of moondust still sprang up; they could see them clearly against the gray and black shadows.

"They're still falling," said Fowler. "Nothing to do but sweat them out. Call you later. Out." And he and McIntosh sat down. A nation sweat it out with them. An entire people felt fear strike at their hearts at the thought of two men sitting beside a collapsed dome amidst a shower of invisible cosmic motes traveling at unthinkable speeds. But though the entire nation felt the horror of their position and wished them well with all its heart, it was not of the slightest aid to the two men on the Moon.

Quiet they sat and dumb. The meteors, forgotten for a moment, were to them now a part of the foreboding moonscape, challenging the presence of men in such a place. A mere light touch from a cosmic pebble, and a human life would snuff out. They sat quiet and dumb looking at the moonscape grim as death. A touch on the hand, the foot, is enough; it would take so little. They were something apart from the human race, men, yet not men. For no man could be so alone as they, such a speck, a trifle; a nothing, so alone were they. Quiet they sat and dumb. But each man's heart beat thick and quick—like a madman on a drum. And the meteors fell.

"Mac."

"Yes."

"Why do we sit here? Why don't we fix it?"

"Suppose it gets hit again?"

"Suppose it does. It'll be hit whether it's collapsed or full. At least we'll have these holes patched. Maybe it'll be easier for the next team. Let's patch the holes anyway and then see what's happening."

McIntosh stood up. "Of course," he said. "We can get that much done no matter what happens."

Fowler stood up and began to turn to the sled to climb up. A tiny spot of brightness suddenly appeared on McIntosh's left shoulder. With a feeling of blackness closing in on his body, Fowler flung himself at McIntosh and clamped a hand over the spot where the glow had been. The weight of his body knocked McIntosh down but Fowler clung to him, kept his hand pressed firmly against the spot where the meteor had hit.

"Mac," said Fowler with the taste of copper in his mouth. "Mac. Can you hear me?"

"I hear you fine. What's the matter with you? You like to scared me to death."

"You got hit. On the left shoulder. Your suit must be punctured. I've got my hand over it."

"Don, I didn't even feel it. There can't possibly be a hole there or I'd have felt the air go, or at least some of it. Take a look."

They got to their feet. Fowler kept his hand in place while he retrieved the flashlight. He got it going and quickly removed his hand and showed the light over the spot to look. At first he saw nothing, so he held his helmet closer. Then he saw it. A tiny crater so small as to amount to nothing beyond a slight disturbance of the shiny surface of the suit. Smaller than the head of a pin it was and not as deep as it was broad.

He let the light go out and said in a choked voice, "Must have been a small one, smaller than a grain of sand. No damage at all."

"Good. Let's go to work."

They cut out two four-foot squares of dome material and several chunks of flooring plastic. They filled the bottom of the hole in the floor with five inches of insulation. They plugged in a wedge-shaped soldering iron and melted the plastic and worked it in to the top three inches of flooring, making an undercut to seal the hole solidly. And the floor was fixed.

Fowler pulled over the squares of dome material while McIntosh adjusted the temperature of the iron to that just below the melting point of the material. Fowler placed the first square inside the hole in the inner layer. He ran the hot blade around the ridge of fused plastic. It sealed well; the thick, leaded, shiny, dome material stiffly flowed together and solidified. Fowler sealed the patches in place with a series of five fused circles concentric to the hole and spaced about three inches apart. The inner hole was hard to work with, for he had to reach through the outer hole, but he managed it. The outer hole went fast. And when they finished they were certain that the dome was as good as ever.

They stood up from their work and looked around. Out onto the moonscape they looked long and carefully. And nowhere could they see one of the dread dust fountains. Slowly and carefully they walked to the edge of the sled and dropped off. They sat down and looked some more, carefully preventing their imaginations from picturing things more fantastic than what was already there. After ten minutes there was no doubt about it, the meteor shower was over.

"Let's blow her up," said Fowler.

McIntosh checked the heated outlet from the air cylinder and then passed current through the coils that heated the cylinder itself. At his O.K., Fowler cracked the valve and air began to flow into the dome. They watched it carefully as it rose, looking for the tell-tale white streams that told of a leak. There were none detectable in either layer. And in half an hour the dome stood full and taut with a good five pounds pressure inside. They went in through the lock together.

McIntosh started the light tube while Fowler began a check of the gauges. In ten minutes it was apparent that things were in order. The dome was warming up too, so they took off their helmets, keeping a wary eye on the gauges. Soon they took off their suits.

The radio was still on, so Fowler called in to Earth that everything was in order. The voice was warm and friendly, congratulating them on their work and passing on the reassurances of men everywhere. They learned that their replacements were on schedule, so far. Fowler signed off.

The two men looked up at the patch on the ceiling, with its corners dangling downward. They looked at each other and Fowler started to make tea. McIntosh walked to a window and as he got there his feet started to slip out from under him. He caught himself and bent to see what he had slipped on. He found a thin sheet of ice on the floor.

"Where'd this come from?" he asked.

Fowler looked over and smiled and said, "That's from the cup of tea you dropped when you saw the first meteor. Remember?"

"Oooh, yes." And McIntosh chipped it up and put it in the waste pot to be purified and used on the pottet.

They had their tea, and they slept long and restlessly. They picked up their work schedule, and very soon they could see the brightness on the mountain tops to the west. The sun was coming back.

But it brought no *joy*. They were beyond any emotional response to night or day. Bright gray or dark gray, it did not matter. It was the Moon they were on and the lightness and darkness were all the same.

On the second Earth-day of sunlight they spoke to the approaching spaceship and made preparations to leave. The laundry was all done and ready for use. The dome was tidy. Their last job was to brew tea and put it in the thermos to keep it hot for their replacements; they would need it.

They donned their spacesuits for the last time on the Moon and went out the lock together. They watched the little flame in the black sky grow larger.

The ship landed and the dust settled immediately. Fowler and McIntosh walked slowly toward the ship; they did not hurry. The door in the side opened, a ladder dropped out, and two suited figures climbed awkwardly to the Moon's surface.

Before they had a chance to look around, McIntosh called, "Over here. The dome is over here."

The four men came together and shook hands. Fowler said, "You can see the dome there." He pointed to it a half mile away. "We've left some hot tea for you there. The terrain is pretty rough so watch yourself moving around for a few days. Good luck." They shook hands. The replacements headed for the dome while Fowler and McIntosh went to the ship and climbed in without looking back. They dogged home the lock, removed their suits, stretched out on the accelerator bunks, and called "O.K." into the intercom.

"Right," said the pilot from his compartment. "Welcome aboard and stand by."

In a moment they felt the acceleration steadily mounting. But it soon eased off, and they slept. For most of the five-day journey they slept. And if they had thought to look at each other during their few waking hours, they would have seen nothing unusual—a few incipient, almost invisible lines around the eyes, nothing more. Neither Fowler nor McIntosh had the far look.

The ship reached the space station and tied to it. Fowler and McIntosh transferred to the shuttle and swiftly dropped toward Earth. They heard the air whistle as the air thickened.

The television cameras first picked up the ship as a small dot. People the world over craned forward to watch as the belly-skids touched the sand—people who did not know that the ship carried two Moon men who did not have the far look. The people watched the ship skid to a halt amidst a slowly settling cloud of dust.

And as they watched, the door amidships swung in. The sun slanted in through the door and showed two figures standing there. The figures moved to a point just inside the door and stopped. They stood there motionless, looking out for what seemed an interminable period.

As Fowler and McIntosh looked out the door, they saw the shimmering sands of the New Mexican desert. But they saw more than that. They saw more than home. They saw the spawning place of the human race. In a roaring rush of recognition, they knew they had done more than simply return to Earth. They had rejoined the human race. They had been apart and were now one again with that brawling, pesky, restless race in which all were brothers, all were one. This was not a return to Earth. This was a return to the womb, to the womb that had nourished them and made them men. A flood of sympathy and heart-felt understanding poured through them as they stared out at the shimmering sands. The kinks and twists of personality fell away and left men of untrammeled mind.

Fowler and McIntosh looked at each other, nodded, and jumped out the door. They fell to their knees in the unaccustomed gravity. They quickly arose, knocked the dust from their clothes, and started walking to where the helicopters were waiting.

The zoom lenses on the television cameras went to work and the faces of Fowler and McIntosh side by side flashed across the country.

And the eyes were different. A network of deep tiny creases laced out from both corners of each eye. The crinkled appearance of the eyes made each man appear older than he actually was. And there was a look in those eyes of things seen from deep inside. It was a far look, a compelling look, a powerful look set in the eyes of normal men.

For a Journal Entry . . .

"The Far Look" has far fewer words in its vocabulary list than "Call Me Joe." Reread both stories carefully and come to some conclusion about the lessened need for an extensive vocabulary in "The Far Look." Both stories deal with psychological development as well as with scientific exploration of a hellish environment. How do they differ (other than in the obvious points of setting, vocabulary, and so on)? How do they resemble each other?

For Your Consideration . . .

1. Why do Earthmen want to establish a permanent scientific base on the moon?
2. This story was first published in 1956, many years prior to America's first actual expedition to the moon. How well did Thomas anticipate the actuality? Where does his projection differ from what really happened?
3. Do the reasons Thomas suggests for the appearance of the far look convince you that the internal change that the look represents has actually taken place? In other words, does Thomas make it seem that the far look is real? How so?
4. The last five paragraphs of the story are crucial to its understanding. Although hints of its development are given when the men are still on the moon, why doesn't the genuine look appear until the men are back on earth?
5. From the evidence given in the story, what do you think will be the future of the "supermen" who possess the far look?
6. From newspaper accounts or any other source of information, can you discover if any of America's astronauts have undergone a profound change in their life styles after returning to Earth?

Notes

PAGE

77   *wizened*—wrinkled
80   *Homo superior*—a man presumably superior to *Homo sapiens*
83   *igneous*—a kind of rock found on the moon
83   *plagioclose*—a kind of rock found on the moon

84   *Mare Imbrium*—a lunar crater
86   *hi-vac*—high vacuum, a training facility on earth imitating lunar conditions
86   *pottet*—a machine containing chemicals used for making oxygen, as well as the oxygen-making substance itself
94   *scintillation counter*—a meter used to measure radioactivity

East Wind, West Wind

Frank M. Robinson

We know that smog is not good for us—that it even kills us if we are too weak. Yet mankind seems incapable of doing anything about this kind of pollution. But we *must* do something, because if we do not we will end up with the kind of world in this story. Frank M. Robinson, who fled the smog of Chicago for the clean air of northern California, is the co-author of the book *The Towering Inferno,* upon which the film was based.

I_T wasn't going to be just another bad day, it was going to be a terrible one. The inversion layer had slipped over the city four days before and it had been like putting a lid on a kettle; the air was building up to a real Donora, turning into a chemical soup so foul I wouldn't have believed it if I hadn't been trying to breathe the stuff. Besides sticking in my throat, it made my eyes feel like they were being bathed in acid. You could hardly see the sun—it was a pale, sickly disc floating in a mustard-colored sky—but even so, the streets were an oven and the humidity was so high you could have wrung the water out of the air with your bare hands . . . dirty water, naturally.

On the bus a red-faced salesman with denture breath recognized my Air Central badge and got pushy. I growled that we didn't *make* the air—not yet, at any rate—and finally I took off the badge and put it in my pocket and tried to shut out the coughing and the complaints around me by concentrating on the faint, cheery sound of the "corn poppers" laundering the bus's exhaust. Five would have gotten you ten, of course, that their effect was strictly psychological, that they had seen more than twenty thousand miles of service and were now absolutely worthless. . . .

At work I hung up my plastic sportscoat, slipped off the white surgeon's mask (black where my nose and mouth had been) and filled my lungs with good machine-pure air that smelled only faintly of oil and electric motors; one of the advantages of working for Air Central was that our office air was the best in the city. I dropped a quarter in the coffee vendor, dialed it black, and inhaled the fumes for a second while I shook the sleep from my eyes and speculated about what Wanda would have for me at the Investigator's Desk. There were thirty-nine other Investigators besides myself but I was junior and my daily assignment card was usually just a listing of minor complaints and violations that had to be checked out.

Wanda was young and pretty and redhaired and easy to spot even in a secretarial pool full of pretty girls. I offered her some of my coffee and looked over her shoulder while she flipped through the assignment cards. "That stuff out there is easier to swim through than to breathe," I said, "What's the index?"

"Eighty-four point five," she said quietly. "And rising."

I just stared at her. I had thought it was bad, but hardly that bad, and for the first time that day I felt a sudden flash of panic. "And no alert? When it hits seventy-five this city's supposed to close up like a clam!"

She nodded down the hall to the Director's office. "Lawyers from Sanitary Pick-Up, Oberhausen Steel, and City Light and Power got an injunction—they were here to break the news to Monte at eight sharp. Impractical, unnecessary, money-wasting, and fifteen thousand employees would be thrown out of work if they had to shut down the furnaces and incinerators. They got an okay right from the top of Air Shed Number Three."

My jaw dropped. "How could they? Monte's supposed to have the last word!"

"So go argue with the politicians—if you can stand the hot

air." She suddenly looked very fragile and I wanted to run out and slay a dragon or two for her. "The chicken-hearts took the easy way out, Jim. Independent Weather's predicting a cold front for early this evening and rising winds and rain for tomorrow."

The rain would clean up the air, I thought. But Independent Weather could be bought and as a result it had a habit of turning in cheery predictions that frequently didn't come true. Air Central had tried for years to get IW outlawed but money talks and their lobbyist in the capital was quite a talker. Unfortunately, if they were wrong this time, it would be as if they had pulled a plastic bag over the city's head.

I started to say something, then shut up. If you let it get to you, you wouldn't last long on the job. "Where's my list of smallfry?"

She gave me an assignment card. It was blank except for *See Me* written across its face. "Humor him, Jim, he's not feeling well."

This worried me a little because Monte was the father of us all—a really sweet old guy, which hardly covers it all because he could be hard as nails when he had to. There wasn't anyone who knew more about air control than he.

I took the card and started up the hall and then Wanda called after me. She had stretched out her long legs and hiked up her skirt. I looked startled and she grinned. "Something new—sulfur-proof nylons." Which meant they wouldn't dissolve on a day like today when a measurable fraction of the air we were trying to breathe was actually dilute sulfuric acid. . . .

When I walked into his office, old Monte was leaning out the window, the fly ash clinging to his bushy gray eyebrows like cinnamon to toast, trying to taste the air and predict how it would go today. We had eighty Sniffers scattered throughout the city, all computerized and delivering their data in neat, graphlike form, but Monte still insisted on breaking internal air security and seeing for himself how his city was doing.

I closed the door. Monte pulled back inside, then suddenly broke into one of his coughing fits.

"Sit down, Jim," he wheezed, his voice sounding as if it were being wrung out of him, "be with you in a minute." I pretended not to notice while his coughing shuddered to a halt and he rummaged through the desk for his little bottle of pills. It was a plain office, as executive offices went, except for Monte's own paintings on the wall—the type I liked to call Twentieth Century Romantic. A mountain scene with a crystal clear lake in the foreground and anglers battling huge trout, a city scene with palm trees lining the boulevards, and finally, one of a man standing by an old automobile on a winding mountain road while he looked off at a valley in the distance.

Occasionally Monte would talk to me about his boyhood around the Great Lakes and how he actually used to go swimming in them. Once he tried to tell me that orange trees used to grow within the city limits of Santalosdiego and that the oranges were as big as tennis balls. It irritated me and I think he knew it; I was the youngest Investigator for Air Central but that didn't necessarily make me naive.

When Monte stopped coughing I said hopefully, "IW claims a cold front is coming in."

He huddled in his chair and dabbed at his mouth with a handkerchief, his thin chest working desperately trying to pump his lungs full of air. "IW's a liar," he finally rasped. "There's no cold front coming in, it's going to be a scorcher for three more days."

I felt uneasy again. "Wanda told me what happened," I said.

He fought a moment longer for his breath, caught it, then gave a resigned shrug. "The bastards are right, to an extent. Stop garbage pick-ups in a city this size and within hours the rats will be fighting us in the streets. Shut down the power plants and you knock out all the air conditioners and purifiers—right during the hottest spell of the year. Then try telling the yokels that the air on the outside will be a whole lot cleaner if only they let the air on the inside get a whole lot dirtier."

He hunched behind his desk and drummed his fingers on the

top while his face slowly turned to concrete. "But if they don't let me announce an alert by tomorrow morning," he said quietly, "I'll call in the newspapers and. . . ." The coughing started again and he stood up, a gnomelike little man slightly less alive with every passing day. He leaned against the windowsill while he fought the spasm. "And we think this is bad," he choked, half to himself. "What happens when the air coming in is as dirty as the air already here? When the Chinese and the Indonesians and the Hottentots get toasters and ice-boxes and all the other goodies?"

"Asia's not that industrialized yet," I said uncomfortably.

"Isn't it?" He turned and sagged back into his chair, hardly making a dent in the cushion. I was bleeding for the old man but I couldn't let him know it. I said in a low voice, "You wanted to see me," and handed him the assignment card.

He stared at it for a moment, his mind still on the Chinese, then came out of it and croaked, "That's right, give you something to chew on." He pressed a button on his desk and the wall opposite faded into a map of the city and the surrounding area, from the ocean on the west to the low-lying mountains on the east. He waved at the section of the city that straggled off into the canyons of the foothills. "Internal combustion engine—someplace back there." His voice was stronger now, his eyes more alert. "It isn't a donkey engine for a still or for electricity, it's a private automobile."

I could feel the hairs stiffen on the back of my neck. Usually I drew minor offenses, like trash burning or secret cigarette smoking, but owning or operating a gasoline-powered automobile was a felony, one that was sometimes worth your life.

"The Sniffer in the area confirms it," Monte continued in a tired voice, "but can't pinpoint it."

"Any other leads?"

"No, just this one report. But—we haven't had an internal combustion engine in more than three years." He paused. "Have fun with it, you'll probably have a new boss in the morning." *That* was something I didn't even want to think about. I had my hand on the doorknob when he said quietly, "The trouble with being boss is that you have to play Caesar and his Legions all the time."

It was as close as he came to saying good-bye and good luck. I didn't know what to say in return, or how to say it, and found myself staring at one of his canvases and babbling, "You sure used a helluva lot of blue."

"It was a fairly common color back then," he growled. "The sky was full of it."

And then he started coughing again and I closed the door in a hurry; in five minutes I had gotten so I couldn't stand the sound.

I had to stop in at the lab to pick up some gear from my locker and ran into Dave Ice, the researcher in charge of the Sniffers. He was a chubby, middle-aged little man with small, almost feminine hands; it was a pleasure to watch him work around delicate machinery. He was our top-rated man, after Monte, and I think if there was anybody whose shoes I wanted to step into someday, it would have been Dave Ice. He knew it, liked me for it, and usually went out of his way to help.

When I walked in he was changing a sheet of paper in one of the smoke shade detectors that hung just outside the lab windows. The sheet he was taking out looked as if it had been coated with lampblack.

"How long an exposure?"

He looked up, squinting over his bifocals. "Hi, Jim—a little more than four hours. It looks like it's getting pretty fierce out there."

"You haven't been out?"

"No, Monte and I stayed here all night. We were going to call an alert at nine this morning but I guess you know what happened."

I opened my locker and took out half a dozen new masks and a small canister of oxygen; if you were going to be out in traffic for any great length of time, you had to go prepared. Allowable vehicles were buses, trucks, delivery vans, police electrics and the like. Not all exhaust control devices worked very well and even the electrics gave off a few acid fumes. And if you were stalled in a tunnel, the carbon monoxide ratings really zoomed. I hesitated at the bottom of the locker and then took out my small Mark II gyrojet and shoulder holster. It was pretty deadly stuff: no recoil and the tiny rocket pellet had twice the punch of a .45.

Dave heard the clink of metal and without looking up asked quietly, "Trouble?"

"Maybe," I said. "Somebody's got a private automobile—gasoline—and I don't suppose they'll want to turn it in."

"You're right," he said, sounding concerned, "they won't." And then: "I heard something about it; if it's the same report, it's three days old."

"Monte's got his mind on other things," I said. I slipped the masks into my pocket and belted on the holster. "Did you know he's still on his marching Chinese kick?"

Dave was concentrating on one of the Sniffer drums slowly rolling beneath its scribing pens, logging a minute-by-minute record of the hydrocarbons and the oxides of nitrogen and sulfur that were sickening the atmosphere. "I don't blame him," he said, absently running a hand over his glistening scalp. "They've started tagging chimney exhausts in Shanghai, Djakarta and Mukden with radioactives—we should get the first results in another day or so."

The dragon's breath, I thought. When it finally circled the globe it would mean earth's air sink had lost the ability to cleanse itself and all of us would start strangling a little faster.

I got the rest of my gear and just before I hit the door, Dave said: "Jim?" I turned. He was wiping his hands on a paper towel and frowning at me over his glasses. "Look, take care of yourself, huh, kid?"

"Sure thing," I said. If Monte was my professional father, then Dave was my uncle. Sometimes it was embarrassing but right then it felt good. I nodded good-bye, adjusted my mask, and left.

Outside it seemed like dusk; trucks and buses had turned on their lights and almost all pedestrians were wearing masks. In a lot across the street some kids were playing tag and the thought suddenly struck me that nowadays most kids seemed small for their age; but I envied them . . . the air never seemed to bother kids. I watched for a moment, then started up the walk. A few doors down I passed an apartment building, half hidden in the growing darkness, that had received a "political influence" exemption a month before. Its incinerator was going full blast now, only instead of floating upward over the city the small charred bits of paper and garbage were falling straight down the building like a kind of oily black snow.

I suddenly felt I was suffocating and stepped out into the street and hailed a passing electricab. Forest Hills, the part of the city that Monte had pointed out, was wealthy and the homes were large, though not so large that some of them couldn't be hidden away in the canyons and gullies of the foothills. If you lived on a side road or at the end of one of the canyons it might even be possible to hide a car out there and drive it only at night. And if any of your neighbors found out . . . well, the people who lived up in the relatively pure air of the highlands had a different view of things than those who lived down in the atmospheric sewage of the flats. *But where would a man get a gasoline automobile in the first place?*

And did it all really matter? I thought, looking out the window of the cab at the deepening dusk and feeling depressed. Then I shook my head and leaned forward to give the driver instructions. Some places could be checked out relatively easily.

The Carriage Museum was elegant—and crowded, considering that it was a weekday. The main hall was a vast cave of black marble housing a parade of ancient internal combustion vehicles shining under the subdued lights; most of them were painted a lustrous black though there was an occasional gray and burst of red and a few sparkles of old gold from polished brass head lamps and fittings.

I felt like I was in St. Peter's, walking on a vast sea of marble while all about me the crowds shuffled along in respectful silence. I kept my eyes to the floor, reading off the names on the small bronze plaques: *Rolls Royce Silver Ghost, Mercer Race-about, Isotta-Fraschini, Packard Runabout, Hispano-Suiza, Model J Duesenberg, Flying Cloud Reo, Cadillac Imperial V16, Pierce Arrow,* the first of the *Ford V8s, Lincoln Zephyr, Chrysler Windsor Club Coup.* . . . And in small halls off to the side, the lesser breeds: *Hudson Terraplane, Henry J., Willys Knight,* something called a *Jeepster, the Mustang, Knudsen,* the 1986 *Volkswagen,* the last *Chevrolet.* . . .

The other visitors to the museum were all middle-aged or older; the look on their faces was something I had never seen before—something that was not quite love and not quite lust. It flowed across their features like ripples of water whenever they brushed a fender or stopped at a hood that had been opened so they could stare at the engine, all neatly chromed or painted. They were like my father, I thought. They had owned cars when they were young, before Turn-In Day and the same date a year later when even most private steam and electrics were banned because of congestion. For a moment I wondered what it had been like to own one, then canceled the thought. The old man had tried to tell me often enough, before I had stormed out of the house for good, shouting how could he love the damned things so much when he was coughing his lungs out. . . .

The main hall was nothing but bad memories. I left it and looked up the office of the curator. His secretary was on a coffee break so I rapped sharply and entered without waiting for an answer. On the door it had said "C. Pearson," who turned out to be a thin, overdressed type, all regal nose and pencil moustache, in his mid-forties. "Air Central," I said politely, flashing my wallet ID at him.

He wasn't impressed. "May I?" I gave it to him and he reached for the phone. When he hung up he didn't bother apologizing for the double check, which I figured made us even. "I have nothing to do with the heating system or the air-conditioning," he said easily, "but if you'll wait a minute I'll—"

"I only want information," I said.

He made a small tent of his hands and stared at me over his fingertips. He looked bored. "Oh?"

I sat down and he leaned toward me briefly, then thought better of it and settled back in his chair. "How easy would it be," I asked casually, "to steal one of your displays?"

His moustache quivered slightly. "It wouldn't be easy at all —they're bolted down, there's no gasoline in their tanks, and the batteries are dummies."

"Then none ever have been?"

A flicker of annoyance. "No, of course not."

I flashed my best hat-in-hand smile and stood up. "Well, I guess that's it, then, I won't trouble you any further." But before I turned away I said, "I'm really not much on automobiles but I'm curious. How did the museum get started?"

He warmed up a little. "On Turn-In Day a number of museums like this one were started up all over the country. Some by former dealers, some just by automobile lovers. A number of models were donated for public display and. . . ."

When he had finished I said casually, "Donating a vehicle to a museum must have been a great ploy for hiding private ownership."

"Certainly the people in your bureau would be aware of how strict the government was," he said sharply.

"A lot of people must have tried to hide their vehicles," I persisted.

Dryly. "It would have been difficult . . . like trying to hide an elephant in a playpen."

But still, a number would have tried, I thought. They might even have stockpiled drums of fuel and some spare parts. In the city, of course, it would have been next to impossible. But in remote sections of the country, in the mountain regions out west or in the hills of the Ozarks or in the forests of northern Michigan or Minnesota or in the badlands of the Dakotas. . . . A few would have succeeded, certainly, and perhaps late at night a few weedgrown stretches of highway would have been briefly lit by the headlights of automobiles flashing past with muffled exhausts, tires singing against the pavement. . . .

I sat back down. "Are there many automobile fans around?"

"I suppose so, if attendance records here are any indication."

"Then a smart man with a place in the country and a few

automobiles could make quite a bit of money renting them out, couldn't he?"

He permitted himself a slight smile. "It would be risky. I really don't think anybody would try it. And from everything I've read, I rather think the passion was for actual ownership— I doubt that rental would satisfy that."

I thought about it for a moment while Pearson fidgeted with a letter opener and then, of course, I had it. "All those people who were fond of automobiles, there used to be clubs of them, right?"

His eyes lidded over and it grew very quiet in his office. But it was too late and he knew it. "I believe so," he said after a long pause, his voice tight, "but. . . ."

"But the government ordered them disbanded," I said coldly. "Air Control regulations thirty-nine and forty, sections three through seven, 'concerning the dissolution of all organizations which in whole or in part, intentionally or unintentionally, oppose clean air.'" I knew the regulations by heart. "But there still are clubs, aren't there? Unregistered clubs? Clubs with secret membership files?" A light sheen of perspiration had started to gather on his forehead. "You would probably make a very good membership secretary, Pearson. You're in the perfect spot for recruiting new members—"

He made a motion behind his desk and I dove over it and pinned his arms behind his back. A small address book had fallen to the floor and I scooped it up. Pearson looked as if he might faint. I ran my hands over his chest and under his arms and then let him go. He leaned against the desk, gasping for air.

"I'll have to take you in," I said.

A little color was returning to his cheeks and he nervously smoothed down his damp black hair. His voice was on the squeaky side. "What for? You have some interesting theories but. . . ."

"My theories will keep for court," I said shortly. "You're under arrest for smoking—section eleven thirty point five of the health and safety code." I grabbed his right hand and spread the fingers so the tell-tale stains showed. "You almost offered me a cigarette when I came in, then caught yourself. I would guess that ordinarily you're pretty relaxed and sociable, you probably smoke a lot—and you're generous with your tobacco. Bottom right hand drawer for the stash, right?" I jerked it open and they were there, all right. "One cigarette's a misdemeanor, a carton's a felony, Pearson. We can accuse you of dealing and make it stick." I smiled grimly. "But we're perfectly willing to trade, of course."

I put in calls to the police and Air Central and sat down to wait for the cops to show. They'd sweat Pearson for all the information he had but I couldn't wait around a couple of hours. The word would spread that Pearson was being held, and Pearson himself would probably start remembering various lawyers and civil rights that he had momentarily forgotten. My only real windfall had been the address book. . . .

I thumbed through it curiously, wondering exactly how I could use it. The names were scattered all over the city, and there were a lot of them. I could weed it down to those in the area where the Sniffer had picked up the automobile, but that would take time and nobody was going to admit that he had a contraband vehicle hidden away anyway. The idea of paying a visit to the club I was certain must exist kept recurring to me and finally I decided to pick a name, twist Pearson's arm for anything he might know about him, then arrange to meet at the club and work out from there.

Later, when I was leaving the museum, I stopped for a moment just inside the door to readjust my mask. While I was doing it the janitor showed up with a roll of weatherstripping and started attaching it to the edge of the doorway where what looked like thin black smoke was seeping in from the outside. I was suddenly afraid to go back out there. . . .

The wind was whistling past my ears and a curve was coming up. I feathered the throttle, downshifted, and the needle on the tach started to drop. The wheel seemed to have a life of its own and twitched slightly to the right. I rode high on the outside of the track, the leafy limbs of trees that lined the asphalt dancing just outside my field of vision. The rear started to come around in a skid and I touched the throttle again and then the wheel twitched back to center and I was away. My eyes were riveted on Number Nine, just in front of me. It was the last lap and if I could catch him there would be nothing between me and the checkered flag. . . .

I felt relaxed and supremely confident, one with the throbbing power of the car. I red-lined it and through my dirt-streaked goggles I could see I was crawling up on the red splash that was Number Nine and next I was breathing the fumes from his twin exhausts. I took him on the final curve and suddenly I was alone in the world of the straightaway with the countryside peeling away on both sides of me, placid cows and ancient barns flowing past and then the rails lined with people. I couldn't hear their shouting above the scream of my car. Then I was flashing under banners stretched across the track and thundering toward the finish. There was the smell of burning rubber and spent oil and my own perspiration, the heat from the sun, the shimmering asphalt, and out of the corner of my eye a blur of grandstands and cars and a flag swooping down. . . .

And then it was over and the house lights had come up and I was hunched over a toy wheel in front of me, gripping it with both hands, the sweat pouring down my face and my stomach burning because I could still smell exhaust fumes and I wanted desperately to put on my face mask. It had been far more real than I had thought it would be—the curved screen gave the illusion of depth and each chair had been set up like a driver's seat. They had even pumped in odors. . . .

The others in the small theatre were stretching and getting ready to leave and I gradually unwound and got to my feet, still feeling shaky. "Lucky you could make it, Jim," a voice graveled in my ear. "You missed Joe Moore and the lecture but the documentary was just great, really great. Next week we've got *Meadowdale '73* which has its moments but you don't feel like you're really there and getting an eyeful of cinders, if you know what I mean."

"Who's Joe Moore?" I mumbled.

"Old time race track manager—full of anecdotes, knew all the great drivers. Hey! You okay?"

I was finding it difficult to come out of it. The noise and the action and the smell, but especially the feeling of actually driving. . . . It was more than just a visceral response. You had to be raised down in the flats where you struggled for your breath every day to get the same feeling of revulsion, the same feeling of having done something dirty. . . .

"Yeah, I'm okay," I said. "I'm feeling fine."

"Where'd you say you were from, anyway?"

"Bosnywash," I lied. He nodded and I took a breath and time out to size him up. Jack Ellis was bigger and heavier than Pearson and not nearly as smooth or as polished—Pearson perspired, my bulky friend sweated. He was in his early fifties, thinning brown hair carefully waved, the beginning of a small paunch well hidden by a lot of expensive tailoring, and a hulking set of shoulders that were much more than just padding. A business bird, I thought. The hairy-chested genial backslapper. . . .

"You seen the clubrooms yet?"

"I just got in," I said. "First time here."

"Hey, great! I'll show you around!" He talked like he was programmed. "A little fuel and a couple of stiff belts first, though—dining room's out of this world. . . ."

And it almost was. We were on the eighty-seventh floor of the new Trans-America building and Ellis had secured a window seat. Above, the sky was almost as bright a blue as Monte had used in his paintings. I couldn't see the street below.

"Have a card," Ellis said, shoving the pasteboard at me. It read *Warshawsky & Warshawsky*, Automotive Antiques, with an address in the Avenues. He waved a hand at the room. "We decorated all of this—pretty classy, huh?"

I had to give him that. The walls were covered with murals of old road races, while from some hidden sound system came a faint, subdued purring—the roaring of cars drifting through the esses of some long-ago race. In the center of the room was a pedestal holding a highly-chromed engine block that slowly revolved under a baby spot. While I was admiring the setting a waitress came up and set down a lazy Susan; it took a minute to recognize it as an old-fashioned wooden steering wheel, fitted with sterling silver hors d'oeuvre dishes between the spokes.

Ellis ran a thick thumb down the menu. "Try a Barney Oldfield," he suggested. "Roast beef and American cheese on pumpernickel."

While I was eating I got the uncomfortable feeling that he was looking me over and that somehow I didn't measure up. "You're pretty young," he said at last. "We don't get many young members—or visitors, for that matter."

"Grandfather was a dealer," I said easily. "Had a Ford agency in Milwaukee—I guess it rubbed off."

He nodded around a mouthful of sandwich and looked mournful for a moment. "It used to be a young man's game, kids worked on engines in their backyards all the time. Just about everybody owned a car. . . ."

"You, too?"

"Oh sure—hell, the old man ran a gas station until Turn-In Day." He was lost in his memories for a moment, then said, "You got a club in Bosnywash?"

"A few, nothing like this," I said cautiously. "And the law's pretty stiff." I nodded at the window. "They get pretty uptight about the air back east . . ." I let my voice trail off.

He frowned. "You don't *believe* all that guff, do you? Biggest goddamn pack of lies there ever was, but I guess you got to be older to know it. Power plants and incinerators, they're the ones to blame, always have been. Hell, people, too—every time you exhale you're polluting the atmosphere, ever think of that? And Christ, man, think of every time you work up a sweat. . . ."

"Sure," I nodded, "Sure, it's always been blown up." I made a mental note that someday I'd throw the book at Ellis.

He finished his sandwich and started wiping his flat face like he was erasing a blackboard. "What's your interest? Mine's family sedans, the old family workhorse. Fords, Chevys, Plymouths—got a case of all the models from '50 on up, one-eighteenth scale. How about you?"

I didn't answer him, just stared out the window and worked with a toothpick for a long time until he began to get a little nervous. Then I let it drop. "I'm out here to buy a car," I said.

His face went blank, as if somebody had just pulled down a shade. "Damned expensive hobby," he said, ignoring it. "Should've taken up photography instead."

"It's for a friend of mine," I said. "Money's no object."

The waitress came around with the check and Ellis initialed it. "Damned expensive," he repeated vaguely.

"I couldn't make a connection back home," I said. "Friends suggested I try out here."

He was watching me now. "How would you get it back east?"

"Break it down," I said. "Ship it east as crates of machine parts."

"What makes you think there's anything for sale out here?"

I shrugged. "Lots of mountains, lots of forests, lots of empty space, lots of hiding places. Cars were big out here, there must have been a number that were never turned in."

"You're a stalking horse for somebody big, aren't you!"

"What do you think?" I said. "And what difference does it make anyway? Money's money."

If it's true that the pupil of the eye expands when it sees something that it likes, it's also true that it contracts when it doesn't—and right then his were in the cold buckshot stage.

"All right," he finally said. "Cash on the barrelhead and remember, when you have that much money changing hands, it can get dangerous." He deliberately leaned across the table so that his coat flapped open slightly. The small gun and holster were almost lost against the big man's girth. He sat back and spun the lazy Susan with a fat forefinger, spearing an olive as it slid past. "You guys run true to form," he continued quietly. "Most guys from back east come out to buy—I guess we've got a reputation." He hesitated. "We also try and take all the danger out of it."

He stood up and slapped me on the back as I pushed to my feet. It was the old Jack Ellis again, he of the instant smile and the sparkling teeth.

"That is, we try and take the danger out of it for *us*," he added pleasantly.

It was late afternoon and the rush hour had started. It wasn't as heavy as usual—businesses had been letting out all day—but it was bad enough. I slipped on a mask and started walking toward the warehouse section of town, just outside the business district. The buses were too crowded and it would be impossible to get an electricab that time of day. Besides, traffic was practically standing still in the steamy murk. Headlights were vague yellow dots in the gathering darkness and occasionally I had to shine my pocket flash on a street sign to determine my location.

I had checked in with Monte who said the hospitals were filling up fast with bronchitis victims; I didn't ask about the city morgue. The venal bastards at Air Shed Number Three were even getting worried; they had promised Monte that if it didn't clear by morning, he could issue his alert and close down the city. I told him I had uncovered what looked like a car ring but he sounded only faintly interested. He had bigger things on his mind; the ball was in my court and what I was going to do with it was strictly up to me.

A few more blocks and the crowds thinned. Then I was alone on the street with the warehouses hulking up in the gloom around me, ancient monsters of discolored brick and concrete layered with years of soot and grime. I found the address I wanted, leaned against the buzzer by the loading dock door, and waited. There was a long pause, then faint steps echoed inside and the door slid open. Ellis stood in the yellow dock light, the smile stretching across his thick face like a rubber band. "Right on time," he whispered. "Come on in, Jim, meet the boys."

I followed him down a short passageway, trying not to brush up against the filthy whitewashed walls. Then we were up against a steel door with a peephole. Ellis knocked three times, the peephole opened, and he said, "Joe sent me." I started to panic. *For God's sake, why the act?* Then the door opened and it was as if somebody had kicked me in the stomach. What lay beyond was a huge garage with at least half a dozen ancient cars on the tool-strewn floor. Three mechanics in coveralls were working under the overhead lights; two more were waiting inside the door. They were bigger than Ellis and I was suddenly very glad I had brought along the Mark II.

"Jeff, Ray, meet Mr. Morrison." I held out my hand. They nodded at me, no smiles. "C'mon," Ellis said, "I'll show you the set-up." I tagged after him and he started pointing out the wonders of his domain. "Completely equipped garage—my old man would've been proud of me. Overhead hoist for pulling motors, complete lathe set-up . . . a lot of parts we have to machine ourselves, can't get the originals anymore and of course the last of the junkers was melted down a long time ago." He stopped by a .workbench with a large rack full of tools gleaming behind it. "One of the great things about being in the antique business—you hit all the country auctions and you'd be surprised at what you can pick up. Complete sets of torque wrenches, metric socket sets, spanner wrenches, feeler gauges, you name it."

I looked over the bench—he was obviously proud of the assortment of tools—then suddenly felt the small of my back grow cold. It was phony, I thought, the whole thing was phony. But I couldn't put my finger on just why.

Ellis walked over to one of the automobiles on the floor and patted a fender affectionately. Then he unbuttoned his coat so that the pistol showed, hooked his thumbs in his vest, leaned against the car behind him and smiled. Someplace he had even found a broomstraw to chew on.

"So what can we do for you, Jim? Limited stock, sky-high prices, but never a dissatisfied customer!" He poked an elbow against the car behind him. "Take a look at this '73 Chevy Biscayne, probably the only one of its kind in this condition in the whole damned country. Ten thou and you can have it—and that's only because I like you." He sauntered over to a monster in blue and silver with grillwork that looked like a set of kitchen knives. "Or maybe you'd like a '76 Caddy convertible, all genuine simulated-leather upholstery, one of the last of the breed." He didn't add why but I already knew—in heavy traffic the high levels of monoxide could be fatal to a driver in an open car.

"Yours," Ellis was saying about another model, "for a flat fifteen"—he paused and shot me a friendly glance—"oh hell, for you, Jim, make it twelve and a half and take it from me, it's a bargain. Comes with the original upholstery and tires and there's less than ten thousand miles on it—the former owner was a little old lady in Pasadena who only drove it to weddings."

He chuckled at that, looking at me expectantly. I didn't get it. "Maybe you'd just like to look around. Be my guest, go right ahead." His eyes were bright and he looked very pleased with himself; it bothered me.

"Yeah," I said absently, "I think that's what I'd like to do." There was a wall phone by an older model and I drifted over to it.

"That's an early Knudsen two-seater," Ellis said. "Popular make for the psychedelic set, that paint job is the way they really came. . . ."

I ran my hand lightly down the windshield, then turned to face the cheerful Ellis. "You're under arrest," I said. "You and everybody else here."

His face suddenly looked like shrimp in molded gelatin. One of the mechanics behind him moved and I had the Mark II out winging a rocket past his shoulder. No noise, no recoil, just a sudden shower of sparks by the barrel and in the far end of the garage a fifty-gallon oil drum went *karrump* and there was a hole in it you could have stuck your head through.

The mechanic went white. "*Jesus Christ, Jack, you brought in some kind of nut!*" Ellis himself was pale and shaking, which surprised me; I thought he'd be tougher than that.

"Against the bench," I said coldly, waving the pistol. "Hands in front of your crotch and don't move them." The mechanics were obviously scared stiff and Ellis was having difficulty keeping control. I took down the phone and called in.

After I hung up, Ellis mumbled, "What's the charge?"

"Charges," I corrected. "Sections three, four and five of the Air Control laws. Maintenance, sale and use of internal combustion engines."

Ellis stared at me blankly. "You don't know?" he asked faintly.
"Know what?"

"I don't handle internal combustion engines." He licked his lips. "I really don't, it's too risky, it's . . . it's against the law."

The workbench, I suddenly thought. The goddamned workbench. I knew something was wrong then, I should have cooled it.

"You can check me," Ellis offered weakly. "Lift a hood, look for yourself."

He talked like his face was made of panes of glass sliding against one another. I waved him forward. "*You* check it, Ellis, you open one up." Ellis nodded like a dipping duck, waddled over to one of the cars, jiggled something inside, then raised the hood and stepped back.

I took one glance and my stomach slowly started to knot up. I was no motor buff but I damned well knew the difference between a gasoline engine and water boiler. Which explained the workbench—the tools had been window dressing. Most of them were brand new because most of them had obviously never been used. There had been nothing to use them on.

"The engines are steam," Ellis said, almost apologetically. "I've got a license to do restoration work and drop in steam engines. They don't allow them in cities but it's different on farms and country estates and in some small towns." He looked at me. "The license cost me a goddamned fortune."

It was a real handicap being a city boy, I thought. "Then why the act? Why the gun?"

"This?" he asked stupidly. He reached inside his coat and dropped the pistol on the floor; it made a light thudding sound and bounced, a pot metal toy. "The danger, it's the sense of danger, it's part of the sales pitch." He wanted to be angry now but he had been frightened too badly and couldn't quite make it. "The customers pay a lot of dough, they want a little drama. That's why—you know—the peephole and everything." He took a deep breath and when he exhaled it came out as a giggle, an incongruous sound from the big man. I found myself hoping he didn't have a heart condition. "I'm well known," he said defensively. "I take ads. . . ."

"The club," I said. "It's illegal."

Even if it was weak, his smile was genuine and then the score became crystal clear. The club was like a speakeasy during the Depression, with half the judges and politicians in town belonging to it. Why not? Somebody older wouldn't have my bias. . . . Pearson's address book had been all last names and initials but I had never connected any of them to anybody prominent; I hadn't been around enough to know what connection to make.

I waved Ellis back to the workbench and stared glumly at the group. The mechanic I had frightened with the Mark II had a spreading stain across the front of his pants and I felt sorry for him momentarily.

Then I started to feel sorry for myself. Monte should have given me a longer briefing, or maybe assigned another Investigator to go with me, but he had been too sick and too wrapped up with the politics of it all. So I had gone off half-cocked and come up with nothing but a potential lawsuit for Air Central that would probably amount to a million dollars by the time Ellis got through with me.

It was a black day inside as well as out.

I holed up in a bar during the middle part of the evening, which was probably the smartest thing I could have done. Despite their masks, people on the street had started to retch and vomit and I could feel my own nausea grow with every step. I saw one man try and strike a match to read a street sign; it wouldn't stay lit, there simply wasn't enough oxygen in the air. The ambulance sirens were a steady wail now and I knew it was going to be a tough night for heart cases. They'd be going like flies before morning, I thought. . . .

Another customer slammed through the door, wheezing and coughing and taking huge gulps of the machine-pure air of the bar. I ordered another drink and tried to shut out the sound; it was too reminiscent of Monte hacking and coughing behind his desk at work.

And come morning, Monte might be out of a job, I thought. I for certain would be; I had loused up in a way that would cost the department money—the unforgivable sin in the eyes of the politicians.

I downed half my drink and started mentally reviewing the events of the day, giving myself a passing score only on figuring out that Pearson had had a stash. I hadn't known about Ellis' operation, which in one sense wasn't surprising. Nobody was going to drive something that looked like an old gasoline-burner around a city—the flatlanders would stone him to death.

But somebody still had a car, I thought. Somebody who was rich and immune from prosecution and a real nut about cars in the first place. . . . But it kept sliding away from me. Really rich men were too much in the public eye, ditto politicians. They'd be washed up politically if anybody ever found out. If nothing else, some poor bastard like the one at the end of the bar trying to flush out his lungs would assassinate him.

Somebody with money, but not too much. Somebody who was a car nut—they'd have to be to take the risks. And somebody for whom those risks were absolutely minimal. . . .

And then the lightbulb flashed on above my head, just like in the old cartoons. I wasn't dead certain I was right but I was willing to stake my life on it—and it was possible I might end up doing just that.

I slipped on a mask and almost ran out of the bar. Once outside, I sympathized with the guy who had just come in and who had given me a horrified look as I plunged out into the darkness.

It was smothering now, though the temperature had dropped a little so my shirt didn't cling to me in dirty, damp folds. Buses were being led through the streets; headlights died out completely within a few feet. The worst thing was that they left tracks in what looked like a damp, grayish ash that covered the street. Most of the people I bumped into—mere shadows in the night—had soaked their masks in water, trying to make them more effective. There were lights still on in the lower floors of most of the office buildings and I figured some people hadn't tried to make it home at all; the air was probably purer among the filing cabinets than in their own apartments. Two floors up, the buildings were completely hidden in the smoky darkness.

It took a good hour of walking before the sidewalks started to slant up and I knew I was getting out toward the foothills . . . I thanked God the business district was closer to the mountains than the ocean. My legs ached and my chest hurt and I was tired and depressed but at least I wasn't coughing anymore.

The buildings started to thin out and the streets finally became completely deserted. Usually the cops would pick you up if they caught you walking on the streets of Forest Hills late at night, but that night I doubted they were even around. They were probably too busy ferrying cases of cardiac arrest to St. Francis. . . .

The Sniffer was located on the top of a small, ancient building off on a side street. When I saw it I suddenly found my breath hard to catch again—a block down, the street abruptly turned into a canyon and wound up and out of sight. I glanced back at the building, just faintly visible through the grayed-down moonlight. The windows were boarded up and there was a For Rent sign on them. I walked over and flashed my light on the sign. It was old and peeling and had obviously been there for years; apparently nobody had ever wanted to rent the first floor. Ever? Maybe somebody had, I thought, but had decided to leave it boarded up. I ran my hand down the boards and suddenly paused at a knothole; I could feel heavy plate glass through it. I knelt and flashed my light at the hole and looked at a dim reflection of myself staring back. The glass had been painted black on the inside so it acted like a black marble mirror.

I stepped back and something about the building struck me. The boarded-up windows, I thought, the huge, oversized windows. . . . And the oversized, boarded-up doors. I flashed the light again at the concrete facing just above the doors. The words were there all right, blackened by time but still readable, cut into the concrete itself by order of the proud owner a handful of decades before. But you could still noodle them out: *RICHARD SIEBEN LINCOLN-MERCURY*.

Jackpot, I thought triumphantly. I glanced around—there was nobody else on the street—and listened. Not a sound, except for the faint murmur of traffic still moving in the city far away. A hot muggy night in the core city, I thought, but this night the parks and the fire escapes would be empty and five million people would be tossing and turning in their cramped little bedrooms; it'd be suicide to try and sleep outdoors.

In Forest Hills it was cooler—and quieter. I glued my ear to the boards over the window and thought I could hear the faint shuffle of somebody walking around and, once the faint clink of metal against metal. I waited a moment, then slipped down to the side door that had "Air Central" on it in neat black lettering. All Investigators had master keys and I went inside. Nobody was upstairs; the lights were out and the only sound was the soft swish of the Sniffer's scribing pens against the paper roll. There was a stairway in the back and I walked silently down it. The door at the bottom was open and I stepped through it into a short hallway. Something, maybe the smell of the air, told me it had been used recently. I closed the door after me and stood for a second in the darkness. There was no sound from the door beyond. I tried the knob and it moved silently in my grasp.

I cracked the door open and peered through the slit—nothing —then eased it open all the way and stepped out onto the showroom floor. There was a green-shaded lightbulb hanging from the ceiling, swaying slightly in some minor breeze so the shadows chased each other around the far corners of the room. Walled off at the end were two small offices where salesmen had probably wheeled and dealed long ago. There wasn't much else, other than a few tools scattered around the floor in the circle of light.

And directly in the center, of course, the car.

I caught my breath. There was no connection between it and Jack Ellis' renovated family sedans. It crouched there on the floor, a mechanical beast that was almost alive. Sleek curving fenders that blended into a louvered hood with a chromed steel bumper curving flat around the front to give it an oddly shark-like appearance. The headlamps were set deep into the fenders, the lamp wells outlined with chrome. The hood flowed into a windshield and that into a top which sloped smoothly down in back and tucked in neatly just after the rear wheels. The wheels themselves had wire spokes that gleamed wickedly in the light, and through a side window I could make out a neat array of meters and rocker switches, and finally bucket seats covered with what I instinctively knew was genuine black leather.

Sleek beast, powerful beast, I thought. I was unaware of

walking up to it and running my hand lightly over a fender until a voice behind me said, "It's beautiful, isn't it?"

I turned like an actor in a slow-motion film. "Yeah, Dave," I said, "it's beautiful." Dave Ice of Air Central. In charge of all the Sniffers.

He must have been standing in one of the salesman's offices; it was the only way I could have missed him. He walked up and stood on the other side of the car and ran his left hand over the hood with the same affectionate motion a woman might use in stroking her cat. In his right hand he held a small Mark II pointed directly at my chest.

"How'd you figure it was me?" he asked casually.

"I thought at first it might be Monte," I said. "Then I figured you were the real nut about machinery."

His eyes were bright, too bright. "Tell me," he asked curiously, "would you have turned in Monte?"

"Of course," I said simply. I didn't add that it would have been damned difficult; that I hadn't even been able to think about that part of it.

"So might've I, so might've I," he murmured. "When I was your age."

"For a while the money angle threw me," I said.

He smiled faintly. "It's a family heirloom. My father bought it when he was young, he couldn't bring himself to turn it in." He cocked his head. "Could you?" I looked at him uneasily and didn't answer and he said casually, "Go ahead, Jimmy, you were telling me how you cracked the case."

I flushed. "It had to be somebody who knew—who was absolutely sure—that he wasn't going to get caught. The Sniffers are pretty efficient, it would have been impossible to prevent their detecting the car—the best thing would be to censor the data from them. And Monte and you were the only ones who could have done that."

Another faint smile. "You're right."

"You slipped up a few nights ago," I said.

He shrugged. "Anybody could've. I was sick, I didn't get to the office in time to doctor the record."

"It gave the game away," I said. "Why only once? The Sniffer should have detected it far more often than just once."

He didn't say anything and for a long moment both of us were lost in admiration of the car.

Then finally, proudly: "It's the real McCoy, Jim. Six cylinder in-line engine, 4.2 liters displacement, nine-to-one compression ratio, twin overhead cams and twin Zenith-Stromberg carbs . . ." He broke off. "You don't know what I'm talking about, do you?"

"No," I confessed, "I'm afraid not."

"Want to see the motor?"

I nodded and he stepped forward, waved me back with the Mark II, and opened the hood. To really appreciate it, of course, you had to have a thing for machinery. It was clean and polished and squatted there under the hood like a beautiful mechanical pet—so huge I wondered how the hood could close at all.

And then I realized with a shock that I hadn't been reacting like I should have, that I hadn't reacted like I should have ever since the movie at the club. . . .

"You can sit in it if you want to," Dave said softly. "Just don't touch anything." His voice was soft. "Everything works on it, Jim, everything works just dandy. It's oiled and greased and the tank is full and the battery is charged and if you wanted to, you could drive it right off the showroom floor."

I hesitated. "People in the neighborhood—"

"—mind their own business," he said. "They have a different attitude, and besides, it's usually late at night and I'm out in the hills in seconds. Go ahead, get in." Then his voice hardened into command: "Get in!"

I stalled a second longer, then opened the door and slid into the seat. The movie was real now, I was holding the wheel and could sense the gearshift at my right and in my mind's eye I could feel the wind and hear the scream of the motor. . . .

There was something hard pressing against the side of my head. I froze. Dave was holding the pistol just behind my ear and in the side mirror I could see his finger tense on the trigger and pull back a millimeter. *Dear God. . . .*

He relaxed. "You'll have to get out," he said apologetically. "It would be appropriate, but a mess just the same."

I got out. My legs were shaking and I had to lean against the car. "It's a risky thing to own a car," I chattered. "Feeling runs pretty high against cars. . . ."

He nodded. "It's too bad."

"You worked for Air Central for years," I said. "How could you do it, and own this, too?"

"You're thinking about the air," he said carefully. "But Jim" —his voice was patient—"machines don't foul the air, men do. They foul the air, the lakes, and the land itself. And there's no way to stop it." I started to protest and he held up a hand. "Oh sure, there's always a time when you care—like you do now. But time . . . you know, time wears you down, it really does, no matter how eager you are. You devote your life to a cause and then you find yourself suddenly growing fat and bald and you discover nobody gives a damn about your cause. They're paying you your cushy salary to buy off their own consciences. So long as there's a buck to be made, things won't change much. It's enough to drive you—" He broke off. "You don't *really* think that anybody gives a damn about anybody else, do you?" He stood there looking faintly amused, a pudgy little man whom I should've been able to take with one arm tied behind my back. But he was ten times as dangerous as Ellis had ever imagined himself to be. "Only suckers care, Jim. I. . . ."

I dropped to the floor then, rolling fast to hit the shadows beyond the circle of light. His Mark II sprayed sparks and something burned past my shirt collar and squealed along the concrete floor. I sprawled flat and jerked my own pistol out. The first shot went low and there was the sharp sound of scored metal and I cursed briefly to myself—I must have brushed the car. Then there was silence and I scrabbled further back into the darkness. I wanted to pot the light but the bulb was still swaying back and forth and chances were I'd miss and waste the shot. Then there was the sound of running and I jumped to my feet and saw Dave heading for the door I had come in by.

He seemed oddly defenseless—he was chubby and slow and knocked-kneed and ran like a woman.

"Dave!" I screamed. "Dave! STOP!"

It was an accident, there was no way to help it. I aimed low and to the side, to knock him off his feet, and at the same time he decided to do what I had done and sprawl flat in the shadows. If he had stayed on his feet, the small rocket would have brushed him at knee level. As it was, it smashed his chest.

He crumpled and I ran up and caught him before he could hit the floor. He twisted slightly in my arms so he was staring at the car as he died. I broke into tears. I couldn't help that, either. I would remember the things Dave had done for me long after I had forgotten that one night he had tried to kill me. A threat to kill is unreal—actual blood and shredded flesh has its own reality.

I let him down gently and walked slowly over to the phone in the corner. Monte should still be in his office, I thought. I dialed and said, "The Director, please," and waited for the voice-actuated relay to connect me. "Monte, Jim Morrison here. I'm over at——" I paused. "I'm sorry, I though it was Monte ——" And then I shut up and let the voice at the other end of the line tell me that Monte had died with the window open and the night air filling his lungs with urban vomit. "I'm sorry," I said faintly, "I'm sorry, I'm very sorry," but the voice went on and I suddenly realized that I was listening to a recording and that there was nobody in the office at all. Then, as the voice continued, I knew why.

I let the receiver fall to the floor and the record started in again, as if expecting condolences from the concrete.

I should call the cops, I thought. I should——

But I didn't. Instead, I called Wanda. It would take an hour or more for her to collect the foodstuffs in the apartment and to catch an electricab but we could be out of the city before morning came.

And that was pretty funny because morning was never coming. The recording had said dryly that the tagged radioactive chimney exhausts had arrived, that the dragon's breath had circled the globe and the winds blowing in were as dirty as the air already over the city. Oh, it wouldn't happen right away, but it wouldn't be very long, either. . . .

Nobody had given a damn, I thought; not here nor any other place. Dave had been right, dead right. They had finally turned it all into a sewer and the last of those who cared had coughed his lungs out trying for a breath of fresh air that had never come, too weak to close a window.

I walked back to the car sitting in the circle of light and ran a finger down the scored fender where the small rocket had scraped the paint. Dave would never have forgiven me, I thought. Then I opened the door and got in and settled slowly back into the seat. I fondled the shift and ran my eyes over the instrument panel, the speedometer and the tach and the fuel and the oil gauges and the small clock. . . . The keys dangled from the button at the end of the hand brake. It was a beautiful piece of machinery. I thought again. I had never really loved a piece of machinery . . . until now.

I ran my hands around the wheel, then located the starter switch on the steering column. I jabbed in the key and closed my eyes and listened to the scream of the motor and felt its power shake the car and wash over me and thunder through the room. The movie at the club had been my only lesson but in its own way it had been thorough and it would be enough. I switched off the motor and waited.

When Wanda got there we would take off for the high ground. For the mountains and the pines and that last clear lake and that final glimpse of blue sky before it all turned brown and we gave up in final surrender to this climate of which we're so obviously proud. . . .

For a Journal Entry . . .

If you knew that the kind of civilization we now have was very probably going to come to an end and you could get away before it happened, would you leave or would you stay to help try to save civilization? What are the arguments for both choices? And for that matter, when is the best time to try to begin saving the world?

For Your Consideration . . .

1. What is the atmospheric condition described as "a real Donora" in the first paragraph of the story? Could it have been prevented?

2. Robinson predicts that atmospheric pollution will get worse and worse. What actions have been taken in the story to prevent the final death of the air? Why weren't they taken soon enough? Why didn't people believe the seriousness of the situation when there was time to prevent the final catastrophe?

3. In conflicts between pollution control and economics, who usually wins? Give examples from the story. Can you think of other examples from the energy crisis of the 1970's?

4. The story begins with a shocking impact. Do you feel that the author is overstating his point? Does he gain or lose your interest by his use of specific detail?

5. It has been said that "East Wind, West Wind," is really about America's 75-year-long love affair with the automobile. Defend or attack this idea.

6. Toward the end of the story Dave says, "Machines don't foul the air, men do." Do you believe this? Why or why not?

7. Is Dave's cynicism convincing? Do you think that "Only suckers care"?

8. Does the vision of the mountains and pines and blue sky in the last paragraph hold any real hope?

Notes

PAGE

111   *injunction*—a court order

116   *gyrojet*—gun

118   *curator*—person in charge of a museum

122   *anecdotes*—short stories, usually of a personal nature

123   *visceral*—physical, bodily

123   *genial*—friendly

126   *venal*—corrupt

127   *lathe*—machine for shaping wood or metal

129   *incongruous*—unbelievable, inconsistent

The Streets of Ashkelon

Harry Harrison

One man's belief can be another man's poison. This is one of the main
reasons why, in the United States, we allow freedom of religion.
Nor do we have a state religion that tells us what we *must* believe.
"The Streets of Ashkelon" is the story of a distant world where
mankind's disparate beliefs have been imported and what happens
to the creatures there who try to understand the differences between them. Harry Harrison, as well as writing this story, co-
edited this anthology. As an editor he is known for his annual
Best SF anthologies and the *Nova* series of original SF stories. His
writing shows a concern for the future of mankind, perhaps best
seen in his novel *Make Room! Make Room!* which was filmed as
Soylent Green.

W. E. McN.

Somewhere above, hidden by the eternal clouds of Wesker's World, a thunder rumbled and grew. Trader John Garth
stopped when he heard it. . . .

"That noise is the same as the noise of your sky-ship," Itin
said, with stolid Wesker logicality, slowly pulverizing the idea in
his mind and turning over the bits one by one for closer examination. "But your ship is still sitting where you landed it. It
must be, even though we cannot see it, because you are the only
one who can operate it. And even if anyone else could operate
it we would have heard it rising into the sky. Since we did not,
and if this sound is a sky-ship sound, then it must mean . . ."

"Yes, another ship," Garth said, too absorbed in his own thoughts to wait for the laborious Weskerian chains of logic to clank their way through to the end. . . .

"You better go ahead, Itin," he said. "Use the water so you can get to the village quickly. Tell everyone to get back into the swamps, well clear of the hard ground. That ship is landing on instruments and anyone underneath at touchdown is going to be cooked."

This immediate threat was clear enough to the little Wesker amphibian. Before Garth finished speaking Itin's ribbed ears had folded like a bat's wing and he slipped silently into the nearby canal. Garth squelched on through the mud, making as good time as he could over the clinging surface. He had just reached the fringes of the village clearing when the rumbling grew to a head-splitting roar and the spacer broke through the low-hanging layer of clouds above. Garth shielded his eyes from the down-reaching tongue of flame and examined the growing form of the grey-black ship with mixed feelings.

After almost a standard year on Wesker's World he had to fight down a longing for human companionship of any kind. While this buried fragment of herd-spirit chattered for the rest of the monkey tribe, his trader's mind was busily drawing a line under a column of figures and adding up the total. This could very well be another trader's ship, and if it were his monopoly of the Wesker trade was at an end. Then again, this might not be a trader at all, which was the reason he stayed in the shelter of the giant fern and loosened his gun in its holster.

The ship baked dry a hundred square metres of mud, the roaring blast died, and the landing feet crunched down through the crackling crust. Metal creaked and settled into place while the cloud of smoke and steam slowly drifted lower in the humid air.

"Garth, where are you?" the ship's speaker boomed. The lines of the spacer had looked only slightly familiar, but there was no mistaking the rasping tones of that voice. Garth wore a smile when he stepped out into the open and whistled shrilly through two fingers. A directional microphone ground out of its casing on the ship's fin and turned in his direction.

"What are you doing here, Singh?" he shouted towards the mike. . . .

"I am on course to a more fairly atmosphered world where a
fortune is waiting to be made. I only stopped here since an opportunity presented to turn an honest credit by running a taxi
service. I bring you friendship, the perfect companionship, a
man in a different line of business who might help you in yours.
I'd come out and say hello myself, except I would have to decon
for biologicals. I'm cycling the passenger through the lock so I
hope you won't mind helping with his luggage."

At least there would be no other trader on the planet now,
that worry was gone. But Garth still wondered what sort of
passenger would be taking one-way passage to an uninhabited
world. And what was behind that concealed hint of merriment
in Singh's voice? He walked around to the far side of the spacer
where the ramp had dropped, and looked up at the man in the
cargo lock who was wrestling ineffectually with a large crate.
The man turned towards him and Garth saw the clerical dog-
collar and knew just what it was Singh had been chuckling
about.

"What are you doing here?" Garth asked; in spite of his attempt at self control he snapped the words. If the man noticed
this he ignored it, because he was still smiling and putting out
his hand as he came down the ramp.

"Father Mark," he said. "Of the Missionary Society of Brothers.
I'm very pleased to . . ."

"I said what are you doing here." Garth's voice was under
control now, quiet and cold. He knew what had to be done,
and it must be done quickly or not at all.

"That should be obvious," Father Mark said, his good nature
still unruffled. "Our missionary society has raised funds to send
spiritual emissaries to alien worlds for the first time. I was lucky
enough . . ."

"Take your luggage and get back into the ship. You're not
wanted here and have no permission to land. You'll be a liability
and there is no one on Wesker to take care of you. Get back
into the ship."

"I don't know who you are, sir, or why you are lying to me,"
the priest said. He was still calm but the smile was gone. "But I
have studied galactic law and the history of this planet very

well. There are no diseases or beasts here that I should have any particular fear of. It is also an open planet, and until the Space Survey changes that status I have as much right to be here as you do."

The man was of course right, but Garth couldn't let him know that. He had been bluffing, hoping the priest didn't know his rights. But he did. There was only one distasteful course left for him, and he had better do it while there was still time.

"Get back in that ship," he shouted, not hiding his anger now. With a smooth motion his gun was out of the holster and the pitted black muzzle only inches from the priest's stomach. The man's face turned white, but he did not move.

"What the hell are you doing, Garth!" Singh's shocked voice grated from the speaker. "The guy paid his fare and you have no rights at all to throw him off the planet."

"I have this right," Garth said, raising his gun and sighting between the priest's eyes. "I give him thirty seconds to get back aboard the ship or I pull the trigger."

"Well I think you are either off your head or playing a joke," Singh's exasperated voice rasped down at them. "If a joke, it is in bad taste, and either way you're not getting away with it. Two can play at that game, only I can play it better."

There was the rumble of heavy bearings and the remote-controlled four-gun turret on the ship's side rotated and pointed at Garth. "Now—down gun and give Father Mark a hand with the luggage," the speaker commanded, a trace of humour back in the voice now. "As much as I would like to help, Old Friend, I cannot. I feel it is time you had a chance to talk to the father; after all, I have had the opportunity of speaking with him all the way from Earth."

Garth jammed the gun back into the holster with an acute feeling of loss. Father Mark stepped forward, the winning smile back now and a bible taken from a pocket of his robe, in his raised hand. "My son," he said.

"I'm not your son," was all Garth could choke out as defeat welled up in him. His fist drew back as the anger rose, and the best he could do was open the fist so he struck only with the flat of his hand. Still the blow sent the priest crashing to the ground and fluttered the pages of the book splattering into the thick mud.

Itin and the other Weskers had watched everything with seemingly emotionless interest, and Garth made no attempt to answer their unspoken questions. He started towards his house, but turned back when he saw they were still unmoving.

"A new man has come," he told them. "He will need help with the things he has brought. If he doesn't have any place for them, you can put them in the big warehouse until he has a place of his own."

He watched them waddle across the clearing towards the ship, then went inside and gained a certain satisfaction from slamming the door hard enough to crack one of the panes. There was an equal amount of painful pleasure in breaking out one of the remaining bottles of Irish whiskey that he had been saving for a special occasion. Well this was special enough, though not really what he had had in mind. The whiskey was good and burned away some of the bad taste in his mouth, but not all of it. If his tactics had worked, success would have justified everything. But he had failed and in addition to the pain of failure there was the acute feeling that he had made a horse's ass out of himself. Singh had blasted off without any good-byes. There was no telling what sense he had made of the whole matter, though he would surely carry some strange stories back to the trader's lodge. Well, that could be worried about the next time Garth signed in. Right now he had to go about setting things right with the missionary. Squinting out through the rain he saw the man struggling to erect a collapsible tent while the entire population of the village stood in ordered ranks and watched. Naturally none of them offered to help.

By the time the tent was up and the crates and boxes stowed inside it the rain had stopped. The level of fluid in the bottle was a good bit lower and Garth felt more like facing up to the unavoidable meeting. In truth, he was looking forward to talking to the man. This whole nasty business aside, after an entire solitary year any human companionship looked good. *Will you join me now for dinner. John Garth,* he wrote on the back of an old invoice. But maybe the guy was too frightened to come? Which was no way to start any kind of relationship. Rummaging under the bunk, he found a box that was big enough and put his pistol inside. Itin was of course waiting outside the door when he opened it, since this was his tour as Knowledge Collector. He handed him the note and the box.

"Is the new man's name New Man?" Itin asked.

"No, it's not!" Garth snapped. "His name is Mark. But I'm only asking you to deliver this, not get involved in conversation."

As always when he lost his temper, the literal-minded Weskers won the round. "You are not asking for conversation," Itin said slowly, "but Mark may ask for conversation. And others will ask me his name, if I do not know his na . . ." The voice cut off as Garth slammed the door. This didn't work in the long run either because next time he saw Itin—a day, a week, or even a month later—the monologue would be picked up on the very word it had ended and the thought rambled out to its last frayed end. Garth cursed under his breath and poured water over a pair of the tastier concentrates that he had left.

"Come in," he said when there was a quiet knock on the door. The priest entered and held out the box with the gun.

"Thank you for the loan, Mr. Garth, I appreciate the spirit that made you send it. I have no idea of what caused the unhappy affair when I landed, but I think it would be best forgotten if we are going to be on this planet together for any length of time."

"Drink?" Garth asked, taking the box and pointing to the bottle on the table. He poured two glasses full and handed one to the priest. "That's about what I had in mind, but I still owe you an explanation of what happened out there." He scowled into his glass for a second, then raised it to the other man. "It's a big universe and I guess we have to make out as best we can. Here's to Sanity."

"God be with you," Father Mark said, and raised his glass as well.

"Not with me or with this planet," Garth said firmly. "And that's the crux of the matter." He half-drained the glass and sighed.

"Do you say that to shock me?" the priest asked with a smile. "I assure you it doesn't."

"Not intended to shock. I meant it quite literally. I suppose

I'm what you would call an atheist, so revealed religion is no concern of mine. While these natives, simple and unlettered stone-age types that they are, have managed to come this far with no superstitions or traces of deism whatsoever. I had hoped that they might continue that way."

"What are you saying?" the priest frowned. "Do you mean they have no gods, no belief in the hereafter? They must die . . . ?"

"Die they do, and to dust returneth like the rest of the animals. They have thunder, trees, and water without having thunder-gods, tree sprites, or water nymphs. They have no ugly little gods, taboos, or spells to hag-ride and limit their lives. They are the only primitive people I have ever encountered that are completely free of superstition and appear to be much happier and sane because of it. I just wanted to keep them that way."

"You wanted to keep them from God—from salvation?" The priest's eyes widened and he recoiled slightly.

"No," Garth said. "I wanted to keep them from superstition until they knew more and could think about it realistically without being absorbed and perhaps destroyed by it."

"You're being insulting to the Church, sir, to equate it with superstition . . ."

"Please," Garth said, raising his hand. "No theological arguments. I don't think your society footed the bill for this trip just to attempt a conversion on me. Just accept the fact that my beliefs have been arrived at through careful thought over a period of years, and no amount of undergraduate metaphysics will change them. I'll promise not to try and convert you—if you will do the same for me."

"Agreed, Mr. Garth. As you have reminded me, my mission here is to save these souls, and that is what I must do. But why should my work disturb you so much that you try and keep me from landing? Even threaten me with your gun and . . ." the priest broke off and looked into his glass.

"And even slug you?" Garth asked, suddenly frowning. "There was no excuse for that, and I would like to say that I'm sorry. Plain bad manners and an even worse temper. Live alone long enough and you find yourself doing that kind of thing." He brooded down at his big hands where they lay on the table, reading memories into the scars and callouses patterned there. "Let's just call it frustration, for lack of a better word. In your business you must have had a lot of chance to peep into the darker places in men's minds and you should know a bit about motives and happiness. I have had too busy a life to ever consider settling down and raising a family, and right up until recently I never missed it. Maybe leakage radiation is softening up my brain, but I had begun to think of these furry and fishy Weskers as being a little like my own children, that I was somehow responsible to them."

"We are all His children," Father Mark said quietly.

"Well, here are some of His children that can't even imagine His existence," Garth said, suddenly angry at himself for allowing gentler emotions to show through. Yet he forgot himself at once, leaning forward with the intensity of his feelings. "Can't you realize the importance of this? Live with these Weskers awhile and you will discover a simple and happy life that matches the state of grace you people are always talking about. They get *pleasure* from their lives—and cause no one pain. By circumstances they have evolved on an almost barren world, so have never had a chance to grow out of a physical stone age culture. But mentally they are our match—or perhaps better. They have all learned my language so I can easily explain the many things they want to know. Knowledge and the gaining of knowledge gives them real satisfaction. They tend to be exasperating at times because every new fact must be related to the structure of all other things, but the more they learn the faster this process becomes. Someday they are going to be man's equal in every way, perhaps surpass us. If—would you do me a favour?"

"Whatever I can."

"Leave them alone. Or teach them if you must—history and science, philosophy, law, anything that will help them face the realities of the greater universe they never even knew existed before. But don't confuse them with your hatreds and pain, guilt, sin, and punishment. Who knows the harm . . ."

"You are being insulting, sir!" the priest said, jumping to his feet. The top of his gray head barely came to the massive space-man's chin, yet he showed no fear in defending what he believed. Garth, standing now himself, was no longer the penitent. They faced each other in anger, as men have always stood, unbending in the defence of that which they think right.

"Yours is the insult," Garth shouted. "The incredible egotism to feel that your derivative little mythology, differing only slightly from the thousands of others that still burden men, can do anything but confuse their still fresh minds! Don't you realize that they believe in truth—and have never heard of such a thing as a lie. They have not been trained yet to understand that other kinds of minds can think differently from theirs. Will you spare them this . . . ?"

"I will do my duty which is His will, Mr. Garth. These are God's creatures here, and they have souls. I cannot shirk my duty, which is to bring them His word, so that they may be saved and enter into the kingdom of heaven."

When the priest opened the door the wind caught it and blew it wide. He vanished into the stormswept darkness and the door swung back and forth and a splatter of raindrops blew in. Garth's boots left muddy footprints when he closed the door, shutting out the sight of Itin sitting patiently and uncomplaining in the storm, hoping only that Garth might stop for a moment and leave with him some of the wonderful knowledge of which he had so much.

By unspoken consent that first night was never mentioned again. After a few days of loneliness, made worse because each knew of the other's proximity, they found themselves talking on carefully neutral grounds. Garth slowly packed and stowed away his stock and never admitted that his work was finished and he could leave at any time. He had a fair amount of interesting drugs and botanicals that would fetch a good price. And the Wesker Artifacts were sure to create a sensation in the sophisticated galactic market. Crafts on the planet here had been limited before his arrival, mostly pieces of carving painfully chipped into the hard wood with fragments of stone. He had supplied tools and a stock of raw metal from his own supplies, nothing more than that. In a few months the Weskers had not only learned to work with the new materials, but had translated their own designs and forms into the most alien—but most beautiful artifacts that he had ever seen. All he had to do was release these on the market to create a primary demand, then return for a new supply. The Weskers wanted only books and tools and knowledge in return, and through their own efforts he knew they would pull themselves into the galactic union.

This is what Garth had hoped. But a wind of change was blowing through the settlement that had grown up around his ship. No longer was he the centre of attention and focal point of the village life. He had to grin when he thought of his fall from power; yet there was very little humour in the smile. Serious and attentive Weskers still took turns of duty as Knowledge Collectors, but their recording of dry facts was in sharp contrast to the intellectual hurricane that surrounded the priest.

Where Garth had made them work for each book and machine, the priest gave freely. Garth had tried to be progressive in his supply of knowledge, treating them as bright but unlettered children. He had wanted them to walk before they could run, to master one step before going on the next.

Father Mark simply brought them the benefits of Christianity. The only physical work he required was the construction of a church, a place of worship and learning. More Weskers had appeared out of the limitless planetary swamps and within days the roof was up, supported on a framework of poles. Each morning the congregation worked a little while on the walls, then hurried inside to learn the all-promising, all-encompassing, all-important facts about the universe.

Garth never told the Weskers what he thought about their new interest, and this was mainly because they never asked him. Pride or honour stood in the way of his grabbing a willing listener and pouring out his grievances. Perhaps it would have been different if Itin was on Collecting duty; he was the brightest of the lot; but Itin had been rotated the day after the priest had arrived and Garth had not talked to him since.

It was a surprise then when after seventeen of the treblylong Wesker days, he found a delegation at his doorstep when he emerged after breakfast. Itin was their spokesman, and his mouth was open slightly. Many of the other Weskers had their mouths open as well, one even appearing to be yawning, clearly revealing the double row of sharp teeth and the purple-black throat. The mouths impressed Garth as to the seriousness of the meeting: this was the one Wesker expression he had learned to recognize. An open mouth indicated some strong emotion; happiness, sadness, anger, he could never be really sure which. The Weskers were normally placid and he had never seen enough open mouths to tell what was causing them. But he was surrounded by them now.

"Will you help us, John Garth," Itin said. "We have a question."

"I'll answer any question you ask," Garth said, with more than a hint of misgiving. "What is it?"

"It there a God?"

"What do you mean by 'God'?" Garth asked in turn. What should he tell them?

"God is our Father in Heaven, who made us all and protects us. Whom we pray to for aid, and if we are saved will find a place . . ."

"That's enough," Garth said. "There is no God."

All of them had their mouths open now, even Itin, as they looked at Garth and thought about his answer. The rows of pink teeth would have been frightening if he hadn't known these creatures so well. For one instant he wondered if perhaps they had been already indoctrinated and looked upon him as a heretic, but he brushed the thought away.

"Thank you," Itin said, and they turned and left.

Though the morning was still cool, Garth noticed that he was sweating and wondered why.

The reaction was not long in coming. Itin returned that same afternoon. "Will you come to the church?" he asked. "Many of the things that we study are difficult to learn, but none as difficult as this. We need your help because we must hear you and Father talk together. This is because he says one thing is true and you say another is true and both cannot be true at the same time. We must find out what is true."

"I'll come, of course," Garth said, trying to hide the sudden feeling of elation. He had done nothing, but the Weskers had come to him anyway. There could still be grounds for hope that they might yet be free.

It was hot inside the church, and Garth was surprised at the number of Weskers who were there, more than he had seen gathered at any one time before. There were many open mouths. Father Mark sat at a table covered with books. He looked unhappy but didn't say anything when Garth came in. Garth spoke first.

"I hope you realize this is their idea—that they came to me of their own free will and asked me to come here?"

"I know that," the priest said resignedly. "At times they can be very difficult. But they are learning and want to believe, and that is what is important."

"Father Mark, Trader Garth, we need your help," Itin said. "You both know many things that we do not know. You must help us come to religion which is not an easy thing to do." Garth started to say something, then changed his mind. Itin went on. "We have read the bibles and all the books that Father Mark gave us, and one thing is clear. We have discussed this and we are all agreed. These books are very different from the ones that Trader Garth gave us. In Trader Garth's books there is the universe which we have not seen, and it goes on without God, for He is mentioned nowhere; we have searched very carefully. In Father Mark's books He is everywhere and nothing can go without Him. One of these must be right and the other must be wrong. We do not know how this can be, but after we find out which is right then perhaps we will know. If God does not exist . . ."

"Of course He exists, my children," Father Mark said in a voice of heartfelt intensity. "He is our Father in Heaven who has created us all . . ."

"Who created God?" Itin asked and the murmur ceased and everyone of the Weskers watched Father Mark intensely. He recoiled a bit under the impact of their eyes, then smiled.

"Nothing created God, since He is the Creator. He always was . . ."

"If He always was in existence—why cannot the universe have

always been in existence? Without having had a creator?" Itin
broke in with a rush of words. The importance of the question
was obvious. The priest answered slowly, with infinite patience.

"Would that the answers were that simple, my children. But
even the scientists do not agree about the creation of the universe. While they doubt—we who have seen the light *know*.
We can see the miracle of creation all about us. And how can
there be a creation without a Creator? That is He, our Father,
our God in Heaven. I know you have doubts; that is because
you have souls and free will. Still, the answer is so simple. Have
faith, that is all you need. Just believe."

"How can we believe without proof?"

"If you cannot see that this world itself is proof of His existence, then I say to you that belief needs no proof—if you have
faith!"

A babble of voices arose in the room and more of the Wesker
mouths were open now as they tried to force their thoughts
through the tangled skein of words and separate the thread
of truth.

"Can you tell us, Garth?" Itin asked, and the sound of his
voice quieted the hubbub.

"I can tell you to use the scientific method which can examine
all things—including itself—and give you answers that can
prove the truth or falsity of any statement."

"That is what we must do," Itin said, "we had reached the
same conclusion." He held a thick book before him and a ripple
of nods ran across the watchers. "We have been studying the
bible as Father Mark told us to do, and we have found the
answer. God will make a miracle for us, thereby proving that
He is watching us. And by this sign we will know Him and
go to Him."

"That is the sin of false pride," Father Mark said. "God needs
no miracles to prove His existence."

"But *we* need a miracle!" Itin shouted, and though he wasn't
human there was need in his voice. "We have read here of many
smaller miracles, loaves, fishes, wine, snakes—many of them, for
much smaller reasons. Now all He need do is make a miracle
and He will bring us all to Him—the wonder of an entire new

world worshipping at His throne as you have told us, Father Mark. And you have told us how important this is. We have discussed this and find that there is only one miracle that is best for this kind of thing."

His boredom at the theological wrangling drained from Garth in an instant. He had not been really thinking or he would have realized where all this was leading. He could see the illustration in the bible where Itin held it open, and knew in advance what picture it was. He rose slowly from his chair, as if stretching, and turned to the priest behind him.

"Get ready!" he whispered. "Get out the back and get to the ship; I'll keep them busy here. I don't think they'll harm me."

"What do you mean . . . ?" Father Mark asked, blinking in surprise.

"Get out, you fool!" Garth hissed. "What miracle do you think they mean? What miracle is supposed to have converted the world to Christianity?"

"No!" Father Mark said. "It cannot be. It just cannot be . . . !"

"GET MOVING!" Garth shouted, dragging the priest from the chair and hurling him towards the rear wall. Father Mark stumbled to a halt, turned back. Garth leaped for him, but it was already too late. The amphibians were small, but there were so many of them. Garth lashed out and his fist struck Itin, hurling him back into the crowd. The others came on as he fought his way towards the priest. He beat at them but it was like struggling against waves. The furry, musky bodies washed over and engulfed him. He fought until they tied him, and he still struggled until they beat on his head until he stopped. Then they pulled him outside where he could only lie in the rain and curse and watch.

Of course the Weskers were marvellous craftsmen, and everything had been constructed down to the last detail, following the illustration in the bible. There was the cross, planted firmly on the top of a small hill, the gleaming metal spikes, the hammer. Father Mark was stripped and draped in a carefully pleated loincloth. They led him out of the church.

At the sight of the cross he almost fainted. After that he held his head high and determined to die as he had lived, with faith.

Yet this was hard. It was unbearable even for Garth, who only watched. It is one thing to talk of crucifixion and look at the gentle carved bodies in the dim light of prayer. It is another to see a man naked, ropes cutting into his skin where he hangs from a bar of wood. And to see the needle-tipped spike raised and placed against the soft flesh of his palm, to see the hammer come back with the calm deliberation of an artisan's measured stroke. To hear the thick sound of metal penetrating flesh.

Then to hear the screams.

Few are born to be martyrs; Father Mark was not one of them. With the first blows, the blood ran from his lips where his clenched teeth met. Then his mouth was wide and his head strained back and the guttural horror of his screams sliced through the susurration of the falling rain. It resounded as a silent echo from the masses of watching Weskers, for whatever emotion opened their mouths was now tearing at their bodies with all its force, and row after row of gaping jaws reflected the crucified priest's agony.

Mercifully he fainted as the last nail was driven home. Blood ran from the raw wounds, mixing with the rain to drip faintly pink from his feet as the life ran out of him. At this time, somewhere at this time, sobbing and tearing at his own bonds, numbed from the blows on the head, Garth lost consciousness.

He awoke in his own warehouse and it was dark. Someone was cutting away the woven ropes they had bound him with. The rain still dripped and splashed outside.

"Itin," he said. It could be no one else.

"Yes," the alien voice whispered back. "The others are all talking in the church. Lin died after you struck his head, and Inon is very sick. There are some that say you should be crucified too, and I think that is what will happen. Or perhaps killed by stoning on the head. They have found in the bible where it says . . ."

"I know." With infinite weariness. "An eye for an eye. You'll find lots of things like that once you start looking. It's a wonderful book." His head ached terribly.

"You must go, you can get to your ship without anyone seeing you. There has been enough killing." Itin as well, spoke with a new-found weariness.

Garth experimented, pulling himself to his feet. He pressed his head to the rough wood of the wall until the nausea stopped. "He's dead." He said it as a statement, not a question.

"Yes, some time ago. Or I could not have come away to see you."

"And buried of course, or they wouldn't be thinking about starting on me next."

"And buried!" There was almost a ring of emotion in the alien's voice, an echo of the dead priest's. "He is buried and he will rise on High. It is written and that is the way it will happen. Father Mark will be so happy that it has happened like this." The voice ended in a sound like a human sob.

Garth painfully worked his way towards the door, leaning against the wall so he wouldn't fall.

"We did the right thing, didn't we?" Itin asked. There was no answer. "He will rise up, Garth, won't he rise?"

Garth was at the door and enough light came from the brightly lit church to show his torn and bloody hands clutching at the frame. Itin's face swam into sight close to his, and Garth felt the delicate, many fingered hands with the sharp nails catch at his clothes.

"He will rise, won't he, Garth?"

"No," Garth said, "he is going to stay buried right where you put him. Nothing is going to happen because he is dead and he is going to stay dead."

The rain runnelled through Itin's fur and his mouth opened so wide that he seemed to be screaming into the night. Only with effort could he talk, squeezing out the alien thoughts in an alien language.

"Then we will not be saved? We will not become pure?"

"You were pure," Garth said, in a voice somewhere between a sob and a laugh. "That's the horrible ugly dirty part of it. You were pure. Now you are . . ."

"Murderers," Itin said, and the water ran down from his lowered head and streamed away into the darkness.

For a Journal Entry . . .

Harrison's story is really concerned with the meeting of two differing cultures and differing attitudes toward that meeting. If SF takes its examples from the past and projects them to the future, can you think of some specific cases in Earth's history of the tragic meeting of two cultures. Consider the missionaries in Hawaii, for example. What happened to Hawaiian customs, habits, modes of dress, religion, language, or music? What about present-day Australian reactions to the Bushmen? And what about your own religion's attitude toward so-called pagans. Why not investigate what your own denomination teaches about the rights of missionaries and the rights of natives to whom they are sent.

For Your Consideration . . .

1. The inhabitants of Wesker's World are presented as being very, very logical and very, very literal. Are there any early indications of these traits? Why are these traits so central to the point of the story?
2. Did the ending come as either a surprise or a shock to you? Why or why not?
3. What other ways could religion develop on other worlds?
4. Would you advocate sending missionaries along on space flights to other planets or stars? Why or why not?
5. Do you think the attitude presented in the story is hostile or sympathetic to religion, or neither?
6. Is the fact that religion is the central issue in the story crucial to its point? Would the same effect be achieved if the people from Earth had been merely advocates of two different economic or political systems?
7. What do you think the life of the Weskers will be like after their exposure to Garth and Father Mark?

Notes

PAGE
142   *ineffectually*—without success
145   *crux*—decisive point

146   *deism*—a generalized belief in God
146   *equate*—to state the equality of
148   *penitent*—one who confesses sin
148   *proximity*—nearness
154   *susurration*—soft whisper
155   *runnelled*—streamed

Omnilingual

H. Beam Piper

What would happen if we found the remains of an ancient civilization on Mars? How could we possibly read their lost writings when there are ancient inscriptions here on Earth that we will never be able to read? Yet they *could* be understood if we had the right clues. H. Beam Piper was a railroad detective when he began writing science fiction—and he did it so successfully that he soon became a full-time author.

Martha Dane paused, looking up at the purple-tinged copper sky. The wind had shifted since noon, while she had been inside, and the dust storm that was sweeping the high deserts to the east was now blowing out over Syrtis. The sun, magnified by the haze, was a gorgeous magenta ball, as large as the sun of Terra, at which she could look directly. Tonight, some of that dust would come sifting down from the upper atmosphere to add another film to what had been burying the city for the last fifty thousand years.

The red loess lay over everything, covering the streets and the open spaces of park and plaza, hiding the small houses that had been crushed and pressed flat under it and the rubble that had come down from the tall buildings when roofs had caved in and walls had toppled outward. Here where she stood, the ancient streets were a hundred to a hundred and fifty feet below the surface; the breach they had made in the wall of the building behind her had opened into the sixth story. She could look down on the cluster of prefabricated huts and sheds, on the brush-grown flat that had been the waterfront when this place had been a seaport on the ocean that was now Syrtis Depression; already, the bright metal was thinly coated with red dust. She thought, again, of what clearing this city would mean, in terms of time and labor, of people and supplies and equipment brought across fifty million miles of space. They'd have to use machinery; there was no other way it could be done. Bulldozers and power shovels and draglines; they were fast, but they were rough and indiscriminate. She remembered the digs around Harappa and Mohenjo-Daro, in the Indus Valley, and the careful, patient native laborers—the painstaking foremen, the pickmen and spademen, the long files of basketmen carrying away the earth. Slow and primitive as the civilization whose ruins they were uncovering, yes, but she could count on the fingers of one hand the times one of her pickmen had damaged a valuable object in the ground. If it hadn't been for the underpaid and uncomplaining native laborer, archaeology would still be back where Wincklemann had found it. But on Mars there was no native labor; the last Martian had died five hundred centuries ago.

Something started banging like a machine gun, four or five hundred yards to her left. A solenoid jackhammer; Tony Lattimer must have decided which building he wanted to break into next. She became conscious, then, of the awkward weight of her equipment, and began redistributing it, shifting the straps of her oxy-tank pack, slinging the camera from one shoulder and the board and drafting tools from the other, gathering the notebooks and sketchbooks under her left arm. She started walking down the road, over hillocks of buried rubble, around snags of wall jutting up out of the loess, past buildings still standing, some of them already breached and explored, and across the brush-grown flat to the huts.

There were ten people in the main office room of Hut One when she entered. As soon as she had disposed of her oxygen equipment, she lit a cigarette, her first since noon, then looked

from one to another of them. Old Selim von Ohlmhorst, the
Turco-German, one of her two fellow archaeologists, sitting at
the end of the long table against the farther wall, smoking his
big curved pipe and going through a looseleaf notebook. The
girl ordnance officer, Sachiko Koremitsu, between two droplights
at the other end of the table, her head bent over her work.
Colonel Hubert Penrose, the Space Force CO, and Captain Field,
the intelligence officer, listening to the report of one of the airdyne pilots, returned from his afternoon survey flight. A couple
of girl lieutenants from Signals, going over the script of the
evening telecast, to be transmitted to the *Cyrano*, on orbit five
thousand miles off planet and relayed from thence to Terra via
Lunar. Sid Chamberlain, the Trans-Space News Service man,
was with them. Like Selim and herself, he was a civilian; he
was advertising the fact with a white shirt and a sleeveless blue
sweater. And Major Lindemann, the engineer officer, and one
of his assistants, arguing over some plans on a drafting board.
She hoped, drawing a pint of hot water to wash her hands and
sponge off her face, that they were doing something about the
pipeline.

She started to carry the notebooks and sketchbooks over to
where Selim von Ohlmhorst was sitting, and then, as she always
did, she turned aside and stopped to watch Sachiko. The Japanese girl was restoring what had been a book, fifty thousand
years ago; her eyes were masked by a binocular loup, the black
headband invisible against her glossy black hair, and she was
picking delicately at the crumbled page with a hair-fine wire
set in a handle of copper tubing. Finally, loosening a particle as
tiny as a snowflake, she grasped it with tweezers, placed it on
the sheet of transparent plastic on which she was reconstruct-
ing the page, and set it with a mist of fixitive from a little
spraygun. It was a sheer joy to watch her; every movement was
as graceful and precise as though done to music after being
rehearsed a hundred times.

"Hello, Martha. It isn't cocktail time yet, is it?" The girl at the
table spoke without raising her head, almost without moving
her lips, as though she were afraid that the slightest breath
would disturb the flaky stuff in front of her.

"No, it's only fifteen-thirty. I finished my work, over there. I didn't find any more books, if that's good news for you."

Sachiko took off the loup and leaned back in her chair, her palms cupped over her eyes.

"No, I like doing this. I call it micro-jigsaw puzzles. This book, here, really is a mess. Selim found it lying open, with some heavy stuff on top of it; the pages were simply crushed." She hesitated briefly. "If only it would mean something, after I did it."

There could be a faintly critical overtone to that. As she replied, Martha realized that she was being defensive.

"It will, some day. Look how long it took to read Egyptian hieroglyphics, even after they had the Rosetta Stone."

Sachiko smiled. "Yes, I know. But they did have the Rosetta Stone."

"And we don't. There is no Rosetta Stone, not anywhere on Mars. A whole race, a whole species, died while the first Crô-Magnon cave-artist was daubing pictures of reindeer and bison, and across fifty thousand years and fifty million miles there was no bridge of understanding.

"We'll find one. There must be something, somewhere, that will give us the meaning of a few words, and we'll use them to pry meaning out of more words, and so on. We may not live to learn this language, but we'll make a start, and some day somebody will."

Sachiko took her hands from her eyes, being careful not to look toward the unshaded lights, and smiled again. This time Martha was sure that it was not the Japanese smile of politeness, but the universally human smile of friendship.

"I hope so, Martha; really I do. It would be wonderful for you to be the first to do it, and it would be wonderful for all of us to be able to read what these people wrote. It would really bring this dead city to life again." The smile faded slowly. "But it seems so hopeless."

"You haven't found any more pictures?"

Sachiko shook her head. Not that it would have meant much if she had. They had found hundreds of pictures with captions; they had never been able to establish a positive relationship between any pictured object and any printed word. Neither of them said anything more, and after a moment Sachiko replaced the loup and bent her head forward over the book.

Selim von Ohlmhorst looked up from his notebook, taking his pipe out of his mouth.

"Everything finished, over there?" he asked, releasing a puff of smoke.

"Such as it was." She laid the notebooks and sketches on the table. "Captain Gicquel's started airsealing the building from the fifth floor down, with an entrance on the sixth; he'll start putting in oxygen generators as soon as that's done. I have everything cleared up where he'll be working."

Colonel Penrose looked up quickly, as though making a mental note to attend to something later. Then he returned his attention to the pilot, who was pointing something out on a map.

Von Ohlmhorst nodded. "There wasn't much to it, at that," he agreed. "Do you know which building Tony has decided to enter next?"

"The tall one with the conical thing like a candle extinguisher on top, I think. I heard him drilling for the blasting shots over that way."

"Well, I hope it turns out to be one that was occupied up to the end."

The last one hadn't. It had been stripped of its contents and fittings, a piece of this and a bit of that, haphazardly, apparently over a long period of time, until it had been almost gutted. For centuries, as it had died, this city had been consuming itself by a process of auto-cannibalism. She said something to that effect.

"Yes. We always find that—except, of course, at places like Pompeii. Have you seen any of the other Roman cities in Italy?" he asked, "Minturnae, for instance? First the inhabitants tore down this to repair that, and then, after they had vacated the city, other people came along and tore down what was left, and burned the stones for lime, or crushed them to mend roads, till there was nothing left but the foundation traces. That's where we are fortunate; this is one of the places where the Martian race perished, and there were no barbarians to come later and destroy what they had left." He puffed slowly at his pipe. "Some of these days, Martha, we are going to break into one of these buildings and find that it was one in which the last of these people died. Then we will learn the story of the end of this civilization."

And if we learn to read their language, we'll learn the whole story, not just the obituary. She hesitated, not putting the thought into words. "We'll find that, sometime, Selim," she said, then looked at her watch. "I'm going to get some more work done on my lists, before dinner."

For an instant, the old man's face stiffened in disapproval; he started to say something, thought better of it, and put his pipe back into his mouth. The brief wrinkling around his mouth and the twitch of his white mustache had been enough, however; she knew what he was thinking. She was wasting time and effort, he believed; time and effort belonging not to herself but to the expedition. He could be right, too, she realized. But he had to be wrong; there had to be a way to do it. She turned from him silently and went to her own packing-case seat, at the middle of the table.

Photographs, and photostats of restored pages of books, and transcripts of inscriptions, were piled in front of her, and the notebooks in which she was compiling her lists. She sat down, lighting a fresh cigarette, and reached over to a stack of unexamined material, taking off the top sheet. It was a photostat of what looked like the title page and contents of some sort of a periodical. She remembered it; she had found it herself, two days before, in a closet in the basement of the building she had just finished examining.

She sat for a moment, looking at it. It was readable, in the sense that she had set up a purely arbitrary but consistently pronounceable system of phonetic values for the letters. The long vertical symbols were vowels. There were only ten of them; not too many, allowing separate characters for long and short sounds. There were twenty of the short horizontal letters, which meant that sounds like -ng or -ch or -sh were single letters. The odds were millions to one against her system being anything like the original sound of the language, but she had listed several thousand Martian words, and she could pronounce all of them.

And that was as far as it went. She could pronounce between three and four thousand Martian words, and she couldn't assign a meaning to one of them. Selim von Ohlmhorst believed that she never would. So did Tony Lattimer, and he was a great deal less reticent about saying so. So, she was sure, did Sachiko Koremitsu. There were times, now and then, when she began to be afraid that they were right.

The letters on the page in front of her began squirming and dancing, slender vowels with fat little consonants. They did that, now, every night in her dreams. And there were other dreams, in which she read them as easily as English; waking, she would try desperately and vainly to remember. She blinked, and looked away from the photostated page; when she looked back, the letters were behaving themselves again. There were three words at the top of the page, over-and-underlined, which seemed to be the Martian method of capitalization. *Mastharnorvod Tadavas Sornhulva.* She pronounced them mentally, leafing through her notebooks to see if she had encountered them before, and in what contexts. All three were listed. In addition, *masthar* was a fairly common word, and so was *norvod,* and so was *nor,* but *-vod* was a suffix and nothing but a suffix. *Davas,* was a word, too, and *ta-* was a common prefix; *sorn* and *hulva* were both common words. This language, she had long ago decided, must be something like German; when the Martians had needed a new word, they had just pasted a couple of existing words together. It would probably turn out to be a grammatical horror. Well, they had published magazines, and one of them had been called *Mastharnorvod Tadavas Sornhulva.* She wondered if it had been something like the *Quarterly Archaeological Review,* or something more on the order of *Sexy Stories.*

A smaller line, under the title, was plainly the issue number and date; enough things had been found numbered in series to enable her to identify the numerals and determine that a deci-

mal system of numeration had been used. This was the one
thousand and seven hundred and fifty-fourth issue, for Doma,
14837; then Doma must be the name of one of the Martian
months. The word had turned up several times before. She
found herself puffing furiously on her cigarette as she leafed
through notebooks and piles of already examined material.

Sachiko was speaking to somebody, and a chair scraped at the
end of the table. She raised her head, to see a big man with red
hair and a red face, in Space Force green, with the single star of
a major on his shoulder, sitting down. Ivan Fitzgerald, the
medic. He was lifting weights from a book similar to the one
the girl ordnance officer was restoring.

"Haven't had time, lately," he was saying, in reply to Sachiko's
question. "The Finchley girl's still down with whatever it is she
has, and it's something I haven't been able to diagnose yet. And
I've been checking on bacteria cultures, and in what spare time
I have, I've been dissecting specimens for Bill Chandler. Bill's
finally found a mammal. Looks like a lizard, and it's only four
inches long, but it's a real warm-blooded, gamogenetic, placental, viviparous mammal. Burrows, and seems to live on what
pass for insects here."

"Is there enough oxygen for anything like that?" Sachiko was
asking.

"Seems to be, close to the ground." Fitzgerald got the headband of his loup adjusted, and pulled it down over his eyes.
"He found this thing in a ravine down on the sea bottom—Ha,
this page seems to be intact; now, if I can get it out all in one
piece—"

He went on talking inaudibly to himself, lifting the page a
little at a time and sliding one of the transparent plastic sheets
under it, working with minute delicacy. Not the delicacy of the
Japanese girl's small hands, moving like the paws of a cat wash-
ing her face, but like a steam-hammer cracking a peanut. Field
archaeology requires a certain delicacy of touch, too, but
Martha watched the pair of them with envious admiration. Then
she turned back to her own work, finishing the table of contents.

The next page was the beginning of the first article listed; many of the words were unfamiliar. She had the impression that this must be some kind of scientific or technical journal; that could be because such publications made up the bulk of her own periodical reading. She doubted if it were fiction; the paragraphs had a solid, factual look.

At length, Ivan Fitzgerald gave a short, explosive grunt.

"Ha! Got it!"

She looked up. He had detached the page and was cementing another plastic sheet onto it.

"Any pictures?" she asked.

"None on this side. Wait a moment." He turned the sheet. "None on this side, either." He sprayed another sheet of plastic to sandwich the page, then picked up his pipe and relighted it.

"I get fun out of this, and it's good practice for my hands, so don't think I'm complaining," he said, "but Martha, do you honestly think anybody's ever going to get anything out of this?"

Sachiko held up a scrap of the silicone plastic the Martians had used for paper with her tweezers. It was almost an inch square.

"Look; three whole words on this piece," she crowed. "Ivan, you took the easy book."

Fitzgerald wasn't being sidetracked. "This stuff's absolutely meaningless," he continued. "It had a meaning fifty thousand years ago, when it was written, but it has none at all now."

She shook her head. "Meaning isn't something that evaporates with time," she argued. "It has just as much meaning now as it ever had. We just haven't learned how to decipher it."

"That seems like a pretty pointless distinction," Selim von Ohlmhorst joined the conversation. "There no longer exists a means of deciphering it."

"We'll find one." She was speaking, she realized, more in self-encouragement than in controversy.

"How? From pictures and captions? We've found captioned pictures, and what have they given us? A caption is intended to explain the picture, not the picture to explain the caption. Suppose some alien to our culture found a picture of a man with a white beard and mustache sawing a billet from a log. He would think the caption meant, 'Man Sawing Wood.'" How would he know that it was really 'Wilhelm II in Exile at Doorn?'"

Sachiko had taken off her loup and was lighting a cigarette. "I can think of pictures intended to explain their captions," she said. "These picture language-books, the sort we use in the Service—little line drawings, with a word or phrase under them."

"Well, of course, if we found something like that," von Ohlmhorst began.

"Michael Ventris found something like that, back in the Fifties," Hubert Penrose's voice broke in from directly behind her.

She turned her head. The colonel was standing by the archaeologists' table; Captain Field and the airdyne pilote had gone out.

"He found a lot of Greek inventories of military stores," Penrose continued. "They were in Cretan Linear B script, and at the head of each list was a little picture, a sword or a helmet or a cooking tripod or a chariot wheel. That's what gave him the key to the script."

"Colonel's getting to be quite an archaeologist," Fitzgerald commented. "We're all learning each other's specialties, on this expedition."

"I heard about that long before this expedition was even contemplated." Penrose was tapping a cigarette on his gold case. "I heard about that back before the Thirty Days' War, at Intelligence School, when I was a lieutenant. As a feat of cryptanalysis, not an archaeological discovery."

"Yes, cryptanalysis," von Ohlmhorst pounced. "The reading of a known language in an unknown form of writing. Ventris' lists were in the known language, Greek. Neither he nor anybody else ever read a word of the Cretan language until the finding of the Greek-Cretan bilingual in 1963, because only with a bilingual text, one language already known, can an unknown ancient language be learned. And what hope, I ask you, have we of finding anything like that here? Martha, you've been working on these Martian texts ever since we landed here—for the last six months. Tell me, have you found a single word to which you can positively assign a meaning?"

"Yes, I think I have one." She was trying hard not to sound

too exultant. "*Doma*. It's the name of one of the months of the Martian calendar."

"Where did you find that?" von Ohlmhorst asked. "And how did you establish—?"

"Here." She picked up the photostat and handed it along the table to him. "I'd call this the title page of a magazine."

He was silent for a moment, looking at it. "Yes. I would say so, too. Have you any of the rest of it?"

"I'm working on the first page of the first article, listed there. Wait till I see; yes, here's all I found, together, here." She told him where she had gotten it. "I just gathered it up, at the time, and gave it to Geoffrey and Rosita to photostat; this is the first I've really examined it."

The old man got to his feet, brushing tobacco ashes from the front of his jacket, and came to where she was sitting, laying the title page on the table and leafing quickly through the stack of photostats.

"Yes, and here is the second article, on page eight, and here's the next one." He finished the pile of photostats. "A couple of pages missing at the end of the last article. This is remarkable; surprising that a thing like a magazine would have survived so long."

"Well, this silicone stuff the Martians used for paper is pretty durable," Hubert Penrose said. "There doesn't seem to have been any water or any other fluid in it originally, so it wouldn't dry out with time."

"Oh, it's not remarkable that the material would have survived. We've found a good many books and papers in excellent condition. But only a really vital culture, an organized culture, will publish magazines, and this civilization had been dying for hundreds of years before the end. It might have been a thousand years before the time they died out completely that such activities as publishing ended."

"Well, look where I found it; in a closet in a cellar. Tossed in there and forgotten, and then ignored when they were stripping the building. Things like that happen."

Penrose had picked up the title page and was looking at it.

"I don't think there's any doubt about this being a magazine, at all." He looked again at the title, his lips moving silently.

"*Mastharnorvod Tadavas Sornhulva*. Wonder what it means. But you're right about the date—*Doma* seems to be the name of a month. Yes, you have a word, Dr. Dane."

Sid Chamberlain, seeing that something unusual was going on, had come over from the table at which he was working. After examining the title page and some of the inside pages, he began whispering into the stenophone he had taken from his belt.

"Don't try to blow this up to anything big, Sid," she cautioned. "All we have is the name of a month, and Lord only knows how long it'll be till we even find out which month it was."

"Well, it's a start, isn't it?" Penrose argued. "Grotefend only had the word for 'king' when he started reading Persian cuneiform."

"But I don't have the word for month; just the name of a month. Everybody knew the names of the Persian kings, long before Grotefend."

"That's not the story," Chamberlain said. "What the public back on Terra will be interested in is finding out that the Martians published magazines, just like we do. Something familiar; make the Martians seem more real. More human."

Three men had come in, and were removing their masks and helmets and oxy-tanks, and peeling out of their quilted coveralls. Two were Space Force lieutenants; the third was a youngish civilian with close-cropped blond hair, in a checked woolen shirt. Tony Lattimer and his helpers.

"Don't tell me Martha finally got something out of that stuff?" he asked, approaching the table. He might have been commenting on the antics of the village half-wit, from his tone.

"Yes; the name of one of the Martian months." Hubert Penrose went on to explain, showing the photostat.

Tony Lattimer took it, glanced at it, and dropped it on the table.

"Sounds plausible, of course, but just an assumption. That word may not be the name of a month, at all—could mean 'published' or 'authorized' or 'copyrighted' or anything like that. Fact is, I don't think it's more than a wild guess that that thing's anything like a periodical." He dismissed the subject and turned to Penrose. "I picked out the next building to enter; that tall one with the conical thing on top. It ought to be in pretty good shape inside; the conical top wouldn't allow dust to accumulate, and from the outside nothing seems to be caved in or crushed. Ground level's higher than the other one, about the seventh floor. I found a good place and drilled for the shots; tomorrow I'll blast a hole in it, and if you can spare some people to help, we can start exploring it right away."

"Yes, of course, Dr. Lattimer. I can spare about a dozen, and I suppose you can find a few civilian volunteers," Penrose told him. "What will you need in the way of equipment?"

"Oh, about six demolition-packets; they can all be shot together. And the usual thing in the way of lights, and breaking and digging tools, and climbing equipment in case we run into broken or doubtful stairways. We'll divide into two parties. Nothing ought to be entered for the first time without a qualified archaeologist along. Three parties, if Martha can tear herself away from this catalogue of systematized incomprehensibilities she's making long enough to do some real work."

She felt her chest tighten and her face become stiff. She was pressing her lips together to lock in a furious retort when Hubert Penrose answered for her.

"Dr. Dane's been doing as much work, and as important work, as you have," he said brusquely. "More important work, I'd be inclined to say."

Von Ohlmhorst was visibly distressed; he glanced once toward Sid Chamberlain, then looked hastily away from him. Afraid of a story of dissension among archaeologists getting out.

"Working out a system of pronunciation by which the Martian language could be transliterated was a most important contribution," he said. "And Martha did that almost unassisted."

"Unassisted by Dr. Lattimer, anyway," Penrose added. "Captain Field and Lieutenant Koremitsu did some work, and I helped out a little, but nine-tenths of it she did herself."

"Purely arbitrary," Lattimer disdained. "Why, we don't even know that the Martians could make the same kind of vocal sounds we do."

"Oh, yes, we do," Ivan Fitzgerald contradicted, safe on his own ground. "I haven't seen any actual Martian skulls—these people seem to have been very tidy about disposing of their dead—but from statues and busts and pictures I've seen, I'd say that their vocal organs were identical with our own."

"Well, grant that. And grant that it's going to be impressive to rattle off the names of Martian notables whose statues we find, and that if we're ever able to attribute any place names, they'll sound a lot better than this horse-doctors' Latin the old astronomers splashed all over the map of Mars," Lattimer said. "What I object to is her wasting time on this stuff, of which nobody will ever be able to read a word if she fiddles around with those lists till there's another hundred feet of loess on this city, when there's so much real work to be done and we're as shorthanded as we are."

That was the first time that had come out in just so many words. She was glad Lattimer had said it and not Selim von Ohlmhorst.

"What you mean," she retorted, "is that it doesn't have the publicity value that digging up statues has."

For an instant, she could see that the shot had scored. Then Lattimer, with a side glance at Chamberlain, answered:

"What I mean is that you're trying to find something that any archaeologist, yourself included, should know doesn't exist. I don't object to your gambling your professional reputation and making a laughing stock of yourself; what I object to is that the blunders of one archaeologist discredit the whole subject in the eyes of the public."

That seemed to be what worried Lattimer most. She was framing a reply when the communication-outlet whistled shrilly, and then squawked: "Cocktail time! One hour to dinner; cocktails in the library, Hut Four!"

The library, which was also lounge, recreation room, and general gathering-place, was already crowded; most of the crowd was at the long table topped with sheets of glasslike plastic that had been wall panels out of one of the ruined buildings. She poured herself what passed, here, for a martini, and carried it over to where Selim von Ohlmhorst was sitting alone.

For a while, they talked about the building they had just

finished exploring, then drifted into reminiscences of their work on Terra—von Ohlmhorst's in Asia Minor, with the Hittite Empire, and hers in Pakistan, excavating the cities of the Harappa Civilization. They finished their drinks—the ingredients were plentiful; alcohol and flavoring extracts synthesized from Martian vegetation—and von Ohlmhorst took the two glasses to the table for refills.

"You know, Martha," he said, when he returned, "Tony was right about one thing. You are gambling your professional standing and reputation. It's against all archaeological experience that a language so completely dead as this one could be deciphered. There was a continuity between all the other ancient languages —by knowing Greek, Champollion learned to read Egyptian; by knowing Egyptian, Hittite was learned. That's why you and your colleagues have never been able to translate the Harappa hieroglyphics; no such continuity exists there. If you insist that this utterly dead language can be read, your reputation will suffer for it."

"I heard Colonel Penrose say, once, that an officer who's afraid to risk his military reputation seldom makes much of a reputation. It's the same with us. If we really want to find things out, we have to risk making mistakes. And I'm a lot more interested in finding things out than I am in my reputation."

She glanced across the room, to where Tony Lattimer was sitting with Gloria Standish, talking earnestly, while Gloria sipped one of the counterfeit martinis and listened. Gloria was the leading contender for the title of Miss Mars, 1996, if you liked big bosomy blondes, but Tony would have been just as attentive to her if she'd looked like the Wicked Witch in "The Wizard of Oz," because Gloria was the Pan-Federation Telecast System commentator with the expedition.

"I know you are," the old Turco-German was saying. "That's why, when they asked me to name another archaeologist for this expedition, I named you."

He hadn't named Tony Lattimer; Lattimer had been pushed onto the expedition by his university. There'd been a lot of high-level string-pulling to that; she wished she knew the whole story. She'd managed to keep clear of universities and university politics; all her digs had been sponsored by nonacademic foundations or art museums.

"You have an excellent standing; much better than my own, at your age. That's why it disturbs me to see you jeopardizing it by this insistence that the Martian language can be translated. I can't, really, see how you can hope to succeed."

She shrugged and drank some more of her cocktail, then lit another cigarette. It was getting tiresome to try to verbalize something she only felt.

"Neither do I, now, but I will. Maybe I'll find something like the picture-books Sachiko was talking about. A child's primer, maybe; surely they had things like that. And if I don't, I'll find something else. We've only been here six months. I can wait the rest of my life, if I have to, but I'll do it sometime."

"I can't wait so long," von Ohlmhorst said. "The rest of my life will only be a few years, and when the *Schiaparelli* orbits in, I'll be going back to Terra on the *Cyrano*."

"I wish you wouldn't. This is a whole new world of archaeology. Literally."

"Yes." He finished the cocktail and looked at his pipe as though wondering whether to re-light it so soon before dinner, then put it in his pocket. "A whole new world—but I've grown old, and it isn't for me. I've spent my life studying the Hittites. I can speak the Hittite language, though maybe King Muwatallis wouldn't be able to understand my modern Turkish accent. But the things I'd have to learn, here—chemistry, physics, engineering, how to run analytic tests on steel girders and beryllosilver alloys and plastics and silicones. I'm more at home with a civilization that rode in chariots and fought with swords and was just learning how to work iron. Mars is for young people. This expedition is a cadre of leadership—not only the Space Force people, who'll be the commanders of the main expedition, but us scientists, too. And I'm just an old cavalry general who can't learn to command tanks and aircraft. You'll have time to learn about Mars. I won't."

His reputation as the dean of Hittitologists was solid and secure, too, she added mentally. Then she felt ashamed of the thought. He wasn't to be classed with Tony Lattimer.

"All I came for was to get the work started," he was continuing. "The Federation Government felt that an old hand should do that. Well, it's started, now; you and Tony and whoever come out on the *Schiaparelli* must carry it on. You said it, yourself; you have a whole new world. This is only one city, of the last Martian civilization. Behind this, you have the Late Upland Culture, and the Canal Builders, and all the civilizations and races and empires before them, clear back to the Martian Stone Age." He hesitated for a moment. "You have no idea what all you have to learn, Martha. This isn't the time to start specializing too narrowly."

They all got out of the truck and stretched their legs and looked up the road to the tall building with the queer conical cap askew on its top. The four little figures that had been busy against its wall climbed into the jeep and started back slowly, the smallest of them, Sachiko Koremitsu, paying out an electric cable behind. When it pulled up beside the truck, they climbed out; Sachiko attached the free end of the cable to a nuclear-electric battery. At once, dirty gray smoke and orange dust puffed out from the wall of the building, and, a second later, the multiple explosion banged.

She and Tony Lattimer and Major Lindemann climbed onto the truck, leaving the jeep stand by the road. When they reached the building, a satisfyingly wide breach had been blown in the wall. Lattimer had placed his shots between two of the windows; they were both blown out along with the wall between, and lay unbroken on the ground. Martha remembered the first building they had entered. A Space Force officer had picked up a stone and thrown it at one of the windows, thinking that would be all they'd need to do. It had bounced back. He had drawn his pistol —they'd all carried guns, then, on the principle that what they didn't know about Mars might easily hurt them—and fired four shots. The bullets had ricochetted, screaming thinly; there were four coppery smears of jacketmetal on the window, and a little surface spalling. Somebody tried a rifle; the 4000-f.s. bullet had cracked the glasslike pane without penetrating. An oxyacetylene torch had taken an hour to cut the window out; the lab crew, aboard the ship, were still trying to find out just what the stuff was.

Tony Lattimer had gone forward and was sweeping his flashlight back and forth, swearing petulantly, his voice harshened and amplified by his helmet-speaker.

"I thought I was blasting into a hallway; this lets us into a room. Careful; there's about a two-foot drop to the floor, and a lot of rubble from the blast just inside."

He stepped down through the breach; the others began dragging equipment out of the trucks—shovels and picks and crowbars and sledges, portable floodlights, cameras, sketching materials, an extension ladder, even Alpinists' ropes and crampons and pickaxes. Hubert Penrose was shouldering something that looked like a surrealist machine gun but which was really a nuclear-electric jackhammer. Martha selected one of the spike-shod mountaineer's ice axes, with which she could dig or chop or poke or pry or help herself over rough footing.

The windows, grimed and crusted with fifty millennia of dust, filtered in a dim twilight; even the breach in the wall, in the morning shade, lighted only a small patch of floor. Somebody snapped on a floodlight, aiming it at the ceiling. The big room was empty and bare; dust lay thick on the floor and reddened the once-white walls. It could have been a large office, but there was nothing left in it to indicate its use.

"This one's been stripped up to the seventh floor!" Lattimer exclaimed. "Street level'll be cleaned out, completely."

"Do for living quarters and shops, then," Lindemann said. "Added to the others, this'll take care of everybody on the *Schiaparelli*."

"Seem to have been a lot of electric or electronic apparatus over along this wall," one of the Space Force officers commented. "Ten or twelve electric outlets." He brushed the dusty wall with his glove, then scraped on the floor with his foot. "I can see where things were pried loose."

The door, one of the double sliding things the Martians had used, was closed. Selim von Ohlmhorst tried it, but it was stuck fast. The metal latch-parts had frozen together, molecule bonding itself to molecule, since the door had last been closed. Hubert Penrose came over with the jackhammer, fitting a spear-point chisel into place. He set the chisel in the joint between the doors, braced the hammer against his hip, and squeezed the trigger-switch. The hammer banged briefly like the weapon it resembled, and the doors popped a few inches apart, then stuck. Enough dust had worked into the recesses into which it was supposed to slide to block it on both sides.

That was old stuff; they ran into that every time they had to force a door, and they were prepared for it. Somebody went outside and brought in a power-jack and finally one of the doors inched back to the door jamb. That was enough to get the lights and equipment through; they all passed from the room to the hallway beyond. About half the other doors were open; each had a number and a single word, *Darfhulva*, over it.

One of the civilian volunteers, a woman professor of natural ecology from Penn State University, was looking up and down the hall.

"You know," she said, "I feel at home here. I think this was a college of some sort, and these were classrooms. That word, up there; that was the subject taught, or the department. And those electronic devices, all where the class would face them; audio-visual teaching aids."

"A twenty-five-story university?" Lattimer scoffed. "Why, a building like this would handle thirty thousand students."

"Maybe there were that many. This was a big city, in its prime," Martha said, moved chiefly by a desire to oppose Lattimer.

"Yes, but think of the snafu in the halls, every time they changed classes. It'd take half an hour to get everybody back and forth from one floor to another." He turned to von Ohlmhorst. "I'm going up above this floor. This place has been looted clean up to here, but there's a chance there may be something above," he said.

"I'll stay on this floor, at present," the Turco-German replied. "There will be much coming and going, and dragging things in and out. We should get this completely examined and recorded first. Then Major Lindemann's people can do their worst, here."

"Well, if nobody else wants it, I'll take the downstairs," Martha said.

"I'll go along with you," Hubert Penrose told her. "If the lower floors have no archaeological value, we'll turn them into living quarters. I like this building; it'll give everybody room to keep out from under everybody else's feet." He looked down the hall. "We ought to find escalators at the middle."

The hallway, too, was thick underfoot with dust. Most of the open rooms were empty, but a few contained furniture, including small seat-desks. The original proponent of the university theory pointed these out as just what might be found in classrooms. There were escalators, up and down, on either side of the hall, and more on the intersecting passage to the right.

"That's how they handled the students, between classes," Martha commented. "And I'll bet there are more ahead, there."

They came to a stop where the hallway ended at a great square central hall. There were elevators, there, on two of the sides, and four escalators, still usable as stairways. But it was the walls, and the paintings on them, that brought them up short and staring.

They were clouded with dirt—she was trying to imagine what they must have looked like originally, and at the same time estimating the labor that would be involved in cleaning them—but they were still distinguishable, as was the word, *Darfhulva*, in golden letters above each of the four sides. It was a moment before she realized, from the murals, that she had at last found a meaningful Martian word. They were a vast historical panorama, clockwise around the room. A group of skin-clad savages squatting around a fire. Hunters with bows and spears, carrying the carcass of an animal slightly like a pig. Nomads riding long-legged, graceful mounts like hornless deer. Peasants sowing and reaping; mud-walled hut villages, and cities; processions of priests and warriors; battles with swords and bows, and with cannon and muskets; galleys, and ships with sails, and ships without visible means of propulsion, and aircraft. Changing costumes and weapons and machines and styles of architecture. A richly fertile landscape, gradually merging into barren deserts and bushlands—the time of the great planet-wide drought. The Canal Builders—men with machines recognizable as steam-shovels and derricks, digging and quarrying and driving across the empty plains with aqueducts. More cities—seaports on the shrinking oceans; dwindling, half-deserted cities; an abandoned city, with four tiny humanoid figures and a thing like a combat-car in the middle of a brush-grown plaza, they and their vehicle dwarfed by the huge lifeless buildings around them. She had not the least doubt; *Darfhulva* was History.

"Wonderful!" von Ohlmhorst was saying. "The entire history of this race. Why, if the painter depicted appropriate costumes and weapons and machines for each period, and got the architecture right, we can break the history of this planet into eras and periods and civilizations."

"You can assume they're authentic. The faculty of this university would insist on authenticity in the *Darfhulva*—History—Department," she said.

"Yes! *Darfhulva*—History! And your magazine was a journal of *Sornhulva!*" Penrose exclaimed. "You have a word, Martha!" It took her an instant to realize that he had called her by her first name, and not Dr. Dane. She wasn't sure if that weren't a bigger triumph than learning a word of the Martian language. Or a more auspicious start. "Alone, I suppose that *hulva* means something like science or knowledge, or study; combined, it would be equivalent to our 'ology. And *darf* would mean something like past, or old times, or human events, or chronicles."

"That gives you three words, Martha!" Sachiko jubilated. "You did it."

"Let's don't go too fast," Lattimer said, for once not derisively. "I'll admit that *darfhulva* is the Martian word for history as a subject of study; I'll admit that *hulva* is the general word and *darf* modifies it and tells us which subject is meant. But as for assigning specific meanings, we can't do that because we don't know just how the Martians thought, scientifically or otherwise."

He stopped short, startled by the blue-white light that blazed as Sid Chamberlain's Kliegettes went on. When the whirring of the camera stopped, it was Chamberlain who was speaking:

"This is the biggest thing yet; the whole history of Mars, stone age to the end, all on four walls. I'm taking this with the fast shutter, but we'll telecast it in slow motion, from the beginning to the end. Tony, I want you to do the voice for it—

running commentary, interpretation of each scene as it's shown. Would you do that?"

Would he do that! Martha thought. If he had a tail, he'd be wagging it at the very thought.

"Well, there ought to be more murals on the other floors," she said. "Who wants to come downstairs with us?"

Sachiko did; immediately, Ivan Fitzgerald volunteered. Sid decided to go uptairs with Tony Lattimer, and Gloria Standish decided to go upstairs, too. Most of the party would remain on the seventh floor, to help Selim von Ohlmhorst get it finished. After poking tentatively at the escalator with the spike of her ice axe, Martha led the way downward.

The sixth floor was *Darfhulva*, too; military and technological history, from the character of the murals. They looked around the central hall, and went down to the fifth; it was like the floors above except that the big quadrangle was stacked with dusty furniture and boxes. Ivan Fitzgerald, who was carrying the floodlight, swung it slowly around. Here the murals were of heroic-sized Martians, so human in appearance as to seem members of her own race, each holding some object—a book, or a testtube, or some bit of scientific apparatus, and behind them were scenes of laboratories and factories, flame and smoke, lightning-flashes. The word at the top of each of the four walls was one with which she was already familiar—*Sornhulva*.

"Hey, Martha; there's that word," Ivan Fitzgerald exclaimed. "The one in the title of your magazine." He looked at the paintings. "Chemistry, or physics."

"Both," Hubert Penrose considered. "I don't think the Martians made any sharp distinction between them. See, the old fellow with the scraggly whiskers must be the inventor of the spectroscope; he has one in his hands, and he has a rainbow behind him. And the woman in the blue smock, beside him, worked in organic chemistry; see the diagrams of long-chain molecules behind her. What word would convey the idea of chemistry and physics taken as one subject?"

"*Sornhulva*," Sachiko suggested. "If *hulva's* something like science, *sorn* must mean matter, or substance, or physical object.

You were right, all along, Martha. A civilization like this
would certainly leave something like this, that would be self-
explanatory."

"This'll wipe a little more of that superior grin off Tony Lattimer's face," Fitzgerald was saying, as they went down the
motionless escalator to the floor below. "Tony wants to be a big
shot. When you want to be a big shot, you can't bear the possibility of anybody else being a bigger big shot, and whoever
makes a start on reading this language will be the biggest big
shot archaeology ever saw."

That was true. She hadn't thought of it, in that way, before,
and now she tried not to think about it. She didn't want to be a
big shot. She wanted to be able to read the Martian language,
and find things out about the Martians.

Two escalators down, they came out on a mezzanine around a
wide central hall on the street level, the floor forty feet below
them and the ceiling thirty feet above. Their lights picked out
object after object below—a huge group of sculptured figures in
the middle; some kind of a motor vehicle jacked up on trestles
for repairs; things that looked like machine-guns and auto-
cannon; long tables, tops littered with a dust-covered miscellany;
machinery; boxes and crates and containers.

They made their way down and walked among the clutter,
missing a hundred things for every one they saw, until they
found an escalator to the basement. There were three base-
ments, one under another, until at last they stood at the bottom
of the last escalator on a bare concrete floor, swinging the portable floodlight over stacks of boxes and barrels and drums, and
heaps of powdery dust. The boxes were plastic—nobody had
ever found anything made of wood in the city—and the barrels
and drums were of metal or glass or some glasslike substance.
They were outwardly intact. The powdery heaps might have
been anything organic, or anything containing fluid. Down here,
where wind and dust could not reach, evaporation had been the
only force of destruction after the minute life that caused putrefaction had vanished.

They found refrigeration rooms, too, and using Martha's ice
axe and the pistollike vibratool Sachiko carried on her belt, they

pounded and pried one open, to find desiccated piles of what had been vegetables, and leathery chunks of meat. Samples of that stuff, rocketed up to the ship, would give a reliable estimate, by radio-carbon dating, of how long ago this building had been occupied. The refrigeration unit, radically different from anything their own culture had produced, had been electrically powered. Sachiko and Penrose, poking into it, found the switches still on; the machine had only ceased to function when the power-source, whatever that had been, had failed.

The middle basement had also been used, at least toward the end, for storage; it was cut in half by a partition pierced by but one door. They took half an hour to force this, and were on the point of sending above for heavy equipment when it yielded enough for them to squeeze through. Fitzgerald in the lead with the light, stopped short, looked around, and then gave a groan that came through his helmet-speaker like a foghorn.

"Oh, no! *No!*"

"What's the matter, Ivan?" Sachiko, entering behind him, asked anxiously.

He stepped aside. "Look at it, Sachi! Are we going to have to do all that?"

Martha crowded through behind her friend and looked around, then stood motionless, dizzy with excitement. Books. Case on case of books, half an acre of cases, fifteen feet to the ceiling. Fitzgerald, and Penrose, who had pushed in behind her, were talking in rapid excitement; she only heard the sound of their voices, not their words. This must be the main stacks of the university library—the entire literature of the vanished race of Mars. In the center, down an aisle between the cases, she could see the hollow square of the librarians' desk, and stairs and a dumbwaiter to the floor above.

She realized that she was walking forward, with the others, toward this. Sachiko was saying: "I'm the lightest; let me go first." She must be talking about the spidery metal stairs.

"I'd say they were safe," Penrose answered. "The trouble we've had with doors around here shows that the metal hasn't deteriorated."

In the end, the Japanese girl led the way, more catlike than

ever in her caution. The stairs were quite sound, in spite of their
fragile appearance, and they all followed her. The floor above
was a duplicate of the room they had entered, and seemed to
contain about as many books. Rather than waste time forcing
the door here, they returned to the middle basement and came
up by the escalator down which they had originally descended.

The upper basement contained kitchens—electric stoves, some
with pots and pans still on them—and a big room that must
have been, originally, the students' dining room, though when
last used it had been a workshop. As they expected, the library
reading room was on the street-level floor, directly above the
stacks. It seemed to have been converted into a sort of common
living room for the building's last occupants. An adjoining audi-
torium had been made into a chemical works; there were vats
and distillation apparatus, and a metal fractionating tower that
extended through a hole knocked in the ceiling seventy feet
above. A good deal of plastic furniture of the sort they had been
finding everywhere in the city was stacked about, some of it
broken up, apparently for reprocessing. The other rooms on the
street floor seemed also to have been devoted to manufacturing
and repair work; a considerable industry, along a number of
lines, must have been carried on here for a long time after the
university had ceased to function as such.

On the second floor, they found a museum; many of the exhibits remained, tantalizingly half-visible in grimed glass cases.
There had been administrative offices there, too. The doors of
most of them were closed, and they did not waste time trying
to force them, but those that were open had been turned into
living quarters. They made notes, and rough floor-plans, to
guide them in future, more thorough examination; it was almost
noon before they had worked their way back to the seventh floor.

Selim von Ohlmhorst was in a room on the north side of the
building, sketching the position of things before examining them
and collecting them for removal. He had the floor checker-
boarded with a grid of chalked lines, each numbered.

"We have everything on this floor photographed," he said. "I
have three gangs—all the floodlights I have—sketching and
making measurements. At the rate we're going, with time out
for lunch, we'll be finished by the middle of the afternoon."

"You've been working fast. Evidently you aren't being high-church about a 'qualified archaeologist' entering rooms first," Penrose commented.

"Ach, childishness!" the old man exclaimed impatiently. "These officers of yours aren't fools. All of them have been to Intelligence School and Criminal Investigation School. Some of the most careful amateur archaeologists I ever knew were retired soldiers or policemen. But there isn't much work to be done. Most of the rooms are either empty or like this one—a few bits of furniture and broken trash and scraps of paper. Did you find anything down on the lower floors?"

"Well, yes," Penrose said, a hint of mirth in his voice. "What would you say, Martha?"

She started to tell Selim. The others, unable to restrain their excitement, broke in with interruptions. Von Ohlmhorst was staring in incredulous amazement.

"But this floor was looted almost clean, and the buildings we've entered before were all looted from the street level up," he said, at length.

"The people who looted this one lived here," Penrose replied. "They had electric power to the last; we found refrigerators full of food, and stoves with the dinner still on them. They must have used the elevators to haul things down from the upper floor. The whole first floor was converted into workshops and laboratories. I think that this place must have been something like a monastery in the Dark Ages in Europe, or what such a monastery would have been like if the Dark Ages had followed the fall of a highly developed scientific civilization. For one thing, we found a lot of machine-guns and light auto-cannon on the street level, and all the doors were barricaded. The people here were trying to keep a civilization running after the rest of the planet had gone back to barbarism; I suppose they'd have to fight off raids by the barbarians now and then."

"You're not going to insist on making this building into expedition quarters, I hope, colonel?" von Ohlmhorst asked anxiously.

"Oh, no! This place is an archaeological treasure-house. More than that; from what I saw, our technicians can learn a lot, here. But you'd better get this floor cleaned up as soon as you can, though. I'll have the subsurface part, from the sixth floor down, airsealed. Then we'll put in oxygen generators and power units, and get a couple of elevators into service. For the floor above, we can use temporary airsealing floor by floor, and portable equipment; when we have things atmosphered and lighted and heated, you and Martha and Tony Lattimer can go to work systematically and in comfort, and I'll give you all the help I can spare from the other work. This is one of the biggest things we've found yet."

Tony Lattimer and his companions came down to the seventh floor a little later.

"I don't get this, at all," he began, as soon as he joined them. "This building wasn't stripped the way the others were. Always, the procedure seems to have been to strip from the bottom up, but they seem to have stripped the top floors first, here. All but the very top. I found out what that conical thing is, by the way. It's a wind-rotor, and under it there's an electric generator. This building generated its own power."

"What sort of condition are the generators in?" Penrose asked.

"Well, everything's full of dust that blew in under the rotor, of course, but it looks to be in pretty good shape. Hey, I'll bet that's it! They had power, so they used the elevators to haul stuff down. That's just what they did. Some of the floors above here don't seem to have been touched, though." He paused momentarily; back of his oxy-mask, he seemed to be grinning. "I don't know that I ought to mention this in front of Martha, but two floors above we hit a room—it must have been the reference library for one of the departments—that had close to five hundred books in it."

The noise that interrupted him, like the squawking of a Brobdingnagian parrot, was only Ivan Fitzgerald laughing through his helmet-speaker.

Lunch at the huts was a hasty meal, with a gabble of full-mouthed and excited talking. Hubert Penrose and his chief subordinates snatched their food in a huddled consultation at one end of the table; in the afternoon, work was suspended on everything else and the fifty-odd men and women of the expedition concentrated their efforts on the University. By the middle of the afternoon, the seventh floor had been completely examined, photographed and sketched, and the murals in the square central hall covered with protective tarpaulins, and Laurent Gicquel and his airsealing crew had moved in and were at work. It had been decided to seal the central hall at the entrances. It took the French-Canadian engineer most of the afternoon to find all the ventilation-ducts and plug them. An elevator-shaft on the north side was found reaching clear to the twenty-fifth floor; this would give access to the top of the building; another shaft, from the center, would take care of the floors below. Nobody seemed willing to trust the ancient elevators, themselves; it was the next evening before a couple of cars and the necessary machinery could be fabricated in the machine shops aboard the ship and sent down by landing-rocket. By that time, the airsealing was finished, the nuclear-electric energy-converters were in place, and the oxygen generators set up.

Martha was in the lower basement, an hour or so before lunch the day after, when a couple of Space Force officers came out of the elevator, bringing extra lights with them. She was still using oxygen-equipment; it was a moment before she realized that the newcomers had no masks, and that one of them was smoking. She took off her own helmet-speaker, throat-mike and mask and unslung her tank-pack, breathing cautiously. The air was chilly, and musty-acrid with the odor of antiquity—the first Martian odor she had smelled—but when she lit a cigarette, the lighter flamed clear and steady and the tobacco caught and burned evenly.

The archaeologists, many of the other civilian scientists, a few of the Space Force officers and the two news-correspondents, Sid Chamberlain and Gloria Standish, moved in that evening, setting up cots in vacant rooms. They installed electric stoves and a refrigerator in the old Library Reading Room, and put in a bar and lunch counter. For a few days, the place was full of noise and activity, then, gradually, the Space Force people and all but a few of the civilians returned to their own work. There was still the business of airsealing the more habitable of the buildings already explored, and fitting them up in readiness for the arrival, in a year and a half, of the five hundred members of

the main expedition. There was work to be done enlarging the
landing field for the ship's rocket craft, and building new chem-
ical-fuel tanks.

There was the work of getting the city's ancient reservoirs
cleared of silt before the next spring thaw brought more water
down the underground aquaducts everybody called canals in
mistranslation of Schiaparelli's Italian word, though this was
proving considerably easier than anticipated. The ancient Canal-
Builders must have anticipated a time when their descendants
would no longer be capable of maintenance work, and had prepared against it. By the day after the University had been made
completely habitable, the actual work there was being done by
Selim, Tony Lattimer and herself, with half a dozen Space Force
officers, mostly girls, and four or five civilians, helping.

They worked up from the bottom, dividing the floor-surfaces
into numbered squares, measuring and listing and sketching and
photographing. They packaged samples of organic matter and
sent them up to the ship for Carbon-14 dating and analysis;
they opened cans and jars and bottles, and found that everything fluid in them had evaporated, through the porosity of glass
and metal and plastic if there were no other way. Wherever they
looked, they found evidence of activity suddenly suspended and
never resumed. A vise with a bar of metal in it, half cut through
and the hacksaw beside it. Pots and pans with hardened remains
of food in them; a leathery cut of meat on a table, with the
knife ready at hand. Toilet articles on washstands; unmade
beds, the bedding ready to crumble at a touch but still retaining
the impress of the sleeper's body; papers and writing materials
on desks, as though the writer had gotten up, meaning to return
and finish a fifty-thousand-year-ago moment.

It worried her. Irrationally, she began to feel that the Martians had never left this place; that they were still around her,
watching disapprovingly every time she picked up something
they had laid down. They haunted her dreams, now, instead of
their enigmatic writing. At first, everybody who had moved into
the University had taken a separate room, happy to escape the
crowding and lack of privacy of the huts. After a few nights,
she was glad when Gloria Standish moved in with her, and ac-

cepted the newswoman's excuse that she felt lonely without somebody to talk to before falling asleep. Sachiko Koremitsu joined them the next evening, and before going to bed, the girl officer cleaned and oiled her pistol, remarking that she was afraid some rust may have gotten into it.

The others felt it, too. Selim von Ohlmhorst developed the habit of turning quickly and looking behind him, as though trying to surprise somebody or something that was stalking him. Tony Lattimer, having a drink at the bar that had been improvised from the librarian's desk in the Reading Room, set down his glass and swore.

"You know what this place is? It's an archaeological *Marie Celeste!*" he declared. "It was occupied right up to the end—we've all seen the shifts these people used to keep a civilization going here—but what was the end? What happened to them? Where did they go?"

"You didn't expect them to be waiting out front, with a red carpet and a big banner, *Welcome Terrans*, did you, Tony?" Gloria Standish asked.

"No, of course not; they've all been dead for fifty thousand years. But if they were the last of the Martians, why haven't we found their bones, at least? Who buried them, after they were dead?" He looked at the glass, a bubble-thin goblet, found, with hundreds of others like it, in a closet above, as though debating with himself whether to have another drink. Then he voted in the affirmative and reached for the cocktail pitcher. "And every door on the old ground level is either barred or barricaded from the inside. How did they get out? And why did they leave?"

The next day, at lunch, Sachiko Koremitsu had the answer to the second question. Four or five electrical engineers had come down by rocket from the ship, and she had been spending the morning with them, in oxy-masks, at the top of the building.

"Tony, I thought you said those generators were in good shape," she began, catching sight of Lattimer. "They aren't. They're in the most unholy mess I ever saw. What happened, up there, was that the supports of the wind-rotor gave way, and weight snapped the main shaft, and smashed everything under it."

"Well, after fifty thousand years, you can expect something like that," Lattimer retorted. "When an archaeologist says something's in good shape, he doesn't necessarily mean it'll start as soon as you shove a switch in."

"You didn't notice that it happened when the power was on, did you?" one of the engineers asked, nettled at Lattimer's tone. "Well, it was. Everything's burned out or shorted or fused together; I saw one busbar eight inches across melted clean in two. It's a pity we didn't find things in good shape, even archaeologically speaking. I saw a lot of interesting things, things in advance of what we're using now. But it'll take a couple of years to get everything sorted out and figure what it looked like originally."

"Did it look as though anybody'd made any attempt to fix it?" Martha asked.

Sachiko shook her head. "They must have taken one look at it and given up. I don't believe there would have been any possible way to repair anything."

"Well, that explains why they left. They needed electricity for lighting, and heating, and all of their industrial equipment was electrical. They had a good life, here, with power; without it, this place wouldn't have been habitable."

"Then why did they barricade everything from the inside, and how did they get out?" Lattimer wanted to know.

"To keep other people from breaking in and looting. Last man out probably barred the last door and slid down a rope from upstairs," von Ohlmhorst suggested. "This Houdini-trick doesn't worry me too much. We'll find out eventually."

"Yes, about the time Martha starts reading Martian," Lattimer scoffed.

"That may be just when we'll find out," von Ohlmhorst replied seriously. "It wouldn't surprise me if they left something in writing when they evacuated this place."

"Are you really beginning to treat this pipe dream of hers as a serious possibility, Selim?" Lattimer demanded. "I know, it would be a wonderful thing, but wonderful things don't happen just because they're wonderful. Only because they're possible, and this isn't. Let me quote that distinguished Hittitologist, Johannes Friedrich: 'Nothing can be translated out of nothing.' Or that later but not less distinguished Hittitologist, Selim von Ohlmhorst: 'Where are you going to get your bilingual?' "

"Friedrich lived to see the Hittite language deciphered and read," von Ohlmhorst reminded him.

"Yes, when they found Hittite-Assyrian bilinguals." Lattimer measured a spoonful of coffee-powder into his cup and added hot water. "Martha, you ought to know, better than anybody, how little chance you have. You've been working for years in the Indus Valley; how many words of Harappa have you or anybody else ever been able to read?"

"We never found a university, with a half-million-volume library, at Harappa or Mohenjo-Daro."

"And, the first day we entered this building, we established meanings for several words," Selim von Ohlmhorst added.

"And you've never found another meaningful word since," Lattimer added. "And you're only sure of general meaning, not specific meaning of word-elements, and you have a dozen different interpretations for each word."

"We made a start," von Ohlmhorst maintained. "We have Grotefend's word for 'king.' But I'm going to be able to read some of those books, over there, if it takes me the rest of my life here. It probably will, anyhow."

"You mean you've changed your mind about going home on the *Cyrano?*" Martha asked. "You'll stay on here?"

The old man nodded. "I can't leave this. There's too much to discover. The old dog will have to learn a lot of new tricks, but this is where my work will be, from now on."

Lattimer was shocked. "You're nuts!" he cried. "You mean you're going to throw away everything you've accomplished in Hittitology and start all over again here on Mars? Martha, if you've talked him into this crazy decision, you're a criminal!"

"Nobody talked me into anything," von Ohlmhorst said roughly. "And as for throwing away what I've accomplished in Hittitology, I don't know what the devil you're talking about. Everything I know about the Hittite Empire is published and available to anybody. Hittitology's like Egyptology; it's stopped being research and archaeology and become scholarship and history. And I'm not a scholar or a historian; I'm a pick-and-shovel field archaeologist—a highly skilled and specialized grave-robber and junk-picker—and there's more pick-and-shovel work on this planet than I could do in a hundred lifetimes. This is something new; I was a fool to think I could turn my back on it and go back to scribbling footnotes about Hittite kings."

"You could have anything you wanted, in Hittitology. There are a dozen universities that'd sooner have you than a winning football team. But no! You have to be the top man in Martiology, too. You can't leave that for anybody else—" Lattimer shoved his chair back and got to his feet, leaving the table with an oath that was almost a sob of exasperation.

Maybe his feelings were too much for him. Maybe he realized, as Martha did, what he had betrayed. She sat, avoiding the eyes of the others, looking at the ceiling, as embarrassed as though Lattimer had flung something dirty on the table in front of them. Tony Lattimer had, desperately, wanted Selim to go home on the *Cyrano*. Martiology was a new field; if Selim entered it, he would bring with him the reputation he had already built in Hittitology, automatically stepping into the leading role that Lattimer had coveted for himself. Ivan Fitzgerald's words echoed back to her—when you want to be a big shot, you can't bear the possibility of anybody else being a bigger big shot. His derision of her own efforts became comprehensible, too. It wasn't that he was convinced that she would never learn to read the Martian language. He had been afraid that she would.

Ivan Fitzgerald finally isolated the germ that had caused the Finchly girl's undiagnosed illness. Shortly afterward the malady turned into a mild fever, from which she recovered. Nobody else seemed to have caught it. Fitzgerald was still trying to find out how the germ had been transmitted.

They found a globe of Mars, made when the city had been a seaport. They located the city, and learned that its name had been Kukan—or something with a similar vowel-consonant ratio. Immediately, Sid Chamberlain and Gloria Standish began giving their telecasts a Kukan dateline, and Hubert Penrose used the name in his official reports. They also found a Martian calendar;

the year had been divided into ten more or less equal months, and one of them had been Doma. Another month was Nor, and that was a part of the name of the scientific journal Martha had found.

Bill Chandler, the zoologist, had been going deeper and deeper into the old sea bottom of Syrtis. Four hundred miles from Kukan, and at fifteen thousand feet lower altitude, he shot a bird. At least, it was something with wings and what were almost but not quite feathers, though it was more reptilian than avian in general characteristics. He and Ivan Fitzgerald skinned and mounted it, and then dissected the carcass almost tissue by tissue. About seven-eighths of its body capacity was lungs; it certainly breathed air containing at least half enough oxygen to support human life, or five times as much as the air around Kukan.

That took the center of interest away from archaeology, and started a new burst of activity. All the expedition's aircraft— four jetticopters and three wingless airdyne reconnaissance fighters—were thrown into intensified exploration of the lower sea bottoms, and the bio-science boys and girls were wild with excitement and making new discoveries on each flight.

The University was left to Selim and Martha and Tony Lattimer, the latter keeping to himself while she and the old Turco-German worked together. The civilian specialists in other fields, and the Space Force people who had been holding tape lines and making sketches and snapping cameras, were all flying to lower Syrtis to find out how much oxygen there was and what kind of life it supported.

Sometimes Sachiko dropped in; most of the time she was busy helping Ivan Fitzgerald dissect specimens. They had four or five species of what might loosely be called birds, and something that could easily be classed as a reptile, and a carnivorous mammal the size of a cat with birdlike claws, and a herbivore almost identical with the piglike thing in the big *Darfhulva* mural, and another like a gazelle with a single horn in the middle of its forehead.

The high point came when one party, at thirty thousand feet below the level of Kukan, found breathable air. One of them had a mild attack of *sorroche* and had to be flown back for treatment in a hurry, but the others showed no ill effects. The daily newscasts from Terra showed a corresponding shift in interest at home. The discovery of the University had focused attention on the dead past of Mars; now the public was interested in Mars as a possible home for humanity. It was Tony Lattimer who brought archaeology back into the activities of the expedition and the news at home.

Martha and Selim were working in the museum on the second floor, scrubbing the grime from the glass cases, noting contents, and grease-penciling numbers; Lattimer and a couple of Space Force officers were going through what had been the administrative offices on the other side. It was one of these, a young second lieutenant, who came hurrying in from the mezzanine, almost bursting with excitement.

"Hey, Martha! Dr. von Ohlmhorst! he was shouting. "Where are you? Tony's found the Martians!"

Selim dropped his rag back in the bucket; she laid her clipboard on top of the case beside her.

"Where?" they asked together.

"Over on the north side." The lieutenant took hold of himself and spoke more deliberately. "Little room, back of one of the old faculty offices—conference room. It was locked from the inside, and we had to burn it down with a torch. That's where they are. Eighteen of them, around a long table—"

Gloria Standish, who had dropped in for lunch, was on the mezzanine, fairly screaming into a radiophone extension:

". . . Dozen and a half of them! Well, of course they're dead. What a question! They look like skeletons covered with leather. No, I do not know what they died of. Well, forget it; I don't care if Bill Chandler's found a three-headed hippopotamus. Sid, don't you get it? We've found the *Martians!*"

She slammed the phone back on its hook, rushing away ahead of them.

Martha remembered the closed door; on the first survey, they hadn't attempted opening it. Now it was burned away at both sides and lay, still hot along the edges, on the floor of the big office room in front. A floodlight was on in the room inside, and Lattimer was going around looking at things while a Space Force officer stood by the door. The center of the room was filled by a long table; in armchairs around it sat the eighteen men and women who had occupied the room for the last fifty millennia. There were bottles and glasses on the table in front of them, and, had she seen them in a dimmer light, she would have thought that they were merely dozing over their drinks. One had a knee hooked over his chair-arm and was curled in foetus-like sleep. Another had fallen forward onto the table, arms extended, the emerald set of a ring twinkling dully on one finger. Skeletons covered with leather, Gloria Standish had called them, and so they were—faces like skulls, arms and legs like sticks, the flesh shrunken onto the bones under it.

"Isn't this something!" Lattimer was exulting. "Mass suicide, that's what it was. Notice what's in the corners?"

Braziers, made of perforated two-gallon-odd metal cans, the white walls smudged with smoke above them. Von Ohlmhorst had noticed them at once, and was poking into one of them with his flashlight.

"Yes; charcoal. I noticed a quantity of it around a couple of hand-forges in the shop on the first floor. That's why you had so much trouble breaking in; they'd sealed the room on the inside." He straightened and went around the room, until he found a ventilator, and peered into it. "Stuffed with rags. They must have been all that were left, here. Their power was gone, and they were old and tired, and all around them their world was dying. So they just came in here and lit the charcoal, and sat drinking together till they all fell asleep. Well, we know what became of them, now, anyhow."

Sid and Gloria made the most of it. The Terran public wanted to hear about Martians, and if live Martians couldn't be found, a room full of dead ones was the next best thing. Maybe an even better thing; it had been only sixty-odd years since the Orson Welles invasion-scare. Tony Lattimer, the discoverer, was beginning to cash in on his attentions to Gloria and his ingratiation with Sid; he was always either making voice-and-image talks for telecast or listening to the news from the home planet. Without question, he had become, overnight, the most widely known archaeologist in history.

"Not that I'm interested in all this, for myself," he disclaimed, after listening to the telecast from Terra two days after his discovery. "But this is going to be a big thing for Martian archaeology. Bring it to the public attention; dramatize it. Selim, can you remember when Lord Carnarvon and Howard Carter found the tomb of Tutankhamen?"

"In 1923? I was two years old, then," von Ohlmhorst chuckled. "I really don't know how much that publicity ever did for Egyptology. Oh, the museums did devote more space to Egyptian exhibits, and after a museum department head gets a few extra showcases, you know how hard it is to make him give them up. And, for a while, it was easier to get financial support for new excavations. But I don't know how much good all this public excitement really does, in the long run."

"Well, I think one of us should go back on the *Cyrano,* when the *Schiaparelli* orbits in," Lattimer said. "I'd hoped it would be you; your voice would carry the most weight. But I think it's important that one of us go back, to present the story of our work, and what we have accomplished and what we hope to accomplish, to the public and to the universities and the learned societies, and to the Federation Government. There will be a great deal of work that will have to be done. We must not allow the other scientific fields and the so-called practical interests to monopolize public and academic support. So, I believe I shall go back at least for a while, and see what I can do—"

Lectures. The organization of a Society of Martian Archaeology, with Anthony Lattimer, Ph.D., the logical candidate for the chair. Degrees, honors; the deference of the learned, and the adulation of the lay public. Positions, with impressive titles and salaries. Sweet are the uses of publicity.

She crushed out her cigarette and got to her feet. "Well, I still have the final lists of what we found in *Halvhulva*—Biology —department to check over. I'm starting on Sornhulva tomorrow, and I want that stuff in shape for expert evaluation."

That was the sort of thing Tony Lattimer wanted to get away

from, the detail-work and the drudgery. Let the infantry do the slogging through the mud; the brass-hats got the medals.

She was halfway through the fifth floor, a week later, and was having midday lunch in the reading room on the first floor when Hubert Penrose came over and sat down beside her, asking her what she was doing. She told him.

"I wonder if you could find me a couple of men, for an hour or so," she added. "I'm stopped by a couple of jammed doors at the central hall. Lecture room and library, if the layout of that floor's anything like the ones below it."

"Yes. I'm a pretty fair door-buster, myself." He looked around the room. "There's Jeff Miles; he isn't doing much of anything. And we'll put Sid Chamberlain to work, for a change, too. The four of us ought to get your doors open." He called to Chamberlain, who was carrying his tray over to the dish washer. "Oh, Sid; you doing anything for the next hour or so?"

"I was going up to the fourth floor, to see what Tony's doing."

"Forget it. Tony's bagged his season limit of Martians. I'm going to help Martha bust in a couple of doors; we'll probably find a whole cemetery full of Martians."

Chamberlain shrugged. "Why not. A jammed door can have anything back of it, and I know what Tony's doing—just routine stuff."

Jeff Miles, the Space Force captain, came over, accompanied by one of the lab-crew from the ship who had come down on the rocket the day before.

"This ought to be up your alley, Mort," he was saying to his companion. "Chemistry and physics department. Want to come along?"

The lab man, Mort Tranter, was willing. Seeing the sights was what he'd come down from the ship for. She finished her coffee and cigarette, and they went out into the hall together, gathered equipment and rode the elevator to the fifth floor.

The lecture hall door was the nearest; they attacked it first. With proper equipment and help, it was no problem and in ten minutes they had it open wide enough to squeeze through with the floodlights. The room inside was quite empty, and, like most of the rooms behind closed doors, comparatively free from dust. The students, it appeared, had sat with their backs to the door, facing a low platform, but their seats and the lecturer's table and equipment had been removed. The two side walls bore inscriptions: on the right, a pattern of concentric circles which she recognized as a diagram of atomic structure, and on the left a complicated table of numbers and words, in two columns. Tranter was pointing at the diagram on the right.

"They got as far as the Bohr atom, anyhow," he said. "Well, not quite. They knew about electron shells, but they have the nucleus pictured as a solid mass. No indication of proton-and-neutron structure. I'll bet, when you come to translate their scientific books, you'll find that they taught that the atom was the ultimate and indivisible particle. That explains why you people never found any evidence that the Martians used nuclear energy."

"That's a uranium atom," Captain Miles mentioned.

"It is?" Sid Chamberlain asked, excitedly. "Then they did know about atomic energy. Just because we haven't found any pictures of A-bomb mushrooms doesn't mean—"

She turned to look at the other wall. Sid's signal reactions were getting away from him again; uranium meant nuclear power to him, and the two words were interchangeable. As she studied the arrangement of the numbers and words, she could hear Tranter saying:

"Nuts, Sid. We knew about uranium a long time before anybody found out what could be done with it. Uranium was discovered on Terra in 1789, by Klaproth."

There was something familiar about the table on the left wall. She tried to remember what she had been taught in school about physics, and what she had picked up by accident afterward. The second column was a continuation of the first: there were forty-six items in each, each item numbered consecutively—

"Probably used uranium because it's the largest of the natural atoms," Penrose was saying. "The fact that there's nothing beyond it there shows that they hadn't created any of the transuranics. A student could go to that thing and point out the outer electron of any of the ninety-two elements."

Ninety-two! That was it; there were ninety-two items in the table on the left wall! Hydrogen was Number One, she knew; One, *Sarfaldsorn*. Helium was Two; that was *Tirfaldsorn*. She couldn't remember which element came next, but in Martian it was *Sarfalddavas*. *Sorn* must mean matter, or substance, then. And *davas;* she was trying to think of what it could be. She turned quickly to the others, catching hold of Hubert Penrose's arm with one hand and waving her clipboard with the other.

"Look at this thing, over here," she was clamoring excitedly. "Tell me what you think it is. Could it be a table of the elements?"

They all turned to look. Mort Tranter stared at it for a moment.

"Could be. If I only knew what those squiggles meant—"

That was right; he'd spent his time aboard the ship.

"If you could read the numbers, would that help?" she asked, beginning to set down the Arabic digits and their Martian equivalents. "It's decimal system, the same as we use."

"Sure. If that's a table of elements, all I'd need would be the numbers. Thanks," he added as she tore off the sheet and gave it to him.

Penrose knew the numbers, and was ahead of him. "Ninety-two items, numbered consecutively. The first number would be the atomic number. Then a single word, the name of the element. Then the atomic weight—"

She began reading off the names of the elements. "I know hydrogen and helium; what's *tirfalddavas*, the third one?"

"Lithium," Tranter said. "The atomic weights aren't run out past the decimal point. Hydrogen's one plus, if that double-hook dingus is a plus sign; Helium's four-plus, that's right. And lithium's given as seven, that isn't right. It's six-point-nine-four-oh. Or is that thing a Martian minus sign?"

"Of course! Look! A plus sign is a hook, to hang things together; a minus sign is a knife, to cut something off from something—see, the little loop is the handle and the long pointed loop is the blade. Stylized, of course, but that's what it is. And the fourth element, *kiradavas;* what's that?"

"Beryllium. Atomic weight given as nine-and-a-hook; actually it's nine-point-oh-two."

Sid Chamberlain had been disgruntled because he couldn't get a story about the Martians having developed atomic energy. It took him a few minutes to understand the newest development, but finally it dawned on him.

"Hey! You're reading that!" he cried. "You're reading Martian!"

"That's right," Penrose told him. "Just reading it right off. I don't get the two items after the atomic weight, though. They look like months of the Martian calendar. What ought they to be, Mort?"

Tranter hesitated. "Well, the next information after the atomic weight ought to be the period and group numbers. But those are words."

"What would the numbers be for the first one, hydrogen?"

"Period One, Group One. One electron shell, one electron in the outer shell," Tranter told her. "Helium's period one, too, but it has the outer—only—electron shell full, so it's in the group of inert elements."

"*Trav, Trav. Trav's* the first month of the year. And helium's *Trav, Yenth; Yenth* is the eighth month."

"The inert elements could be called Group Eight, yes. And the third element, lithium, is Period Two, Group One. That check?"

"It certainly does. *Sanv, Trav; Sanv's* the second month. What's the first element in Period Three?"

"Sodium Number Eleven."

"That's right; it's *Krav, Trav.* Why, the names of the months are simply numbers, one to ten, spelled out."

"*Doma's* the fifth month. That was your first Martian word, Martha," Penrose told her. "The word for five. And if *davas* is the word for metal, and *sornhulva* is chemistry and/or physics, I'll bet *Tadavas Sornhulva* is literally translated as: 'Of-Metal Matter-Knowledge.' Metallurgy, in other words. I wonder what *Mastharnorvod* means." It surprised her that, after so long and with so much happening in the meantime, he could remember that. "Something like 'Journal,' or 'Review,' or maybe 'Quarterly.'"

"We'll work that out, too," she said confidently. After this, nothing seemed impossible. "Maybe we can find—" Then she stopped short. "You said 'Quarterly.' I think it was 'Monthly,' instead. It was dated for a specific month, the fifth one. And if *nor* is ten, *Mastharnorvod* could be 'Year-Tenth.' And I'll bet we'll find that *masthar* is the word for year." She looked at the table on the wall again. "Well, let's get all these words down, with translations for as many as we can."

"Let's take a break for a minute," Penrose suggested, getting out his cigarettes. "And then, let's do this in comfort. Jeff, suppose you and Sid go across the hall and see what you find in the other room in the way of a desk or something like that, and a few chairs. There'll be a lot of work to do on this."

Sid Chamberlain had been squirming as though he were afflicted with ants, trying to contain himself. Now he let go with an excited jabber.

"This is really it! *The* it, not just it-of-the-week, like finding the reservoirs or those statues or this building, or even the animals and the dead Martians! Wait till Selim and Tony see this! Wait till Tony sees it; I want to see his face! And when I get this on telecast, all Terra's going to go nuts about it!" He turned to Captain Miles. "Jeff, suppose you take a look at that other door, while I find somebody to send to tell Selim and Tony. And Gloria; wait till she sees this—"

"Take it easy, Sid," Martha cautioned. "You'd better let me have a look at your script, before you go too far overboard on the telecast. This is just a beginning; it'll take years and years before we're able to read any of those books downstairs."

"It'll go faster than you think, Martha," Hubert Penrose told her. "We'll all work on it, and we'll teleprint material to Terra, and people there will work on it. We'll send them everything we can . . . everything we work out, and copies of books, and copies of your word-lists—"

And there would be other tables—astronomical tables, tables in physics and mechanics, for instance—in which words and numbers were equivalent. The library stacks, below, would be full of them. Transliterate them into Roman alphabet spellings and Arabic numerals, and somewhere, somebody would spot each numerical significance, as Hubert Penrose and Mort Tranter and she had done with the table of elements. And pick out all the chemistry textbooks in the Library; new words would take on meaning from contexts in which the names of elements appeared. She'd have to start studying chemistry and physics, herself—

Sachiko Koremitsu peeped in through the door, then stepped inside.

"Is there anything I can do—?" she began. "What's happened? Something important?"

"Important?" Sid Chamberlain exploded. "Look at that, Sachi! We're reading it! Martha's found out how to read Martian!" He grabbed Captain Miles by the arm. "Come on, Jeff; let's go. I want to call the others—" He was still babbling as he hurried from the room.

Sachi looked at the inscription. "Is it true?" she asked, and then, before Martha could more than begin to explain, flung her arms around her. "Oh, it really is! You are reading it! I'm so happy!"

She had to start explaining again when Selim von Ohlmhorst entered. This time, she was able to finish.

"But, Martha, can you be really sure? You know, by now, that learning to read this language is as important to me as it is to you, but how can you be so sure that those words really mean things like hydrogen and helium and boron and oxygen? How do you know that their table of elements was anything like ours?"

Tranter and Penrose and Sachiko all looked at him in amazement.

"That isn't just the Martian table of elements; that's *the* table of elements. It's the only one there is," Mort Tranter almost exploded. "Look, hydrogen has one proton and one electron. If it had more of either, it wouldn't be hydrogen, it'd be something else. And the same with all the rest of the elements. And hydrogen on Mars is the same as hydrogen on Terra, or on Alpha Centauri, or in the next galaxy—"

"You just set up those numbers, in that order, and any first-year chemistry student could tell you what elements they represented," Penrose said. "Could if he expected to make a passing grade, that is."

The old man shook his head slowly, smiling. "I'm afraid I wouldn't make a passing grade. I didn't know, or at least didn't realize, that. One of the things I'm going to place an order for, to be brought on the *Schiaparelli*, will be a set of primers in chemistry and physics, of the sort intended for a bright child of ten or twelve. It seems that a Martiologist has to learn a lot of things the Hittites and the Assyrians never heard about."

Tony Lattimer, coming in, caught the last part of the explanation. He looked quickly at the walls and, having found out just what had happened, advanced and caught Martha by the hand.

"You really did it, Martha! You found your bilingual! I never believed that it would be possible; let me congratulate you!"

He probably expected that to erase all the jibes and sneers of the past. If he did, he could have it that way. His friendship would mean as little to her as his derision—except that his friends had to watch their backs and his knife. But he was going home on the *Cyrano*, to be a big shot. Or had this changed his mind for him again?

"This is something we can show the world, to justify any expenditure of time and money on Martian archaeological work. When I get back to Terra, I'll see that you're given full credit for this achievement—"

On Terra, her back and his knife would be out of her watchfulness.

"We won't need to wait that long," Hubert Penrose told him dryly. "I'm sending off an official report, tomorrow; you can be sure Dr. Dane will be given full credit, not only for this but for her previous work, which made it possible to exploit this discovery."

"And you might add, work done in spite of the doubts and discouragements of her colleagues," Selim von Ohlmhorst said. "To which I am ashamed to have to confess my own share."

"You said we had to find a bilingual," she said. "You were right, too."

"This is better than a bilingual, Martha," Hubert Penrose said. "Physical science expresses universal facts; necessarily it is a universal language. Heretofore archaeologists have dealt only with pre-scientific cultures."

For a Journal Entry . . .

This story is another about the contacts of two cultures, one dead and one alive, meeting after untold centuries. How does this meeting compare with the meeting in "The Streets of Ashkelon" or "Call Me Joe" or "Black Destroyer"? What are some of the similarities and differences in these meetings? What are some of the conventional attitudes today about Martians? What is the source of these attitudes?

From the hints and suggestions in this story, what do you think the ancient Martians looked like? What can you guess about aspects of their culture? Was their educational system much different from ours? Do you think the Martians would have been friendly? What do you think their reaction would have been to the Earth expedition if they had been alive when it landed?

For Your Consideration . . .

1. What are the similarities between the Martian civilization and our own? What are the differences?
2. Do the descriptions in the story indicate that the Martians were scientifically more advanced than the Earthmen?
3. What indications are there that Earthmen had put aside major international differences?
4. Early in the story the Rosetta Stone is mentioned. What is the Rosetta Stone? Why is it so important to Martha Dane that she find a "Rosetta Stone" on Mars?
5. What do you think caused the extinction of the Martian civilization?

6. Piper doesn't talk about the problems of getting to Mars and back in any detail. From the hints given in the story, what do you think they must have been?
7. If there were no obstacles to sending a manned expedition to Mars now, would you favor such an expedition? Why or why not?
8. "Sweet are the uses of publicity," the author remarks on page 194. Discuss this concept, pointing out the adverse aspects of publicity as well.

Notes

PAGE
158 *loess*—yellowish-brown dust
162 *conical*—cone-shaped
162 *haphazardly*—randomly, without order
164 *reticent*—to keep silent
165 *gamogenetic*—having genes
165 *placental*—having reproductive organs
165 *viviparous*—bearing live young
166 *decipher*—decode
167 *cryptanalysis*—decoding ciphers or cryptograms
169 *plausible*—believable
173 *beryllosilver alloys*—a metal mixture of beryllium and silver
174 *spalling*—chipping
175 *petulantly*—angrily, almost sulking
180 *mezzanine*—middle of three stories
180 *putrefaction*—decay, erosion
185 *tarpaulin*—canvas covering
185 *antiquity*—history before Christ, any ancient times
186 *enigmatic*—baffling, puzzling
188 *busbar*—part of a machine, usually carrying a heavy electrical load
191 *herbivore*—an animal that feeds on grass or other plants
192 *sorroche*—an illness
193 *foetus-like*—an embryo, resembling the curled-up positions of babies before birth
193 *braziers*—portable containers for fire
193 *ingratiation*—bring oneself into favor
196 *transuranics*—elements on the periodic chart beyond uranium

The Asian Shore

Thomas M. Disch

On the surface, this is the story of an American who is visiting Turkey.
He appears to have problems with the Turkish way of life—and
some Turkish people as well. Little by little, we realize that his
problems go deeper than that. They *may* be his problems and his
alone. Thomas M. Disch, poet and author, loves to travel, and he
is living in Italy at the present time. His poetry pervades his
fiction, perhaps one of the reasons why his writing is among the
most highly respected in science fiction.

I

THERE were voices on the cobbled street, and the sounds of
motors. Footsteps, slamming doors, whistles, footsteps. He lived
on the ground floor, so there was no way to avoid these evidences of the city's too abundant life. They accumulated in the
room like so much dust, like the heaps of unanswered correspondence on the mottled tablecloth.

Every night he would drag a chair into the unfurnished back
room—the guest room, as he liked to think of it—and look out
over the tiled roofs and across the black waters of the Bosphorus
at the lights of Usküdar. But the sounds penetrated this room
too. He would sit there, in the darkness, drinking wine, waiting
for her knock on the back door.

Or he might try to read: histories, books of travel, the long
dull biography of Ataturk. A kind of sedation. Sometimes he
would even begin a letter to his wife:

"Dear Janice,

"No doubt you've been wondering what's become of me these last few months. . . ."

But the trouble was that once that part had been written, the frail courtesies, the perfunctory reportage, he could not bring himself to say what *had* become of him.

Voices . . .

It was just as well that he couldn't speak the language. For a while he had studied it, taxiing three times a week to Robert College in Bebek, but the grammar, based on assumptions wholly alien to any other language he knew, with its wavering boundaries between verbs and nouns, nouns and adjectives, withstood every assault of his incorrigibly Aristotelian mind. He sat at the back of the classroom, behind the rows of American teen-agers, as sullen as convicts, as comically out-of-context as the machineries melting in a Dali landscape—sat there and parroted innocuous dialogues after the teacher, taking both roles in turn, first the trustful, inquisitive JOHN, forever wandering alone and lost in the streets of Istanbul and Ankara, then the helpful, knowing AHMET BEY. Neither of these interlocutors would admit what had become increasingly evident with each faltering word that JOHN spoke—that he would wander these same streets for years, inarticulate, cheated, and despised.

But these lessons, while they lasted, had one great advantage. They provided an illusion of activity, an obelisk upon which the eye might focus amid the desert of each new day, something to move toward and then something to leave behind.

After the first month it had rained a great deal, and this provided him with a good excuse for staying in. He had mopped up the major attractions of the city in one week, and he persisted at sightseeing long afterward, even in doubtful weather, until at last he had checked off every mosque and ruin, every museum and cistern cited in boldface in the pages of his Hachette. He visited the cemetery of Eyup, and he devoted an entire Sunday to the land walls, carefully searching out, though he could not read Greek, the inscriptions of the various Byzantine emperors. But more and more often on these excursions he would see the woman, or the child, or the woman and the child together, until he came almost to dread the sight of any woman or any child in the city. It was not an unreasonable dread.

And always, at nine o'clock, or ten at the very latest, she would come knocking at the door of the apartment. Or, if the outer door of the building had not been left ajar by the people upstairs, at the window of the front room. She knocked patiently, in little clusters of three or four raps spaced several seconds apart, never very loud. Sometimes, but only if she were in the hall, she would accompany her knocking with a few words in Turkish, usually *Yavuz! Yavuz!* He had asked the clerk at the mail desk of the Consulate what this meant, for he couldn't find it in his dictionary. It was a common Turkish name, a man's name.

His name was John. John Benedict Harris. He was an American.

She seldom stayed out there for more than half an hour any one night, knocking and calling to him, or to this imaginary Yavuz, and he would remain all that while in the chair in the unfurnished room, drinking Kavak and watching the ferries move back and forth on the dark water between Kabataş and Üsküdar, the European and the Asian shore.

He had seen her first outside the fortress of Rumeli Hisar. It was the day, shortly after he'd arrived in the city, that he had come out to register at Robert College. After paying his fees and inspecting the library, he had come down the hill by the wrong path and there it had stood, mammoth and majestically improbable, a gift. He did not know its name, and his Hachette was at the hotel. There was just the raw fact of the fortress, a mass of gray stone, its towers and crenellations, the gray Bosphorus below. He angled for a photograph, but even this far away it was too big—one could not frame the whole of it in a single shot.

He left the road, taking a path through dry brush that promised to circle the fortress. As he approached, the walls reared higher and higher. Before such walls there could be no question of an assault.

He saw her when she was about fifty feet away. She came

toward him on the footpath, carrying a large bundle wrapped in newspaper and bound with twine. Her clothes were the usual motley of washed-out cotton prints that all the poorer women of the city went about in, but she did not, like most other women of her kind, attempt to pull her shawl across her face when she noticed him.

But perhaps it was only that her bundle would have made this conventional gesture of modesty awkward, for after that first glance she did at least lower her eyes to the path. No, it was hard to discover any clear portent in this first encounter.

As they passed each other he stepped off the path, and she did mumble some word in Turkish. Thank you, he supposed. He watched her until she reached the road, wondering whether she would look back, and she didn't.

He followed the walls of the fortress down the steep crumbling hillside to the shore road without finding an entrance. It amused him to think that there might not be one. Between the water and the barbicans there was only a narrow strip of highway.

An absolutely daunting structure.

The entrance, which did exist, was just to the side of the central tower. He paid five lire admission and another two and a half lire to bring in his camera.

Of the three principal towers, visitors were allowed to climb only the one at the center of the eastern wall that ran along the Bosphorus. He was out of condition and mounted the enclosed spiral staircase slowly. The stone steps had evidently been pirated from other buildings. Every so often he recognized a fragment of a classic entablature or a wholly inappropriate intaglio design—a Greek cross or some crude Byzantine eagle. Each footfall became a symbolic conquest: one could not ascend these stairs without becoming implicated in the fall of Constantinople.

This staircase opened out onto a kind of wooden catwalk clinging to the inner wall of the tower at a height of about sixty feet. The silo-like space was resonant with the coo and flutter of invisible pigeons, and somewhere the wind was playing with a metal door, creaking it open, banging it shut. Here, if he so wished, he might discover portents.

He crept along the wooden platform, both hands grasping the iron rail stapled to the stone wall, feeling just an agreeable amount of terror, sweating nicely. It occurred to him how much this would have pleased Janice, whose enthusiasm for heights had equaled his. He wondered when, if ever, he would see her again, and what she would be like. By now undoubtedly she had begun divorce proceedings. Perhaps she was already no longer his wife.

The platform led to another stone staircase, shorter than the first, which ascended to the creaking metal door. He pushed it open and stepped out amid a flurry of pigeons into the full dazzle of the noon, the wide splendor of the elevation, sunlight above and the bright bow of water beneath—and, beyond the water, the surreal green of the Asian hills, hundred-breasted Cybele. It seemed, all of this, to demand some kind of affirmation, a yell. But he didn't feel up to yelling, or large gestures. He could only admire, at this distance, the illusion of tactility, hills as flesh, an illusion that could be heightened if he laid his hands, still sweaty from his passage along the catwalk, on the rough warm stone of the balustrade.

Looking down the side of the tower at the empty road he saw her again, standing at the very edge of the water. She was looking up at him. When he noticed her she lifted both hands above her head, as though signaling, and shouted something that, even if he could have heard it properly, he would surely not have understood. He supposed that she was asking to have her picture taken, so he turned the setting ring to the fastest speed to compensate for the glare from the water. She stood directly below the tower, and there seemed no way to frame an interesting composition. He released the shutter. Woman, water, asphalt road: it would be a snapshot, not a photograph, and he didn't believe in taking snapshots.

The woman continued to call up to him, arms raised in that same hieratic gesture. It made no sense. He waved to her and smiled uncertainly. It was something of a nuisance really. He would have preferred to have this scene to himself. One climbed towers, after all, in order to be alone.

Altin, the man who had found his apartment for him, worked as a commission agent for carpet and jewelry shops in the Grand Bazaar. He would strike up conversations with English and

American tourists and advise them what to buy, and where, and how much to pay. They spent one day looking and settled on an apartment building near Taksim, the commemorative traffic circle that served the European quarter of the city as a kind of Broadway. The several banks of Istanbul demonstrated their modern character here with neon signs, and in the center of the traffic circle, life-size, Ataturk led a small but representative group of his countrymen toward their bright, Western destiny.

The apartment was thought (by Altin) to partake of this same advanced spirit: it had central heating, a sit-down toilet, a bathtub, and a defunct but prestigious refrigerator. The rent was six hundred lire a month, which came to sixty-six dollars at the official rate but only fifty dollars at the rate Altin gave. He was anxious to move out of the hotel, so he agreed to a six-month lease.

He hated it from the day he moved in. Except for the shreds of a lousy sofa in the guest room, which he obliged the landlord to remove, he left everything as he found it. Even the blurry pinups from a Turkish girlie magazine remained where they were to cover the cracks in the new plaster. He was determined to make no accommodations: he might have to live in this city; it was not required that he *enjoy* it.

Every day he picked up his mail at the Consulate. He sampled a variety of restaurants. He saw the sights and made notes for his book.

On Thursdays he visited a hamam to sweat out the accumulated poisons of the week and to be kneaded and stomped by a masseur.

He supervised the growth of his young mustache.

He rotted, like a jar of preserves left open and forgotten on the top shelf of a cupboard.

He learned that there was a special Turkish word for the rolls of dirt that are scraped off the skin after a steambath, and another that imitated the sound of boiling water: *fuker, fuker, fuker.* Boiling water signified, to the Turkish mind, the first stages of sexual arousal. It was roughly equivalent to the stateside notion of "electricity."

Occasionally, as he began to construct his own internal map

of the unpromising alleyways and ruinous staircase streets of his
neighborhood, he fancied that he saw her, that same woman.
It was hard to be certain. She would always be some distance
away, or he might catch just a glimpse out of the corner of his
eye. If it were the same woman there was nothing at this stage
to suggest that she was pursuing him. It was, at most, a coin-
cidence.

In any case, he was not certain. Her face had not been unusual,
and he did not have the photograph to consult, for he had
spoiled the entire roll of film removing it from the camera.

Sometimes after one of these failed encounters he would feel
a slight uneasiness. It amounted to no more than that.

He met the boy in Üsküdar. It was during the first severe cold
spell, in mid-November. His first trip across the Bosphorus, and
when he stepped off the ferry onto the very soil (or, anyhow,
the very asphalt) of this new continent, the largest of all, he
could feel the great mass of it beckoning him toward its vast
eastward vortex, tugging at him, sucking at his soul.

It had been his first intention, back in New York, to stop
two months at most in Istanbul, learn the language; then into
Asia. How often he had mesmerized himself with the litany of
its marvels: the grand mosques of Kayseri and Sivas, of Beysehir
and Afyonkarahisar; the isolate grandeur of Ararat and then,
still moving east, the shores of the Caspian; Meshed, Kabul, the
Himalayas. It was all these that reached out to him now, singing,
stretching forth their siren arms, inviting him to their whirlpool.

And he? He refused. Though he could feel the charm of the
invitation, he refused. Though he might have wished very much
to unite with them, he still refused. For he had tied himself
to the mast where he was proof against their call. He had his
apartment in that city which stood just outside their reach, and
he would stay there until it was time to return. In the spring he
was going back to the States.

But he did allow the sirens this much—that he would abandon
the rational mosque-to-mosque itinerary laid down by his Hachette and entrust the rest of the day to serendipity. While the

sun still shone that afternoon they might lead him where they would.

Asphalt gave way to cobbles, and cobbles to packed dirt. The squalor here was on a much less majestic scale than in Stambul, where even the most decrepit hovels had been squeezed by the pressure of population to heights of three and four stories. In Usküdar the same wretched buildings sprawled across the hills like beggars whose crutches had been kicked out from under them, supine; through their rags of unpainted wood one could see the scabbed flesh of mud-and-wattle. As he threaded his way from one dirt street to the next and found each of them sustaining this one unvarying tone, without color, without counterpoint, he began to conceive a new Asia, not of mountains and vast plains, but this same slum rolling on perpetually across grassless hills, a continuum of drabness, the sheer dumb extent.

Because he was short and because he would not dress the part of an American, he could go through these streets without calling attention to himself. The mustache, too, probably, helped. Only his conscious, observing eyes (the camera had spoiled a second roll of film and was being repaired) would have betrayed him as a tourist today. Indeed, Altin had assured him (intending, no doubt, a compliment) that as soon as he learned to speak the language he would pass for a Turk.

It grew steadily colder throughout the afternoon. The wind moved a thick veil of mist over the sun and left it there. As the mists thinned and thickened, as the flat disk of sun, sinking westward, would fade and brighten, the vagaries of light whispered conflicting rumors about these houses and their dwellers. But he did not wish to stop and listen. He already knew more concerning these things than he wanted to. He set off at a quicker pace in the supposed direction of the landing stage.

The boy stood crying beside a public fountain, a water faucet projecting from a crude block of concrete, at the intersection of two narrow streets. Five years old, perhaps six. He was carrying a large plastic bucket of water in each hand, one bright red, the other turquoise. The water had splashed over his thin trousers and bare feet.

At first he supposed he cried only because of the cold. The damp ground must be near to freezing. To walk on it in bare wet feet . . .

Then he saw the slippers. They were what he would have called shower slippers, small die-stamped ovals of blue plastic with a single thong that had to be grasped between the first and second toe.

The boy would stoop over and force the thongs between his stiff, cold-reddened toes, but after only a step or two the slippers would again fall off his numb feet. With each frustrated progress more water would slop over the sides of the buckets. He could not keep the slippers on his feet and he would not walk off without them.

With this understanding came a kind of horror, a horror of his own helplessness. He could not go up to the boy and ask him where he lived, lift him and carry him—he was so small—to his home. Nor could he scold the child's parents for having sent him out on this errand without proper shoes or winter clothes. He could not even take up the buckets and have the child lead him to his home. For each of these possibilities demanded that he be able to *speak* to the boy, and this he could not do.

What *could* he do? Offer money? As well offer him, at such a moment, a pamphlet from the U.S. Information Agency!

There was, in fact, nothing, *nothing* he could do.

The boy had become aware of him. Now that he had a sympathetic audience he let himself cry in earnest. Lowering the two buckets to the ground and pointing at these and at the slippers, he spoke pleadingly to this grown-up stranger, to this rescuer, words in Turkish.

He took a step backward, a second step, and the boy shouted at him, what message of pain or uncomprehending indignation he would never know. He turned away and ran back along the street that had brought him to this crossway. It was another hour before he found the landing stage. It had begun to snow.

As he took his seat inside the ferry he found himself glancing at the other passengers, as though expecting to find her there among them.

The next day he came down with a cold. The fever rose through the night. He woke several times, and it was always their two faces that he carried with him from the dreams, like souvenirs whose origin and purpose have been forgotten; the woman at Rumeli Hisar, the child in Usküdar: some part of his mind had already begun to draw the equation between them.

II

It was the thesis of his first book that the quiddity of architecture, its chief claim to an aesthetic interest, was its arbitrariness. Once the lintels were lying on the posts, once some kind of roof had been spread across the hollow space, then anything else that might be done was gratuitous. Even the lintel and the post, the roof, the space below, these were gratuitous as well. Stated thus it was a mild enough notion; the difficulty was in training the eye to see the whole world of usual forms—patterns of brick, painted plaster, carved and carpentered wood—not as "buildings" and "streets" but as an infinite series of free and arbitrary choices. There was no place in such a scheme for orders, styles, sophistication, taste. Every artifact of the city was anomalous, unique, but living there in the midst of it all you could not allow yourself too fine a sense of this fact. If you did . . .

It had been his task, these last three or four years, to reeducate his eye and mind to just this condition of innocence. His was the very reverse of the Romantics' aims, for he did not expect to find himself, when this ideal state of "raw" perception was reached (it never would be, of course, for innocence, like justice, is an absolute; it may be approached but never attained), any closer to nature. Nature, as such, did not concern him. What he sought, on the contrary, was a sense of the great artifice of things, of structures, of the immense interminable wall that has been built just to exclude nature.

The attention that his first book had received showed that he had been at least partially successful, but he knew (and who better?) how far short his aim had fallen, how many clauses of the perceptual social contract he had never even thought to question.

So, since it was now a matter of ridding himself of the sense of the familiar, he had had to find some better laboratory for this purpose than New York, somewhere that he could be, more naturally, an alien. This much seemed obvious to him.

It had not seemed so obvious to his wife.

He did not insist. He was willing to be reasonable. He would talk about it. He talked about it whenever they were together— at dinner, at her friends' parties (his friends didn't seem to give parties), in bed—and it came down to this, that Janice objected not so much to the projected trip as to his entire program, the thesis itself.

No doubt her reasons were sound. The sense of the arbitrary did not stop at architecture; it embraced—or it would, if he let it—all phenomena. If there were no fixed laws that governed the furbelows and arabesques out of which a city is composed, there were equally no laws (or only arbitrary laws, which is the same as none at all) to define the relationships woven into the lattice of that city, relationships between man and man, man and woman, John and Janice.

And indeed this had already occurred to him, though he had not spoken of it to her before. He had often had to stop, in the midst of some quotidian ritual like dining out, and take his bearings. As the thesis developed, as he continued to sift away layer after layer of preconception, he found himself more and more astonished at the size of the demesne that recognized the sovereignty of convention. At times he even thought he could trace in his wife's slightest gesture, or in her aptest phrase, or in a kiss, some hint of the Palladian rulebook from which it had been derived. Perhaps with practice one would be able to document the entire history of her styles—here an echo of the Gothic Revival, there an imitation of Mies.

When his application for a Guggenheim was rejected, he decided he would make the trip by himself, using the bit of money that was still left from the book. Though he saw no necessity for it, he had agreed to Janice's request for a divorce. They parted on the best of terms. She had even seen him to the boat.

The wet snow would fall for a day, two days, forming knee-deep drifts in the open spaces of the city, in paved courtyards, on vacant lots. Cold winds polished the slush of streets and sidewalks to dull-gleaming lumpy ice. The steeper hills became impassable. The snow and the ice would linger a few days and then a sudden thaw would send it all pouring down the cobbled hillside in a single afternoon, brief Alpine cataracts of refuse and brown water. A patch of tolerable weather might follow this flood, and then another blizzard. Altin assured him that this was an unusually fierce winter, unprecedented.

A spiral diminishing.

A tightness.

And each day the light fell more obliquely across the white hills and was more quickly spent.

One night returning from a movie he slipped on the iced cobbles just outside the door of his building, tearing both knees of his trousers beyond any possibility of repair. It was the only winter suit he had brought. Altin gave him the name of a tailor who could make another suit quickly and for less money than he would have had to pay for a readymade. Altin did all the bargaining with the tailor and even selected the fabric, a heavy wool-rayon blend of a sickly and slightly iridescent blue, the muted, imprecise color of the more unhappy breeds of pigeons. He understood nothing of the fine points of tailoring and so he could not decide what it was about this suit—whether the shape of the lapels, the length of the back vent, the width of the pants legs—that made it seem so different from other suits he had worn, so much . . . smaller. And yet it fitted his figure with the exactness one expects of a tailored suit. If he looked smaller now, and thicker, perhaps that was how he *ought* to look and his previous suits had been telling lies about him all these years. The color, too, performed some nuance of metamorphosis: his skin, balanced against this blue-gray sheen, seemed less "tan" than sallow. When he wore it he became, to all appearances, a Turk.

Not that he wanted to look like a Turk. Turks were, by and large, a homely lot. He only wished to avoid the other Americans who abounded here even at this nadir of the off-season. As their numbers decreased, their gregariousness grew more implacable. The smallest sign—a copy of *Newsweek* or the *Herald Tribune*, a word of English, an airmail letter with its telltale canceled stamp—could bring them down at once in the full fury of their good-fellowship. It was convenient to have some kind of camouflage, just as it was necessary to learn their haunts in order to avoid them: Divan Yolu and Cumhuriyet Cadessi, the American Library and the Consulate, as well as some eight or ten of the principal well-touristed restaurants.

Once the winter had firmly established itself he also put a stop to his sightseeing. Two months of Ottoman mosques and Byzantine rubble had brought his sense of the arbitrary to so fine a pitch that he no longer required the stimulus of the monumental. His own rooms—a rickety table, the flowered drapes, the blurry lurid pinups, the intersecting planes of walls and ceilings —could present as great a plenitude of "problems" as the grand mosques of Suleiman or Sultan Ahmet with all their mihrabs and minbars, their stalactite niches and faienced walls.

Too great a plenitude actually. Day and night the rooms nagged at him. They diverted his attention from anything else he might try to do. He knew them with the enforced intimacy with which a prisoner knows his cell—every defect of construction, every failed grace, the precise incidence of the light at each hour of the day. He had taken the trouble to rearrange the furniture, to put up his own prints and maps, to clean the windows and scrub the floors, to fashion some kind of bookcase (all his books remained in their two shipping cases); he might have been able to blot out these alien presences by the sheer strength of self-assertion, as one can mask bad odors with incense or the smell of flowers. But this would have been admitting defeat. It would have shown how unequal he was to his own thesis.

As a compromise he began to spend his afternoons in a café a short distance down the street on which he lived. There he would sit, at the table nearest the front window, contemplating the spirals of steam that rose from the small corolla of his tea glass. At the back of the long room, beneath the tarnished brass tea urn, there were always two old men playing backgammon. The other patrons sat by themselves and gave no indication that their thoughts were in any way different from his. Even when no one was smoking, the air was pungent with the charcoal fires of nargilehs. Conversation of any kind was rare. The nargilehs bubbled, the tiny die rattled in its leather cup, a newspaper rustled, a glass chinked against its saucer.

His red notebook always lay ready to hand on the table, and on the notebook his ballpoint pen. Once he had placed them there, he never touched them again till it was time to leave.

Though less and less in the habit of analyzing sensation and motive, he was aware that the special virtue of this café was as a bastion, the securest he possessed, against the now omnipresent influence of the arbitrary. If he sat here peacefully, observing the requirements of the ritual, a decorum as simple as the rules of backgammon, gradually the elements in the space about him would cohere. Things settled, unproblematically, into their own contours. Taking the flower-shaped glass as its center, this glass that was now and only and exactly a glass of tea, his perceptions slowly spread out through the room, like the concentric ripples passing across the surface of an ornamental pond, embracing all its objects at last in a firm, noumenal grasp. Just so. The room was just what a room should be. It contained him.

He did not take notice of the first rapping on the café window, though he was aware, by some small cold contraction of his thoughts, of an infringement of the rules. The second time he looked up.

They were together. The woman and the child.

He had seen them each on several occasions since his trip to Usküdar three weeks before. The boy once on the torn-up sidewalk outside the Consulate, and another time sitting on the railing of the Karaköy bridge. Once, riding in a dolmus to

Taksim, he had passed within a scant few feet of the woman and they had exchanged a glance of unambiguous recognition. But he had never seen them together before.

But could he be certain, now, that it *was* those two? He saw a woman and a child, and the woman was rapping with one bony knuckle on the window for someone's attention. For his? If he could have seen her face . . .

He looked at the other occupants of the café. The backgammon players. A fat unshaven man reading a newspaper. A dark-skinned man with spectacles and a flaring mustache. The two old men, on opposite sides of the room, puffing on nargilehs. None of them paid any attention to the woman's rapping.

He stared resolutely at his glass of tea, no longer a paradigm of its own necessity. It had become a foreign object, an artifact picked up out of the rubble of a buried city, a shard.

The woman continued to rap at the window. At last the owner of the café went outside and spoke a few sharp words to her. She left without making a reply.

He sat with his cold tea another fifteen minutes. Then he went out into the street. There was no sign of them. He returned the hundred yards to his apartment as calmly as he could. Once inside he fastened the chain lock. He never went back to the café.

When the woman came that night, knocking at his door, it was not a surprise.

And every night, at nine or, at the very latest, ten o'clock.

Yavuz! Yavuz! Calling to him.

He stared at the black water, the lights of the other shore. He wondered, often, when he would give in, when he would open the door.

But it was surely a mistake. Some accidental *resemblance*. He was not Yavuz.

John Benedict Harris. An American.

If there had ever been one, if there had ever been a Yavuz. The man who had tacked the pinups on the walls?

Two women, they might have been twins, in heavy eye make-up, garter belts, mounted on the same white horse. Lewdly smiling.

A bouffant hairdo, puffy lips. Drooping breasts with large brown nipples. A couch.

A beachball. Her skin dark. Bikini. Laughing. Sand. The water unnaturally blue.

Snapshots.

Had these ever been *his* fantasies? If not, why could he not bring himself to take them off the walls? He had prints by Piranesi. A blowup of Sagrada Familia in Barcelona. The Tchernikov sketch. He could have covered the walls.

He found himself trying to imagine of this Yavuz . . . what he must be like.

III

Three days after Christmas he received a card from his wife, postmarked from Nevada. Janice, he knew, did not believe in Christmas cards. It showed an immense stretch of white desert —a salt-flat, he supposed—with purple mountains in the distance, and above the purple mountains, a heavily retouched sunset. Pink. There were no figures in this landscape, nor any sign of vegetation. Inside she had written:

"Merry Christmas! Janice."

The same day he received a manila envelope with a copy of *Art News*. A noncommittal note from his friend Raymond was paperclipped to the cover: "Thought you might like to see this. R."

In the back pages of the magazine there was a long and unsympathetic review of his book by F. R. Robertson. Robertson was known as an authority on Hegel's aesthetics. He maintained that *Homo Arbitrans* was nothing but a compendium of truisms and—without seeming to recognize any contradiction in this— a hopelessly muddled reworking of Hegel.

Years ago he had dropped out of a course taught by Robertson after attending the first two lectures. He wondered if Robertson could have remembered this.

The review contained several errors of fact, one misquotation, and failed to mention his central argument, which was not, ad-

mittedly, dialectical. He decided he should write a reply and
laid the magazine beside his typewriter to remind himself. The
same evening he spilled the better part of a bottle of wine on it,
so he tore out the review and threw the magazine into the
garbage with his wife's card.

The necessity for a movie had compelled him into the streets and
kept him in the streets, wandering from marquee to marquee,
long after the drizzle of the afternoon had thickened to rain.
In New York when this mood came over him he would take in
a double bill of science-fiction films or Westerns on Forty-second
Street, but here, though cinemas abounded in the absence of
television, only the glossiest Hollywood kitsch was presented with
the original soundtrack. B-movies were invariably dubbed in
Turkish.

So obsessive was this need that he almost passed the man in
the skeleton suit without noticing him. He trudged back and
forth on the sidewalk, a sodden refugee from Halloween, followed by a small Hamelin of excited children. The rain had
curled the corners of his poster (it served him now as an um-
brella) and caused the inks to run. He could make out:

KIL G

STA   LDA

After Ataturk, the skeleton-suited "Kiling" was the principal
figure of the new Turkish folklore. Every newsstand was heaped
with magazines and comics celebrating his adventures, and here
he was himself, or his avatar at least, advertising his latest movie.
Yes, and there, down the side street, was the theater where it
was playing: KILING ISTANBULDA. Or: *Kiling in Istanbul.*
Beneath the colossal letters a skull-masked Kiling threatened to
kiss a lovely and obviously reluctant blonde, while on the larger
poster across the street he gunned down two well-dressed men.
One could not decide, on the evidence of such tableaux as these,
whether Kiling was fundamentally good, like Batman, or bad,
like Fantomas. So . . .

He bought a ticket. He would find out. It was the name that intrigued him. It was, distinctly, an English name.

He took a seat four rows from the front just as the feature began, immersing himself gratefully into the familiar urban imagery. Reduced to black-and-white and framed by darkness, the customary vistas of Istanbul possessed a heightened reality. New American cars drove through the narrow streets at perilous speeds. An old doctor was strangled by an unseen assailant. Then for a long while nothing of interest happened. A tepid romance developed between the blond singer and the young architect, while a number of gangsters, or diplomats, tried to obtain possession of the doctor's black valise. After a confusing sequence in which four of these men were killed in an explosion, the valise fell into the hands of Kiling. But it proved to be empty.

The police chased Kiling over tiled rooftops. But this was a proof only of his agility, not of his guilt: the police can often make mistakes in these matters. Kiling entered, through a window, the bedroom of the blond singer, waking her. Contrary to the advertising posters outside, he made no attempt to kiss her. He addressed her in a hollow bass voice. The editing seemed to suggest that Kiling was actually the young architect whom the singer loved, but as his mask was never removed this too remained in doubt.

He felt a hand on his shoulder.

He was certain it was her and he would not turn around. Had she followed him to the theater? If he rose to leave, would she make a scene? He tried to ignore the pressure of the hand, staring at the screen where the young architect had just received a mysterious telegram. His hands gripped tightly into his thighs. His hands: the hands of John Benedict Harris.

"Mr. Harris, hello!"

A man's voice. He turned around. It was Altin.

"Altin."

Altin smiled. His face flickered. "Yes. Do you think it is anyone?"

"Anyone else?"

"Yes."

"No."

"You are seeing this movie?"

"Yes."

"It is not in English. It is in Turkish."

"I know."

Several people in nearby rows were hissing for them to be quiet. The blond singer had gone down into one of the city's large cisterns. Binbirdirek. He had been there himself. The editing created an illusion that it was larger than it actually was.

"We will come up there." Altin whispered.

He nodded.

Altin sat on his right, and Altin's friend took the seat remaining empty on his left. Altin introduced his friend in a whisper. His name was Yavuz. He did not speak English.

Reluctantly he shook hands with Yavuz.

It was difficult, thereafter, to give his full attention to the film. He kept glancing sideways at Yavuz. He was about his own height and age, but then this seemed to be true of half the men in Istanbul. An unexceptional face, eyes that glistened moistly in the half-light reflected from the screen.

Kiling was climbing up the girders of a building being constructed on a high hillside. In the distance the Bosphorus snaked past misted hills.

There was something so unappealing in almost every Turkish face. He had never been able to pin it down: some weakness of bone structure, the narrow cheekbones; the strong vertical lines that ran down from the hollows of the eyes to the corner of the mouth; the mouth itself, narrow, flat, inflexible. Or some subtler disharmony among all these elements?

Yavuz. A common name, the mail clerk had said.

In the last minutes of the movie there was a fight between two figures dressed in skeleton suits, a true and a false Kiling. One of them was thrown to his death from the steel beams of the unfinished building. The villain, surely—but had it been the true or the false Kiling who died? And come to think of it, which of them had frightened the singer in her bedroom, strangled the old doctor, stolen the valise?

"Do you like it?" Altin asked as they crowded toward the exit.

"Yes, I did."

"And do you understand what the people say?"

"Some of it. Enough."

Altin spoke for a while to Yavuz, who then turned to address his new friend from America in rapid Turkish.

He shook his head apologetically. Altin and Yavuz laughed.

"He says to you that you have the same suit."

"Yes, I noticed that as soon as the lights came on."

"Where do you go now, Mr. Harris?"

"What time is it?"

They were outside the theater. The rain had moderated to a drizzle. Altin looked at his watch. "Seven o'clock. And a half."

"I must go home now."

"We will come with you and buy a bottle of wine. Yes?"

He looked uncertainly at Yavuz. Yavuz smiled.

And when she came tonight, knocking at his door and calling for Yavuz?

"Not tonight, Altin."

"No?"

"I am a little sick."

"Yes?"

"Sick. I have a fever. My head aches." He put his hand, mimetically, to his forehead, and as he did this he *could* feel both the fever and the headache. "Some other time perhaps. I'm sorry."

Altin shrugged skeptically.

He shook hands with Altin and then with Yavuz. Clearly, they both felt they had been snubbed.

Returning to his apartment he took an indirect route that avoided the dark side streets. The tone of the movie lingered, like the taste of a liqueur, to enliven the rhythm of cars and crowds, deepen the chiaroscuro of headlights and shop windows. Once, leaving the Eighth Street Cinema after *Jules et Jim,* he had discovered all the street signs of the Village translated into French; now the same law of magic allowed him to think that he could understand the fragmented conversation of passersby. The meaning of an isolated phrase registered with the self-evident uninterpreted immediacy of "fact," the nature of the words mingling with the nature of things. Just so. Each knot in the net of language slipped, without any need of explication, into place. Every nuance of glance and inflection fitted, like a tailored suit, the contours of that moment, this street, the light, his conscious mind.

Inebriated by this fictive empathy he turned into his own darker street at last and almost walked past the woman—who fitted, like every other element of the scene, so well the corner where she'd taken up her watch—without noticing her.

"You!" he said and stopped.

They stood four feet apart, regarding each other carefully. Perhaps she had been as little prepared for this confrontation as he.

Her thick hair was combed back in stiff waves from a low forehead, falling in massive parentheses to either side of her thin face. Pitted skin, flesh wrinkled in concentration around small pale lips. And tears—yes, tears—just forming in the corners of her staring eyes. With one hand she held a small parcel wrapped in newspaper and string; with the other she clutched the bulky confusion of her skirts. She wore several layers of clothing, rather than a coat, against the cold.

A slight erection stirred and tangled in the flap of his cotton underpants. He blushed. Once, reading a paperback edition of Krafft-Ebing, the same embarrassing thing had happened. That time it had been a description of necrophilia.

God, he thought, *if she notices!*

She whispered to him, lowering her gaze. To him, to Yavuz.

To come home with her . . . Why did he . . . ? Yavuz, Yavuz, Yavuz. . . . she needed . . . and his son . . .

"I don't *understand* you," he insisted. "Your words make no sense to me. I am an American. My name is John Benedict Harris, not Yavuz. You're making a mistake—can't you see that?"

She nodded her head. "Yavuz."

"*Not* Yavuz! *Yok! Yok, yok!*"

And a word that meant "love" but not exactly that. Her hand tightened in the folds of her several skirts, raising them to show the thin, black-stockinged ankles.

"No!"

She moaned.

. . . wife . . . his home . . . Yalova . . . his life.

"Damn you, go away!"

Her hand let go her skirts and darted quickly to his shoulder, digging into the cheap cloth. Her other hand shoved the wrapped parcel at him. He pushed her back but she clung fiercely, shrieking his name: *Yavuz!* He struck her face.

She fell on the wet cobbles. He backed away. The greasy parcel was in his left hand. She pushed herself up to her feet. Tears flowed along the vertical channels from eyes to mouth. A Turkish face. Blood dripped slowly out of one nostril. She began to walk away in the direction of Taksim.

"And don't return, do you understand? Stay away from me!" His voice cracked.

When she was out of sight he looked at the parcel in his hand. He knew he ought not to open it, that the wisest course was to throw it into the nearest garbage can. But even as he warned himself, his fingers had snapped the string.

A large lukewarm doughy mass of borek. And an orange. The saliva sprouted in his mouth at the acrid smell of the cheese.

No!

He had not had dinner that night. He was hungry. He ate it. Even the orange.

During the month of January he made only two entries in his notebook. The first, undated, was a long extract copied from A. H. Lybyer's book on the Janissaries, the great slave-corps of the sultans, *The Government of the Ottoman Empire in the Time of Suleiman the Magnificent*. The passage read:

> Perhaps no more daring experiment has been tried on a large scale upon the face of the Earth than that embodied in the Otto-man Ruling Institution. Its nearest ideal analogue is found in the Republic of Plato, its nearest actual parallel in the Mamluk system of Egypt; but it was not restrained within the aristocratic Hellenic limitations of the first, and it subdued and outlived the second. In the United States of America men have risen from the rude work of the backwoods to the Presidential chair, but they have done so

by their own effort and not through the gradations of a system carefully organized to push them forward. The Roman Catholic can still train a peasant to become a pope, but it has never begun by choosing its candidates almost exclusively from families which profess a hostile religion. The Ottoman system deliberately took slaves and made them ministers of state. It took boys from the sheep-run and the plough-tail and made them courtiers and the husbands of princesses; it took young men whose ancestors had borne the Christian name for centuries and made them rulers in the greatest of Muhammedan states, and soldiers and generals in invincible armies whose chief joy it was to beat down the Cross and elevate the Crescent. It never asked its novices "Who was your father?" or "What do you know?" or even "Can you speak our tongue?" but it studied their faces and their frames and said: "*You* shall be a soldier and if you show yourself worthy, a general," or "*You* shall be a scholar and a gentleman and, if the ability lies in you, a governor and a prime minister." Grandly disregarding the fabric of fundamental customs which is called "human nature," and those religious and social prejudices which are thought to be almost as deep as life itself, the Ottoman system took children for ever from parents, discouraged family cares among its members through their most active years, allowed them no certain hold on property, gave them no definite promise that their sons and daughters would profit by their success and sacrifice, raised and lowered them with no regard for ancestry or previous distinction, taught them a strange law, ethics, and religion, and ever kept them conscious of a sword raised above their heads which might put an end at any moment to a brilliant career along a matchless path of human glory.

The second and briefer entry was dated the twenty-third of January and read as follows:

"Heavy rains yesterday. I stayed in drinking. She came around at her usual hour. This morning when I put on my brown shoes to go out shopping they were *wet through*. Two hours to dry them out over the heater. Yesterday I wore only my sheepskin slippers—*I did not leave the building once*."

IV

A human face is a construction, an artifact. The mouth is a little door, and the eyes are windows that look at the street, and all the rest of it, the flesh, the bone beneath, is a wall to which any manner of ornament may be affixed, gewgaws of whatever style or period one takes a fancy to—swags hung below the cheeks and chin, lines chiseled or smoothed away, a recession emphasized, a bit of vegetation here and there. Each addition or subtraction, however minor in itself, will affect the entire composition. Thus, the hair that he has had trimmed a bit closer to the temples restores hegemony to the vertical elements of a face that is now noticeably *narrower*. Or is this exclusively a matter of proportion and emphasis? For he has lost weight too (one cannot stop eating regularly without some shrinkage), and the loss has been appreciable. A new darkness has given definition to the always incipient pouches below his eyes, a darkness echoed by the new hollowness of his cheeks.

But the chief agent of metamorphosis is the mustache, which has grown full enough now to obscure the modeling of his upper lip. The ends, which had first shown a tendency to droop, have developed, by his nervous habit of twisting them about his fingers, the flaring upward curve of a scimitar (or *pala*, after which in Turkey this style of mustache is named, *pala biyik*). It is this, the baroque mustache, not a face, that he sees when he looks in a mirror.

Then there is the whole question of "expression," its quickness, constancy, the play of intelligence, the characteristic "tone" and the hundreds of possible gradations within the range of that tone, the eyes' habits of irony and candor, the betraying tension or slackness of a lip. Yet it is scarcely necessary to go into this at all, for his face, when he sees it, or when anyone sees it, could not be said to *have* an expression. What was there, after all, for him to express?

The blurring of edges, whole days lost, long hours awake in bed, books scattered about the room like little animal corpses to be nibbled at when he grew hungry, the endless cups of tea, the tasteless cigarettes. Wine, at least, did what it was supposed to do—it took away the sting. Not that he felt the sting these days with any poignance. But perhaps without the wine he *would* have.

He piled the nonreturnable bottles in the bathtub, exercising in this act (if in no other) the old discrimination, the "compulsive tact" he had made so much of in his book.

The drapes were always drawn. The lights were left burning at all hours, even when he slept, even when he was out, three sixty-watt bulbs in a metal chandelier hanging just out of plumb.

Voices from the street impinged. Vendors in the morning, and the metallic screak of children. At night the radio in the apartment below, drunken arguments. Scatterings of words, like illuminated signs glimpsed driving on a thruway, at high speeds, at night.

Two bottles of wine were not enough if he started early in the afternoon, but three could make him sick.

And though the hours crawled, like wounded insects, so slowly across the floor, the days rushed by in a torrent. The sunlight slipped across the Bosphorus so quickly that there was scarcely time to rise and see it.

One morning when he woke there was a balloon on a stick propped in the dusty flower vase atop his dresser. A crude Mickey Mouse was stenciled on the bright red rubber. He left it there, bobbing in the vase, and watched it shrivel day by day, the face turning small and black and wrinkled.

The next time it was ticket stubs, two of them, from the Kabataş-Üsküdar ferry.

Till that moment he had told himself it was a matter only of holding out until the spring. He had prepared himself for a siege, believing that an assault was not possible. Now he realized that he would have actually to go out there and fight.

Though it was mid-February the weather accommodated his belated resolution with a series of bright blue days, a wholly unseasonable warmth that even tricked early blossoms from a few unsuspecting trees. He went through Topkapi once again, giving a respectful, indiscriminate, and puzzled attention to the celadon ware, to golden snuffboxes, to pearl-embroidered pillows, to the portrait miniatures of the sultans, to the fossil footprint of the Prophet, to Iznik tiles, to the lot. There it was, all spread out before him, heaps and masses of it: beauty. Like a salesclerk tying price tags to items of merchandise, he would attach this favorite word of his, provisionally, to these sundry bibelots, then step back a pace or two to see how well or poorly it "matched." Was *this* beautiful? Was *that*?

Amazingly, none of it was beautiful. The priceless baubles all just sat there on their shelves, behind the thick glass, as unresplendent as the drab furniture back in his own room.

He tried the mosques: Sultan Ahmet, Beyazit, Şehazade, Yeni Camii, Laleli Camii. The old magic, the Vitruvian trinity of "commodity, firmness, and delight," had never failed him so enormously before. Even the shock of scale, the gape-mouthed peasant reverence before thick pillars and high domes, even this deserted him. Go where he would through the city, he could not get out of his room.

Then the land walls, where months before he had felt himself rubbing up against the very garment of the past. He stood at the same spot where he had stood then, at the point where Mehmet the Conqueror had breached the walls. Quincunxes of granite cannonballs decorated the grass; they reminded him of the red balloon.

As a last resort he returned to Eyup. The false spring had reached a tenuous apogee, and the February light flared with deceiving brilliance from the thousand facets of white stone blanketing the steep hillside. Small flocks of three or four sheep browsed between the graves. The turbaned shafts of marble jutted in every direction but the vertical (which it was given to the cypresses to define) or lay, higgledy-piggledy, one atop another. No walls, no ceilings, scarcely a path through the litter: this was an architecture supremely abstract. It seemed to him to have been piled up here, over the centuries, just to vindicate the thesis of his book.

And it worked. It worked splendidly. His mind and his eye came alive. Ideas and images coalesced. The sharp slanting light of the late afternoon caressed the jumbled marble with a cold careful hand, like a beautician adding the last touches to an elaborate coiffure. Beauty? Here it was. Here it was abundantly!

He returned the next day with his camera, redeemed from the repairshop where it had languished for two months. To be on the safe side he had asked the repairman to load it for him. He composed each picture with mathematic punctilio, fussing over the depth of field, crouching or climbing atop sepulchers for a better angle, checking each shot against the reading on the light meter, deliberately avoiding picturesque solutions and easy effects. Even taking these pains he found that he'd gone through the twenty exposures in under two hours.

He went up to the small café on the top of the hill. Here, his Hachette had noted respectfully, the great Pierre Loti had been wont to come of a summer evening, to drink a glass of tea and look down the sculptured hills and through the pillars of cypress at the Fresh Waters of Europe and the Golden Horn. The café perpetuated the memory of this vanished glory with pictures and mementoes. Loti, in a red fez and savage mustachios, glowered at the contemporary patrons from every wall. During the World War Loti had remained in Istanbul, taking the part of his friend, the Turkish sultan, against his native France.

He ordered a glass of tea from a waitress who had been got up as a harem girl. Apart from the waitress he had the café to himself. He sat on Pierre Loti's favorite stool. It was delicious. He felt right at home.

He opened his notebook and began to write.

Like an invalid taking his first walk out of doors after a long convalescence, his renascent energies caused him not only the predictable and welcome euphoria of resurrection but also a pronounced intellectual giddiness, as though by the simple act of rising to his feet he had thrust himself up to some really dangerous height. This dizziness became most acute when, in trying to draft a reply to Robertson's review, he was obliged to return to passages in his own book. Often as not what he found there struck him as incomprehensible. There were entire chapters that might as well have been written in ideograms or futhore for all the sense they made to him now. But occasionally, cued by some remark so irrelevant to any issue at hand as to be squeezed into an embarrassed parenthesis, he would sprint off toward the most unforeseen—and undesirable—conclusions. Or rather, each of these tangents led, asymptotically, to a single conclusion: to wit, that his book, or any book he might yet conceive, was worthless, and worthless not because his thesis was wrong but precisely because it might be right.

There was a realm of judgment and a realm of fact. His book, if only because it was a book, existed within the bounds of the first. There was the trivial fact of its corporeality, but, in this case as in most others, he discounted that. It was a work of criticism, a systematization of judgment, and to the extent that his system was complete its critical apparatus must be able to measure its own scales of mensuration, and judge the justice of its own decrees. But could it? Was not his "system" as arbitrary a construction as any silly pyramid? What was it, after all? A string of words, of more or less agreeable noises, politely assumed to correspond to certain objects and classes of objects, actions and groups of actions, in the realm of fact. And by what subtle magic was this correspondence to be verified? Why, by just the assertion that it was so!

This, admittedly, lacked clarity. It had come to him thick and fast, and it was colored not a little by cheap red wine. To fix its outlines a bit more firmly in his own mind he tried to "get it down" in his letter to *Art News*:

Sirs:
    I write to you concerning F. R. Robertson's review of my book, though the few words I have to say bear but slightly upon Mr. Robertson's oracles, as slightly perhaps as these bore upon *Homo Arbitrans*.
    Only this—that, as Gödel has demonstrated in mathematics, Wittgenstein in philosophy, and Duchamp, Cage, and Ashbery in their respective fields, the final statement of any system is a self-denunciation, a demonstration of how its particular little tricks are done—not by magic (as magicians have always known) but by the readiness of the magician's audience to be deceived, which readiness is the very glue of the social contract.
    Every system, including my own and Mr. Robertson's, is a system

of more or less interesting lies, and if one begins to call these lies into question, then one ought really to begin with the first. That is to say, with the very questionable proposition on the title page: *Homo Arbitrans* by John Benedict Harris.

Now I ask you, Mr. Robertson, what could be more improbable than that? More tentative? More arbitrary?

He sent the letter off, unsigned.

V

He had been promised his photos by Monday, so Monday morning, before the frost had thawed on the plate glass window, he was at the shop. The same immodest anxious interest to see his pictures of Eyup possessed him as once he had felt to see an essay or a review in print. It was as though these items, the pictures, the printed words, had the power to rescind, for a little while, his banishment to the realm of judgment, as though they said to him: "Yes, look, here we are, right in your hand. We're real, and so you must be too."

The old man behind the counter, a German, looked up mournfully to gargle a mournful *ach.* "Ach, Mr. Harris! Your pictures are not ready yet. Come back soon at twelve o'clock."

He walked through the melting streets that were, this side of the Golden Horn, jokebooks of eclecticism. No mail at the Consulate, which was only to be expected. Half past ten.

A pudding at a pudding shop. Two lire. A cigarette. A few more jokes: a bedraggled caryatid, an Egyptian tomb, a Greek temple that had been changed by some Circean wand into a butcher shop. Eleven.

He looked, at the bookshop, at the same shopworn selection of books that he had looked at so often before. Eleven thirty. Surely, they would be ready by now.

"You are here, Mr. Harris. Very good."

Smiling in anticipation, he opened the envelope, removed the slim warped stack of prints.

No.

"I'm afraid these aren't mine." He handed them back. He didn't want to feel them in his hand.

"What?"

"Those are the wrong pictures. You've made a mistake."

The old man put on a pair of dirty spectacles and shuffled through the prints. He squinted at the name on the envelope. "You are Mr. Harris."

"Yes, that is the name on the envelope. The envelope's all right, the pictures aren't."

"It is not a mistake."

"These are *somebody else's* snapshots. Some family picnic. You can see that."

"I myself took out the roll of film from your camera. Do you remember, Mr. Harris?"

He laughed uneasily. He hated scenes. He considered just walking out of the shop, forgetting all about the pictures. "Yes, I do remember. But I'm afraid you must have gotten that roll of film confused with another. I *didn't* take these pictures. I took pictures at the cemetery in Eyup. Does that ring a bell?"

Perhaps, he thought, "ring a bell" was not an expression a German would understand.

As a waiter whose honesty has been called into question will go over the bill again with exaggerated attention, the old man frowned and examined each of the pictures in turn. With a triumphant clearing of his throat he laid one of the snapshots face up on the counter. "Who is that, Mr. Harris?"

It was the boy.

"Who! I . . . I don't know his name."

The old German laughed theatrically, lifting his eyes to a witnessing heaven. "It is you, Mr. Harris! It is you!"

He bent over the counter. His fingers still refused to touch the print. The boy was held up in the arms of a man whose head was bent forward as though he were examining the close-cropped scalp for lice. Details were fuzzy, the lens having been mistakenly set at infinity.

Was it his face? The mustache resembled his mustache, the crescents under the eyes, the hair falling forward . . .

But the angle of the head, the lack of focus—there was room for doubt.

"Twenty-four lire please, Mr. Harris."

"Yes. Of course." He took a fifty-lire note from his billfold. The old man dug into a lady's plastic coin purse for change.

"Thank you, Mr. Harris."

"Yes. I'm . . . sorry."

The old man replaced the prints in the envelope, handed them across the counter.

He put the envelope in the pocket of his suit. "It was my mistake."

"Good-bye."

"Yes, good-bye."

He stood on the street, in the sunlight, exposed. Any moment either of them might come up to him, lay a hand on his shoulder, tug at his pants leg. He could not examine the prints here. He returned to the sweetshop and spread them out in four rows on a marble-topped table.

Twenty photographs. A day's outing, as commonplace as it had been impossible.

Of these twenty, three were so overexposed as to be meaningless and should not have been printed at all. Three others showed what appeared to be islands or different sections of a very irregular coastline. They were unimaginatively composed, with great expanses of bleached-out sky and glaring water. Squeezed between these the land registered merely as long dark blotches flecked with tiny gray rectangles of buildings. There was also a view up a steep street of wooden houses and naked wintry gardens.

The remaining thirteen pictures showed various people, and groups of people, looking at the camera. A heavyset woman in black, with black teeth, squinting into the sun—standing next to a pine tree in one picture, sitting uncomfortably on a natural stone formation in the second. An old man, dark-skinned, bald, with a flaring mustache and several days' stubble of beard. Then these two together—a very blurred print. Three little girls standing in front of a middle-aged woman, who regarded them with a pleased, proprietorial air. The same three girls grouped around the old man, who seemed to take no notice of them whatever. And a group of five men: the spread-legged shadow of the man taking this picture was roughly stenciled across the pebbled foreground.

And the woman. Alone. The wrinkled sallow flesh abraded to a smooth white mask by the harsh midday light.

Then the boy snuggling beside her on a blanket. Nearby small waves lapped at a narrow shingle.

Then these two still together with the old woman and the three little girls. The contiguity of the two women's faces suggested a family resemblance.

The figure that could be identified as himself appeared on only three of the pictures: once holding the boy in his arms; once with his arm around the woman's shoulders, while the boy stood before them scowling; once in a group of thirteen people, all of whom had appeared in one or another of the previous shots. Only the last of these three was in focus. He was one of the least noticeable figures in this group, but the mustached face smiling so rigidly into the camera was undeniably his own.

He had never seen these people, except, of course, for the woman and the boy. Though he had, hundreds of times, seen people just like them in the streets of Istanbul. Nor did he recognize the plots of grass, the stands of pine, the boulders, the shingle beach, though once again they were of such a generic type that he might well have passed such places a dozen times without taking any notice of them. Was the world of fact really as characterless as *this*? That it *was* the world of fact he never for a moment doubted.

And what had *he* to place in the balance against these evidences? A name? A face?

He scanned the walls of the sweetshop for a mirror. There was none. He lifted the spoon, dripping, from his glass of tea to regard the reflection of his face, blurred and inverted, in the concave surface. As he brought the spoon closer, the image grew less distinct, then rotated through 180 degrees to present, upright, the mirror image of his staring, dilated eye.

He stood on the open upper deck as the ferry churned, hooting, from the deck. Like a man stepping out of doors on a blustery day, the ferry rounded the peninsular tip of the old city, leaving the quiet of the Horn for the rough wind-whitened waters of the Sea of Marmara. A cold south wind stiffened the scarlet star-and-crescent on the stern mast.

From this vantage the city showed its noblest silhouette: first

the great gray horizontal mass of the Topkapi walls, then the
delicate swell of the dome of St. Irena, which had been built
(like a friend carefully chosen to demonstrate, by contrast, one's
own virtues) just to point up the swaggering impossibility of
the neighboring Holy Wisdom, that graceless and abstract issue
of the union commemorated on every capital within by the
twined monograms of the demon-emperor Justinian and his
whore and consort Theodora; then, bringing both the topo-
graphic and historic sequence to an end, the proud finality of
the Blue Mosque.

The ferry began to roll in the rough water of the open sea.
Clouds moved across the sun at quicker intervals to mass in the
north above the dwindling city. It was four thirty. By five
o'clock he would reach Heybeli, the island identified by both
Altin and the mail clerk at the Consulate as the setting of the
photographs.

The airline ticket to New York was in his pocket. His bags, all
but the one he would take on the plane, had been packed and
shipped off in a single afternoon and morning of headlong
drunken fear. Now he was safe. The certain knowledge that tomorrow he would be thousands of miles away had shored up
the crumbling walls of confidence like the promise of a prophet
who cannot err, Tiresias in balmy weather. Admittedly this was
the shameful safety of a rout so complete that the enemy had
almost captured his baggage train—but it was safety for all
that, as definite as tomorrow. Indeed, this "tomorrow" was more
definite, more present to his mind and senses, than the actual
limbo of its preparation, just as, when a boy, he had endured
the dreadful tedium of Christmas Eve by projecting himself into
the morning that would have to follow and which, when it did
finally arrive, was never so real, by half, as his anticipations.

Because he was this safe, he dared today confront the enemy
(if the enemy would confront *him*) head on. It risked nothing
and there was no telling what it might yield. Though if it were
the *frisson* that he was after, then he should have stayed and
seen the thing through to its end. No, this last excursion was
more a gesture than an act, bravado rather than bravery. The
very self-consciousness with which he had set out seemed to

insure that nothing really disastrous could happen. Had it not always been their strategy before to catch him unaware?

Finally, of course, he could not explain to himself why he had gone to the ferry, bought his ticket, embarked, except that each successive act seemed to heighten the delectable sense of his own inexorable advance, a sensation at once of almost insupportable tension and of dreamlike lassitude. He could no more have turned back along this path once he had entered on it than at the coda of a symphony he could have refused to listen. Beauty? Oh yes, intolerably! He had *never* known anything so beautiful as this.

The ferry pulled into the quay of Kinali Ada, the first of the islands. People got on and off. Now the ferry turned directly into the wind, toward Burgaz. Behind them the European coast vanished into the haze.

The ferry had left the Burgaz dock and was rounding the tiny islet of Kasik. He watched with fascination as the dark hills of Kasik, Burgaz, and Kinali slipped slowly into perfect alignment with their positions in the photograph. He could almost hear the click of the shutter.

And the other relationships between these simple sliding planes of sea and land—was there not something nearly as *familiar* in each infinitesimal shift of perspective? When he looked at these islands with his eyes half-closed, attention unfocused, he could almost . . .

But whenever he tried to take this up, however gently, between the needle-tipped compasses of analysis, it crumbled into dust.

It began to snow just as the ferry approached Heybeli. He stood at the end of the pier. The ferry was moving eastward, into the white air, toward Buyuk Ada.

He looked up a steep street of wooden houses and naked wintry gardens. Clusters of snowflakes fell on the wet cobbles and melted. At irregular intervals street lamps glowed yellow in the dusk, but the houses remained dark. Heybeli was a summer resort. Few people lived here in the winter months. He walked halfway up the hill, then turned to the right. Certain details of woodwork, the proportion of a window, a sagging roof caught his attention momentarily, like the flicker of wings in the foliage of a tree twenty, fifty, a hundred yards ahead.

The houses were fewer, spaced farther apart. In the gardens snow covered the leaves of cabbages. The road wound up the hill toward a stone building. It was just possible to make out the flag waving against the gray sky. He turned onto a footpath that skirted the base of the hill. It led into the pines. The thick carpet of fallen needles was more slippery than ice. He rested his cheek against the bark of a tree and heard, again, the camera's click, systole and diastole of his heart.

He heard the water, before he saw it, lapping on the beach. He stopped. He focused. He recognized the rock. He walked toward it. So encompassing was his sense of this scene, so inclusive, that he could feel the footsteps he left behind in the snow, feel the snow slowly covering them again. He stopped.

It was here he had stood with the boy in his arms. The woman had held the camera to her eye with reverent awkwardness. He had bent his head forward to avoid looking directly into the glare of the setting sun. The boy's scalp was covered with the scabs of insect bites.

He was ready to admit that all this had happened, the whole impossible event. He did admit it. He lifted his head proudly and smiled, as though to say: *All right—and then? No matter what you do, I'm safe! Because, really, I'm not here at all. I'm already in New York.*

He laid his hands in a gesture of defiance on the outcropping of rock before him. His fingers brushed the resilient thong of the slipper. Covered with snow, the small oval of blue plastic had completely escaped his attention.

He spun around to face the forest, then around again to stare at the slipper lying there. He reached for it, thinking to throw it into the water, then drew his hand back.

He turned back to the forest. A man was standing just outside the line of the trees, on the path. It was too dark to discern any more of his features than that he had a mustache.

On his left the snowy beach ended in a wall of sandstone. To his right the path swung back into the forest, and behind him the sea dragged the shingle back and forth.

"Yes?"

The man bent his head attentively, but said nothing.

"Well, yes? Say it."

The man walked back into the forest.

The ferry was just pulling in as he stumbled up to the quay. He ran onto it without stopping at the booth to buy a ticket. Inside under the electric light he could see the tear in his trousers, and a cut on the palm of his right hand. He had fallen many times, on the pine needles, over rocks in furrowed fields, on cobbles.

He took a seat by the coal stove. When his breath returned to him, he found that he was shivering violently. A boy came round with a tray of tea. He bought a glass for one lira. He asked the boy, in Turkish, what time it was. It was ten o'clock.

The ferry pulled up to the dock. The sign over the ticket booth said BUYUK ADA. The ferry pulled away from the dock.

The ticket taker came for his ticket. He held out a ten-lira note and said, "Istanbul."

The ticket taker nodded his head, which meant no. "*Yok.*"

"No? How much then? *Kaç para?*"

"*Yok Istanbul—Yalova.*" He took the money offered him and gave him back in exchange eight lire and a ticket to Yalova on the Asian coast.

He had got onto a ferry going in the wrong direction. He was not returning to Istanbul, but to Yalova.

He explained, first in slow precise English, then in a desperate fragmentary Turkish, that he could not go to Yalova, that it was impossible. He produced his airline ticket, pointed at the eight o'clock departure time, but he could not remember the Turkish word for "tomorrow." Even in his desperation he could see the

futility of all this: between Buyuk Ada and Yalova there were
no more stops, and there would be no ferries returning to Istanbul that night. When he got to Yalova he would have to get
off the boat.

A woman and a boy stood at the end of the wooden dock, at
the base of a cone of snowy light. The lights were turned off on
the middle deck of the ferry. The man who had been standing
so long at the railing stepped, stiffly, down to the dock. He
walked directly toward the woman and the boy. Scraps of paper
eddied about his feet, then, caught up in a strong gust, sailed
out at a great height over the dark water.

The man nodded sullenly at the woman, who mumbled a few
rapid words of Turkish. Then they set off, as they had so many
times before, toward their home, the man leading the way, his
wife and son following a few paces behind, taking the road
along the shore.

For a Journal Entry . . .

Someone once described a good story as one that ends ten minutes
after you've finished reading it. Is that the case with this story? Or
were you able to catch the hints that the author gives you almost
from the beginning?

What do you think it might be like to be stranded on an island
with no communication with the outside world, or in a country where
no one speaks English and you know nothing of the native language.
Does the author catch something of that spirit?

For Your Consideration . . .

1. There isn't a single mention of any science in this story. What
    then makes it science fiction other than the fact that it was orig-
    inally published in a SF story anthology?
2. Does the large number of relatively unfamiliar words that the
    author uses (see the vocabulary list) affect your opinion of this
    story in any way? Why does he use this large a vocabulary?

3. What reasons could you give for calling this a horror story or a fantasy dealing with the supernatural?
4. What prevented Harris-Yavuz from simply getting on an airplane and "returning" to America?
5. When do you become aware that Harris and Yavuz are really one person? What clues has the author provided prior to your discovery?
6. The noted SF author Samuel R. Delaney has written of this novella: "The sense of mystical horror in . . . "The Asian Shore" does not come from its study of a particularly insidious type of racism, incisive though the study is; nor does it come from the final incidents set frustratingly between the supernatural and the insane. It generates rather in the formal parallels between the protagonist's concepts of Byzantine architecture and the obvious architecture of his own personality." (from "About 5,175 Words," in *SF: The Other Side of Realism*, p. 145.) What do you think Delaney means by this remark? What evidences of racism do you find in the story? And what are the parallels between the hero's ideas about architecture and his personality?

Notes

This story contains a great many references to architectural terms, literary figures, and painters and sculptors. No attempt has been made to define all of them. Reference to a desk dictionary or encyclopedia will readily explain who Dali is or Pierre Loti was, to cite only two examples.

PAGE

204 *Ataturk*—the founder of modern Turkey
205 *innocuous*—innocent, harmless
205 *obelisk*—a tapering, four-sided shaft of stone like the Washington monument
205 *Hachette*—a tourist guidebook
206 *crenellations*—notches on the parapet of a fort
207 *barbicans*—the fortified outposts of a castle
207 *entablature*—the horizontal portion of a temple
207 *intaglio*—carvings upon stone
207 *portents*—signs
208 *surreal*—unreal, beyond reality
208 *Cybele*—nature goddess of Asia Minor

208   *balustrade*—a kind of stone railing
208   *hieratic*—priestly
209   *prestigious*—esteemed, honored
209   *hamam*—a Turkish bath
210   *serendipity*—unexpected good fortune
211   *supine*—laying flat on the back
213   *quiddity*—the essential nature of something
213   *gratuitous*—without cause, unnecessary
213   *artifact*—any object made by man
213   *anomalous*—something deviating from the ordinary
214   *social contract*—the entire social pattern of a culture, with its dos and don'ts, its expectations for everyone
214   *furbelows and arabesques*—architectural ornamentation
214   *quotidian*—daily
214   *demesne*—region or territory
214   *Palladian*—From Palladio, Italian Renaissance architect whose rules governed classic architecture
214   *Mies*—Ludwig Mies van der Rohe, famous modern architect
215   *iridescent*—shining with rainbow colors
215   *metamorphosis*—change, especially in outer form
216   *nadir*—the lowest point
216   *gregariousness*—group friendliness
216   *mihrabs and minbars*—architectural details on a mosque
216   *faienced*—highly decorated, ornate
217   *corolla*—flowerlike, particularly here the radiating light from the center of a glass
217   *nargileh*—Oriental tobacco pipe
217   *bastion*—a fortress or any place of safety
217   *noumenal*—in philosophy, the object of intellectual intuition
217   *dolmus*—a Turkish vehicle
218   *unambiguous*—certain, unquestioned
218   *paradigm*—a pattern or set of forms
219   *Homo Arbitrans*—the title of Harris's book
220   *dialectical*—pertaining to the nature of logical argument
220   *kitsch*—artistic material of low quality
220   *Hamelin*—site of the famous Pied Piper
220   *avatar*—a visible appearance of some celebrated figure or god
221   *tepid*—lukewarm
223   *chiaroscuro*—a pattern of light and dark
224   *necrophilia*—abnormal interest in death
225   *borek*—a Turkish food
225   *analogue*—pattern or similarity

227 *hegemony*—leadership; here, influence or control
227 *baroque*—excessively ornamented
228 *celadon*—a kind of porcelain
229 *bibelot*—a small, rare, beautiful object
229 *quincunx*—an arrangement of five objects in another geometrical figure like a square or circle
229 *apogee*—the highest or most distant point
230 *coiffure*—hair arrangement
230 *punctilio*—a detailed arrangement
230 *renascent*—reborn
230 *euphoria*—a feeling of well being
230 *futhorc*—the runic alphabet
231 *asymptotically*—non-logically
231 *mensuration*—any system of measurement
232 *eclecticism*—selective, diverse
232 *caryatid*—the figure of a woman used like a column
232 *Circean*—Circe, the goddess in the *Odyssey* who changes men into swine
234 *abraded*—worn away
235 *contiguity*—nearness
235 *shingle*—gravel
236 *Tiresias*—a Greek fortune teller or seer
236 *frisson*—a chill or shiver or thrill of expectation
237 *inexorable*—inevitable
237 *lassitude*—laziness or languor
238 *systole and diastole*—normal rhythmic contractions of the heart
239 *quay*—dock or pier

Suggestions for
Further Reading

Suggestions for Further Reading

ALDISS, BRIAN W. *Barefoot in the Head; Frankenstein Unbound; Galaxies Like Grains of Sand; Greybeard; The Ninety Minute Hour; Report on Probability A; Starship*

ANDERSON, POUL. *Brain Wave; The High Crusade; The Starfox; Tau Zero*

ASIMOV, ISSAC. *The Caves of Steel; Foundation; The Gods Themselves; I, Robot; The Naked Sun*

BALLARD, J. G. *The Crystal World; The Drowned World; Terminal World; The Wind From Nowhere*

BALMER, EDWIN AND PHILIP WYLIE. *When Worlds Collide; After Worlds Collide*

BESTER, ALFRED. *The Demolished Man; The Stars My Destination*

BLISH, JAMES. *Black Easter; A Case of Conscience; Cities in Flight*

BOYD, JOHN. *The Last Starship from Earth; The Pollinators of Eden; The Rakehells of Heaven*

BRADBURY, RAY. *Fahrenheit 451; The Martian Chronicles; The October Country*

BRUNNER, JOHN. *The Squares of the City; Stand on Zanzibar*

BUDRYS, ALGYS. *Rogue Moon*

CAMPBELL, JOHN W. *The Mightiest Machine; The Ultimate Weapon*

CLARKE, ARTHUR C. *Childhood's End; The City and the Stars; The Deep Range; Rendezvous with Rama; 2001, A Space Odyssey*

CLEMENT, HAL. *Cycle of Fire; Ice World; Mission of Gravity; Needle*

DICK, PHILIP K. *Do Androids Dream of Electric Sheep?; The Man in the High Castle; Martian Time Slip; The Three Stigmata of Palmer Eldritch*

DICKSON, GORDON A. *The Alien Way; The Genetic General*

DISCH, THOMAS M. *Camp Concentration; One Hundred and Two H Bombs*

FRANK, PAT. *Alas, Babylon!*

GOLDING, WILLIAM. *The Inheritors*

GUNN, JAMES. *The Immortals; The Joymakers; The Listeners*

HARRISON, HARRY. *Bill the Galactic Hero; Deathworld; Make Room! Make Room!; The Technicolor Time Machine; Tunnel through the Deeps*

HEINLEIN, ROBERT A. *Citizen of the Galaxy; Double Star; Glory*

Road; The Moon is a Harsh Mistress; Orphans of the Sky; Stranger in A Strange Land

HENDERSON, ZENA. *Pilgrimage: The Book of the People*

HERBERT, FRANK. *Dune; Dune Messiah; Santaroga Barrier; Under Pressure*

HOYLE, FRED. *The Black Cloud; October the First Is Too Late*

HUXLEY, ALDOUS. *Brave New World*

KEYES, DANIEL. *Flowers for Algernon*

LAFFERTY, R. A. *Fourth Mansions; Nine Hundred Grandmothers; Past Master*

LEGUIN, URSULA. *The Lathe of Heaven; The Left Hand of Darkness; The Wizard of Earthsea*

LEIBER, FRITZ. *Gather Darkness!*

LEWIS, C. S. *Out of the Silent Planet; Perelandra; That Hideous Strength*

MALZBERG, BARRY. *Beyond Apollo; The Falling Astronauts*

MCALLISTER, BRUCE. *Humanity Prime*

MCCAFFREY, ANNE. *Dragonquest*

MILLER, WALTER M. JR. *A Canticle for Leibowitz*

NIVEN, LARRY. *Neutron Star; Ringworld*

ORWELL, GEORGE. *Animal Farm; 1984*

POHL, FREDERICK AND CYRIL KORNBLUTH. *Gladiator-at-Law; The Space Merchants*

RUSS, JOANNA. *And Chaos Died; Picnic on Paradise*

RUSSELL, ERIC FRANK. *Dreadful Sanctuary; Sinister Barrier; Wasp*

SCHMITZ, JAMES H. *Agent of Vega; The Witches of Karres*

SHAW, BOB. *Night Walk; The Palace of Eternity*

SHECKLEY, ROBERT. *Citizen in Space; Dimension of Miracles*

SHUTE, NEVILLE. *On the Beach*

SILVERBERG, ROBERT. *The Book of Skulls; Dying Inside; The Masks of Time; Tower of Glass*

SIMAK, CLIFFORD. *City; Ring Around the Sun; Time and Again*

SMITH, E. E. *Triplanetary; First Lensman; Galactic Patrol; Gray Lensman; Second Stage Lensman; Children of the Lens*

STAPLEDON, OLAF. *First and Last Men; Odd John; Sirius; The Star-Maker*

STEWART, GEORGE O. *Earth Abides*

STURGEON, THEODORE. *E Pluribus Unicorn; More Than Human; Venus Plus X*

TENN, WILLIAM. *The Human Angle*

TUCKER, WILSON. *The Long, Loud Silence; The Year of the Quiet Sun*

Van Vogt, A. E. *Slan; The Voyage of the Space Beagle; The World of Null-A*

Verne, Jules. *Journey to the Center of the Earth; 20,000 Leagues Under the Sea*

Vinge, Vernor. *Grimm's World*

Vonnegut, Kurt Jr. *Player Piano; Cat's Cradle; The Sirens of Titan; Slaughter-House Five*

Wells, H. G. *The Invisible Man; The Island of Dr. Moreau; The Time Machine; War of the Worlds*

Williamson, Jack. *Darker Than You Think; The Humanoids; The Legion of Time*

Wright, Austin T. *Islandia*

Wyndham, John. *Day of the Triffids; The Midwich Cuckoos; Rebirth*

Zelazny, Roger. *Creatures of Light and Darkness; Lord of Light*

Critical Works About
Science Fiction

Critical Works About Science Fiction

AGEL, JEROME, ed. *The Making of Kubrick's 2001.* New York: The New American Library, 1972.

ALDISS, BRIAN. *Billion Year Spree: The True History of Science Fiction.* New York: Doubleday, 1973.

AMIS, KINGSLEY. *New Maps of Hell: A Survey of Science Fiction.* New York: Harcourt, Brace, 1960.

ARMYTAGE, W. H. G. *Yesterdays Tomorrows: A Historical Survey of Future Societies.* London: Routledge & Kegan Paul; Toronto: University of Toronto Press, 1968.

ATHELING, WILLIAM, JR. (pseud. of James Blish). *The Issue at Hand.* Chicago: Advent, 1964.

——. *More Issues at Hand.* Chicago: Advent, 1970.

BAILEY, J. O. *Pilgrims Through Space and Time.* New York: Argus Books, 1947; Westport, Conn.: Greenwood Press, 1972.

BAXTER, JOHN. *Science Fiction in the Cinema.* New York: A. S. Barnes, 1970.

BLEILER, EVERETT F. *The Checklist of Fantastic Literature.* Chicago: Shasta Publishers, 1948; Naperville, Ill.: Fax, 1972.

BRETNOR, REGINALD, ed. *Modern Science Fiction: Its Meaning and Future.* New York: Coward-McCann, 1953.

——. *SF, Today and Tomorrow.* New York: Harper and Row, 1974.

BRINEY, ROBERT AND EDWARD WOOD. *SF Bibliographies: An Annotated Bibliography of Bibliographical Works on Science Fiction and Fantasy.* Chicago: Advent, 1972.

BURGUM, EDWIN BERRY. "Freud and Fantasy in Contemporary Fiction." *Science and Society,* 29 (Spring 1965), 224–231.

CALKINS, ELIZABETH AND BARRY McGHAN. *Teaching Tomorrow: A Handbook of Science Fiction for Teachers.* Dayton, Ohio: Pflaum/Standard, 1973.

CHRISTOPHER, JOSEPH AND JOAN K. OSTLING. *C. S. Lewis: A Checklist.* Kent, Ohio: Kent State University Press, 1974.

CLARESON, THOMAS D. *SF: A Dream of Other Worlds.* College Station, Texas: Texas A&M University Library Miscellaneous Publication 6.

——. *Science Fiction Criticism: An Annotated Checklist.* Kent, Ohio: Kent State University Press, 1972.

————, ed. *SF: The Other Side of Realism*. Bowling Green, Ohio: Bowling Green Popular Press, 1971.

————. *Symbolic Worlds of Science Fiction*. Bowling Green, Ohio: Bowling Green Popular Press, 1974.

CLARKE, I. F. *Voices Prophesying War*. New York & London: Oxford University Press, 1966.

————. *The Tale of the Future: From the Beginning to the Present Time*, 2nd ed. London: The Library Association, 1972.

DAY, BRADFORD M. *The Complete Checklist of Science-Fiction Magazines*. Woodhaven, N.Y.: Science Fiction & Fantasy Publishers, 1961.

————. *The Supplemental Checklist of Fantastic Literature*. New York & Denver: Science Fiction & Fantasy Publishers, 1963.

DAY, DONALD B. *Index to the Science Fiction Magazines 1926–1950*.

DeCAMP, L. SPRAGUE. *Science-Fiction Handbook: The Writing of Imaginative Fiction*. New York: Hermitage House, 1953.

DELANEY, SAMUEL R. "Critical Methods: Speculative Fiction" in *Quark/1*. New York: The Paperback Library, 1970.

ESHBACH, LLOYD ARTHUR, ed. *Of Worlds Beyond: The Science of Science Fiction Writing*. Chicago: Advent, 1964.

GERBER, RICHARD. *Utopian Fantasy: A Study of English Utopian Fiction Since the End of the Nineteenth Century*. London: Routledge & Kegan Paul, 1955; New York: McGraw-Hill, 1973.

GOVE, PHILIP BABCOCK. *The Imaginary Voyage in Prose Fiction*. New York: Columbia University Press, 1941.

HALL, H. W. *SFBRI: Science Fiction Book Review Index*. Bryan, Texas: The Author, 1970—.

HARRISON, HARRY, ed. *The Light Fantastic*. New York: Charles Scribner's Sons, 1970.

HILLEGAS, MARK. *The Future as Nightmare: H. G. Wells and the Anti-Utopians*. New York: Oxford University Press, 1967.

JOHNSON, WILLIAM, ed. *Focus on the Science Fiction Film*. Englewood Cliffs, N.J.: Prentice-Hall, 1972.

KARGARLITSKI, JULIUS. *The Life and Thought of H. G. Wells*. London: Sidgwick and Jackson, 1966.

LEE, WALT. *Reference Guide to Fantastic Films: Science Fiction, Fantasy, & Horror. Volume 1: A-F*. Los Angeles: Chelsea-Lee Books, 1972.

LUNDWALL, SAM J. *Science Fiction: What It's All About*. New York: Ace Books, 1972.

MCNELLY, WILLIS E. "Science Fiction and the Academy," *The CEA*

Critic, November, 1972, continued in the January 1973 and May 1973 issues.

McNELLY, WILLIS E., ed. *Science Fiction: The Academic Awakening.* Centenary College, Louisiana: The College English Association, 1974.

MILLER MARJORIE M. *Asimov: A Checklist of Works Published in the United States March 1939–March 1972.* Kent, Ohio: Kent State University Press, 1973.

NICOLSON, MARJORIE. *Voyages to the Moon.* New York: Macmillan, 1948; Macmillan paperbacks, 1960.

PHILMUS, ROBERT M. *Into the Unknown: The Evolution of Science Fiction from Francis Godwin to H. G. Wells.* Berkeley and Los Angeles: University of California Press, 1970.

PLANK, ROBERT. *The Emotional Significance of Imaginary Beings: A Study of the Interaction Between Psychotherapy, Literature, and Reality in the Modern World.* Springfield, Ill.: Charles C. Thomas, 1968.

SADOUL, JACQUES. *Histoire de la Science-fiction Moderne.* Paris: Albin Michel, 1973.

SCHMERL, RUDOLF B. "Fantasy as Technique," *Virginia Quarterly Review,* 43 (Autumn 1967), 644–656; reprinted in Clareson, *SF: The Other Side of Realism,* pp. 105–115.

SILVERBERG, ROBERT, ed. *The Mirror of Infinity.* San Francisco: Canfield Press, 1970.

STEVENSON, LIONEL. "Purveyors of Myth and Magic," in *Yesterday and After: The History of the English Novel.* New York: Barnes & Noble, 1967.

STRAUSS, ERWIN S. *The MIT Science Fiction Society's Index to the S-F Magazines 1951–1965.* Cambridge, Mass.: MIT Science Fiction Society, 1966.

SWIGART, LESLIE KAY. *Harlan Ellison: A Bibliographical Checklist.* Los Angeles: The Author, 1973.

WILLIAMSON, JACK. *H. G. Wells: Critic of Progress.* Baltimore: The Mirage Press, 1973.

WOLLHEIM, DONALD A. *The Universe Makers: Science Fiction Today.* New York: Harper and Row, 1971.

Scribner Student Paperbacks

Scribner Student Paperbacks